AL SAMAK

Also by Brian Nicholson featuring John Gunn

GWEILO

ASHANTI GOLD

FIRE DRAGON

AL SAMAK

BRIAN NICHOLSON

TRAFFORD PUBLISHING

This book is a work of fiction and all the characters, places and
events in this book are fictitious, and any resemblance to actual persons,
living or dead, is purely coincidental.

Order this book online at www.trafford.com/06-3026
or email orders@trafford.com

Most Trafford titles are also available at major online book retailers.

Note for Librarians: A cataloguing record for this book is available from Library
and Archives Canada at www.collectionscanada.ca/amicus/index-e.html

Printed in Victoria, BC, Canada.

ISBN: 978-1-4251-1267-7

*We at Trafford believe that it is the responsibility of us all, as both individuals
and corporations, to make choices that are environmentally and socially sound.
You, in turn, are supporting this responsible conduct each time you purchase a
Trafford book, or make use of our publishing services. To find out how you are
helping, please visit www.trafford.com/responsiblepublishing.html*

*Our mission is to efficiently provide the world's finest, most comprehensive
book publishing service, enabling every author to experience success.
To find out how to publish your book, your way, and have it available
worldwide, visit us online at www.trafford.com/10510*

Trafford
PUBLISHING

www.trafford.com

North America & international
toll-free: 1 888 232 4444 (USA & Canada)
phone: 250 383 6864 ♦ fax: 250 383 6804
email: info@trafford.com

The United Kingdom & Europe
phone: +44 (0)1865 722 113 ♦ local rate: 0845 230 9601
facsimile: +44 (0)1865 722 868 ♦ email: info.uk@trafford.com

10 9 8 7 6 5 4

AL SAMAK

Al Samak is the phonetic English spelling of the Arabic word for 'The Fish'.

For D, Rugs and Basher

FOREWORD

This is a story about intrigue, treachery, conspiracy, revenge and violence. It's a story of flawed and bungled political manoeuvring before the invasion of Iraq in March 2003. It's the story of Russia's fight to protect its embryo democracy against plotting by die-hard communists. It's the story of Iraq's desperate struggle to achieve a WMD capability to prevent the invasion. It's the story of the desperate measures taken by the intelligence agencies of the coalition to prevent a nuclear holocaust in the Middle East.

It's John Gunn's second assignment with the British Intelligence Directorate, but above all, it's a story.... a story of 21st Century political intrigue and weapons of mass destruction, but this story started as long ago as the 7th Century, as a storm-lashed papyrus raft broke up in the Arabian Sea......but is it a story? ....you decide.

PROLOGUE

In the 7th Century, inspired by the new religion preached by Mohammed, the Arabs left the desert for the more fertile lands of Mesopotamia to spread the word of the Prophet and create an Empire which would eventually stretch from the Atlantic Ocean to the River Indus. The creation of the Empire was preceded by missionaries fired with fervour by their visit to the Black Stone in the Kaaba of the great mosque at Mecca. By the year 632 AD, the Arab Empire had spread to the extremities of Mesopotamia and beyond. The fervour to spread the faith did not accept physical barriers, such as oceans, and so in order to expand the Empire even further, a group of missionaries set sail on a raft made of papyrus reeds, collected from the delta swamps of the Euphrates, to carry the word of the Prophet across the uncharted expanse of the Arabian Sea.

The five missionaries were alternately seared by heat or drenched by mountainous seas until the raft became waterlogged and their numbers were reduced by sickness and exhaustion. Of the surviving three, two were swept from the raft in a storm. Eventually, one man, Hazrat Ubaidulla, was washed onto the white sands of an atoll in the Arabian Sea, entangled in a fishing net amongst dead and dying fish. The island was uninhabited, but fishermen from the islands to the south found the missionary and took him back to their island. Hazrat Ubaidulla subsequently converted the islands to the faith of Islam and the island where he had been found was named 'Al Samak' - The Fish.

*

He was being burnt alive. White-hot needles of pain seared every morsel of exposed flesh, which erupted into raw and suppurating blisters. All his senses were overwhelmed by the pain from the condensing droplets of the deadly cocktail of Sarin, Lewisite and mustard gas which the wind had blown into every corner and crevice of his village, five miles to the west of Halabjah in the foothills of Kurdistan. He sensed, rather than heard, the diminishing roar of the Tumansky turbofan engines of the three Sukoi Su-7/22 fighter-ground-attack aircraft as they disappeared over the hills to the south on the return journey to the air force base at Karbala, to the south of Baghdad. There were no markings on any of the aircraft. That was

7

the last thing he had noticed before he was blinded by the gas as it vaporised from the spray pumped out of the drop-tanks, slung below the wings of the FGA aircraft.

The village had been celebrating his return after nearly twenty years, in an attempt to show its gratitude for all the lavish gifts he had given to the people of his birthplace. The latest offerings were two articulated low-loaders, each with three gleaming red tractors and all the mechanical attachments which stood deserted, like abandoned dinosaurs, in the centre of the village. There wasn't a sound and nothing moved; there was nothing to move. Life in every human, animal, insect and plant had been extinguished in less than three minutes by the burning, persistent chemical sprayed from the aircraft.

*

A small cloud of dust drifted across the dried-up floor of the valley. There was no wind and the fierce mid-afternoon sun bounced and shimmered off the rocks and stones in the dried-up riverbed. The source of the dust cloud came from the wheels of two, white-painted Willys jeeps which were following a boulder-strewn track beside the river bed. There were four men in each jeep; all wore dust-grimed pale blue berets, dark-lensed goggles and had scarves wrapped over the lower part of their faces. On the left side of each jeep was a short metal mast from which fluttered a large blue flag with the white emblem of the United Nations. On a pintle mount, just to the rear of the front seats was a Bofors 7.62, belt-fed machine gun - barrel pointed skywards and covered to protect the working parts from the dust. All the soldiers were from NORCON - the Norwegian Contingent of the United Nations Military Observer Group in Iran (UNIMOG) - which was responsible for policing a demilitarised buffer zone extending ten kilometres either side of the Iraq/Iran border.

At 1315 hours that afternoon, the Headquarters of the Northern Division of Iraqi Forces had come through to UN Headquarters on the HF guard net to report that there had been a sighting of three, F-4 Phantoms carrying the red, white and green colours of the Iranian Air Force. They were reported to be well inside Iraqi airspace near the village of Sarikamis at grid reference Wiskey 541, November 327. It appeared that no ordnance had been dropped from the aircraft, but there was no contact with the village via the one line into the post office. The village lay inside the UN demilitarised zone agreed after the cessation of hostilities after the Iraq/Iran war. Because of this, the Iraqi Divisional Commander had asked if a UN patrol could report on the situation in that area and convey his President's condemnation

8

of this breach of the recently negotiated cease-fire to the Security Council of the UN. The village lay in the Tactical Area of Operational Responsibility of NORCON and the two-jeep patrol had left the NORCON HQ within ten minutes of the receipt of the task from UNIMOG Operational Command HQ, to investigate the reported incident in its TAOR.

The track left the dry, dusty valley and started to climb into the foothills of the long spine of mountains stretching from the Black Sea to the Gulf of Oman. The army captain, sitting in the front right seat of the leading jeep bent forward and studied the map encased in a plastic folder on his lap. He brushed away the dust, studied the map closely and then turned and spoke to the corporal driver on his left who nodded. The two jeeps bounced and ground their way onto a saddle of ground overlooking the village lying in a small depression in the hills some three miles away. There was a properly graded road to the village, but that approached it from the west and was outside the UN Zone, clearly overprinted on the captain's map.

The patrol commander turned in his seat and spoke to the men behind him and then dismounted from the jeep. The captain made a signal to the men in the second jeep who all dismounted and, like the men in the lead jeep, started to pull on their Nuclear, Biological and Chemical protective clothing. The captain checked the wind direction, tightened up the lacing of the rubber over-boots and pulled on his respirator. He removed the one-colour detector paper from its foil protection and attached it to the Velcro strip on his left forearm, as did all the other soldiers in the patrol.

His crew climbed back into the jeep, the plastic cover was removed from the machine gun and a quick flick of the cocking lever chambered the first 7.62mm round of the belt. The front jeep moved forward, but the rear one didn't move until it was some 200 metres away; it then swung away to the right, on the orders of the vehicle commander and approached the village from a flank, all the while covering the lead jeep. Bitter experience of UN patrols driving into undisclosed or unmarked minefields and small groups of deserters from the Iraqi Army who had no knowledge of the cease-fire, had quickly taught the UN soldiers to drive everywhere with the utmost caution.

The lead jeep stopped and the commander stood up on his seat and held his binoculars close to the eyepieces of the respirator. There wasn't a sign of life anywhere; not even a wisp of smoke rose from any of the stone houses and there wasn't a sheep or goat anywhere. The captain turned to his radio operator in the rear of the jeep and was handed the microphone and earphones. After another scrutiny of the map, he sent the initial contact report to NORCON HQ with a description of the deserted village. He then picked up a small hand-held radio and spoke to the lieutenant in the other jeep. The latter was immediately driven into a fold in the ground from which only its pintle mounted machine gun was visible.

The lead jeep moved forward at little more than walking pace towards the village, each man constantly checking the detector paper. The captain's contact report had been relayed to a Norwegian Bell UH-1B Huey helicopter, which was airborne, patrolling the NORCON Sector. The pilot switched his second radio to the frequency of the jeep patrol and pressed the transmit button on the collective stick in his right hand. The radio operator in the first jeep tapped the captain on the shoulder and once he had his attention pointed in the direction of the valley through which they had just driven. The patrol commander spotted the helicopter as it hugged the terrain until it climbed up the side of the valley and banked in a steep turn over their heads. The captain took the earphones from his operator and spoke to the pilot who acknowledged and swung away towards the village. Once there, the Huey circled the area giving the patrol commander a detailed description of what the pilot and observer could see.

The lead jeep increased speed and within two minutes was in the centre of the village; all the detector papers were discoloured. The captain spoke to the lieutenant in the second jeep, which moved to a position on some high ground up-wind of and with a clear view into the village. The machine-gunner and radio-operator stayed in the jeep and the commander and driver dismounted, unclipped the Uzi carbines from their brackets beside the seats and stared at the revolting sight of putrefying human and animal corpses all round them. Already carrion crows had started to peck out the eyes from the piles of bodies scattered everywhere and then in turn had been contaminated by the persistent chemical agent and lay twitching and flapping helplessly in the dust. Half-an-hour later the two soldiers had completed their search; no one was alive.

The whole incident was identical to the three previous occasions that the Iraqi Commander had protested at an Iranian incursion of Iraqi airspace. The two men returned to the square and the captain paused as his driver walked over to a Chevrolet Charger station wagon parked in front of the two low-loaders. He was about to get into the jeep and talk to the pilot of the Huey circling overhead, when the gesticulations from his driver made him change direction and run - as best he could in the protective clothing - over to the station wagon. The driver had the door open and there was a man - he had a

10

man's figure and was dressed in men's clothing - lying across the front bench seat. His face was unrecognisable as such, but he was alive and must have escaped the worst of the gas by shutting himself in the car.

The station wagon door was quickly shut and the driver produced a plastic bag, a mask and cylinder of compressed air from the back of the jeep. With the help, now, of the other two men in the jeep, the mask was placed over the face where some form of mouth cavity was just recognisable, the air was turned on and the body was placed into the plastic bag which was then sealed. The folding stretcher was placed across the back of the jeep and the body was driven gently upwind of the village until the detector paper failed to react. The Huey landed and the body was transferred onto the left, outside stretcher rack where it was firmly strapped in place. The final task was to tie on a warning label of chemical-contamination and then the helicopter whisked its grizzly patient away to the UN Field Hospital.

The four soldiers in the lead jeep decontaminated each other with calcium hypochlorite and all the protective clothing was sealed into plastic disposal bags. The two jeeps disappeared over the rim of the saddle and the little dust cloud appeared once again in the valley as the two vehicles returned towards Halabjah and the border with Iran.

CHAPTER 1

A gust of wind picked up the leaves and sent them scurrying in fits and starts along the sodden pavement, only to pile up in another drift at the foot of a flight of worn steps, the base of a sycamore tree or amongst other piles of discarded litter. Simeon Bukharin hunched his shoulders against the bitter October cold and the rain-laden wind and hurried towards Block Number 52. On either side of the street was a succession of identical apartment blocks, which were all in the same rundown and dilapidated state.

All were a product of the unimaginative architecture of the 1930s, which had proliferated this concrete ugliness on the outskirts of Moscow and the larger towns and cities of European Russia. The town of Kalinin fell exactly into this category and the rows and rows of identical, grey, five-storey apartment blocks seemed even more depressing than usual. The depressing buildings matched his depressing future, Simeon thought, as he made his way towards Number 52; apartment number 10 would be on the top floor - ten flights of stone stairs.

With relief, he saw the faded number above the entrance and was turning towards it when his attention was caught by a stifled exclamation, carried quickly away by the wind, from a group of people gathered on the pavement outside the next apartment block. Despite his anxiety to get out of the bitter wind, Simeon walked on past Number 52 towards the huddle of people, one of whom turned and pointed up at the flat-roofed apartment block. Their voices were indistinct, carried away on the wind as he approached the group.

In the middle of the group was one of the many piles of litter and leaves and what had looked like an old piece of cloth was revealed as a coat which was still occupied by a body. A pale faced woman, scarf wrapped tightly around her head and lower part of her face, bent down and brushed the leaves and litter away from the face and then stepped back quickly and turned away from the group at the sound of an approaching siren.

A militia patrol car swung into the road from a side street and Simeon turned and headed back towards Number 52. Another patrol car came from the other direction and stopped in front of him. A policeman got out of the car and blocked his access to the apartment block. The man's hand was held out and the single word 'propiski!' was snapped at him.

'My resident's permit?' repeated Simeon absent-mindedly, 'yes, yes of course, a moment please,' and he undid the buttons of his coat which immediately let in the chilling wind. 'Ah! here you are,' and he held out his permit.

'Passport!' was snapped back at him with barely a glance at the permit. Simeon fumbled once again inside his jacket for the passport issued by the Ministry of Internal Affairs, wishing that he still possessed his Special Military Pass which would have wiped the supercilious smirk off the policeman's face. The pass and prestige had all been a part of his appointment as the General in command of Military Construction Troops with the responsibility for all civil and military state construction projects. The pass had made him a member of the 'Elite', which entitled him to use special shops, bars and clubs where only foreign currency and rouble certificates were accepted. The 'old guard', of which he was one, was viewed with great suspicion by the younger, supposedly liberated Russians after the collapse of the communist state.

'Why are you visiting Kalinin?' The barked interrogation snapped Simeon out of his whimsical reverie.

'I'm visiting an old friend of mine who lives in Number 52; there!' and he pointed over the policeman's shoulder.

'Your travel permit expires at midnight. See to it that you are on your way back to Minsk by then. The last train from Kalinin is at 2010 hours. Make sure that you are on it or an earlier one!' and the permit and passport were slapped into Simeon's hand and the policeman walked past him, but then stopped and turned. 'Were you able to identify the body on the pavement,' he was asked, too politely and quietly for Simeon's liking.

'No officer,' Simeon assured the policeman, perhaps too hastily, and then to justify his ignorance he added, 'his face is terribly injured....er, I think it would be difficult, even for a relative, to recognise him.'

'But you were able to identify the body as a 'him' rather than a 'her' and you saw the injuries to the face,' the interrogation persisted.

'Yes, indeed, officer,' Simeon agreed, 'the face has a week's growth of beard and the injuries are both obvious and most unpleasant.' The policeman turned without another word and walked purposefully towards the body where his colleagues were questioning the people who had found it. Simeon turned and climbed the steps to the drab entrance of Number 52.

The stone-flagged hallway was dank and cold and an evil smell of stale cabbage water and boiled fish exuded out of the caretaker's flat at the foot of the stairs. The stone staircase was as damp as the hall and the paint was peeling off the walls and the rusty balustrade. Simeon's breathing became more laboured as he climbed up to the fifth floor. On the third floor he had to pause for breath. 'This is dreadful,' he muttered to himself, 'I'm only 58 and I can't go up more than six flights of stairs without a rest. This bloody climate drains any man's resolve to take exercise or keep fit.' His breathing was under control again so he began the climb up the last four flights to apartment 10.

Apartment 10 was rented by Boris Samsonov, former Colonel General of the Kiev Military District during Brezhnev's benignly corrupt leadership of the Soviet Communist Party. He now lived on his own in a run-down, two-bedroom apartment since his wife, Anna, had left him. She had departed with their three children only six months after the disgrace of his dismissal with ignominy and the removal of all the privileges and perks that went with the appointment of Commander of a Military District. Gorbachev's new regime had found him guilty of corruption and embezzlement of party funds and dismissal with ignominy carried with it the mandatory denial of his military pension. Boris Samsonov was therefore forced to survive on a meagre state pension and the residue of the capital he had managed to keep from the plump and prying fingers of his avaricious wife. Once all the luxuries had vanished, his wife was not long in following them; back to the bosom of her family in Georgia, close to the shores of the Black Sea.

Simeon Bukharin reached the top floor where the door to apartment 9 was ajar, through which came the sound of a man and woman arguing. In the doorway, astride a paint-chipped tricycle, was a child of indiscernible sex who had been watching his ascent to the fifth floor; the forefinger of the right hand was wedged firmly, to the second joint, up the right nostril, distorting the grimy little face. Simeon was reminded of the stone-carved gargoyles supporting the guttering and buttresses of the Orthodox Churches. The bell on number 10 didn't work. The door was opened by Boris Samsonov in response to Simeon's knock,

Simeon had thought that this was to be just another afternoon of reminiscing between two servicemen whose memories and experiences went back many years together and who both now found themselves in very reduced circumstances. Today had to be different because behind Samsonov the pokey little living room was filled with

14

cigarette smoke, slightly obscuring Simeon's view of the people, but not the sound of clinking glasses as they were filled with vodka.

'Come in, come in! Simeon, my old friend,' Boris greeted him, vodka glass and cigar in his left hand and the right one now thumping Simeon on the back. 'You know everyone here,' continued Boris, leading him across the small room to where three other men had risen from the chairs in which they had been sitting. 'Perhaps I should stick to seniority,' chuckled Boris Samsonov with an expansive gesture of his left hand which slopped a fair proportion of his vodka over the worn and threadbare carpet. Simeon recalled Samsonov's addiction to vodka and his hard head and capacity for it, so this would certainly not be the first bottle which he could see amidst the over-spilling ashtrays, partially-filled glasses of the colourless spirit and plates of small, open sandwiches made of brown bread and covered in an assortment of salami, salted herring, caviare and pickled vegetables. 'Marshal Andrey Rokossovsky,' introduced Boris in a slurred voice and over- formal manner, 'erstwhile Commander of the Civil Defence Corps.'

'Oh shut up Boris! You drunken old fool. Simeon! How nice to see you again,' Andrey Rokossovsky had stepped round the large and unsteady bulk of Boris and greeted the new arrival. 'Please forgive Boris, but I don't think that he's been drinking much 'til today and the vodka has gone to his head rather quicker than usual! Now then, let me see.... um,' and he turned, 'you know Ivan Voznesensky,' Andrey had smoothly taken over the introductions while Boris made his way over to the table to replenish the vodka which he had spilt on the floor.

'Yes, of course,' acknowledged Simeon, who well knew his fellow General who had been in charge of the Rear Services Directorate at the same time as he had been in command of the Military Construction Troops. The two men embraced, genuinely pleased to see each other again.

'And another of your fellow logisticians,' interrupted Rokossovsky, 'Peter Milynkov.' Again, Simeon knew him well and the two men greeted each other warmly.

'Vodka?' offered Samsonov.

'Yes I will, thank you,' said Simeon accepting the thick, squat glass.

'Good; that only leaves one more of our number to complete the reunion,' announced Rokossovsky cheerfully.

'Presumably the sixth member of the reunion is Franz,' offered Simeon, taking a sip from his glass and accepting a cigarette from Peter Milynkov.

15

'Yes, you're right, but how did you guess?' queried Samsonov pugnaciously, suspicion and vodka thickening his voice.

'Call it a reasonable assumption,' replied Simeon calmly, unruffled by Boris' aggressive tone.

'How's that as you could've only met Franz a couple of times during your service?' persisted Boris, quickly reverting to the bullying manner he had always adopted when interrogating a suspect.

'Now then Boris, calm down; you haven't given Simeon a chance to tell us how he guessed who the last member of the reunion was to be,' chided Andrey Rokossovsky. Once again the restraining and calming role, but the chilling bite in his voice left no doubt that an explanation from Simeon was required.

'If you all go over to that window,' replied Simeon, 'you will see Franz Sokolovsky, former Marshal of the Air Defence Force of our beloved Motherland, lying on the pavement with his brains splattered around him. At a guess, I would say he's very dead indeed, so if you are planning on arranging a reunion with him, we've all got either a very long wait - and there's certainly not enough vodka for Boris if you choose that option - or we can all jump out of the window and join him. Personally, I suggest that we proceed without Franz and our first toast should be to absent friends, Na'storovia!' and Simeon drained his glass and walked over to the table to refill it.

At that moment, the door to the main bedroom opened and a woman shuffled into the room, bare-footed and dressed only in a man's dressing gown hanging wide open and revealing a remarkable figure. It was remarkable because of the woman's height which was certainly not less than a shade under six foot and with the voluminous proportion of breasts and hips which would have done credit to any cartoonist's wildest fantasies. She appeared to be totally unaware of the guests invited to the apartment until she had advanced some two or three paces into the room in the direction of the kitchen. At this juncture she stopped rubbing the sleep out of her eyes and became aware that she was not alone.

Simeon Bukharin was the only person to have noticed the intrusion, while all the others had their attention focused on the scene in the street below, where the body of Marshal Sokolovsky was being loaded into an ambulance. He was the man ultimately responsible for allowing an 18 year old West German youth to fly a single-engined Cessna 152 into Red Square, successfully avoiding the Soviet Union's entire air defence system. With a composure, which Simeon could only admire, she calmly drew the dressing gown around her, tied the cord, nodded a greeting to Simeon and continued into the kitchen, closing the door quietly behind her.

Simeon shook his head slowly with a wry smile; it was common knowledge that Boris Samsonov's appetite for alcohol was only equalled by the virility of his libido, although for obvious reasons the two were not always compatible. His wife had suffered many ignominious incidents when her husband had been caught 'in flagrante' in brothels from one end of the Soviet Union to the other. There was one story, how genuine Simeon had his doubts, that Boris had even succeeded in seducing the Swedish Military Attache's wife behind the curtains of the drawing room during a reception at the Swedish Embassy in Moscow. It was, therefore, hardly surprising, thought Simeon, that his wife had disappeared with such alacrity, once Boris was unable to provide her with the comforts of life which in the past had made her overlook his frequent acts of infidelity. The departure of the ambulance brought the attention of the four men back into the living room from the scene in the street below.

'When I saw him on the street,' continued Simeon, 'he had at least a week's growth of beard and looked like a vagrant, which is exactly what the police think he is. You're right, Boris, I didn't know him all that well, only a couple of meetings in fact, at official receptions and I had completely lost touch with his movements after he was dismissed by Boris Yeltsin for the incident in Red Square. I would be most interested to know what happened to him. Why have we all been asked to this reunion? If the answers to either of those questions is even mildly sensitive, I would feel considerably more at ease, Boris, if you would ask your lady friend to go and do some shopping or visit her mother - if she ever knew her!'

'How dare you make insults...!' spluttered Samsonov before he was curtly interrupted.

'Shut up, Boris!' ordered Andrey Rokossovsky. 'Simeon is quite right. Go and ask your friend to leave us so that we may reminisce discreetly.'

'Very well, but...'

'Just go and do it,' ordered the ex-Marshal. Boris started towards the bedroom door, but was stopped by Simeon's correction.

'No, you won't find the lady in there; she's in the kitchen.' He changed direction without a word and disappeared into the kitchen, slamming the door behind him.

'Once she's gone,' Rokossovsky broke the silence which followed, 'and thank you Simeon for drawing our attention to the lady's presence,' was added with a courteous nod in his direction, 'I'll explain the purpose of this reunion. Franz's death brings everything

17

into focus, so fill up your glasses, pass round the sandwiches and cigars, be seated and we will reminisce until such time as Boris' girlfriend has gone. Speaking of which, what is Boris up to now?' and the Marshal placed his glass on the table, walked to the kitchen and threw open the door.

The lady in question was lying on her back on the kitchen table. Boris' dressing gown had been removed which revealed all of her very obvious attractions. Boris' trousers were round his ankles and her powerful legs were locked behind his back, firmly clamping him into her. Even Boris' large hands were incapable of grappling with the ample proportions of her breasts and her glazed expression, matched by Boris' accelerated breathing, indicated to the Marshal that there was no point in interrupting at that juncture. He closed the door and rejoined the group in the living room.

'Boris is at it again; we'll have to wait 'til he's finished as he's an essential part of the matter which I wish to discuss with you all. I don't think that there's any danger of the young lady overhearing me as all her senses are focused in a different direction!' chuckled Rokossovsky, taking a seat in an armchair.

'All of us, at one time or another, held positions of considerable importance from which we derived many privileges. All of us were removed by the new regime and were stripped of all those privileges and, I think that I'm correct in saying, every one of us lost his Service pension?' Rokossovsky glanced round the other three men with raised eyebrows for confirmation of the last statement, which brought nods of assent. 'Yes, I thought I was right,' he continued, 'well comrades...' but at that moment there was a loud crash from the kitchen.

Andrey Rokossovsky rose nimbly, for his years, from the armchair and opened the door. The kitchen table had given up the unequal struggle of supporting the fornicating couple and had collapsed in a heap of splintered wood, leaving some of the sharper bits lodged in the buttocks of the fair Kristina. These painful splinters were being removed by Boris, who was looking particularly disgruntled having suffered such a catastrophic form of 'coitus interruptus'. Andrey Rokossovsky closed the door again and resumed his seat in the armchair. 'I have a plan which will make all of us very rich men indeed,' he announced quietly to the three men.

Kristina, whom Boris described as his housekeeper, left the apartment within ten minutes of the collapse of the kitchen table, apparently none the worse for wear and tear. Her exit was as calm and dignified as had been her confrontation with Simeon Bukharin earlier. It was marred by a slight limp, but enhanced by a pause at

18

the door, as she dropped her lipstick, bent over to pick it up thus allowing her short skirt to reveal the majority of charms which so endeared her to Boris and which ensured that all the eyes in the room were focused on that view and none of them saw her hand move to the sideboard by the apartment door.

Once the five men were all seated, Andrey Rokossovsky refilled his glass and began. 'Comrades, I said earlier while we were waiting for Boris,' this was said with an irritated glance in the latter's direction who had slumped into a noticeably relaxed posture, 'that I have a plan to make us all rich men. It's not without risk, but that is something which all of us are used to in one form or another. Our rewarding and comfortable way of life would have continued into our retirement had not Brezhnev died and, three years and three geriatrics later, been replaced by Michail Gorbachev and then by our current revered President.

'That's all now water under the bridge; all of us are living close to the bread line, our wives have left us and there's very little for any of us to look forward to in our old age. Before I go any further, is there any disagreement up to this point?' Rokossovsky paused, searching the four faces for any sign of unease or discomfort; there was none. 'I shall pause like that at various stages of my plan so that any of you who wish to take your leave may do so. There will come a point when you will not be allowed to leave. I hope that my implication is quite clear to you all without having to go into any detail.'

'Now, would any of you like to leave?' For answer, there came a loud snore from Boris Samsonov. It would seem, thought Simeon, that Boris' 'coitus' had not been 'interruptus' after all. Andrey Rokossovsky nodded at Peter Milynkov who brought Boris out of his slumbers with a sharp kick on the ankle.

'If you can't control yourself, Boris, and make an effort to pay attention, then this meeting will be stopped and reconvened in my flat. You, in particular, are well aware of the implication of exclusion from this plan as I've discussed it with you already,' warned Andrey. Samsonov knew that the Marshal's threat was no idle one. He excused himself and disappeared into the bathroom from whence came sounds of running water. He reappeared quickly with the obvious signs of having doused his head in cold water.

'As I have just mentioned exclusion from the plan, I think that I should start by explaining this fully to you all so that there will be no misunderstandings from now on,' continued Rokossovsky once more. 'You were all selected with considerable care, both for the positions you once occupied and the cause of your dismissal, which in all cases involved the misappropriation of state funds. Let's not be squeamish

19

about that any longer nor the shared impecunious state in which we all find ourselves today. Opting out of this plan is not an option being offered to any of you. If you do not support it fully, it has to be assumed that you are against it and therefore constitute a risk I cannot afford to take,' he paused for a sip of his vodka. The proverbial pin could have been heard as the attention of everyone was focused on the Marshal.

'Let me get this quite clear,' interjected Voznesensky, who was a sound logistician, but not gifted with great mental alacrity. 'We are all part of this plan whether we wish to be or not and if our inclination is the latter we will be killed...correct?'

'Correct,' Rokossovsky confirmed.

'That's quite clear; from my point of view, please continue. You have both my full attention and support,' assured the General.

'And mine,' Milynkov added.

'Simeon?' queried the Marshal.

'Yes, Andrey, you have my full support, please continue.'

'Very well,' resumed Rokossovsky, not bothering to get confirmation from Boris as he had already been told what the future held for him if there was dissent or lack of co-operation. 'There's one more administrative point which I must cover before I inform you all of the detail of my plan and the part which each of you will play in it. All of us are in our late fifties or early sixties. We're all still active - some of us more so than others,' this aside was made with a glance at Boris, 'and we are all medically fit. I know that because I've had access to all your medical documents. We do not have youth and stamina on our side nor the specific skills - familiar to all of us, I'm sure - to deal with any enforcement aspect of this plan; just in case any of us lose our resolve.'

'There's one more person who will join us shortly,' and Rokossovsky glanced at his watch, 'who is a product of the old school of the KGB. He joins the group in the same circumstances as all of us - incidentally, he was sacked for killing three political prisoners in his custody, in a manner which was so horrifically unpleasant that it even shocked the hypocritical hierarchy of the KGB. He has nothing to lose; he is a born psychopathic killer of considerable expertise and finesse who will kill each and every one of us without the slightest hesitation should we become a threat to the security or success of the plan. Should you consider this to be an idle threat, please cast your minds back a few minutes to the scene you witnessed in the street outside. Without a shadow of doubt, that was the work of Yuri Volkonoff.'

'At the first meeting I set up with Boris, Franz and Yuri, Sokolovsky was not only openly against the plan, but it was very plain to see that his dismissal over that airspace intrusion had turned him into the alcoholic hobo Simeon saw lying on the pavement. We realised that we had made a very serious mistake to take Franz into our confidence and that he now posed a grave security risk to the plan. Yuri was given the task of eliminating that risk and we decided that we needed both Peter and Simeon to complete the group.'

'You mean that Yuri was told to kill Franz,' Simeon interrupted.

'Yes, if you insist,' Rokossovsky remarked, unperturbed by Simeon's interruption. 'Yuri was given instructions to kill Franz. He was given no direction as to when that should happen, but I suspect that the time was chosen to give all of you a very clear warning of what will happen if any of us fall under suspicion. Yuri will be joining us a little later after I've explained the plan in outline to all of you. I think that now completes the administrative point which I wished to cover so I will move on to the plan itself,' the Marshal paused to re-light his cigar and with a motion of his right hand indicated that everyone should refill their glasses.

When the cigar was well aglow and thick clouds of smoke swirled towards the ceiling, he continued; 'you will remember that we signed the INF Treaty with the USA in December of 1987. In case any of you have forgotten, that was the Intermediate Nuclear Forces Treaty which, very briefly, was an agreement to dismantle and destroy all Soviet and American ballistic and cruise missiles with a range of between 500 and 5000 kilometres. That included all the support systems and the suspension of missile production and testing.' Nods from the four other men confirmed their knowledge of this treaty. 'All of us in this room,' Andrey Rokossovsky continued, 'were involved, in one way or another, with the construction, testing, storing and deployment of our SS20 missiles. What is perhaps more important, is that we know all the key personnel in the Services and the KGB who are responsible for implementing the terms of the treaty, and even more importantly, those who are susceptible to bribes, blackmail and threats to assist us with our plan. You are all, of course, familiar with the procedure involved with the SS20s from their assembly in the factory at Votinsk to their arrival at the arsenal here, at Kalinin. In outline only, this is the plan.'

'Ten, SS20 missiles with their MIRVs - the multiple, independently-targeted, re-entry nuclear warheads - will be removed from those designated for destruction under the terms of the treaty and will be replaced with very convincing fakes.' Rokossovsky paused for a sip of his vodka and a long pull at his cigar sending more smoke to join the thick layer, which was hanging above their heads in the airless room. It bothered none of them as all were smoking. 'These ten missiles will be sold to a third party, through the good offices of a trusted and tried arms dealer, for four million dollars each. I'm sure that all of you have done your mental arithmetic already and have worked out that some 6 million plus dollars will go to each of us.'

'I think that you will all agree that we would find it hard not to be comfortable for the remainder of our retirement with that sort of money. As a show of good faith, I have already been presented with $600,000 in advance to finance this plan and that will be distributed to you in direct proportion to the task which each of you will complete.' Rokossovsky nodded to Samsonov who walked over to a battered roll-top desk from which he retrieved five envelopes, which he handed to the men in the room. Each envelope had a name on it and from their varying thickness, it was obvious that there was a different sum of money in each one.

'Are questions permitted at this stage?' Simeon asked.

'By all means,' offered the Marshal expansively.

'Very well; are we allowed to know where these missiles are going and the name of the arms dealer, who, presumably, is financing the deal?

'Yes, of course: I wouldn't think of asking you all to involve yourselves in such a plan without knowing the stakes and the risks...'

'Bullshit!' thought Simeon to himself as Rokossovsky continued.

'... you were being asked to take. You will all remember that in 1980, the Soviet Union supplied Iraq with the SCUD B missile and launch system to use with conventional explosive and chemical warheads against the Iranians. Well, they did use them - with chemical warheads - supervised by our military advisers. Throughout that futile war, Iraq was negotiating with anyone and everyone to achieve a nuclear capability and delivery means after the Israelis had destroyed their plant for producing enriched uranium. The Iraq/Iran war came to its predictably futile conclusion with massive loss of human life and not one inch of territorial gain to either side.'

'A year later, the Mossad and British Intelligence Directorate uncovered a scheme to build a huge nuclear artillery piece in Iraq - you will remember that many of the parts came from British firms. I have a very close friend in the KGB who is currently a military adviser in Baghdad. He has told me that Saddam Hussein needs a nuclear capability to stalemate the inevitable US/UK military intervention in Iraq and to assist in the expansion of Iraqi territory in the area of the Gulf ports and oilfields and the destruction of Israel. It is the Iraqi intention to use the SS20 warhead on the SCUD B missile and launcher. Saddam's plan is to neutralise the forces of Saudi Arabia, Iran and the USA/UK coalition with the threat of the use of nuclear weapons. Everyone knows that he's mad enough to carry out that threat, but in spite of protestations by the British Prime Minister and the US President in the UN Security Council that Saddam possesses weapons of mass destruction and can deploy them within 45 minutes, he hasn't and he can't. He has no WMDs.

'I see; and who is the arms dealer negotiating this masterly plan?' Peter Milynkov couldn't keep the irony out of his voice.

'You sound less than enthusiastic about the successful outcome to our plan, comrade,' and the malevolence in Rokossovsky's voice was unmistakable.

'I have no doubt about the success of the plan, Comrade Marshal, my only doubt is whether I shall live to spend my share of the money. Who is the arms dealer?' Milynkov asked again.

'We are using the same man whom you used to negotiate the supply of Semtex explosive from Czechoslovakia to the Provisional IRA via Libya - from which, if my research is correct, you made the handsome sum of $50,000 and which subsequently led to your dismissal; right?'

'Correct,' confirmed Milynkov; 'Hassan Hussein is certainly capable of fixing a deal of this size. Have you ever met the man?'

'No, only spoken to him. I'm told that no one is allowed to meet him.'

'Yes, that's the man,' Milynkov acknowledged.

'Well, Peter my friend, you'll find more than $50,000 in the envelope which you have in your hand and that's just for incidental expenses!' was Rokossovsky's smug response. 'Now let's return to the plan. The ten missiles will be transported to Southern China and then shipped to Iraq via Hong Kong. We will be paid our money in three stages; one million each when the missiles leave our country; another million when they leave Hong Kong and the final four million-plus when we part company in the Straits of Hormuz. We will be lifted off the ship by helicopter and taken to Dubai Airport from where we will fly to Tripoli. From there, the choice of destination is up to the individual.'

'The detailed instructions for the jobs which each of you will be required to do are in your envelopes. You will go home and study these instructions and we will meet here at exactly the same time next week.' At that moment the front door opened and one of the largest men Simeon had ever seen walked into the room. 'Ah!' exclaimed

Rokossovsky, 'what perfect timing; comrades, this is Yuri Volkonoff - our sixth member. That now completes the membership of our little conspiracy.'

CHAPTER 2

The stone-flagged, beamed bar of the Flute and Fiddle was packed with people; smoke hung in wreaths which drifted to and fro as the door onto the street was opened and closed. The conversation was loud and light-hearted, as it usually was on a Friday evening when the sailing fraternity gathered for a weekend afloat. Hamble was only one of many towns and villages on the south and east coast of England to which the work-weary and not-so-work-weary rushed from London on a Friday evening to let the sharp, salt-tinged wind blow away the fug-filled, carbon-dioxide-choked air from both brain and lungs.

The navigable length of the River Hamble - for boats of any size - stretched from its mouth where it flowed into the Solent to just north of the bridge which supported the M27 Motorway, a distance of about 4½ miles. The banks of the river were filled with expensive and desirable properties, very expensive and not-so-desirable marinas, boatyards, chandlers, pubs and yacht clubs combining and competing to make as much money as possible out of the rapidly increasing number of people who spent their leisure time messing around in boats in the short season from May to September.

'And why not,' thought John Gunn as he drove south down the B3397 towards the village of Hamble which lay near the mouth of the river of the same name. 'That's what makes the wheels of commerce turn, provides the boat industry with the necessary cash-flow to build boats for those who can afford to buy them and then invite me for a week's sailing.' His train of thought was interrupted by the task of manoeuvring his fire engine red, TR6 along the narrow and congested streets of the small village. It was only a quarter to seven, but already the streets were full of people heading for one pub or another and cars parked illegally with wheels on the pavement. The TR6 was the last of the proper classic British sports cars produced by Triumph before it diverged into mediocrity – and subsequently bankruptcy - with the hideous TR7 and its monocoque construction. Gunn had lavished much time and devotion on his pride and joy which possessed an up-rated 200 bhp, 2½ litre, fuel-injected engine with a skimmed head, balanced crank, fly-wheel and clutch and tuned exhaust.

Like many towns and villages on the coast, which relied on the large influx of people interested in boats and the money they brought with them, Hamble sported a whole range of pubs and restaurants, each trying to find its slot in the market. There were rough and tatty pubs with mind-bendingly loud juke boxes and clattering pool tables, smart pubs with up-market restaurants, not-so-smart ones with bar food, pseudo-chic bistros with over-priced menus and indifferent food and others with good, simple fare. Gunn had tried most of them at one time or another while sailing the yachts available for charter at HMS Hornet - the Joint Services Sailing Centre - in Gosport.

The invitation to spend a week sailing on a large and comfortable yacht with some people whom he'd never met in his life before, had been passed to him by the Assistant Director South-East Asia just before he had finished a month's course at the British Intelligence Directorate's training centre near Maidenhead. Since his return from another assignment eighteen months previously he had done nothing but courses of one sort or another. His recruitment into the Directorate some six years previously was similar in most respects to the way that the majority of field operatives had been brought in to replace their compromised predecessors in the now defunct MI5 and MI6 - the Secret Intelligence Service.

The buildings in Shepherd's Market and Lambeth housing the active and passive organisations of the British Intelligence Services had been retained, as had the organisations themselves, which fulfilled a purely clerical function, dealing with low-grade classified material. They now served a useful purpose as a continuing and purpose-designed target for foreign espionage and subversion while the new Intelligence Directorate was established in a, likewise, purpose-designed building to the west of Sloane Square in Kingsroad House.

Gunn had been recruited by the very simple means of the Intelligence Directorate informing the Ministry of Defence of the urgent requirement for an agent. Officer or non-commissioned rank was immaterial, but he had to speak Chinese - preferably both Cantonese and Mandarin Chinese, be single - as the odds against survival were low - preferably Special Forces trained, have a sound knowledge of Hong Kong and be extremely fit. It had taken the Directorate of Manning's computer at the Ministry of Defence Buildings in Glasgow a matter of seconds to produce a short list of seven names, which came within the parameters of the specification.

Gunn's name was added as an afterthought because he had been the only one who was not Special Air Service or Special Boat Service trained, but had just completed the SAS acceptance course - and had passed it - at the time of the search. The computer had produced the CVs of all eight men which had been sent by a motorbike messenger to Express Delivery Services in Kingsroad House, the home of the British Intelligence Directorate. The Directorate had two other buildings in London and another in Southampton to which the entire Directorate could be transferred - to continue operations within minutes and completely in less than 24 hours - if Kingsroad House should be compromised.

Having successfully completed and passed the SAS selection course, Gunn had been told by the Commanding Officer of 22 SAS Regiment that there had been a most unfortunate mix-up of reports and, regrettably, he had failed the selection. This had achieved exactly what Simon Peters had planned; Gunn had resigned his commission. The Commanding Officer of 22 SAS Regiment had also threatened his resignation. That reaction had also been predicted and the announcement in the London Gazette of the Commanding Officer's accelerated promotion to Brigadier to command a brigade solved that problem.

On return from his first assignment, Gunn had met the Director of BID who had offered him permanent employment, which he had accepted. Other assignments had followed, but for the last nine months, he had been on a succession of courses, which had finished with the one at Maidenhead. He had been invited to join a certain Peter de Havilland at the Royal Hamble Yacht Club at 7.30 pm on that Friday for a week's cruise. The invitation had been passed on to him by his Assistant Director and offered the opportunity of a pleasant break from the testing programme of training as a field operative of the Directorate. On the Monday following the week's cruise he was off to Langley in Virginia to report for a further month's training with the CIA. He had been glad of the offer of the cruise and wondered what sort of yacht Peter de Havilland owned, as he paused to let six or seven people cross the road.

On a Sunday evening, the south coast villages and towns returned to their weekly level of population as the boating fraternity made its way home in preparation for the start of the working week, but on Friday and Saturday evening an extraordinary, frenetic activity took place. It seemed that throughout the evening, everyone who was in one pub wanted to be in another one. Amongst the young, and even the not-so-young, there seemed to be this paranoia about not being 'where it was at'. Each season and sometimes each month, a different pub was deemed to be the 'in place' to be seen drinking, wearing the 'in' clothes and attempting to pick up a member of the opposite sex. And so, from early evening to late at night, this rush of clientele occurred from one hostelry to another to make sure that the 'in crowd' hadn't moved to a new watering hole.

Gunn saw the Flute and Fiddle on his right as he drove towards the car park by the river, a hundred yards further on round a bend in the street. The Flute succeeded in hedging nearly all its bets by having a cocktail bar and a pub bar, a smart restaurant and a bistro and was also an hotel; moreover, it overlooked the river which not many of the other pubs could boast. Its clientele had spilled out onto the patio where there were three or four wooden tables and benches. The clothing was colourful and eye-catching as were the girls and for a moment Gunn's attention was distracted.

A cacophonous and discordant blast of air horns recalled his attention rapidly as a bright-red, mid-engined Nissan 3500 sports car snaked past him up the street, the deep exhaust note from its wide-bore pipes reverberated off the buildings as it scattered the early evening pub-crawlers. The car disappeared followed by much fist shaking, shouts and signals suggesting what the driver might do with him/herself - the sex was impossible to see because of the dark, smoked- glass windows.

'Someone in a hurry,' Gunn muttered as he drove round the final right-hand bend and turned into the car park by the Royal Hamble Yacht Club. He glanced at his watch; half-an-hour before he had to meet his hosts in the bar of the Royal Hamble. He locked the car and headed towards the Flute and Fiddle to get a closer look at what had distracted him earlier. 'Time for a quick pint to wash away the London dust,' he thought with pleasant anticipation which was only mildly spoilt by seeing that the red Nissan 3500 had returned and was parked outside the pub, thoughtlessly blocking nearly half the road.

*

Peter de Havilland reached the table, after struggling through the scrum of people between it and the bar. He placed a glass of white wine in front of his wife, Tricia, and sat down beside her with his pint of beer. 'That's a miracle!' he laughed, 'I said that the Flute would probably be a little more lively than the bar in the Royal Hamble, but I hadn't anticipated this sort of crowd.'

'It's always like this before the start of the first Admiral's Cup Race of the season,' the man opposite Peter offered. 'We've just brought our boat over from Cowes and if you think this is crowded, you should see that place; not a mooring or visitor's berth to be had for love or money. We only just managed to persuade the Royal Hamble to let us have a mooring on the trots opposite the clubhouse.'

'Yes, I know; Cowes is packed as I was working with three of my men on one of the Class I boats in the Groves and Gutteridge Marina,' Peter agreed. 'I think we'll finish these drinks and then go over to the Royal Hamble; we've got to meet someone there in about half-an-hour anyway.' There were four of them at the table in the bay window and Tricia had struck up a conversation with the man's wife.

Peter de Havilland had left the Royal Navy, as a Lt Commander, shortly after the Suez débacle in 1956. He had been the Captain of a minesweeper evacuating what was left of an infantry company cut off and then abandoned in Alexandria during the withdrawal of the British troops. He and the company commander had struck up a friendship that had lasted ever since. Peter had left the Navy shortly after the Suez episode and had made use of his degree in naval architecture to get a job with Osprey Boats Ltd. He had not only risen to be managing director of the company, but had taken over three smaller companies and it was now known as De Havilland Boats plc.

His great friend had stayed on in the Army where he had achieved very fast promotion to high rank, such was his ability. He had resigned his commission as a Major-General commanding an armoured division in the British Army of the Rhine. His resignation had been a protest at the government's handling of the conditions of service for the British servicemen based in West Germany. He had been snapped up by a leading firm of 'head hunters' in London to revitalise an ailing company suffering under obsolete management and three years and two companies later had been persuaded by the Prime Minister to completely reorganise Britain's Intelligence Services. He had achieved this in six months less than the target date, received a knighthood and was created the first Director of the new British Intelligence Directorate. He had succeeded in combining the roles of MI5 and 6 under one roof, to achieve clarity and co-operation rather than confusion and confrontation.

The other factor, which had contributed to the long-standing friendship was the marriage of both men to girls who had shared a flat in London. The third girl in the flat had married a friend whom Peter de Havilland had met at university and who had, on one occasion, taken him to his girlfriend's flat for a party. The aim of this cruise in Peter de Havilland's 60 foot yacht had been a reunion of the three couples, but even the best laid plans had gone wrong. Firstly, Celia and Robin Harris had had to decline as Robin was unable to get away from Hong Kong for their planned leave in UK because of a hiccup in a major ship refitting contract. Secondly, Sir Jeremy Hammond, the head of the British Intelligence Directorate, had had to fly to Washington for a meeting with his opposite number in the

29

CIA to assess the deteriorating situation in Iraq. Then a telex had come from Hong Kong to say that Robin still couldn't get away, but Celia was coming back on the Trans-Siberian railway and would be in UK in time to join the cruise. This message was followed by another from Susan Hammond to say that she did not have to accompany Jeremy to the States and could also make the cruise.

That had left Peter de Havilland with only himself and three women on the boat. He had rung Jeremy Hammond and asked him if he had anyone in his organization, who would like a week's cruise and, ideally, who had a bit of sailing experience. The result had come within 48 hours with a telephone call to Peter's PA, letting her know that a John Gunn would meet them at the Royal Hamble Yacht Club at 7.30 pm on the Friday.

'Peter, aren't those three men part of the crew of that large motor yacht moored behind us on the pontoon?' Tricia asked.

'I suppose they could be,' Peter replied, having identified the three men in the packed bar who, surprisingly, as they appeared to be of middle-east ethnic origin, seemed to have had too much to drink already. Peter knew that many drank alcohol in private, but rarely in public.

'I don't think that the owner of that yacht would be very pleased to see his crew - if that's what they are - in the state which that lot are in. Excuse me Peter, I must just nip to the loo,' and Tricia squeezed out from behind the table and through the packed bar towards the toilets.

'They've been racing up and down the main street in that red sports car,' the man opposite Peter commented. 'They must be miles over the limit and they'll kill someone unless something is done to stop them. I heard their language when I went to the gents and it really is unpleasant - look how everyone has moved away from them.'

'Well, perhaps its time we made a move; I think we'll go over to the Royal Hamble as soon as Tricia gets back. Please excuse us,' and Peter drained his glass and pushed his chair back the only inch or two that he could in the packed bar and started to get up.

'I think we'll come too,' the man's wife said and the trouble started at exactly that moment.

Tricia de Havilland had to pass the three men to get to the pub's toilets and whilst being reasonably broad-minded and resilient, she was totally unprepared for the torrent of obscene language and gestures which were directed at her by the three men. She recoiled in shock and revulsion and then to her intense annoyance and embarrassment, burst into tears. The incident had attracted

30

everyone's attention in the bar and Peter, in a rage of anguish, pushed his way through the crowd towards his wife, followed by the man who had shared the table in the bay window. Tricia had recoiled towards a group of young men who were doing their best to comfort her.

In the silence that followed, the barmen asked the three men to leave the pub or he would have to call the police. Before he had finished his warning a stinging back-hander from a ring-encrusted hand, ripped his cheek open to the bone. Blood from the long and deep wound spurted over the bar and glasses causing one of the barmaids to faint. The barman held a drying-up cloth to his injured cheek and backed away from the three men towards a telephone behind the bar. One of the three men produced a switch-blade knife which appeared in his hand with frightening speed. A young man from the group who was shielding Tricia de Havilland moved towards the man with the knife at the same moment as Peter and his table companion reached the scene.

The stage was set for a most unpleasant and bloody pub brawl between a group of enthusiastic and fairly sober amateurs and three drunken, professional thugs. The young man found himself facing a knife held by someone who, very evidently, knew how to use it. The knife was held well forward and low with the blade tilted up towards the young man's chest. It was moving hypnotically from side to side to make the intended victim concentrate on the knife rather than the face, and in particular, the eyes which would signal the instant and direction of the intended thrust. Like a shower of icy water, the young man realised that he was now the intended victim and the panic-stricken look on his face as he turned for support from his companions, who were backing away rapidly from the confrontation, drew a sneer from the knife-wielder.

To his amazement, the young man was suddenly grasped from behind and sent sprawling at the feet of Peter and his table companion, knocking them over and preventing their intervention in the scene. The knifeman's attention switched to the tangle of humanity on his right for just a split second, but it was enough. His head jerked back from a scything, side-handed blow to his throat, the knife fell from his hand and was kicked away across the flagstones. The other two men reached into their pockets, but their hands never reappeared; their skulls cracked together with a force which fractured both and they slumped unconscious to the floor to join their companion. The plunge into unconsciousness coupled with their large intake of fluid, resulted in involuntary urination and an unpleasant smell rose from the pile of three unconscious men. A matter of seconds before, the three, dark-skinned, swarthy and hirsute men had seemed highly menacing; now all that remained was an unpleasant, smelly pile of bodies looking like something from the heaps of discarded humanity in a refugee camp.

Peter helped his companion off the floor and then reached out for Tricia who had rushed towards him. 'I'm so sorry about that, darling,' and he then turned to the young men who had shielded her from the abuse, 'many thanks for your help. That was very kind of you. Come on, Trish, I think it's time we left,' but at that moment both the police and an ambulance arrived.

First into the Flute and Fiddle were the paramedics from the ambulance, followed by a police inspector and sergeant. Before dealing with the three men on the pub floor, the barman's wound was dressed and he was led out to sit in the ambulance. The driver of the ambulance bent down and checked the pulses on the three men and then turned to the inspector and his partner who had returned from the ambulance. 'This one's dead; his oesophagus and wind pipe have been ruptured and no form of resuscitation will bring him back to life; come on Harry, bring that stretcher over here and we'll get these other two out to the blood wagon.' All three bodies were finally removed and the ambulance departed. Peter de Havilland persuaded one of the barmaids to ring the Royal Hamble and pass a message to the barman there that he would be late for his meeting.

'Right sir,' the inspector was talking to Peter,' I gather that this whole incident started when these men used abusive language to your wife.' Peter explained carefully how the whole incident had started and finished with his description of the way the brawl was brought to a dramatic halt by the intervention of one man. 'And could you identify that man please, Sir,' the inspector requested.

'Yes, I'm fairly certain of that, but he seems to have vanished.'

'Did you see where he went, Sir?'

'No, inspector, I'm afraid I didn't, I was comforting my wife,' Peter replied. The sergeant came into the pub from the patio and spoke with the inspector who nodded and then replied. The sergeant left the pub and walked down the road to the Royal Hamble. Peter de Havilland explained to the inspector where their boat was and the inspector told him that he would come by later and take a statement from them. Names and addresses were taken of all the people who had been in the pub during the incident.

The sergeant reappeared from the Royal Hamble and asked the inspector to join him at the car where they spoke together for three or four minutes. The inspector then returned to the pub as another police car arrived and 'scene of crime' officers carried their equipment into the bar. Photographs were taken - a chalk outline was the sole epitaph of the dead man - and the knife was carefully placed in a plastic bag and labelled. It was a further twenty minutes before the de Havillands were able to leave the pub and walk over to the Royal Hamble.

The de Havillands went into the yacht club after bidding good-night to their table companions, who headed towards the wooden pontoons where they had tied their yacht's tender. Once they were in the reception area of the Club, Tricia remembered that she needed to find the toilets, which had been the start of the whole incident in the pub. Peter decided that he likewise would visit the gents, if for no other reason than to wash away the unpleasantness of the recent incident.   Peter waited in the reception area and when Tricia reappeared, they both went through into the bar. The restaurant was beyond the bar which, in turn, led onto a terrace from which there was a view across the boats in the marina to the river.

'Good evening Mr and Mrs de Havilland; it's nice to see that lovely boat of yours back on its berth in the marina. Hear there's been a spot of bother at the pub,' commented the barman as he recognised Peter.

'Evening Joe; yes its nice to be back and yes, there was a spot of bother at the pub, but that's being sorted out by the police.'

'Can I get you both a drink?' the barman offered.

'Yes, I think I'll have a scotch and a white wine for my wife. Joe, but before you get the drinks, has anyone been in here asking for me. You see, we should have been here at 7.30, but that wretched incident in the Flute and giving statements to the police took so long that I wouldn't be surprised if our guest had given up and gone home. Did you get the message from the Flute that we'd be late?'

'Don't worry, Sir; I got the message and passed it on to the gentleman. He was talking to a police sergeant until a few minutes ago. They were both on the terrace. He told me that he was waiting for you and I pointed out your yacht to him. I expect he's looking at her as I can't see him in the bar.'

'Thanks very much. Could we have our drinks on the terrace please?'

'Very well, Sir; the young girl will be out with them in a couple of minutes,' and Peter and Tricia walked out to the terrace and sat down at one of the tables. Osprey, Peter's yacht was on the farthest pontoon where the water in the small club marina was deepest.

Peter de Havilland had taken delivery of Osprey in the Spring of the previous year. She had been designed by a naval architect whose designs Peter admired for their simplicity, excellence of line and the first class sea-keeping qualities of the finished boats. She had been built by a West Country boatyard under Dutch management, in high quality steel and the interior had been completed to the exact specification and layout stipulated by Peter de Havilland. Osprey's overall length was a shade over 60 feet, which included a short bowsprit. She was ketch-rigged with a self-tacking, roller stays'l, roller-reefed genoa and in-mast, reefed mains'l and mizzen. The yacht could be sailed by two people with ease and by Peter on his own, assisted by the automatic steering. She was broad of beam with a deep, long keel and had twin, turbo-charged diesels all of which made her an extremely comfortable boat, particularly in heavy weather.

Peter had been most anxious to avoid what he called 'the plastic, open-planned unpleasantness and lack of privacy of a caravan,' in the design and decor below decks. A short descent from the large wheelhouse led to the saloon and dining area on the port side and a large galley on the starboard side which was better equipped than most modern, fitted household kitchens. All the navigation equipment, both satellite and coastal systems, radar, radio and automatic steering gyro-compass were positioned on the port side of the wheelhouse with the inside steering station beside them on the starboard side.

Immediately aft of the saloon was the engine room which housed the two, turbo-charged diesels. There was a third, smaller diesel, which generated the boat's electricity. On the port side of the engine room was the aft cabin bathroom and heads and on the starboard side was a small, single berth pilot cabin. In the stern of the boat was Peter's and Tricia's double stateroom. For'ard of the saloon and galley were two more cabins reached by a central companionway. On the port side was a double-bed cabin with its own bathroom and heads and on the starboard side was a two-berth cabin with its own bathroom. For'ard of this was the forepeak which contained all the sail bags, the chain locker and the spare warps and fenders. Osprey could sleep seven people in great comfort and eleven or more if the settees in the saloon and wheelhouse were used.

The waitress from the bar arrived with their drinks and placed them on the table. 'I suppose it's all very serious as that horrible creature in the pub was killed,' Tricia said after taking a sip of her wine. 'I hope this won't prevent us from setting out on our cruise tomorrow morning. It all happened so quickly and unexpectedly.'

'Don't worry; the inspector said that after we've made our statements there's no reason for us to delay our departure. When are you expecting Celia and Susan?' Peter asked. Tricia glanced at her watch, which now showed a quarter to nine.

'They both said they hoped to be here by 9.30. Celia had planned to spend a couple of days with their two girls who are staying with Celia's parents somewhere near Guildford.'

'What are we doing about supper?'

'What you mean is, what am I doing about supper!' corrected Tricia.

'Yes, alright,' smiled Peter, 'What are you doing?'

'Very little.'

'Oh.'

'Don't worry,' he was assured by Tricia, 'you won't starve. I've got a cold supper in the fridge on the boat which we can eat or not depending on how people are feeling when they get here.'

'Ah!' was the monosyllabic response and then Peter changed the subject, 'I wonder what on earth happened to that man who came to your rescue? He seems to have vanished into thin air and the police appear to be remarkably unconcerned about the whole matter.'

'Peter de Havilland?' the voice came from behind Peter. He started, slightly spilling his scotch. His surprise increased considerably when he recognised the man who had come to their rescue in the pub. 'I'm so sorry to startle you; you've very kindly asked me to come sailing with you for the next week. I would've been here earlier, but I've just been making a telephone call. My name's John; John Gunn.'

CHAPTER 3

Celia Harris accepted the offer of assistance from the Chinese 'fuwuren' - her carriage attendant - in his smart, blue uniform, to help her down the steep steps of the carriage onto the platform at Erlian Station. The station lay on the border between China and Mongolia on the Trans-Siberian railway. Celia had been looking forward to this forty-five minute halt to stretch her legs after the eleven hour journey from Beijing. At this stop on the route from Beijing to Moscow, the gauge of the track changed; once all the passengers had disembarked to go through the various customs formalities, the train was shunted into a long shed where the bogies on each carriage were changed from the narrower Chinese gauge to the wider Russian one.

At the time of the matched communist ideals of both nations, the Russians had built the wider gauge track all the way to Beijing, but when ideologies diverged the Chinese reverted to their narrower gauge again - a reasonably accurate reflection of their outlook on the rest of the world, Celia had thought, as the train pulled into the station. The bogey-changing was achieved by a large, overhead gantry crane - similar to those used in container ports - which lifted the carriage, goods wagon or rail flat, and hydraulic jacks which were used to disconnect the bogies.

Most of the non-Chinese passengers, which was the majority and consisted of nearly every nationality in the world, were heading towards the cashier's window within the station building to change their currency from Yuan to US Dollars or Russian Roubles. Celia had been warned against doing this before setting out on the trip. There was never any difficulty in changing a hard foreign currency into Yuan, but the reverse process was always conducted at highly disadvantageous rates and depended entirely on the amount of foreign currency available in the sack by the cashier and whatever form of robbery the latter thought he could get away with.

Every tourist or traveller who made use of the currency exchange facility had to accept what was given which bore not even a distant resemblance to the foreign currency exchange rates. Celia had been advised, when planning this different way of returning to England from Hong Kong, to take a plentiful supply of small denomination US Dollar notes which were still the most acceptable form of barter on the Trans-Siberian railway throughout its five thousand miles. So with time to kill, Celia dug out her little digital camera from her small backpack and wandered towards the shed where the sound of metallic bangs and clanking indicated that the bogie changing operation was in progress.

Celia had married Robin Harris two years after meeting him at a flat party in London. Her flatmate, Tricia, had a boyfriend in the navy and had brought a friend with him who was a marine engineer; they had both met at Southampton University where one had studied naval architecture and the other marine engineering which had led to many shared lectures. The friend was Robin Harris and their honeymoon had been spent cruising around the Brittany Coast in Robin's small Folkboat. Robin Harris had a job with the Swedish marine engineering firm of Astra Nova and was now its managing director in Hong Kong. Their two daughters had gone to Abbottswood, a girl's boarding school some five miles to the south-west of Guildford, on the advice of her erstwhile flatmate and husband who had sent their daughter there.

Celia and Tricia had succeeded in keeping in touch, as had the third girl in the flat, Susan, who had married a man in the army. Meetings frequently coincided with the children's exeats from school and she and Robin had been invited by Tricia and her husband to join them on a week's cruise around the Channel Islands and Brittany Coast. The invitation had been accepted as it coincided perfectly with their annual leave back in the UK and the girls' school holidays. Robin had then successfully landed a major contract to re-engine all the Star Ferries in Hong Kong, starting with all those which had been so badly damaged in a typhoon which had devastated Hong Kong a few years previously.

No sooner had he successfully tendered for and been awarded the contract against keen competition from Taiwan, than a number of serious problems had arisen and with penalty clauses in the contract looming on the horizon, Robin had had to cancel his leave in UK. He had insisted that Celia went back to England because their two daughters, Bridget and Emma, were waiting at Celia's parents' house as the summer holidays had already started.

During their three years in Hong Kong, Celia had visited Southern China a couple of times; once to the bicycle-teeming port of Guangzhou and the other to the mist-shrouded rivers and hills of Guilin. Each visit had intensified her interest in China and her determination to learn more about the huge and ancient nation which was so steeped in historical intrigue, corruption, revolution, brutality and bloodshed on the one hand and such finesse and intricacy of art, literature, culture and drama on the other. Instead of the mundane and very boring, non-stop flight from Hong Kong to London, Celia had decided to return to England on the Trans-Siberian railway. Once the decision had been made, she set about finding out as much as she could about her proposed trip.

She had eventually decided to go by train from Hung Hom Station in Hong Kong's Kowloon to Beijing, China's capital city and from there to Moscow via Mongolia. She had booked herself into the Jianguo Hotel in Beijing, for four nights, with the aim of seeing the Forbidden City, Temple of Heavenly Peace, the Ming Tombs and the Great Wall. The hotel had been chosen for no better reason than its situation close to the embassy area of the city, which she had hoped would simplify the process of acquiring her Mongolian visa. The Wednesday train from Beijing went via Mongolia, whereas the Saturday train went via Manchuria, which, apart from taking longer was supposed to be less interesting than the Mongolian route.

She had no interest in continuing the train journey through Eastern Europe as she intended to save that for a return trip at some future date when she intended to do the entire journey by train - Liverpool Street Station in London to Hung Hom in Hong Kong - the original route of the Orient Express. From Moscow to London would be by the British Airways flight, followed by a night in London at the Inn on the Park - a treat from her husband - a couple of days spent with her daughters, Bridget and Emma, and then down to Hamble to meet up with Tricia and Peter de Havilland.

She had left Hong Kong in a typical July tropical downpour on a Thursday evening and had arrived in Beijing, 1800 miles to the north and two and a half days later on a bright, dry and warm morning. Celia's four nights and three days in Beijing had been both fascinating and hectic. It had been some years since the Tiananmen Square massacre of the students and bystanders protesting for a more democratic form of government. There was still an embargo on any gathering in public places, but the cacophony of the bells on five million bicycles taking their mounts to work each morning was unchanged and her visits to the Wall, tombs, palaces and shopping emporiums had been fascinating.

Her visit to the Mongolian Embassy, which only opened for the issue of visas for one hour, twice a week, had been successful and so at six on the Wednesday morning, Celia was standing on the platform at Xizhimen Station on the northern side of Beijing. Beside her was the gleaming green and gold train; a smartly dressed fuwuren appeared who showed her to a very comfortable, two berth compartment, where she had been presented with a polythene bag containing pristine white sheets and thick, fluffy green blankets; and so the great train journey had begun.

The comfortable, two-berth compartments were much sought after; there was a chair, a small washbasin with mirror and curtains that matched the green of the blankets. Every carriage was heated by a solid-fuel boiler and a constantly boiling samovar at the end of each carriage provided a never-ending supply of hot water for tea, coffee, soup or hot water bottles. All of this was carefully explained to Celia as the large diesel locomotive hauled the twenty-five coaches north, out of Beijing.

The first sights had been of the industrial suburbs, which were dusty, dull, drab and grey and reminded Celia of the only occasion on which she had visited East Berlin on a business trip with Robin some five years previously. After the suburbs, the scenery had changed to flat farm land which had stretched all the way to the foothills which divided China from inner Mongolia.

The train had wound its way through the hills via tunnels, gorges, bridges and steep embankments, eventually reaching a crumbling portion of the Great Wall which followed the crest line of these hills for a further 1200 miles to the west to link up with the Himalayas and so complete this natural and man-made barrier between north and south. The train slowly climbed the steep gradient past the dilapidated portion of the Great Wall - which, in direct contrast to the refurbished portion a short distance away on the road route through the hills, was not on the list of places for tourists to visit. The train had reached Erlian at 5.25 in the evening and even though she had been able - like everyone else - to walk around the train chatting to different groups of fellow travellers, Celia was enjoying the exercise of stepping over the tracks as she made her way towards the train shed.

The sun was sinking towards the horizon in a fiery red glow, giving Celia a preview of the sunsets she would see as the train crossed the Gobi Desert where the rays of the setting sun were refracted off the silicon crystals of sand drifting in the wind. Once her eyes had become accustomed to the change in light inside the shed, Celia realised that there were two trains on the tracks running through the shed. Her train, as she liked to think of it, was the one nearer to her and prevented anyone seeing her entry into the building. Further away was the east-bound track on which was a goods train.

Although she had been told that she must expect to see Russian military personnel from the border onwards and had brought little bribes for them - music casettes, cigarettes, lighters, Western magazines and anything American, particularly small denomination dollar notes - she had not expected to see quite so many so soon. There were at least thirty or more in the train shed and all were armed. 'What on earth are they doing here, in the bogie-changing shed, rather than where all the foreign tourists are, on the station?' Celia whispered aloud as she moved to get a better view of the activity around the goods train.

The wagons of the goods train stretched out of sight into the distance, but in the shed at that moment and receiving the full attention of both the Russian soldiers and all the railway workers were ten low-loading rail flats which were usually used for transporting heavy plant, machinery, cars and lorries. Each of these flats was loaded with tree trunks which were about four feet in diameter and about fifty or sixty feet in length. Celia estimated these dimensions using the size of the men moving around the loaded flats as a measuring guide.

Each flat seemed to have three or four of these huge tree trunks, held in place by two metal rods on either side, at each end and heavy, steel-link chain lashing them down to various strong points. The gantry crane was astride one of the flats and the railway workers were attaching the chains of the lifting cradle to purpose-designed shackles on the flats. On the narrower gauge track beside the goods train were the bogies waiting for each flat to be lowered onto them.

Celia realised that the soldiers had formed a cordon round these ten rail flats. No interest was being taken in any of the other wagons. There was a considerable amount of noise as men shouted, steel hammers clanged on metal cotter pins and clattering diesel engines shunted those wagons, which had been re-bogied. A foreman, Celia presumed, who had been supervising a handful of men working on the hydraulic jacks, shouted something and the chains of the gantry crane began to straighten. Slowly, inch by inch, the flat started to rise from the two sets of bogies. As soon as it was clear, the whine of a powerful electric motor preceded the sideways movement of the crane as it traversed the flat to the bogies on the narrower track.

The accident happened when the flat was exactly midway between the two sets of tracks. There was a sharp, metallic report, which made at least three soldiers unsling their Kalashnikov rifles. The left and foremost lifting chain of the cradle, and the one nearest to Celia, parted. The upper portion of the chain flicked upwards like the end of a giant's bull whip and ripped open the metal roofing of the rail shed. The lower portion did the same in the opposite direction, decapitating one soldier and removing the trunk of another from his legs as cleanly as a cheese slice. The flat lurched down to the left and the tree trunks, despite the retaining chains, slid forward on the flat and crashed onto the concrete floor of the shed.

With considerable presence of mind, the crane operator threw the hoist into governed neutral and the bogie-less flat thumped down onto the space in between the tracks, removing yet another soldier who had been unwise enough to stand under the flat while it was being lifted. This unfortunate accident with its macabre dissection of human limb from body and copious quantities of blood would almost certainly have made Celia turn in horror and make a hasty exit from the place, if it hadn't been for what happened as the tree trunks struck the concrete floor. The load appeared to split apart perfectly symmetrically, revealing a blue, grey cylinder, tapering to a point at the end towards Celia. Even though she had never seen one before, other than on film or photograph, Celia realised that she was looking at a very large missile with tail fins removed which had printing in red along its side in Russian Cyrillic script.

The accident caused near panic-driven anxiety amongst the soldiers to conceal the hidden content of the rail flat and they formed a protective screen around it while the 'container' was resealed. Surprisingly, none of the rail workers were in a position to see what Celia had and if any had been, all eyes were focused on the bloody mess around the flat. Certainly, none of the men changing the bogies on the Trans-Siberian passenger train had seen anything.

Celia immediately left the shed, trying to think of a rational explanation for transporting a missile hidden amongst a load of tree trunks. There wasn't one and presumably ten flats meant ten missiles. That wasn't necessarily so, Celia reasoned to herself as she made her way back over the tracks to the station, but the soldiers had been interested in all ten flats and nothing else, so it was a reasonable assumption. Dusk was falling and as Celia turned back to glance once more at the bogie-changing shed, the setting sun had turned to a blood-red hue, all too appropriate for the incident to which she had just been the sole witness.

The Trans-Siberian coaches were shunted out of the shed and back onto the main line alongside the platform and then the Russian locomotive reversed and was connected to them. The steps were repositioned and the passengers boarded once more. Celia went straight to her compartment and picked up the diary from the fitted table beside the lower berth. She wrote up the events of that day, determined that the incident in the train shed would not spoil the rest of her journey through Mongolia and southern Russia. The route went north across the Gobi Desert, giving Celia a glimpse, every now and then, of groups of 'Yurts' - the low, pudding-bowl-shaped tents in which the itinerant Mongols lived, surrounded by their sheep and yaks. The railway crossed into Siberia at Naushki, circled the southern shore of Lake Baikal, giving Celia a magnificent view of this vast inland sea which was nearly 150 miles in length.

Celia was so fascinated by the changing scenery, the anecdotes told by all her newly-formed acquaintances - of every nationality - and the humour and conviviality at mealtime in the restaurant car, that she had no difficulty in dismissing the incident at Erlian, except at night when she was warmly tucked up in bed with a hot drink and a book. It was then that the gory scene sprang to life once more with all the gruesome details of the dismembered soldiers and the sinister appearance of the missile from inside the tree trunks. Celia searched and searched in her memory to try and think of someone to whom she could talk about what she had seen. There seemed to be little or no point in reporting it officially because she was certain that she would be politely humoured and then equally politely shown the door. These thoughts returned to her nightly as the train steadily made its way westward through Irkutsk, Novosibirsk, Omsk, Kirov and finally, after hundreds of miles of silver birch forests, to Moscow.

As the train covered the last few miles through the Moscow suburbs at lunchtime on that Monday, addresses were exchanged and farewells made; to the Swiss hotelier who had finally resigned his job as manager of one of Beijing's most prestigious hotels because he was not allowed to sack members of the hotel staff who persistently spat and picked their noses in front of the hotel guests; to the Italian journalist who was writing up the itinerary for the Figaro; to the husband and wife from Mongolia who were on their way to Budapest and the Russian guard who was leaving the train with a carrier bag full of little 'presents'.

In contrast to the cleanliness and excellent state of repair of the buildings in Moscow, the Intourist Hotel lived up to its reputation and was predictably awful as Celia had been forewarned; the rooms were scruffy, the food barely edible and the staff were experts at ignoring the guests in the hotel and were totally indifferent to any of the requests for assistance. Celia was saved from putting her stomach through the assault course of wrestling with a hotel meal by the Italian journalist, who had collected all of those who had regularly chatted on the train and took them all out for an hilarious and very tasty meal in a restaurant which bore a striking resemblance to a converted church. Much vodka, caviare and a very palatable form of strogonoff with dumplings were consumed which provided a pleasant form of immunisation to the extremely uncomfortable beds in the hotel.

The British Airways 747 landed at Heathrow at 0708 hours on the Wednesday morning; Celia had arrived back in England two minutes earlier than scheduled after travelling some 8,500 miles. With only a minimal amount of luggage, Celia pushed her trolley down to the Underground and within the hour she was relaxing in a bath at her room in the Inn on the Park. The remainder of the Wednesday was spent shopping in London and buying presents for her daughters and parents whom she would see the following day.

The next morning, she collected the keys of her hire car at reception and drove out of London through Sloane Square, and the King's Road onto the A3 to Guildford. She turned off the A3 at Guildford and fought her way through the traffic to the Cranleigh road. Twenty minutes later, she reached her parents' home in Hascombe where she received a rapturous welcome from her two daughters. The girls had been invited on the cruise, but were both booked on a Pony Club camp, which had far more appeal to them. Celia left her parents' home shortly after six on the Friday evening and once again took the A3 south to Hamble.

*

Peter de Havilland got to his feet and took the hand held out to him; 'Peter de Havilland, John, and this is my wife, Tricia. It really is very good of you to agree to join us and I must apologise for being so late, but you see...'

'Darling, John knows all that; remember, it was he who...'

'Of course! Sorry, the old brain's not as nimble as it used to be,' apologised Peter,

'Not at all; that must've been a particularly unpleasant experience for you, Mrs de Havilland...' Gunn started.

'Tricia, please.'

'Tricia,' he corrected, 'it's I who owe you both an apology; it was silly of me to lose my temper and hit that little creep so hard. If I hadn't killed him, the whole episode would have been over much sooner. Fortunately, that was a very bright police sergeant who knew exactly what to do when I showed him my BID identity card and now that I've phoned my duty officer the whole matter will be handled by the appropriate departments.'

'Thank heavens for that; but won't there be an awful diplomatic fuss from the employer of that man?' Tricia asked.

'I gather not; the police sergeant told me that they're employed by a Mr Hassan Hussein, who owns that very large motor boat astern of you,' Gunn explained. 'All of them have overstayed their work permits and I gather from my office in London that when informed of the death and the manner in which it occurred, the Iraqi Embassy wanted nothing to do with it. They said that they would be very happy if the Home Office arranged for their arrest and removal as illegal immigrants. So it looks as though that will leave your next door neighbour without a crew.

'No fear of that,' Peter commented, 'he's got at least six if not more on that boat and a whole lot more in that extraordinary castle of his in the Channel Islands.'

'Oh, that's who it is; I thought the name was familiar. Didn't one of the weekend colour supplements do an article on him and the castle - Sardrière Island isn't it?' Gunn said and then added, 'there's something odd about the man, now wait...'

'No one's ever seen him - close to, that is,' Tricia volunteered. 'That article you mentioned had photos of him from a distance, but it could have been anyone,' then she glanced at her watch. 'Come on, we must go back to the boat or Celia and Susan will be there before us,' and Tricia got up. 'Where are your things, John?'

'They're already on the boat - the barman very kindly gave me a hand and we wheeled it out on a trolley while you were stuck in the Flute.' The three of them walked off the terrace and then down a sloping concrete ramp onto the floating wooden pontoons of the marina. When they reached Osprey, John was taken below and shown to the single cabin on the starboard side of the engine room and having quickly stowed his gear, returned to the wide cockpit, aft of the wheelhouse, where he was offered a drink by Peter de Havilland.

'Tricia's just getting some food sorted out; what'll you have?'

'A cold beer would do just fine; I never had a chance to drink the one I bought in the pub. I'd just struggled away from the bar, having paid for it, when that foul-mouthed creature started up.'

'Hello Peter!' came from the direction of the wooden finger of the pontoon that led towards Osprey's berth.

'That's Celia,' Peter said, putting his drink down on the small teak table in the cockpit, 'come on, I'll make the introductions,' and the two men jumped down onto the pontoon and went to greet Celia and help her with the trolley which she was pushing. The introductions were conducted briefly on the narrow and slightly wobbly pontoon and once Celia's bags were on board, Gunn offered to return the trolley to the clubhouse. Tricia appeared from the galley below and the two ex-flatmates embraced. Peter poured a glass of wine for Celia and they stood in the cockpit waiting for Gunn's return.

'Where did you find that great hunk of manhood; are you responsible Tricia?' Celia teased.

'Wish I was, Celie; no, Peter found him when he realised that he was to be three to one in the minority of sexes to sail Osprey on our cruise.

'How did you meet him, Peter?' Celia asked.

'That's quite a story and I may be wrong, but I detect a note of disapproval in your voice.'

'Nonsense, Peter, Celie's never met the man before; how could she possibly disapprove after a two second introduction.'

'No, Trish, Peter's right, but it's not disapproval, more disappointment that the original plan for the six of us to meet up again didn't succeed in coming to fruition. We all know each other so well that we can just pick up our friendships where we left them a year or more before. Peter is very perceptive, my initial reaction was of disappointment, but that was silly and I now see that it was much better to have a total stranger to all of us than someone who one or two of us knew, but not the others. That we were unable to make the reunion work was partially our fault, of course, although there was no way poor Robin could get away with those wretched penalty clauses in the contract looming over him.'

'Whatever your first impressions were, Celie, he's the most extraordinary man; I might as well tell you now while he's away,' Tricia continued. 'You'll find it hard to believe, but he has just killed a man!'

'What!' Celia exclaimed, sitting down quickly on the teak woodwork of the cockpit.

'There was a most unpleasant incident in the Flute a bit earlier this evening when we were having a drink while we waited for all of you to arrive. There were these three drunken men from that boat behind us - there,' and she pointed - 'and as I went to the loo, they said some really foul things to me which gave me such a shock that I burst into tears, I regret to say.'

'You poor thing, what foul men.'

'Well there was the ever trusty 'St George' coming to my rescue,' and Tricia nodded towards Peter, 'when suddenly this man appeared and dealt with the whole situation in as many seconds as it's taken me to say that. He killed one of the men and very nearly killed the other two as well and then, just like a fairy tale, he vanished into thin air. It was only a matter of minutes ago that we found that the man who had rescued me was the one we'd invited to come sailing with us. There! that brings you up to date and now you know about as much about John Gunn as we do.'

'Well how did you get his name, for heavens sake?'

'Peter asked Jeremy Hammond if he knew of someone who would like to go sailing and knew a bit about it. A message was sent a couple of days later giving us John's name and that he'd meet us here at 7.30 this evening. He arrived early and did exactly what we did; went to the Flute because it's more lively than the Royal Hamble. In future, I think I'll stick to the staid atmosphere of the yacht club.'

'But how the hell does he get away with killing a man, I mean, I would expect the police to be swarming all over the place?'

'We'd just reached that stage when you arrived so perhaps you'd like to ask him yourself, Celie. Do you know what Jeremy does?' Peter asked.

'I know that he's sorted out lots of ailing companies and got a knighthood for it, but not much more than that,' Celia answered.

'He was given a job to do by Maggie Thatcher which got him his knighthood, Celie, and then he was told to run the organisation which he'd created. Perhaps you'd better ask Susan as she's just about to join us or perhaps Trish can tell you in the galley while you both dish up the food,' Peter had seen Gunn returning with another trolley and Susan Hammond. Susan Hammond preceded her bags onto the boat and after effusive greetings, all three women disappeared below. 'Hope you're not starving, John; the three of them haven't seen each other for about a year so we'll be lucky if food appears before midnight!'

'We heard that!' Tricia's disembodied voice came from below. 'Dinner is served.'

CHAPTER 4

'Peter, would you open the wine; the corkscrew's beside the wine-cooler,' Tricia added as she saw her husband heading towards the drawer where it was usually kept. She had prepared a cold meal of gaspaccio soup followed by fresh salmon and salad. The wine was a crisp, dry Muscadet which had been collected from the cellars of Henri Ries in Cherbourg on Osprey's previous trip to France. Throughout the meal, the three women brought each other up to date on the happenings in each of the families and listened to Celia's anecdotes of her train journey on the Trans-Siberian railway.

The two men found they had a great deal in common with their interest in boats and when Tricia got up to collect the coffee percolator from the galley, the two of them disappeared up to the wheelhouse, where Peter explained all the navigation gadgets which Osprey possessed. They were brought back to the saloon by a call from Tricia to let them know that their coffee was poured and Celia wanted to ask Peter a question.

'Peter,' Celia started as he came down the four steps into the saloon, 'didn't you have a friend who eventually became involved in something to do with security or intelligence?' It was obvious that the time in the galley getting the supper ready had not extended to a revelation by Susan of the job which Jeremy did.

'Yes Celia; you've been talking to his wife for the last hour or so,' he laughed. Susan Hammond had become so used to telling people that her husband worked in the Foreign and Commonwealth Office and then steering the conversation away from any detailed discussion of her husband's job, that it had never occurred to her that Celia had no idea what Jeremy really did. 'I think in this company, Susan won't mind me saying that; why? What's the problem? Don't tell me that you saw all the Soviet Divisions forming up to start World War Three did you?' Peter teased.

'There you are! That's exactly the reaction I expected,' Celia sighed in mock exasperation.

'Oh, shut up Peter! Anyone for more coffee?' Tricia offered. All of them accepted the offer of more coffee and then Celia turned to Susan.

'Do you mind me asking you to mention it to Jeremy? I don't want to know the result, but I'm sure there was something very odd happening and feel that someone ought to know about it.'

'Of course, but I don't have to mention it to Jeremy; John is in the same business, so let's hear what happened and then you can leave it up to him to do whatever has to be done.' Celia turned towards Gunn. On introduction, she had decided that the large man, now sitting beside her, was good to look at, as opposed to good-looking, was very attractive and had lots of sex appeal. Then Peter and Tricia had told her what he'd done in the pub earlier in the evening and she had decided there and then that when the opportunity arose that evening, he was the person to whom she should recount the incident at Erlian. She had addressed her question to Peter merely to get him to steer her to John Gunn.

'Very well,' and for a few seconds Celia collected her thoughts, 'this is what happened.' For the next twenty minutes she recounted the incident which she had seen in the train shed at Erlian. Not a word was said to interrupt her. When she had finished, Gunn was the first to speak.

'Would you be able to recognise those stencilled markings on the missile if you were shown pictures of the same or similar ones? you know, rather like the police do with an identikit.'

'Yes, I'm sure I could, but I think I can do better than that. As soon as I got back to my compartment I drew sketches of what I had seen. Do you mean you believe that they were missiles?' she added, squeezing out from her seat as Gunn got up to make room for her.

'Oh, I don't think there's any doubt about that. What we've got to find out is exactly what they were, why they were being moved into China and the implications - which could be extremely serious,' Gunn added as Celia went forward along the companionway to her cabin on the starboard side of the yacht. She was back in a moment with her diary and sat down again.

'There you are!' she said, holding open the diary and showing Gunn the sketches and notes which she had made.

'Would you let me have that page out of your diary?'

'Yes, here you are,' and she tore it out and handed it to him.

'Do you really think this is very important?'

'Yes I do - I hasten to add,' Gunn continued, 'that I'm not a Russian expert and I certainly don't speak the language, so I'm afraid that the Cyrillic script you've copied so carefully means nothing to me. What I do know is that the Russians, and the Western Nuclear Powers for that matter, take great care to hide the movement of their strategic and tactical nuclear weapons from their own people. You may not believe it, but Russia has almost as many unilateral nuclear disarmament freaks as the NATO Countries. Hiding missiles in log piles is a ploy that has been used before, in fact, some of their launch sites are disguised as logging camps. In just the same way, the Americans move theirs around on underground railways. The two key questions which need rapid answers are; were these missiles governed by the INF Treaty and therefore should have been destroyed and, secondly, what were they doing going into China? Just two questions for you, Celia, if I may.'

'Yes of course.'

'How many of these tree-trunk-loaded-flats were there?'

'Ten.'

'And the soldiers were guarding all ten?'

'Yes, they'd formed a sort of ring all round them.'

'Right; and your estimate of the length of this missile?'

'About 50 or 60 feet,' a pause, then, 'nearer 60 feet. Yes, definitely nearer 60 than 50,' Celia said confidently.

'Many thanks; no further questions,' Gunn smiled and turned to Tricia. 'Would you excuse me for a few minutes if I go and make a quick 'phone call from my car.' He went to the car park, opened the TR6 and sat in the driver's seat. The cellphone on the console between the two front seats looked like just that. It was, in fact, very similar and if the car was stolen - or just the phone for that matter - it would function just like an ordinary cellphone, but it would also identify its location to the communications centre at Kingsroad House resulting in the speedy arrest of the thief. With the correct code tapped out on the touch-sensitive buttons, the speech from the car to Kingsroad House was completely secure. It was the same duty officer to whom Gunn had spoken earlier using the 'phone in the Royal Hamble.

'You're meant to be taking a week's holiday,' he was told.

'And have every intention of doing so, especially as the boss' wife is aboard,' Gunn replied. 'Can you get someone from the Soviet Section to meet me at St Peter Port in Guernsey. We leave tomorrow at about seven in the morning and should get in to St Peter Port at about nine tomorrow night; visitor's berth 162 in the new marina to the north of the ferry harbour. Instead of phoning in at each port of call, I'll take this mobile with me. When you've briefed whoever is coming, please get him to bring that Soviet Military Equipment and Uniform ident' manual with him and ask him to check in with Richard Preston of Asia Section and Simon Peters of South-East Asia.' This was acknowledged and Gunn broke the connection and then lifted the phone clear of its mounting using a small key to unfasten the locking device. From the glove pocket, he removed a plastic envelope, which contained a power lead for connecting the phone to either an AC or DC charging source. He then locked the car and walked back to the boat.

It was a clear night with hardly any breeze - not even enough to cause the familiar frapping noise of cordage against mast. Peter and the three women were sitting in the cockpit when Gunn returned to the boat. 'All OK?' asked Peter. 'What's that?'

This is a slightly special mobile, which I can use on your boat - if that's OK? There'll be someone to meet us at St Peter Port.'

'Yes, that's fine; will you be able to stay on the cruise with us?' was Peter's next inquiry and there was a note of anxiety in his voice.

'Yes of course,' laughed Gunn, 'as I said, my knowledge of Russia and Russian equipment is pretty rudimentary and this is a job for specialised experts. Celia did a really excellent job spotting all the detail of the incident at Erlian. I'll just dump this in the wheelhouse, if I may, and then join you all for a nightcap.' When he reappeared from the wheelhouse, he accepted the scotch offered to him by Peter and sat on the raw teak coaming of the cockpit. 'So that's Hussein's great gin palace,' he observed, nodding in the direction of a gleaming red and white boat astern of Osprey.

'Yes, no beauty is it; I'm told it's capable of nearly fifty knots. I know that he can do the journey to Sardrière in under two hours and that's all of 100 miles,' was Peter's comment.

'What's his background?' Susan asked.

'There's very little known about him,' Tricia answered. 'Other than what I told you in the galley; isn't he an arms dealer, Peter?

'Supposed to be, but that's just like all the stories about him. He's an Iraqi by nationality, but prefers to think of himself as a Kurd. The story is that on a visit to his village he was caught by one of Saddam Hussein's attempts to wipe out the Kurdish population of Northern Iraq. It is said that he was the only survivor and was desperately burned by whatever gas was used. That would certainly explain why he has never been seen or photographed by anyone. There was then a long period in a private clinic in Switzerland when plastic surgeons tried to give him a face - so the story goes. None of this can be verified because the private clinic was burnt to the ground shortly after his departure and - surprise, surprise - all those involved in his treatment, died in that fire. Certainly the bit about the hospital is correct - I checked that out of curiosity. There's an even stranger rumour that the plastic surgery was a disaster, left his face in a frightful mess and that he so detested the sight of himself, he had a mask made - a veritable 'phantom of the opera' for real.'

'Poor man,' muttered Susan.

'How did you discover all this?' Celia asked.

'That boat - the Arabic script on the bow is pronounced 'Al Samak' which means 'fish' - was sent to my yard last Spring for a major service to the engines. I employ an ethnic Arab in the yard - you've met him Trish - Frank Abadi by name, who became quite friendly with the boat's skipper and told me all this shortly after the job was finished. I then did a little bit of my own investigation, once again, purely out of curiosity,' Peter finished. Just at that moment there was a metallic squeak from the wheelhouse. 'What the devil's that?' Peter exclaimed, getting to his feet.

'Sorry, that's my 'phone,' Gunn apologised, putting down his drink.

'I thought you said it had to be connected to a power source?'

'Only to be connected up to recharge like all mobiles,' Gunn answered as he got up and went into the wheelhouse. He picked up the 'phone and listened. When he returned to the cockpit, Peter asked him if all was well. 'Yes fine; that was confirmation of the arrival of an expert in St Peter Port to talk to Celia.'

'I don't know about everyone else, but I know that Peter wants to get away tomorrow shortly after seven and as its now just past midnight, I'm for bed,' and with that Tricia picked up her glass, wished everyone 'goodnight' and went through the wheelhouse and down to the saloon. She was followed by the others and within ten minutes there was no sound except the gurgle and slop of water against the boats' hulls.

*

Peter de Havilland woke with a start and lay quite still for a few moments, trying to think what it was that had woken him. Tricia lay fast asleep beside him on the double bed in the aft stateroom of the yacht. No inexplicable sound or movement of the boat registered with Peter.

It sometimes occurred with houses which people had lived in for many years; perhaps one of the few atavistic instincts which had survived with humans. It nearly always happened with owners or skippers of boats - and sailing boats, in particular. In some way, the boat - by movement, noise or whatever, communicated to the subconscious mind of the person in charge of it to warn them that something unusual was happening or was about to happen. There were numerous accounts of single-handed yachtsmen who had awoken and gone on deck just in time to save their boats from catastrophe.

These thoughts drifted through Peter's sleep-fogged brain as it gradually cleared. He was tired and wanted to go back to sleep and was turning over to do just that when his irritating conscience reminded him of the time he had woken with the same feeling when he had been commanding his minesweeper off Suez in 1956. He had fallen, exhausted, into his bunk and had been asleep for only forty minutes before his ship had woken him. He had only left the bridge, having given the new course to the officer of the watch, when he was satisfied that his ship was clear of the Egyptian mines protecting the navigable channel into the port of Alexandria.

He had picked up Captain Hammond and the remnants of his company, made sure that the best possible attention was given to the wounded and had then sat in the 'driving seat' until his ship was in safe waters. He had got out of his bunk and gone up to the bridge, sensing that something was wrong. When he reached it, all had seemed in order; the coxs'n was at the wheel, the officer of the watch was alert and his navigator was bent over the chart at the back of the bridge making a plot; the port and starboard lookout both appeared to be alert and had binoculars raised as they swept their sectors. He had walked out onto the port wing of the bridge where he glanced at the compass...turned round and dived back into the bridge, reached across the coxs'n and had spun the wheel hard to starboard. For forty minutes the ship had steered a course of 250° instead of 350°, as ordered by him before leaving the bridge. As the minesweeper had swung hard to starboard, the port lookout reported mines off the port quarter; his ship had been saved, by only seconds, from annihilation.

Nothing stirred and through the open scuttle in their cabin, he sensed rather than heard the altering motion of the water as the slack high water turned to an ebbing tide. He sat up and then quietly got out of bed, stepped into a pair of sailing shoes and put on his dressing gown. Tricia stirred and turned over in her sleep; he paused to make sure he hadn't woken her and then slipped out through the cabin door closing it quietly behind him. He stood for a few more moments in the companionway, just aft of the engine room, to listen, but there was no sound other than his own breathing. He turned to the right and went past Gunn's cabin door, into the saloon and then doubled back up the steps into the wheelhouse. He looked at his watch; it was 1.30 and then his heart lurched and missed a beat or two as a firm hand was placed on his shoulder. 'It's me, Peter; John Gunn,' came the whispered reassurance.

'Thank God for that! What's going on and why am I whispering?' he chuckled softly.

'There was rather more to that 'phone call I received just before we turned in.'

'I thought so; none of my business, but it seemed too long a call just to confirm an RV in St Peter Port.'

'I'm not sure I know what's really behind it all, but since my earlier call, they've been looking into Hassan Hussein's dossier on the computer. I was asked if he was on the boat and had to say that I had no idea, but it was most unlikely that he would have allowed any of us to see him after what you told us last night.'

'That's right,' Peter confirmed. 'We came down on Thursday and I can't pretend that I was looking for him, but there hasn't been any sign except for his crew.'

'Anyway, I've been told to go and have a look around his boat.'

'Whatever for? That's taking a risk - the whole bloody boat is wired up with alarms like the crown jewels; I should know because it was my electrician who installed most of it. What's more, you must be target number one for revenge amongst what's left of the crew. What do they expect you to find?'

'No idea; or if they have, I'm not to be privy to that. No, since I'm here, there's something they want to know and its an opportunity that apparently can't be missed.'

'I think it's very risky,' Peter said rather naively and then corrected himself, 'but of course, that's presumably what you're paid for! Right, I'll give you a hand.'

'No you won't, Peter; the best help you can give me is to tell me quickly as much as you know about the security system on that boat. If I'm not back by....' and Gunn glanced at his watch, '3.30, use my 'phone and dial this number,' and in the reflected light of the marina, he jotted down the number on the navigation scribble pad, 'OK?'

'Yes, I've got all that, is there any...'

'No, nothing else; just tell me please, about Hassan's security system,' which Peter did and then Gunn left the wheelhouse.

Peter went back to the aft cabin and quietly collected his jeans and a T-shirt and then returned to the wheelhouse. He went over to the water-boiler, lifted it to see if it was full, checked that the power supply was switched to shore power and then turned it on. He wanted a strong cup of coffee to shake off any drowsiness and sharpen up his wits for the two hour wait for Gunn's return.

*

The pontoon was lit every five metres by low-level lights, which illuminated the planked surface and made it impossible to approach any boat without being seen. Apart from ensuring that people using

53

the pontoon legitimately had a well-lit route to and from their boats, the lights enabled the duty night watchman to ensure that no unauthorised people approached the boats in his care. Gunn lowered himself down into Osprey's dinghy; both Osprey and Al Samak were moored port side to the pontoon. In both cases, the starboard side was in deep shadow.

There was a gap of only five metres between the stern of Osprey and the bow of the motorboat. Gunn had no intention of using the oars, but instead, the warps and the current of the ebbing tide to carry the dinghy under the sheer of the widely flared bows of the motorboat. Just as he reached the point he had selected to tie up the dinghy and climb onto the bow using the starboard anchor stowage, a fine stream of liquid appeared over the side of the boat. This, very conveniently, showed Gunn exactly where the urinating guard was positioned.

He would have been most surprised if there hadn't been a guard; arms dealers had many enemies and the lives of the former were not noted for their longevity. The arms industry was probably the most lucrative and unscrupulous one in the world, second only to drugs. Gunn was well aware that in the arms selling business, every dirty trick in the book - and a few not even in that - was used by the intermediaries between the producers and the customers. It was the arms dealers who took all the risks, particularly when negotiating with third world countries, and it was very much in their interest to lower the odds stacked against them. On the conclusion of a deal, the dealer became a very dispensable item who frequently knew far too much for the comfort of the purchaser. In order to prevent any abrupt end to their dealings, they surrounded themselves with every form of mechanical and electronic security and then backed that with firepower and human muscle.

Richard Preston had told him that both the Middle East and Russian Sections were interested in Hassan Hussein. The latter, Gunn had been told, had succeeded in getting not only arms, but every other form of commodity, into sanction-embargoed countries. He was told that the Deputy Director of the Intelligence Directorate had been contacted when it was realised that an agent was in an opportune position and approval had been given for Gunn to investigate the motorboat. Peter de Havilland had been able to tell Gunn that there were pressure pads under the fitted carpet at every door, including the heads and bathrooms. All the scuttles, windows and hatches were wired to the alarm system. Gunn had been prepared for the guard, but it added a complication that would give him less time for his search of the boat.

He reached up and very gently transferred his weight from the dinghy to the shank of the motorboat's anchor and then using the fluke of the CQR anchor as a foothold, heaved himself onto the deck, where he remained motionless. The guard finished urinating and began to re-stow that part of his anatomy. A man was at no time - except, perhaps one - more vulnerable than when caught with trousers undone and both hands and attention focused on his genitals. He never heard Gunn's approach and the blow, just below and behind his ear, pitched him into unconsciousness without ever knowing what had happened.

The man was wearing jeans, trainers, T-shirt and an anorak. Gunn searched his clothes quickly. He had about fifty pounds in his wallet, but nothing else of any interest there. There was a packet of cigarettes and a cheap, disposable lighter in one anorak pocket and a Beretta automatic in the other. He released the magazine catch and removed it; he then worked the action and ejected the chambered round which he pressed under the retaining lips of the magazine and then replaced it in the butt of the Beretta. He held the ringed hammer and squeezed the trigger, easing the hammer forward and then replaced the automatic in the anorak pocket.

He glanced at his watch. It was already nearly 2.10; he moved silently towards the stern to find an entrance into the yacht. The glass door into the deck saloon was shut. Gunn climbed onto the flying bridge and went to the engine control console as directed by Peter de Havilland. The console was a mass of switches, buttons and dials and under the engine oil gauges was the switch with a safety cap over it. Gunn lifted the cap and moved the switch from 'on' to 'off' and then climbed down the steps to the deck, slid back the glass door and went into the saloon.

The saloon revealed nothing; Gunn went forward into a room he presumed served as Hassan's office when he was on board. It was filled with every state-of-the-art piece of office machinery and teak veneered filing cabinets. There was much less light in this room as the windows looked out on the starboard side away from the marina lighting. Gunn switched on a desk light and bent the angle poise right down so that the shaded bulb was only a few inches off the desk. He took a key ring out of his pocket and selected a metal lockpick, only slightly longer than a household key and with a tip to it similar to a dentist's tooth probe.

There were two cabinets; the first revealed nothing of particular interest and Gunn closed it again. The second one appeared to be equally innocuous and he was just closing the drawer when he saw a piece of paper that was on the bottom of it under the file holders. He pushed the files apart and retrieved the piece of paper; it was a newspaper cutting. The cutting had been stuck to a piece of A4 paper and then the title and date of the newspaper had also been cut out and glued above the article. The article was from the Westdeutsche Zeitung and showed an artist's impression of a rather unusual vessel and in bold type the heading of the article asked, WER HAT DAS SCHIFF GESTOHLEN?

The paper was dated 20th November 1989. Gunn quickly scanned the article; the ship building consortium of Neuberg und Deutschmetal had completed a cargo vessel for South Africa. The pressurized water-cooled reactor for the twin-shaft drive had been provided by South Africa which gave the vessel a reputed 120,000 shaft horsepower and a speed of nearly 30 knots. Throughout the construction of the vessel, the Hamburg Police Department had been kept busy by various factions demonstrating outside the yard against this support for apartheid and the rumour that it was powered by a nuclear reactor.

A crew had been sent from South Africa to complete a fortnight's work-up in the ship and then sail it back with a cargo. The demonstrations had finally prevailed on the German politicians to back down, cancel the cargo and get rid of the vessel as quickly as possible. The ship had been officially handed over by the shipyard to the South African captain in a ceremony which was ordered by the West German Government to be low key and no press were to be admitted. Once the ship had been handed over, a private security company, which had been hired by the South African captain, had been given the task of guarding the ship until it sailed the next day.

That night, the entire crew had gone out for a night on the town and had arrived back from the strip clubs, brothels and massage parlours of the Rieperbahn and Herbertstrasse at four in the morning to find that the ship had vanished. So had all the guards supplied by the security company. Not one single sighting of the vessel had been reported despite a request to all the NATO Navies for assistance. The incident, so the article claimed, had caused intense embarrassment to the South African Government, jubilation for the anti-apartheid lobby and relief to the West German Government who held no responsibility for the ship once it had been handed over.

There was something in the article that rang a chord in Gunn's memory, but he had neither the time nor the concentration to pursue it. He was just removing the article from under the desk light where he had been reading it, when he noticed some indentations on the surface of the paper. He held the paper at an angle to the light and this immediately revealed a line of figures which appeared to resemble a phone number. '0424 130710,' he whispered and repeated it several times and then muttered, 'so did Hassan have something to do with this and why can't I bloody well think what's familiar about something in that article?'

His irritation was interrupted by a noise which came from the companionway for'ard of the office. It sounded like a robotic, computer-generated electronic voice; the language it used appeared to be Arabic and the inflection had indicated a question to a man called Yussuf - presumably the guard on watch? Gunn had no idea, but he certainly wasn't going to stay and find out. He replaced the cutting, closed the drawer, turned out the light and raised it back to its previous position. The name was called again.

Gunn went back into the saloon and closed the door as he went out onto the deck. From there he went up the steps to the flying bridge and switched on the alarm system; a small red light appeared on the console, went out and a green one came on and then that went off. He presumed that that was the arming sequence of the alarm. He was just about to climb down the steps when he heard the soft swish of the sliding door of the saloon being opened.

Gunn was standing by the base of the fin-like mast on which was mounted the boat's radar scanner. Someone had come out onto the deck and was standing quite still, just outside the saloon door below Gunn. Neither of them moved. Gunn's only concealment was the deep shade cast by the mast; the person below him was back-lit by the marina lights making any features impossible to identify. The figure was clothed in a long garment, like a bernous, which covered the entire body. It seemed like five minutes, but was probably less than two, that the two of them stood motionless.

The figure turned to the left and moved slowly away from the steps leading up to the flying bridge and round to the starboard side of the boat. Gunn took a pace towards the steps and then immediately pulled back into the shadow; the figure had reappeared and moved towards the foot of the flying bridge steps. The steps were on the port side of the bridge and only the slim, fin of the mast would separate them if the character below Gunn decided to come up. He did; two gloved hands appeared first at the top of the guardrails, which seemed odd for such a warm night, and then the top part of the body followed, now illuminated by the marina lighting.

Gunn had the greatest difficulty controlling his sharp intake of breath and he physically felt the sweat burst out on his forehead and the palms of his hands. The creature, because that is what had appeared at the top of the steps, came up one further step and paused and called Yussuf quietly once more. Gunn was rooted to the spot, torn by an emotional conflict of horror and compassion for the appalling disfigurement to a human body.

There was no face, as such; no eyes, ears, mouth or hair, it was just a monstrous lump of scar-tissued flesh which slowly turned from side to side, scanning the area of the flying bridge. There was a form of collar around the neck from which a fine wire disappeared down into the bernous. Gunn assumed that this was some sort of voice synthesizer because there was no recognisable mouth to form speech. The skin resembled something that had been dreamt up in the special effects department of a computer-animation film. There had to be eyes because the 'man' could move around the boat without touching things like a blind person. There was no nose, just a deformed aperture where it had once been and it seemed to Gunn that this was being used, almost like an animal, to scent for danger.

The man came up two more steps and still the grotesque head cast from side to side and then stopped, pointing directly at the fin mast. With quite remarkable agility, Hassan - for this could be no other person - came up the last few steps and bounded towards Gunn's hiding place. With matching agility, driven by his horror of the monstrously disfigured body coming towards him, Gunn took one pace towards the side of the bridge and dived over the side.

It was only half an hour or so after high tide and Gunn let himself go deep and then turned to his right away from Osprey. There was no possible chance of anyone seeing in which direction he went, but he had to make sure that he avoided involving the de Havillands if anyone was following him and there was still the dinghy tied up under the bow of Al Samak. John Gunn surfaced by the rudder stock under the counter of an attractive old wooden yacht, moored astern of the motorboat. The pontoons were kept buoyant by rectangular, welded-steel canisters; there was a gap of about eighteen inches between the water and the pontoon and Gunn used this to make his way towards the inshore side of the marina. Using the pontoons to hide his movement, he made his way round the marina until he eventually reached the bow of Osprey again.

The yacht's freeboard was far too high for him to climb over, but by using a fender to help him reach up, he was able to grasp the metal stanchion on the deck and pull himself up. The water increased his weight by nearly a third again and his muscles ached as he heaved himself over the side of the toe-rail. Once again, he was on the starboard side of Osprey, in deep shadow. As his breathing slowed, he was able to take stock of his surroundings. Fortunately, there was a really heavy dew and the teak-laid decks were soaked by it, masking the puddle which was spreading around Gunn. Osprey's fore-hatch was open to allow what breeze there was to circulate through the yacht. The hatch led down into the forepeak store and chain locker; he lowered himself down gently and closed the hatch behind him. He then removed his sodden clothes and shoes and walked silently along the fitted carpet of the companionway into the saloon and then to the heads on the port side of the engine room where he dumped his clothes on the gridded teak floor of the shower stall. He went into his cabin, glancing at his watch as he did so; it was between twenty and twenty-five past three. In a few more minutes, Peter de Havilland would pick up the phone to raise the alarm. Gunn quickly towelled his hair dry, pulled on his dressing gown and went back into the saloon. As he did so, he saw the night watchman approaching the yacht accompanied by what looked like a member of Hassan's crew.

'Peter! I'm back; quick! Come down into the saloon,' he whispered urgently.'

'Christ! You gave me a fright; are you alright?' an anxious Peter asked.

'Yes, fine thanks; quick out of sight, we're about to have visitors and we must convince them that they've just woken us up,' and with that, the two men on the pontoon stepped onto the yacht and tapped on the saloon door.

'Go and put a dressing gown on, or whatever you sleep in and then come back,' Gunn whispered. Peter went aft to his cabin and reappeared almost immediately in a sarong and flip-flops just as there was a rather louder tap on the saloon door.

'Make a show of having been woken up,' Gunn said, 'and you know nothing about Osprey's dinghy being moved. Come and get me to confirm that; OK?'

·   'Yes, got all that,' and Peter went up into the wheelhouse and then stopped. He quickly unplugged the water boiler and handed it to Gunn together with a still warm cup of coffee. 'Stick those in the galley!' and he turned and went to the saloon door and opened it with a very convincing performance of having just woken up.

'What is it?.... Frank, isn't it,' and Peter addressed his question to the night watchman. 'We haven't met,' and he held his hand out to the man standing beside 'Frank'.

'Iddrisu,' was the curt response.

'What's the problem,' and Peter looked brearily at his watch. 'Gracious, it's only just after half past three in the morning; please, come in, come in..... wait a minute,' and Peter switched on the lights in the wheelhouse; 'there we are; now what's the problem?'

'I'm sorry to disturb you, Sir,' apologised the night watchman, 'but this 'gentleman', and the slight emphasis on the word conveyed the night watchman's disapproval, 'tells me that he's had a prowler on his employer's boat and he's found your ship's tender tied up under the bow of the boat.'

'Oh, I see; which boat is that?'

'The one right behi....astern of you, Sir.'

'Mr Hussein's boat? That's dreadful, what can I do? Is the prowler still around? Have you called the police? What do you want me to do?' The acting was brilliant and Gunn could only admire the conviction with which Peter delivered his incredulity.

'No, no, Sir; we haven't called the police yet. We... that's to say, this gentleman, wondered if you had lost anything or seen anything,' Frank finished off rather lamely and then added, 'other than your tender, I mean, Sir.'

'I really haven't the faintest idea. Hang on, I'd better wake my companion and see if he heard anything.'

'Oh no, Sir, please don't go to that trouble, I'm.....'

'No trouble, Frank,' and Peter retired to the saloon where Gunn mouthed the word 'brilliant'. Two minutes later, he followed Peter into the wheelhouse, yawning and rubbing the sleep from his eyes. It was not long before both men left; the crewman said nothing and Frank apologised profusely for the disturbance. When they were some twenty metres away and Peter had switched off the light, Gunn asked, 'what would the name Neuberg und Deutschmetal mean to you, Peter?'

'Probably the ship building world's leading experts on the construction of submarines,' was the instant reply.

CHAPTER 5

It was still dark when the strident ringing of the alarm clock woke Gregorei Malinovsky out of a deep sleep following his exhaustion from the exertions of the previous night. He groped for the clock, but it wasn't in the usual place, nor was it the usual sound and he was unable to find it. His brain gradually cleared and he remembered that he was not in his own bedroom. His hand made contact with the clock and knocked it from the bedside table onto the floor where it continued ringing even more noisily. Cursing and swearing, his hand eventually found it again and brute force rather than mechanical aptitude finally silenced the alarm.

Beside him, the steady breathing of the woman, whom he had met for the first time the previous evening, did not falter. He felt drained of energy and short of sleep because of the insatiable demands of the woman who had insisted on repeat performances, in every imaginable position, until nearly five in the morning. The room was well heated against the biting cold, which proved he supposed, that the stories he had heard about the high standard of living enjoyed by prostitutes were probably correct. She would certainly need a better salary than a Colonel in the Army could provide and no infantry major - to whom she had claimed to be married - in the Russian Army could have possibly afforded to pay the rent of this comfortable apartment on the much sought-after south side of Kalinin. No, she had to be making a living on the side and that had to be prostitution, but, Gregorei foggily recalled, she hadn't asked for any money from him. Still trying to recall what had happened the previous evening, he got off the bed and staggered around in search of a light switch first and the bathroom second.

Colonel Malinovsky was the Commandant of the underground nuclear missile arsenal on the north side of Kalinin. It was a job which carried considerable responsibility, particularly since the signing of the Intermediate Nuclear Forces Treaty, and was known to be a make or break appointment - get it right and promotion was assured; get it wrong and he would never be heard of again. His predecessor had been promoted to Colonel General and Commander of the Kiev Military District, where he'd subsequently been caught with his hand in the till, but then, there, but for the grace of his wonderful Motherland, he thought cynically, nearly all of his contemporaries could have been found guilty and shared the same fate.

Thoughts of promotion immediately reminded him of his mean, frigid and wasp-tongued wife, who was a distant relation to a very senior member of the Russian Government and constantly reminded him of this relationship. Gregorei shuddered at the thought of what his wife's reaction would be if she ever found out what had happened the previous night.

To his surprise, there was a razor in the cupboard above the washbasin and, what was even more of a surprise, the blade was new. As he shaved, his mind drifted back to the previous evening. He had been to a reunion dinner of the 52nd Tank Division, which had been held in the tank battalion barracks eight kilometres to the south of Kalinin. After the dinner and several vodkas, someone had suggested that they go and try out a new club that had just opened in Kalinin. Only high-ranking officers or those in jobs, which carried the perk of Special Military Passes, were allowed to visit the club, which only accepted foreign currency or rouble certificates. Gregorei had realised that he was the only person in the group who possessed such a pass; he had already made arrangements to stay the night in the barracks to avoid his wife's mockery of a drunken homecoming. So why not? he had thought as he briefed his driver and offered a lift to two battalion commanders.

They had arrived at the club, which sported the rather hackneyed title of Club Moulin Rouge, shortly before midnight. The existence of the club had never come to Gregorei's ears, but some of those officers with him had been before and were warmly welcomed by the staff and hostesses.

The lighting was low, the music seductive and the drinks were both exotic and expensive. The club had been well patronised, but not overcrowded. Gregorei had excused himself and left his two colleagues to make his way to the toilets in the small reception area of the club. When he had returned, both his colleagues were already dancing with pretty hostesses.

'Damn! Why do I always miss out?' he had cursed under his breath.

'We both seemed to have missed out; sorry to butt into your thoughts, but perhaps you would be kind enough to let me have a light?' had come from his right and startled, Gregorei had turned towards the woman who had spoken to him. Even a cursory glance had been enough for him to realise that he was standing beside a most striking looking woman who had a superb figure. He had also realised that he had voiced his thoughts out loud; a bad habit for someone with a job like his.

'Sorry...a light? Just a moment,' and he had patted his tunic pockets, embarrassed at his clumsiness and lack of confidence in the presence of this attractive woman. 'Yes, here we are,' and he had produced a really cheap book of matches, which added further to his lack of self-assurance in those surroundings. 'Why couldn't I have had a lighter?' he had mutely reproached himself.

'This is my first visit to this place since it reopened last month; have you been here before?' she had asked him.

'No, I've never been here before,' Gregorei had confessed.

'Do you have a table?' she had then asked.

'Yes, over there,' and Gregorei had pointed to an empty table near the small dance floor.

'Would you mind if I joined you at your table? I feel a little vulnerable sitting at the bar.'

'No, of course not, please do,' and Gregorei had helped her off the barstool and led her across to the table. 'Would you like to dance?'

'Yes, I'd like that,' she had replied and they both edged their way onto the crowded dance floor. Still believing that she was employed at the club, Gregorei had asked her whether she enjoyed the job and the very long hours it must entail. Much to his confusion, she had told him that she didn't work at the club, but was married to a major in the infantry who had been in Iraq for the last eighteen months as a military adviser. They had no children, but were fortunate to have a small, but comfortable apartment in Kalinin. She had told him that when she was bored of television, reading or her own company, she went to the Moulin Rouge to cheer herself up.

'But I thought you needed a Special Pass to get into this place,' he had said, at which she had laughed.

'Not if you have contacts, are a woman and a reasonably attractive one!' Gregorei had felt a twinge of jealousy, realising that a woman as attractive as the one with whom he was dancing must have many 'contacts'. It was either the crowded dance floor which had forced all the couples to dance close together, or it had been her uninhibited behaviour, but within a few minutes she had pressed every possible portion of her body against him to which he had reacted like a gawky, adolescent schoolboy.

After his fumbling courtship, engagement and subsequent marriage to Yelena, his wife, and the arrival of their one and only child, his son Alexei, she had made it quite clear that sex, and particularly childbirth, were both unpleasant and unnecessary. Yelena had become progressively more frigid and the double bed quickly disappeared to be replaced by single beds which, in their turn had given way to separate bedrooms. He and Yelena merely shared a house which kept up appearances and provided a roof over the head of their son. He adored his young, teenage son and the two of them spent as much time as possible together, which merely served to increase his wife's resentment and hostility.

Yelena had progressively developed, what Gregorei had considered to be an unhealthily close relationship with their young and simple-minded housemaid. Only some weeks after his removal to a separate bedroom, he had returned home early from work to find - to his surprise - that the house was empty, or so he had thought. He had gone upstairs to have a bath and it could have only been the two women's preoccupation with what they were doing which prevented them from hearing his arrival and his approach to his bedroom door, which he had found locked.

He had tried to open the door, which had caused considerable confusion on the other side of it. When the door had been opened, it revealed both Yelena and Olga the maid, flushed of cheek and in a highly embarrassed state. His wife's explanation had been a masterpiece of improvisation. She claimed that she had caught Olga asleep in his bedroom when she was supposed to be cleaning it. She had just threatened the girl with her notice if ever caught malingering again. 'Why lock the door?' he had asked rather naively. His wife's improvisation had been exhausted by this question and she had mumbled something to the effect that the lock had always been faulty on that door and had locked her in at least twice before.

'That's why the key's on the inside,' she had thrown over her shoulder as she bustled Olga out of the room. He hadn't thought much about it at that instant, but as he had undressed for his bath, he did.

'Of course the key's on the inside,' he muttered. 'It always has been and so it is in every other bedroom in this and every other house.' He had sat on the bed to remove his socks and while bending down to pull them off, saw something sticking out from under the mattress. He had paused with his sock half off and pulled the object out into the open. They were far too small to be his wife's, so they could only be Olga's knickers. Not that it really mattered whose they were as one or other of the two women had felt it necessary to remove them to indulge in whatever form of activity had been going on when he had interrupted it by his early return. He had carefully pushed them back under the mattress, from where they had vanished the next day.

In the days and weeks that had followed, it had been blatantly obvious that his wife played the dyke role in the lesbian relationship and out of pure mischief and curiosity, Gregorei had decided to search both his wife's and housemaid's rooms. He had no idea what he was looking for until he stumbled across a vibrator hidden inside an umbrella case in his wife's chest of drawers. He removed this and then buried it in the garden in the same place as their small, wire-haired dog buried his bones. His dancing partner mistook the smile on his face as a sign of his enjoyment of the closeness of her body. He was indeed enjoying that, but the smile came from the recollection of the incident that followed the burial of the vibrator.

Not even he could have planned it so perfectly if he had hatched the plot for months. The celebrated relative had arrived unannounced to ask if he might stop at the house for a short pause for tea as he was ahead of his schedule to visit the forestation project to the north of Kalinin. The drawing room had been filled with his staff and acolytes and Yelena had been in her element, preening herself in the reflected glory of her relative's importance.

Olga had been handing round some biscuits and was offering them to the uncle in the Government, when 'Dacha', the scruffy little Malinovsky dog had appeared with the vibrator proudly held in his mouth which he planted on the floor in front of Yelena, who was sitting next to her uncle. Olga had shrieked, turned crimson, dropped the biscuits and fled from the room. Yelena had turned so puce that Gregorei thought she would burst a blood vessel. The uncle, who had got on very well with Gregorei - and vice versa - collapsed with laughter, as had all his staff to the mortification of Yelena who suddenly found herself to be a very unwanted centre of interest, curiosity and amusement.

By their reaction to the incident, both women had revealed their relationship and unable to endure the laughter any longer, Yelena had also fled from the room. The uncle had slapped Gregorei on the back, saying that he had never understood how his shrew of a niece had managed to catch such a red-blooded male and that he must come and stay at their Moscow apartment whenever he wished to. The masculine pronoun had been purposely emphasised in a loud voice, which had carried easily out to the kitchen, which added insult to the injury already inflicted on Yelena. However, within a fortnight of that incident, she was as waspish as ever, but the sting had been drawn and the uncle had never been mentioned again.

It was a long time since Gregorei had held a woman with such an excellent figure so close and his lack of self-control had become abundantly obvious which exacerbated his embarrassment and confusion. On the contrary, his lack of self-control had delighted his partner who made matters even more embarrassing for Gregorei by moving her body rhythmically against him in time to the music. In an agony of embarrassment at her increasing sexual abandon, Gregorei had furtively glanced at the other couples around them, but the combination of the subdued lighting and the other couples' preoccupation with their respective partners, reassured him that his seduction on the dance floor had so far gone unnoticed.

He had realised that he was fast reaching the point of no return if her stimulation continued and the increased pace of her warm breath in his ear indicated a reciprocal state of arousement in his partner. Her hands had been round his waist, but they moved down round his buttocks and pulled him in even harder against her. This final sensual assertion of her lust precipitated both of them into a gasping climax of sexual relief. Holding onto each other for mutual support, there had been a few moments of silence and then she had quietly suggested that they return to her apartment.

He couldn't even remember if he had replied, but he remembered dismissing his driver as she owned her own car. Once they were in it, Gregorei had realised, rather like a lamb being led to the slaughter, that he had bitten off more than he could chew and as she drove she was unable to leave him alone and demanded a reciprocal effort on his part by placing his hand firmly between her thighs. They had reached the apartment at 1.40 in the morning and from then until five she had encouraged him to make love to her in ways which, twenty-four hours previously, he would have thought were physically impossible, until finally, he had collapsed exhausted and totally spent into a deep sleep.

He had managed to shave one side of his face with the diminutive razor and was just positioning the blade to begin on the other side, when two things happened in quick succession. He was grabbed from behind which made him cut himself and before he knew what had happened, he had been mounted once more. Only once his partner had relieved her morning passion was he allowed to shave the other side of his face and get dressed in his uniform. From the kitchen came the sound of her humming a tune and when he went in she was standing by the stove, clad only in a tiny apron as she prepared a delicious breakfast for him, which included French ground coffee. The exertion of the night had not left the slightest impression on her and she looked as though she had just had eight hours of undisturbed sleep. Gregorei could only marvel at both her appetite for sex and the stamina she possessed to sustain it. 'You know,' he began lamely, ' I don't even know your name.'

'Kristina,' she replied, 'now come on and eat your breakfast or you'll be late for work.'

It had been a week later that Gregorei Malinovsky's adjutant had come into his office to announce that he had a visitor and then showed in his predecessor, Boris Samsonov. It looked as though it might be an embarrassing interview because it was well known that Samsonov was very hard up having lost his military pension. However, the offered seat was declined and when the door had closed behind the adjutant, Samsonov had opened his briefcase and produced a large manila envelope, which he handed over the desk to Gregorei.

Barely a word had passed between the two men. Gregorei opened the envelope and one glance was enough to know the purpose of Samsonov's visit. 'What is it that you want,' he asked in a resigned voice and Samsonov had told him while Kristina's mocking smile looked up at him from the pile of explicit pornographic photos which had spilled out of the manila envelope.

It wasn't until Samsonov had left the office, having given his instructions, that Gregorei allowed himself to smile as he recalled the detailed briefing he had received after his encounter with Kristina.

*

The jet-foil turned in a sweeping curve to port as it left the Pearl River estuary and entered the waters of Hong Kong, just to the north of Tree Island. Simeon Bukharin stared in ill-concealed fascination at the changing scenery. On his left were the densely populated towns of the New Territories followed by the yacht marina, Pearl Island and the sprawling suburbs of Kowloon, while in direct contrast on his right was Chek Lap Kok Airport – the state of the art airport built on reclaimed land on the north shore of Lantau Island.

The PA system on the Boeing jet-foil announced in Cantonese and then English that their arrival at the Tai Kok Tsui Pier in Kowloon would be in just under ten minutes. Simeon glanced at his watch and then leant back in the comfortable airline seat. 'Was this really all happening to him,' he thought, 'or was it a dream and he'd wake up soon in that miserably cold flat in Minsk.' It was hard to believe that the train of events which had taken him all the way from the heart of Russia to the unashamed capitalist hub of South-East Asia had really happened.

After the meeting in Samsonov's apartment the previous October, they had all gone home; 'home,' grunted Simeon in derision and then suddenly realised that he had said it aloud in Russian and was being watched apprehensively by the Chinese couple sitting next to him.

He had to be more careful if he wished to stay alive to benefit from his portion of the share-out of the sale of the missiles. Having chided himself for this slip, he then considered the part he had been required to play in the conspiracy. The instructions in his envelope had been detailed and complicated and had involved considerable risk on his part, but he had assumed that it would be the same for all of them. He and Ivor Voznesensky were to work together and then he had read the outline of the whole plan.

After the signing of the INF Treaty, both the Russians and the Americans had arranged a number of highly publicized functions in both Countries during which the appropriate number of missiles would be symbolically destroyed. Although it involved many risks, the plan was both ingenious and simple, with the exception of some individual tasks that were both complicated and planned in great detail. The unpredictable element of the plan was going to be the reaction of those people in the Government, Military, KGB and GRU who had to be bribed or blackmailed to co-operate. All of these people had been selected with great care and all had behaved as predicted in Rokossovsky's assessment. Simeon smiled at the recollection of the 'honey trap' set for the Commandant of Kalinin Arsenal; he'd enjoyed the videos of the bedroom scenes.

Boris Samsonov had been given the task of finding out from the Commandant when missiles were to be removed from the arsenal for destruction. Peter Milynkov had been given the job of procuring the ten fake missiles, which were to be swapped for the real ones. As he had been the Director for Weapons Research, Design and Production, the assignment had proved to be fairly straight-forward and then the three of them, he, Peter and Ivan had had to arrange the exchange of the missiles and the transportation to Southern China.

On receipt of these instructions, all three of them had queried the wisdom of routing the missiles through China and the risks that would be involved. Rokossovsky had explained that the Black Sea ports of Odessa and Rostov were out of the question, as were the ports of Murmansk in the Barent's Sea and Vladivostok in Eastern Manchuria. All of the Russian ports, Rokossovsky had explained, were under close observation, both by satellites and in-country agents of America's CIA; this was the reason for the Trans-Siberian route.

Samsonov had identified the key officials of the Government, the Military and the KGB who required to be suborned to make the plan work. Samsonov had been astutely chosen by Rokossovsky because as Commander of the Kiev Military District, he had kept copious files on everyone of importance or influence and very little happened, particularly of a scandalous or illegal nature, that was not picked up by the sensitive monitoring system deployed by the District Commander.

Samsonov had discovered that the Commandant of the Kalinin Arsenal had a completely clean record and so had had to engineer a situation to trap him. The dubious proprietor of a back street marital aids shop, who had kept both photos and names of all his clients, on interrogation by Samsonov, had provided the latter with the information on Yelena Malinovsky's purchase and a little gentle persuasion had extracted the required information from the Malinovsky's housemaid.

The plan had not only been brilliant in its simplicity and would make them all rich men, but it had the added satisfaction of revenge by destroying the credibility of President Putin, who had been instrumental in their banishment. He would, in turn, be removed from office in disgrace when the final act of the plan was put into effect, which was to inform the USA that Russia had not only cheated on the INF Treaty, but had provided one of the most unstable leaders in the world with a nuclear capability.

Rokossovsky had explained in their instructions that their Country possessed one third of the world's total forest area, which covered some 747 million hectares and contained about 79,000 million cubic metres of wood of which 84% were coniferous. In 2001, the Chinese had suffered the most disastrous series of forest fires in living memory. They had raged for nearly four months despite every human effort to contain them and in the end had been put out by the heavy monsoon rains. China's timber export trade to the world was totally wiped out and at highly advantageous terms to Russia, a trade agreement had been signed whereby China imported timber from Russia and then exported it via Hong Kong to maintain her existing timber trade agreements. Twice a week, the Trans-Siberian railway carried large consignments of timber to Guangzhou via Beijing.

One hundred and fifty miles to the north of Moscow was Lake Rybinskoye, around which grew some of the tallest and widest girthed conifers in the Soviet Union. After felling, these trees were taken to the rail sidings at Vesyegonsk. From the rail sidings, they went on rail flats to the sidings in Kalinin to await collection by diesel shunting engines, which then took them to the Kalinin saw mills. It was by no coincidence that the missile arsenal was collocated by a saw mill. Even with the high-resolution lenses deployed by the US satellites, long, cylindrical trees appeared not dissimilar to long, cylindrical missiles.

The plan had required the concealment of ten, SS20 missiles amongst the tree trunks on the rail flats. The missiles were 55.8 feet in length and 8.2 feet in diameter. Peter Milynkov had had no difficulty in procuring the wooden packing cases for the missiles, which had fitted in snugly with the stabilising fins removed and stowed on either side of the missile. The boxes were transported to the saw mills at Kalinin where it had been the simplest of tasks to swear the State Director of the mills to secrecy and then get him to produce the camouflage which would conceal the distinctive packing cases.

One glance at Volkonoff had been enough to ensure the co-operation of the Director. The conifer tree trunks had been sawn in half lengthways, fixed around the packing cases and then the circular ends of the trunks had been replaced, turning the packing case into what looked like a 'bundle' of three or four huge tree trunks. The cranes of the rail salvage equipment had proved to be tailor-made for the task of placing the real missiles inside the packing cases having replaced them with fakes in the Kalinin Arsenal. The fake missiles were identical to the real SS20s except for the warhead. The two sub-critical masses of enriched plutonium had been removed which, when driven together by the explosive nuclear trigger, would have produced a critical mass and nuclear fission; these had been replaced by a precisely measured amount of cobalt which gave an identical reading of radio-active emission, but in a quantity which could not produce nuclear fission.

The task of providing security for the move of the missiles to the Mongolian/China Border and a credible cover story for the military guard on the rail flats had also fallen to Samsonov. Beyond the border with China, security of their 'pension fund' was up to them. The plan had gone like clockwork and each member of the group had achieved his task on time. Simeon had been horrified to discover how simple it was to bribe and blackmail key personnel to achieve co-operation and how widespread was the corruption, disloyalty and greed in high places throughout the Services, the Government and, particularly, the KGB.

He would never have believed while he had been a serving member of the Soviet Army, that a company of motorised infantry could be tasked to guard ten rail flats loaded with tree trunks on a journey to the Chinese Border. Samsonov had called in a debt owed to him by the commanding officer of a motorised infantry battalion under the pretext that the flats carried spare parts for the SCUD missiles shipped to Iraq for the conflict against Iran.

There had been no hitch to the plan until the accident in the train shed at Erlian. Fortunately, the incident had passed with no one seeing the real content of the packing cases and the three dead soldiers had been buried within thirty minutes of the incident. All the soldiers had been offered a generous bonus to their paltry monthly salary so the death of three of their comrades and the subsequent increase to the bonus for the rest of them ensured their silence. Despite this, the incident had left a nasty taste in Simeon's mouth and brought home to him how vulnerable they and the plan were to the unpredictable.

All of them had stayed together until they reached Beijing and then Simeon had gone on ahead of the others by train to Guangzhou to catch the jet-foil to Hong Kong. They had all shared good compartments in 'soft class' on the Trans-Siberian train. Each compartment had four bunks and Yuri Volkonoff had moved unpredictably from one compartment to another as he watched all of them from under his heavy-lidded eyes whilst he played some form of patience with a greasy pack of cards for hour after hour. He had been delighted to get away from Volkonoff because the train spent four days in the sidings in Beijing and another three on the journey to Guangzhou. The other five had been booked into a very third rate hotel in Beijing and would have to take turns to watch the rail flats 24 hours a day.

Simeon had the task to ensure that all the arrangements were in order for the transfer of the timber cargo from one ship to another in Hong Kong Harbour. His instructions had been to go directly to the typhoon shelter at Yau Ma Tei after arrival in Kowloon where he would be met and taken out to the cargo ship chartered by the arms dealer for the last leg of their journey to the Gulf.

The PA system on the jet-foil startled Simeon from his reverie of the events leading to his arrival in Hong Kong. The Cantonese was unintelligible to him, but the English version told him that they were now arriving at the Tai Kok Tsui Pier in Kowloon and all passengers were required to follow the appropriate signs through immigration and customs.

The jet-foil sank down off its foils onto its hard-chined hull and immediately the smooth ride ceased as the boat wallowed in the lumpy water of the harbour. Once the boat was tied up alongside the pier, Simeon disembarked with the other passengers and followed the sign, which took him through the channel for non-Hong Kong residents where he presented his passport to the official in the Immigration Department. He was now Herr Helmut Sachs; a German businessman returning from a trip to Beijing via Guangzhou.

His passport had all the relevant stamps and he was through the immigration and customs formalities within minutes. His passport for the journey from Moscow to Beijing was now at the bottom of the Pearl River.

As he left the ferry terminal, Simeon was assailed by the sounds, colours, bustle and smells of Kowloon; all his senses were tested to the full, particularly his sense of smell, as he weaved his way through the packed streets towards the typhoon shelter. It was now early evening and all around were neon signs, street stalls, food trollies, restaurants, taxis and always people; he'd never seen so many of every shape, size, colour and ethnic origin and all jostling, pushing, hurrying and shouting to make themselves heard above the incessant roar of the traffic, the eardrum-splitting sound of jack hammers and the strident blare of car horns from the permanent traffic jam that was Hong Kong's solution to its transport problem.

There were stalls everywhere, covered in what looked to Simeon like the most dreadful offal, entrails, flattened ducks, bottled snakes and lizards, herbs, insects and patent remedies for everything from premature baldness to impotence. In direct contrast to the revolting food and bottled horrors, were other stalls covered in bolt after bolt of silks and cottons covering every shade of the spectrum, intricate rattan work and other chinoisery which tantalised and delighted Simeon as he wallowed in the freedom of this frontal assault on his senses.

All too soon, he reached the typhoon shelter and as he turned to follow the proscribed route along its seaward wall, he saw for the first time the lights and skyline of Hong Kong Island. He released his sharp intake of breath slowly at the magical sight of the view. The hills had turned a deep shade of purple and were silhouetted by the setting sun providing a velvety backdrop to the 'son et lumière' of the Hong Kong waterfront. The whimsical moment of the beauty of the fairy-lit island vanished with a blunt return to reality as the stench of the stagnant, sewage-saturated water of the typhoon shelter assailed his nostrils.

Putting his suitcase down, Simeon removed a handkerchief from his pocket which he held over his mouth and nose as he made his way towards the third set of landing steps where he had been told that he would find someone waiting for him. At the foot of the steps, where they disappeared into the solid mass of water-borne refuse and dead or dying animal life, was a small sampan with a lop-sided bamboo, rattan and polythene structure which was its apology for some form of shelter. In the stern, sat a wizened old Chinese crone with only two or three gold-capped, tobacco-stained teeth and a voice like a 1500 watt loud-speaker - tweeters and woofers included -

which she was using at maximum volume to prevent another sampan from usurping her pole position at the foot of the steps.

On a large, once white, piece of cardboard, pinned to a bamboo pole was his name, he presumed - SACKS. Simeon went down the slippery steps, carrying his suitcase and trying to avoid putting his feet in the dog and human faeces which was scattered liberally on each one and at the same time trying to judge the rise and fall of the tyre-wrapped, blunt bow of the sampan. He timed his jump and landed on the short, planked foredeck whereupon the old crone rammed the gear lever astern and the throttle to full. Simeon just saved himself from being hurled backwards into the cesspool-like water of the typhoon shelter as his sampan barged through the other water taxis jockeying to grab the pole position that was now free. As soon as the sampan was clear, the lever was thrust forward and the small boat surged towards the opening in the breakwater.

Once out of the shelter of the breakwater, the sampan bounced horribly over the lumpy seas of the harbour. He had been told that the cargo ship was in the Western Anchorage, but that had meant little to him at the time when he was reading his instructions and he hadn't bothered to compare the scale of the map with the distance to the anchorage. It was just after 7.30 and full dark, but the harbour was alive with a myriad of lights on tugs, ferries, pleasure craft and boats of all sizes which criss-crossed the harbour throughout the night. Simeon was no sailor, but even he understood the need for navigation lights; the four, dim Christmas tree lights which the old hag had draped over the canopy could not have been seen more than ten metres away.

Puffing away on a small, long-stemmed pipe gripped between the few remaining stained teeth which she possessed, the wizened old Chinese skipper of the sampan drove it forward with reckless abandon, barrel-rolling over the swell and swerving past the bows and counters of huge container vessels, which certainly hadn't noticed the passage of such a small, ill-lit craft through the water and would have crushed it into matchwood and spewed it out at the stern to join all the other mass of flotsam swilling around the harbour.

Glancing to his right, Simeon identified the outline of what had once been Stonecutters Island, but was now joined to Kowloon and the huge container terminal. He realised to his misery that they were barely halfway to the anchorage. The Western Anchorage had been chosen with care because it was usually fairly deserted and because of its distance from the commercial centre of the harbour, attracted much lower harbour dues. The crews of merchant vessels and warships hated it because it was a good 1½ hours in a water taxi from the bars, discos, massage parlours and one-roomed brothels of Mong Kok and Wanchai. It also meant a long literage journey for the agent bringing out the new cargo to a vessel. The charge for the extra fuel and time invariably exceeded the money saved on the cheaper dues, so all in all, the Western Anchorage was to be avoided unless you commanded a nuclear-powered vessel or one with a very deep draught.

There were no such ships that night in the Western Anchorage and gradually the lights became fewer and fewer as the small sampan wallowed into the inky black night. There was no compass for the old hag to steer by, no stars in the overcast sky to guide her and Simeon wondered whether he had taken all the risks merely to sink without trace in the polluted waters of Hong Kong harbour.

The anchorage lay just to the south of the Pun Shan Shek light, but Simeon was unused to the tricks that lights, darkness and a low position in the sea can play even on an experienced seaman and it wasn't until he suddenly realised that a darker piece of the night was the slab steel side of a large ship that his miserable voyage was at an end. The sampan ran up to the foot of a companionway which was held in place by steel hawsers which vanished into the night above Simeon's head. He staggered clumsily to his feet and more by good luck than agility, managed to get both his suitcase and himself onto the foot of the companionway without getting either wet.

He turned, fumbling with the unfamiliar money in his pocket to pay the old hag, but the sampan had vanished into the night and he was now on his own. The wind coming off the sea made him shiver so he grasped his case and holding on firmly to the guardrail, made his way carefully up to the deck. At the top of the companionway he was met by a man who seemed to be of Caucasian rather than Asian origin and without a word of greeting he was led towards the stern of the ship. Simeon took little note of his surroundings which were totally unfamiliar to him as he had never been to sea before; his trip on the jet-foil was his first venture onto water other than a very dull hour's cruise on a pleasure steamer on the River Dnieper in Kiev. He was guided through a steel door which closed automatically behind them on large hydraulic rams and then along corridors and down metal ladders until he was totally disorientated. His guide stopped and opened another steel door and indicated that he should enter. He went into a luxurious cabin with its own bathroom and a small study; suddenly everything seemed better.

His guide touched his sleeve and then pointed to a notice on the back of the door. Simeon nodded his thanks and the man left, closing the door behind him. Simeon put his suitcase down and walked round the cabin; it seemed odd that there were no portholes or scuttles and then he wandered over to the notice on the back of the door. It told him when meals would be served and the place to which he should go in case of emergency. While he was reading, he lowered his hand to the door handle with the intention of doing some exploring before going to bed. There wasn't one. He looked down; the surface of the steel door was unblemished by any protuberance which could possibly assist in opening it. He was locked in. With a weary sigh, Simeon walked over to the bed, sat down and buried his head in his hands.

CHAPTER 6

'Wake up! Here's your tea. I thought we were supposed to be making an early start today, or did I not hear you correctly last night,' and Tricia pulled back the scuttle curtains letting the bright morning sunlight flood into the aft cabin. Peter struggled awake, remembering all his good intentions to make the most of the west-going tide down the Solent. He swore as he propped himself up on one elbow and sipped at the hot tea.

'Anyone else up?'

'Yes; your female crew is up, but not a sign of the men. Breakfast is ready, the newspaper has been delivered and we're ready to go. Come on, show a leg or we'll have to go round by the Nab Tower.'

'Is John up?'

'He wasn't the last time I checked his room and gave him his tea,' and with that Tricia left the cabin throwing over her shoulder as she went, 'breakfast in five minutes or you can have it while we're under way.' Peter finished his tea, showered, shaved and dressed and walked out of the cabin where he met Gunn emerging from his.

'Morning John; I've rather overslept. Sorry about that; I gather that breakfast is nearly ready. If you could nip up topsides and get us ready to leave, I'll check the engines and fire them up.'

'Sure,' and then Gunn added quietly, 'Al Samak left at six this morning; on my way,' and he disappeared up the steps into the wheelhouse. Gunn had heard the preparations for the departure of Hassan's boat, but had no intention of appearing on deck. He was reasonably confident that neither he nor Osprey were under suspicion because only three members of the crew had seen him and of those, one was dead and two were still suffering from concussion in hospital. Yussuf certainly hadn't seen him and Hassan could have only seen his back as he dived over the side of the motorboat. No other boat had occupied the vacant berth astern of Osprey which would make their departure that much easier.

First the port and then the starboard engine rumbled into life and the black diesel smoke drifted low across the water to be dispersed in a flurry as soon as it was caught by the wind out on the river. Gunn brought the two warps on board, which were acting as springs to prevent Osprey moving to and fro on the pontoon berth. He then changed the bow and stern warps so that they ran from the boat round the bollards on the pontoon and back onto the boat. In this way, they merely had to be uncleated and hauled round the bollard and back on board without anyone going ashore to cast them off. Having completed that task, he secured the dinghy – presumably Al Samak's crew had returned it - into the davit snap shackles and hauled it up out of the water on the davit's electric winch. Peter was now behind the wheel astern of the cockpit. Before getting back on board, Gunn had one final check and then unplugged their shore-power line and brought it on board, closing the gate in the guard rail as he did so.

He turned to Peter, 'ready when you are. I'll check the sheets and outhauls when we're under way.' He noticed that Peter had raised a white ensign on the staff at the stern. There was only one yacht club in the world with the charter to fly it and that was the Royal Yacht Squadron whose splendid, grey-stoned solemnity watched over the start of the majority of the Admiral's Cup and other off-shore races from its vantage point on Castle Hill in West Cowes.

Many were the skippers who had attempted to show-off some flashy manoeuvre or sail-change in front of the red and white striped awning of the Royal Yacht Squadron only to limp shame-faced into the Groves and Gutteridge Marina with a sheet wrapped round the propeller, a spinnaker ripped to shreds or a crew member trailing in the water at the end of a safety line. It was the one yacht club, Gunn could remember being told by a retired naval officer instructor from HMS Hornet, where title, status and bank balance meant nothing when trying to gain membership; who you knew and what you knew about the sea and ships was what mattered.

'Thanks John;' because of the ebbing tide, the bow warp was taught and doing all the work while the stern warp was taking no strain. What breeze there was in the sheltered marina of the Royal Hamble Yacht Club was coming from a couple of points to the west of south which blew the ensign back over the stern of Osprey, wrapping it round the mizzen mast backstay.

'Cast off aft!' As Gunn hauled the warp back on board the yacht, Peter spun the wheel clockwise. The combined effect of the ebbing tide and the rudder blade turned to starboard, pushed the bows of the boat out from the pontoon. When he gave the order to 'cast off for'ard!' and the warp was released by Gunn, Osprey neatly swung her bow out assisted by the port bow-thruster. Peter engaged the drive to the port propeller. They were, in fact, only half an hour behind schedule as Peter brought the ketch out into the Hamble River and turned south towards Southampton Water and the Solent. The unusually fine weather was still holding and the scattered, low-level cumulus cloud foretold a perfect sailing day.

All the sails could be set from the cockpit and once Gunn had done his checks round the foredeck, he came aft and asked Peter if he would like a forecast from one of the coastal stations.

'It's alright; I've got a little fellow whom I've christened 'Charlie' who saves me getting up at six in the morning to listen to the shipping forecast. He's that box of tricks on the port side of the wheelhouse. Charlie will have recorded the shipping forecast and then wound back his tape. All you have to do is press the 'play' button and you will get the shipping forecast. If you want to see what it looks like, press the HC button on the weatherfax and that'll produce you a hard copy of the Atlantic weather chart. The wind's right on the nose, so you go down and have your breakfast in peace; Tricia's already given me my coffee and some toast. If the wind stays in the south, there's no point in putting up the sails until we start turning westwards round Calshot Spit.' John went into the wheelhouse where the aroma of fresh ground coffee and hot rolls made him bypass the weatherfax in favour of breakfast.

'It's always the same, however corny it sounds, but that sea air really does give me an appetite. When I'm living in London, I can never face more than a cup of coffee and a piece of toast,' Gunn said to no one in particular as he joined the three women in the saloon.

'Right, there's every type of egg, sausages, tomatoes, mushrooms and fried potatoes; what'll it be?' Tricia offered as she got up from her place at the table and headed for the galley.

'Yes please; fried eggs will be fine.'

'Well what made you two get up so late this morning,' Celia asked as she poured more coffee from the percolator. Celia was given a hard look by Susan Hammond, which she chose to ignore.

'That phone call I had last night told me to take the opportunity of having a look inside Hassan's boat, so I did and Peter kept a lookout for me back here on Osprey; we got to bed at about a quarter to four this morning. Could you pass the milk please Susan?' Gunn's reply was a conversation killer and there was dead silence in the saloon - the only noise was Gunn's breakfast sizzling on the cooker.

'Oh well, ask a silly question...' sighed Celia breaking the silence. 'Do we get to hear what happened or does that come under the Official Secrets Act, or whatever it's called these days.'

'Celia...' started Susan.

'No really, it would be a great help to discuss what I found, but I would like Peter to be present as I need his knowledge of ships and ship-building. Just like the best thrillers there's a clue or riddle which requires solving and I've yet to meet the male who can better a female at riddle solving!'

'Right, here's your breakfast,' announced Tricia placing a steaming fry-up in front of John. 'Grab a knife and fork and take it up to the cockpit. We'll bring all the rest of the things. If you think I'm going to sit here waiting for you to eat that while we wait to hear what happened you've another think coming. Go on, I'll bring your coffee,' and with that he was hustled out of the saloon and in less than two minutes the breakfast table had been set up in the cockpit.

'Good heavens, Tricia, have you burnt the breakfast or can't you all bear to be without my company,' a startled Peter remarked as he watched the rapid exodus from the saloon into the cockpit.

'Neither; John's about to tell us what happened last... this morning. He needs your advice about something to do with boats and he wants us to solve a riddle. Is that cup being held out for more coffee?'

'Yes please.'

'Blast; don't you dare start without me,' and Tricia rushed down to the saloon to refill Peter's coffee cup. She reappeared, handed over the cup and sat down. 'Right we're all ready,' and Gunn told them what had happened in the early hours of the morning. There wasn't a murmur from his audience as Osprey cut across Southampton Water to the Calshot Spit light. When he had finished, no one said anything and all that broke the sound of Osprey's muted rumble of diesels and the cries of gulls was the distant roar of the 9 am, red and white hydrofoil ferry from Southampton to Cowes.

'And the riddle?' Celia broke the silence.

'It was something I found at the bottom of a drawer in a filing cabinet in Hassan's study.'

'What was it?'

'It was a cutting from a German newspaper - the Westdeutsche Zeitung and the article was dated 20th November 1989.'

'You speak German?' asked Tricia.

'Yes, I've kept it going ever since I left school - mainly for skiing, I suppose, but I took it as an optional subject at university. Where was I? Oh yes; the article was captioned 'Who has stolen the ship?' and it went on to describe how a cargo vessel, which was being built for a South African shipping line, had been stolen from the ship building yard of Neuberg und Deutschmetal.'

'How on earth was a ship stolen from its yard?' this came from Peter who was clearly outraged at the thought of a ship being stolen from its builder's yard.

'It was really very simple,' and Gunn repeated what had been reported in the article.

'How very odd.'

'Yes, I suppose it is,' Gunn agreed.

'No, no, no...sorry, I was thinking aloud. You see.....' and again Peter paused, 'why on earth would Neuberg and Deutschmetal build a cargo ship for South Africa when that Country is more than capable of building as many ships as it wants at a fraction of the cost that old man Neuberg would charge for a ship. Not only that, and I expect I'm generalising, but to my knowledge, Neuberg has never built anything but submarines.'

'Interesting....' began Gunn, but he was interrupted by Peter.

'I wonder... sorry, I interrupted you.'

'No, go on.'

'Tell me, what's your knowledge like on the problems in South Africa?'

'Pretty thin, I regret to say; I haven't even been there.' There was silence for a few moments while Peter collected his thoughts and Osprey continued her course, keeping close to the line of port hand markers in the channel round the Calshot Spit and the Bramble Bank. Peter looked up at the triangular cruising burgee at the top of the main mast.

'Let's put the sails up and then we'll have a short history lesson on South Africa which might help with your riddle.'

'Can we help?' came from Susan Hammond.

'You can indeed,' and Gunn gave each of the women a sheet or out-haul to put round a winch. Peter brought Osprey into the wind and in less than a minute, the genoa was unfurled and the in-mast main and mizzen out-hauls had set the sails and had been made fast. Peter brought Osprey back on course and she heeled over gracefully to starboard as the sails filled close-hauled on a port tack. Peter pressed the de-compressors on the diesels and all mechanical noise ceased, to be replaced by the swish and gurgle of the sea below the leeward gun'le and the creak of rigging and terylene sails. While the cordage from sheets and out-hauls in the cockpit was being tidied, Tricia went into the wheelhouse, heated up the water in the boiler and reappeared with a tray filled with mugs of steaming coffee and a plate of biscuits.

'I'm not going back any further than Soweto in 1976,' Peter began. 'Does that incident mean anything to you?'

'Yes, I think so; unfortunately, there've been so many 'incidents' in that country that I find it very easy to get them muddled. Was that the one where the police opened fire on a demonstration by black South Africans?'

'Yes, that's it; so that's my starting point. The reason that I know a little about South Africa is because I was appointed to a frigate in the early fifties, which was based in Simonstown. I not only became very fond of the country, but also took a keen interest in its people and problems which, incidentally, I've kept up to this day. After Soweto, the situation in South Africa gradually deteriorated as the ANC increased in number and its activities were better co-ordinated and more sophisticated. The culmination of the improved organisation and expertise was the successful explosion of two bombs at two plants belonging to SASOL - that's a company which produces oil from coal, incidentally - one was in the Orange Free State and the other was in the Transvaal. This was followed in....' and here Peter paused as he glanced down at the chart which was clamped to a small angled chart table mounted in front of the binnacle.

It was now just over three hours after high water in Southampton Water; most of the rise or fall in a tide occurred in the third and fourth hour of its six-hour cycle in the sea around the British and French Coasts. They were into that third hour now and yet there was a large sloop, with spinnaker set on a broad port reach cutting across the Bramble Bank.

'That silly sod's taking a hell of a risk,' and the others turned to follow the direction in which Peter was looking.

'What's the problem?' Celia asked.

'We're on spring tides; that means a larger range of rise and fall between high and low tide. At low water springs, you can see the sand of the Bramble Bank and that's exactly where that yacht is heading.'

'Perhaps he's done his navigational sums really well, or has a swing keel,' Tricia offered. 'It really is a very colourful spinnaker isn't it.'

'I'm afraid it's neither of those reasons; I know that boat; it's been into the yard to have the hull cleaned and re-anti-fouled,' and now Peter was studying her through his binoculars. 'It's a charter job and certainly doesn't'... and the yacht struck the bank at precisely that moment with its own speed of nine knots and another three of tide slamming it into the sand bank. Inside the boat the effect would have been similar to driving a car into a concrete wall at nearly 20mph. The mast snapped just above the deck and a welter of rigging and sails collapsed across the foredeck of the yacht. The fin keel had been sheared from the hull, which flipped the yacht onto its side and then it capsized.

'Oh God! They'll all be drowned,' Tricia exclaimed in horror. Peter had already started both engines and without being asked, Gunn had started taking off all the sail from Osprey. The sails were furled and stowed in a trice and at a cautious speed with one eye glued to the digital readout of the depth gauge, Peter steered the big ketch towards the capsized yacht.

'Tricia, can you get some blankets ready please. John, can you put our swimming ladder over the side and stand by to lower the dinghy, but first would you give a shout for help on channel 16. Can you all go and put on your safety harnesses so that we don't add to this disaster!' All these directions were given in a matter-of-fact manner and everyone did as they were told. Gunn reappeared from the wheelhouse.

'The Calshot boat's on its way. They were also watching the yacht and launched before she struck. That's her astern of us now.' A large bow wave almost hid the speeding inshore lifeboat, which would reach the yacht only shortly after Osprey. Gunn had removed a long, lightweight spinnaker sheet from a seat locker in the cockpit and placed it ready for use. 'They'll be trapped under the hull; I'll tie this round my waist and the girls can hang onto it and help me back on board.'

'Well done; I'll come up on her windward side away from all the ropes and rigging and pray that the tide and wind has carried her over the shoal. We certainly can't hang around for long on a falling tide.' Gunn tied a bowline round his waist, handed the other end to Tricia and as Peter skilfully brought Osprey broadside on to the capsized sloop, he dived over the side. Two men had been thrown clear and were hanging on to the underside of the upturned hull. The water was cold, but not chillingly so and Gunn surfaced inside the open centre cockpit of the sloop where the air had been trapped. There was an indescribable mess of broken and tangled equipment, food, cooking utensils and cutlery but no people.

Gunn realised that his safety line would now be more of a hindrance than a safety precaution so he removed it and tied it round a winch drum. He then took a deep breath from the air trapped under the hull, ducked under the surface and swam into the saloon where he surfaced with his head well clear of the shallow bilge of that design of light-displacement boat. There were three men, one of whom was supporting an unconscious woman who had a very deep gash on her forehead.

'There are two men in the water beside the hull and four of you here. Are there any more?' Gunn quizzed the dazed trio. It seemed as though they thought he had been on the boat and their brains were clearly functioning at dead slow. 'I'm here to rescue you,' he shouted at them, there's a lifeboat out there,' and he pointed. 'Are you all here?' The man supporting the woman was the first to come to his senses.

'Gary and Carol,' he muttered feebly.

'Where were they?'

'I..I think in the cabin at the front,' and he pointed feebly behind him. Gunn drew a deep breath and dived down, pushing his way through plastic cushions, clothes, fruit, tins of food, books and other junk as he fought his way past the for'ard heads into the forepeak cabin. A man and a woman were there; both as naked as the day they were born and both drowned or very close to that state. Gunn dragged the woman out first and handed her to one of the men in the saloon and then returned for the man, whom he handed over again to another man. He then grabbed hold of the woman and pulled her out into the cockpit where he retrieved his safety line and tied it round her waist. He took another deep breath and pushed her under the upturned gun'le and swam clear of the boat pulling her behind him. He surfaced right beside the lifeboat, which had changed places with Osprey. Two of the lifeboat crew reached down and pulled the unconscious woman on board.

'Any more in there?' someone shouted and John held up his hand with fingers spread before ducking under the surface and swimming back under the boat. When he reached the surface again with the naked man from the forepeak cabin, there were two lifeboat men ready to take over who dived under the hull; Gunn was pulled on board the lifeboat where a large blanket was wrapped round him. On the deck, two members of the crew were attempting to resuscitate the man and woman. Osprey was tied up, outboard of the lifeboat. Gunn walked across the boat and climbed over the guardrail onto Osprey assisted by Tricia and Celia.

'Many thanks; I think I'll nip down and get into some dry clothes,' and Gunn disappeared into the wheelhouse.

'Leave all your wet clothes on the floor of the shower. I'll wash them and stick them in the tumble dryer,' Tricia shouted after him.

Both wind and tide were carrying the three boats in a north-westerly direction away from the Bramble Bank, into deeper water. The Search and Rescue, Sea King helicopter from Lee-on-Solent appeared and hovered above the three boats. In order to make it easier for winching up the crew of the capsized yacht, Peter cast off from the lifeboat and took Osprey 100 metres clear. The Sea King then took up station above the lifeboat and the crew of the sloop was winched up. The naked woman had recovered, but the man had died from a broken neck, which must have happened when the boat struck the sandbank. As soon as all the crew had been winched up, the helicopter banked away heading for Southampton Hospital. The radio in the wheelhouse burst into life.

'Osprey, Osprey, Osprey this is the Calshot lifeboat, channel 67, over.' Peter heard the message on the extension speaker beside the wheel, went into the wheelhouse, punched the digital tuner to read channel 67 and picked up the microphone from its clip.

'Calshot lifeboat this is Osprey, send your message, over.'

'Osprey, this is the Calshot lifeboat, Skipper Hamilton speaking. Very grateful for your most professional and gallant assistance to the crew of the capsized yacht Sea Breeze Two. At least one and probably more owe their lives to your boat handling and the bravery of your crew-member who dived under the capsized yacht. Most grateful if you would let me know the name of skipper and crew member for our records, over.' Gunn had just reappeared in the wheelhouse and caught Peter's eye; he shook his head and Peter nodded.

'Calshot lifeboat this is Osprey, Skipper Peter de Havilland speaking, Managing Director of De Havilland Boats - might as well get some free advertising,' Peter thought, as he knew that by now every boat in the Solent would be listening' - my crew member prefers to remain anonymous. Delighted to have been of assistance. Rule Britannia! over.'

'Calshot lifeboat, my sentiments exactly; happy and safe sailing, out.'

'It was jolly brave too,' and Celia threw her arms round Gunn and kissed him full on the lips and then did the same to Peter. She was followed by both Tricia and Susan and then all hell broke loose as one after another, boats came up on channel 67 to congratulate Osprey. It was nearly eleven before they set sail once more with only an hour of west-going tide remaining. As they bore away round the East Lepe buoy, Peter asked Gunn to set the cruising chute which sent Osprey's speed up to nine knots, so with only ten miles to go to Hurst Point, the lost hour of their rescue of the crew of the capsized yacht would make very little difference. They were once more seated in the cockpit with cups of coffee and Gunn now had the wheel.

'Before I was so rudely interrupted by that moron skippering the sloop, I was successfully boring you all about South Africa. I shall now continue because I hope that you will soon see the relevance to your newspaper cutting. Now, where had I got to before all that drama?'

'You had just told us about the bombs at the two SASOL plants,' Gunn prompted Peter.

'Ah yes, right; well, those two bomb incidents were followed by another in December '82 at South Africa's nuclear power station at Koeburg - that's quite near Capetown - and then in March '85, in fact 25 March '85, which was the anniversary of the Sharpville Massacre, the police opened fire on a peaceful black procession at Uitenhage, near Port Elizabeth. I think about 20 people were killed and from that moment on the situation deteriorated very rapidly. The frequency of riots in open defiance of the South African Government increased. Black policemen, community leaders, and suspected informers were ritualistically murdered with burning necklaces - you know, John, tyres soaked in petrol. In July '85, the South African Government declared a state of emergency and censorship was clamped on every form of media reporting. That's all background; now we come to the bit which I think might shed some light on your newspaper cutting.

The South African Government realised that there would be worldwide condemnation, which would probably lead to a censorship motion by the UN - that's about the only motion other than a bowel one that ever occurs in that moribund organisation - to impose international sanctions against South Africa.'

'Southern Rhodesia managed perfectly well after Ian Smith declared UDI, and it's a fact that the shops in Cecil Rhodes Avenue in Salisbury were far better stocked during UDI than they are now in Zimbabwe's corrupt, one-party dictatorship. If Rhodesia managed so easily with no coastline at all, how much easier was it going to be for South Africa with every type of mineral resource she needed and some 1500 miles of coast for sanction busting. Now, John, from this point on what I say is hearsay and rumour; none of it is substantiated by any proof whatsoever. Even prior to UN Resolution, whatever number it was, which called for sanctions against South Africa, it is claimed that the South African Government commissioned a German boatyard to build five submersible cargo ships.'

'What!' exclaimed Gunn, 'is that possible?'

'Good heavens above, yes. The rumour goes that these vessels were to be of about 20,000 tons displacement with a maximum submerged depth of a couple of hundred feet and an underwater speed of anything up to about 30 knots. Their design was to be such that when operating as a conventional, surface cargo ship they would attract no undue attention, but were rumoured to have a surface speed of over 30 knots and were to be powered by a South African designed, pressurised water-cooled reactor. Now compare that specification with the Russian Typhoon Class SSBN - sorry girls - surface-to-surface ballistic nuclear submarine, which has a displacement of 29,000 tons, is over 560 feet long and can travel at 24 knots submerged. The whole business was a closely guarded secret and BOSS - that's the South African equivalent...oh damn! I'm trying to teach my grandmother to suck eggs.'

'Not a bit, the girls need to hear it all as we're all going to try and solve this riddle.'

'Right, everyone knows what BOSS is the South African Secret Service?' and nods indicated that they did. Good, so where was I? Oh yes, it had to be kept a closely guarded secret so that the EU and other countries didn't find out that West Germany – as it was then, before reunification - was sanction busting and had taken on this highly lucrative contract. Neuberg and Deutschmetal is a private company, just like the West German company which was discovered to be providing the Libyans with the wherewithal to build a chemical plant to produce chemical and biological gas.'

'Did they build these ships?'

'To be honest, I don't think anyone knows. The first partial confirmation of those rumours is your discovery of that newspaper cutting. I believe that they were built; perhaps not all five, but certainly a couple and it seems that our friend Hassan may know where one of them is. Just imagine what a marvellous means of transport a submersible cargo vessel would be for an arms dealer and the recipient of those arms.'

'Wouldn't this ship be very obvious as a submersible vessel?' Tricia asked.

'No, not at all; you see there are three essential differences to the design of a submersible ship and a submarine. The latter is designed to go to great depths, move at speeds of nearly 40 knots submerged and run silently to avoid detection. The submersible cargo ship requires none of these attributes. It only needs to submerge just below the surface of the sea and so doesn't require an immensely strong pressure hull. It neither needs to move fast nor silently. I agree that it would be an advantage to have a reasonably clean profile - unlike a surface cargo ship - but that advantage would be outweighed by the requirement for the ship to be unnoticeable amongst other cargo ships. Self-stowing derricks have been a feature on cargo ships for some years now to decrease the wind resistance of a vessel's superstructure.'

'I can't believe that it would be very difficult, from a marine engineering point of view, to make other parts of the ship movable - like the variable geometry of a fighter aircraft - to improve the streamlining of a ship and hence its submerged performance. Do remember that this vessel doesn't have to move fast underwater. All it has to do is approach its destination by night with no lights and then just before it appears over the radar horizon and is detected, it submerges and creeps towards the coast or an RV at a mere handful of knots. Yes, the whole concept is perfectly feasible and is just the sort of solution that would appeal to the South Africans.'

'So you believe that the cutting was kept by Hassan because it was he who stole that ship from the German shipbuilders,' Susan commented.

'It's not an unreasonable assumption; someone stole the ship and of anyone, Hassan has the ideal place to keep it.'

'At Sardrière Island! Come on,' Susan argued, 'it would have been spotted ages ago.'

'Not if it was sitting on the seabed. Look, I'll show you,' and Peter got up and went into the wheelhouse from where he returned with a Stanford Chart of the Channel Islands. Tricia removed the coffee mugs from the teak table in the cockpit and wiped it down, knowing how pernickety Peter was about stains on his charts. Peter spread out the chart so that the three women could see it. 'The soundings - that's the depth of water - are in fathoms at chart datum. That's lower than the water would ever be except for, possibly, during a period of lowest and highest astronomical tides which occurs about every seventy years or so. The last one was in September '94.'

'Now here's Sardrière Island, seven miles due south of St Martin's Point on Guernsey and look at the depth of water,' and Peter produced a pair of brass dividers. 'Within four cables - that's about 800 metres - its 24 fathoms and two nautical miles away,' he continued as he measured the gap between the points of the dividers against the latitude scale on the side of the chart, 'it's 35 fathoms - that's 210 feet. He could keep a whole armada of submersible ships there and no one would be any the wiser. I wonder...?'

'What is it Peter?' Gunn could see that Peter was absorbed by the task he had set himself of solving, or at least coming up with a rational and plausible solution, to the newspaper cutting.

'Since both the British and American Navies have based their SSBN subs in the Firth of Clyde, there've been a number of incidents of both British and Irish fishing boats getting their nets snagged by submarines. Some boats have disappeared without trace. In fact, I think there's a lawsuit going through the courts at the moment to get compensation for an Irish boat, which radioed that its nets had been snagged by a submarine. That was the last transmission until bits of wreckage of the boat were washed ashore in Anglesey. No bodies were ever recovered.'

'What's the connection with Sardrière Island?' Celia asked.

'I think it would be worth asking the Guernsey Coastguard if any fishing vessels have disappeared without trace or explanation since November '89 and where their last reported position was before they disappeared.'

'That sounds like a thoroughly logical line to take, but what do you make of that number pressed into the cutting and do you think there's a connection with what Celia saw in the train shed at Erlian?' Gunn asked.

'What was the number again?' Tricia queried.

'0424 130710.'

'It must be a telephone number.'

'Or a number disguised to look like a telephone number. Peter, could you take the wheel for a moment while I contact the Directorate on my phone.'

'Yes, of course,' and he took over the wheel as Osprey was approaching Hurst Point. Although the sun was warm there was a fresh force four to five blowing and the women retired into the wheelhouse to read newspapers and magazines. John called the Directorate and briefly recounted what had happened during his search of Hassan's boat and then returned to take the wheel back from Peter. 'Alright?'

'Yes, fine; I spoke to the man who runs the Middle East Section. He's got the head of the Russian Section and South-East Asia Section in his office and I was told to expect a return call. He asked for our position, which was very easy to give as I was looking straight at the lighthouse on Hurst Castle.'

'I suspect that they'll want you back in London.'

'I asked that, but for the moment they're quite keen for me to stick with Hassan and Osprey is providing the perfect cover for that. Incidentally, do you carry diving gear on Osprey?'

'Yes, I do; pretty sophisticated stuff too, even though I say so myself. The compressor comes up through the forepeak hatch. There's a fibreglass tank, which is also placed on deck and filled with water so that the air-bottles can be filled submerged to prevent accidents. There are four complete sets of equipment including wet suits and a little aqua-scooter. Thinking of taking a look at Sardrière Island?'

'Yes, I was, but I'm loathe to drag you, your boat and the women in any further than I've done already. I get the feeling that we've stumbled into something that is being played for very high stakes where the lives of the people on this boat will count for very little,' he paused as there appeared to be a mild commotion inside the wheelhouse. 'What's all that about?' For answer, Tricia rushed out of the wheelhouse, waving the business section of the Times, which had been delivered to the boat that morning.

'What's up, Trish? Have you won the Lottery?'

'Don't be silly, not on a Saturday morning. I think I've found a piece of the jigsaw that's part of the riddle which John's set us to solve.' Susan and Celia looked just as excited as Tricia. 'Come on then, what is it?'

'In a way you're right, darling; I was looking at the financial section, but my eye was caught by an article on the facing page when I opened out the paper. Its a whole page devoted to business opportunities in China and so on, but the particular article which caught my eye and you can see why,' and she held open the paper at the appropriate page and pointed to a photo of tree trunks being cross-loaded from one ship to another. The article was titled, CHINA WINS BATTLE TO SAVE TIMBER EXPORTS - BUT AT A PRICE. 'It seems that in 2001, and Celia has confirmed this, China suffered the most dreadful forest fires which destroyed thousands of hectares of the Country's most mature timber. Everything they tried failed to extinguish the fires until they were finally put out by the arrival of the monsoon in that part of China. The Chinese Government immediately blamed the fires on arson and accused the Pro-Democracy student movement for starting them.'

'China was unable to honour her timber trade agreements with overseas customers of whom - here comes the crunch - the Middle East was the largest customer. In order to save these trade agreements, China has been forced to import all its timber from Russia at highly disadvantageous prices. The timber has been transported from Russia on the Trans-Siberian railway to Guangzhou - that's Canton, Celie told me - where it's shipped to Hong Kong and then cross-loaded - that's the photograph - to other ships for the last leg of the journey to China's clients in the Middle East.'

'That article explains why Russia was exporting timber to China, but doesn't tell us if the missiles went to China, the Middle East or somewhere else. What is terrifying is the possibility that all this reduction of missiles is a complete sham to catch the USA off guard. If it is proved that the Russian President has reneged on the INF Treaty and, worse still, is flogging nuclear missiles to one of the most unstable regimes in the Middle East, then I wouldn't rule out a pre-emptive strike by the USA and the start of World War 3,' Gunn remarked as he brought Osprey a couple of points to port onto a course of 233° to keep her clear of the Shingles sandbank.

'You don't think that article shows a possible connection with our friend Hassan,' Celia stated rather than asked.

'No, I didn't say that; there could well be a connection between what you saw and Hassan's arms dealing because he is one of the wealthiest and most unscrupulous dealers in the world. Arms dealers sell to buyers all over the world, not just the Middle East. What that article does is to validate what you saw and proves that there is a very convenient cover cargo to hide the move of missiles from Russia to Hong Kong and from there to the Middle East amongst many other places. Hassan could well be involved, but I think it's time we handed all this information to my Directorate in London,' and smack on cue, Gunn's phone buzzed in the wheelhouse.

CHAPTER 7

The afternoon summer sun shone through the long sash windows casting trapeziums of light on the polished wood-block floor of Vladimir Putin's large and comfortable office of the Russian President. The office overlooked the inner courtyard of the beautifully proportioned Kremlin building with its classical, pillared facade. From this building came the decisions and judgements of the Russian Government and its President. The office was empty except for the man seated behind the desk. There was only one file on the desk and that was open, in front of the President. While continuing to read the top folio of the file, he reached out and pressed a button on the intercom. 'Yes, Sir,' came from the speaker on his desk.

'I'll see Major Petrovsky now please.'

'Straight away, Sir.' The long panelled double doors opened to admit the President's visitor.

'Please take a seat here,' and he indicated a comfortable chair just to the right of his desk. There was complete silence as he finished reading the report in the file.

'A clear and concise report; well done.'

'Thank you, Sir.'

'I find that the number of people willing to betray their country and conspiring for my removal is a little larger than I had expected, but their backgrounds and identities really hold no surprises.'

'Agreed, Sir; your instructions to me were very precise.'

'Are you quite certain that there have been no mistakes?'

'Quite certain.'

'You recommend that I inform the President Bush, through diplomatic channels, at this stage of the plan.

'Yes, Sir; that was part of your plan.'

'Indeed it was, I'm not questioning that, only the method of communication. Diplomats have an uncanny knack of misleading heads of state in the fond belief that they know better and we can't afford any misunderstandings with this little scheme.'

'Indeed not, Sir.'

'You're quite certain that there has been no leak of this scheme to the Western Intelligence Services?'

'Quite certain, Sir.'

'Thank you, Major; because of that assurance, we will keep this to ourselves for just a little longer. Please let me have your report when the second stage of the plan is complete.'

'Very well, Sir.'

'Thank you, you may go now.' Major Petrovsky rose from the chair, saluted and walked to the door. As the double doors closed, President Putin glanced at his watch, did a quick mental calculation of time zones and then picked up a red telephone from his desk.

*

Gunn's telephone buzzed impatiently in the wheelhouse. 'I think you'd better answer that John; I'll take the wheel,' and Peter de Havilland came round and took Osprey's wheel.

'Still on a course of 210°, Peter, and that's the Bridge cardinal buoy astern of us,' with a wave of his arm, Gunn indicated the black and yellow buoy which marked the western limit of the Needles rocks.

'Thanks John; the GPS is on and we don't have a way point until we're just to the north of Alderney. There's six hours of east-going Springs under us now,' Peter added as Gunn disappeared into the wheelhouse and picked up the telephone.

'John Gunn,' and then there was a one-sided conversation, in which Gunn was the listener and did little more than acknowledge with an affirmative or negative until he cleared the line and replaced the telephone.

'Everything alright?' Tricia asked, failing to hide her intense curiosity to know what was going on.

'Yes, fine; I'll just go and have a word with Peter and then let you all know what's happening.'

'Problems?' Peter inquired as Gunn reappeared from the wheelhouse.

'No, but a lot's been happening and I'm wanted back in London.'

'I guessed as much; I'll put you ashore in Lymington and you can catch the train to London.'

'No, there's no need for that. If we could take all the sail off Osprey as soon as we see a chopper coming up astern, I'll be winched up off the deck. I'll then change helicopters at HMS Daedalus at Lee-on-Solent and be back in London in no time.'

'They don't waste any time do they.'

'They weren't prepared to tell me too much, even on that phone,' and Gunn jerked his head in the direction of the wheelhouse, but it seems that Celia has stumbled onto something which has very sinister implications.'

'I'm sorry that you can't stay with us,' Tricia had appeared from the wheelhouse.

'Oh no, you're not getting rid of me that easily. Once I've been to this debrief in London, I'm being taken straight back to Southampton where I can catch the flight to Guernsey; I might even be in St Peter Port before you!'

'Excellent! We'll have'... but Peter's plans for the reunion in St Peter Port were interrupted by the sound of the approaching Sea King. He started both engines and turned Osprey into the wind while Gunn furled the genoa and the three women helped by winding the main and mizzen sails into the masts. Peter set the engine revolutions to 1200 rpm and Osprey moved into the seas at a shade over 4 knots. The Sea King approached Osprey from her port quarter and as it steadied in the hover, a petty officer swung out from the open fuselage door and descended towards the ketch.

'What on earth's that fishing rod thing he's holding?' Celia shouted to make herself heard above the noise of the twin Rolls Royce Gnome engines.

'A chopper generates a huge charge of static electricity which it earths when it lands on the ground, but in the hover that steel cable has to be earthed,' John shouted back at her and she nodded because speech was now impossible. The man on the end of the line swung the pole down and Celia saw that he was holding a heavily insulated handle. Sparks flew as the tip of the pole touched the steel hull of Osprey. Gunn walked forward, a yellow collar was placed over his head and under his arms and then both of them rose together until they disappeared inside the Sea King. The helicopter banked hard to port and from his canvas seat in the fuselage, Gunn saw the sails reappear on Osprey as she returned to her course for Guernsey.

The Sea King landed at HMS Daedalus where there was an Army Lynx helicopter waiting with rotors turning. Gunn jumped from the Sea King, walked out from under the swept arc of its rotor blades and then went forward to indicate to the pilot that he was clear. His thumbs-up was acknowledged with a wave. Gunn turned and repeated the procedure in reverse at the Lynx; his raised thumb received the same response from the pilot and he went round and climbed into the rear bench seat of the helicopter.

The roar of the twin gas-turbines rose as the engine revolutions increased to give the helicopter maximum power for lift-off and once he was strapped in, the sergeant pilot pulled up on the collective stick and the Lynx lifted off the ground, swung round to check for an unobstructed ascent and then dipped its nose and climbed rapidly to an operating height of 1000 feet. At a speed of 140 mph, the Lynx covered the 70 miles to London in a little under half an hour, assisted by the southerly wind and landed at Battersea Heliport beside the Thames. Gunn had been told that this procedure would be quicker than sending one of the Express Delivery Gazelles. It had been decided that military helicopters would not be allowed to land on the helipad on the roof of the Intelligence Directorate, so that a reasonable level of security about the real purpose of the building might be preserved. As soon as Gunn was clear of the helicopter, it took off and returned to its base at Netheravon in Wiltshire.

Gunn was still dressed in jeans, T-shirt, sailing shoes and a light cotton anorak and as he walked out into York Road, he followed his instructions and bent to retie the lace on one of his shoes. He heard a powerful motorbike start up and out of the corner of his eye, saw it pull in to the kerb beside him. He took the offered helmet, put it on and then climbed onto the pillion seat. The exhausts crackled and the machine was soon weaving through the early lunchtime traffic over Battersea Bridge, followed by a right turn into King's Road and then a number of lefts and rights which led to a multi-storey National Car Park beside an unimpressive modern building called Kingsroad House, the main London distribution centre of the Express Delivery Services plc.

The motorbike went to the sixth floor of the car park and stopped by the doors leading to the lifts. Gunn stepped off the pillion seat, removed his helmet, which he gave to the rider of the bike and then went through a swing door to the lifts. He summoned the right-hand lift and when the doors opened he stepped in and pressed out the day's sequence of floor buttons. Had there been anyone standing outside the lift, the panel indicating its position showed that it was descending to the ground floor; in fact, it stayed on the sixth floor. The blank, polished brushed-metal side of the lift opposite the doors swung back to reveal a lighted, reinforced concrete corridor. Gunn walked out of the lift and the door shut behind him.

The lift would now go to the ground floor where it would ascend and descend with its 'legitimate' load of people leaving or returning to their cars. The moment that the correct sequence was pressed out on the buttons in the lift, a CCTV camera was switched on and the occupant of the lift was identified by the security office, which monitored all access to Kingsroad House, the headquarters of Britain's Intelligence Directorate. It was just possible that a child playing with the lift buttons could tap out the correct sequence for the day and the camera prevented any security breach of this nature. Once the occupant of the lift had been identified, the door, which gave access to Kingsroad House was opened. The three buildings in

London and the one in Southampton housed a genuine company operated by staff who had been positively vetted and all were run on a strictly commercial basis producing a profit which offset the cost to the taxpayer of Britain's intelligence service.

Gunn walked along the corridor and stopped in front of another steel door. Having placed the palm of his right hand on a screen to the right of the door and tapped out a code on a keyboard below it with his left hand, the steel door divided into two at the centre, one half disappearing into the ceiling and the other into the floor. As Gunn reached the lifts in the centre of a long, carpeted corridor, the doors in one of the lifts opened and he was greeted by Simon Peters who ran the South-East Asia Section.

'Sorry to interrupt your sailing trip; we'll go straight to the conference room where the Deputy Director is running your debrief as Sir Jeremy is away at Langley.' The lift stopped on the 4th floor and Simon led the way out of the lift and through an open door into a purpose-designed conference room which had no windows and was physically and electronically 'sealed' from the outside world once the door was shut. As soon as the two men came into the room, the Deputy Director, Miles Thompson, pressed a button on a small console let into the conference table beside him and the door closed. Gunn was shown to the 'hot seat' opposite the Deputy Director and Simon Peters sat on his right. Also seated at the conference table was Richard Preston who headed the Asia Section, James Rayner for Russia and Donald Hastings for the Middle East.

General Sir Jeremy Hammond, the Head of Britain's Intelligence Directorate, who had long since discarded his military rank, had been given a free hand in recruiting his staff. A brilliant linguist with a Cambridge honours degree, Sir Jeremy had been given the task by the Prime Minister in 1986 of totally reorganising the British Intelligence Services. The men and women who had been recruited into the Intelligence Directorate - in almost every case - had had nothing to do with MI5 and 6. They had been selected because they were acknowledged experts on the people, politics, geography, history and languages of the nation or area, which they represented. The operatives or agents had been recruited for specific tasks and believed that they were working for MI6. Once their ability, integrity and motivation had been proved, they were brought into the organisation at Kingsroad House; the controllers of the agents had been recruited in much the same way. What Sir Jeremy had ruthlessly welded together was a totally professional organisation bereft of nepotism, and pseudo-intellectualism.

Miles Thompson, the Deputy Director, had been head-hunted off the Civil Service; he was the youngest Principal Private Secretary in the Service and was tipped to become Head of the Civil Service. The challenge of the new appointment had appealed to him; he had abandoned the assured knighthood with barely a second thought and had devoted his wealth of administrative skills to mould the Directorate into a highly efficient, effective and secure intelligence-gathering agency for the government.

'Right, gentlemen, let's get on with the debrief of Mr Gunn,' he began, once everyone was seated. He then pressed another button on the console and small, red lights appeared on the four microphones placed around the table. The Deputy announced the date and time for the benefit of the tape recorder and then looked at Gunn. 'Right, we've all listened to the recording which was made of your report on the incident on the Trans-Siberian railway, so could you now tell us what you discovered from your search of Hassan's boat.'

Gunn described what had happened in the early hours of that morning in the Royal Hamble Yacht Club Marina. As he spoke, the Deputy made notes on a jotting pad in front of him. When Gunn had finished his report, the Deputy asked him what significance he placed on the newspaper cutting and the figures pressed onto the surface of the paper.

'A submersible ship is the ideal mode of transport for an arms dealer; I believe that the article was cut from the paper because Hassan had acquired or wanted to acquire such a ship. The figures could have no more significance than a telephone number, but I would prefer to leave that to our experts here.'

'Thank you Mr Gunn, that's a very clear account of what happened. Simon, have you had confirmation from our man in the Embassy in Beijing, whether that consignment of timber has continued on to Guangzhou?'

'Not yet, Sir; Tim Driscoll left last night for Hong Kong to see if the cargo follows the usual route from Guangzhou to Hong Kong.'

'Yes, thank you; who's his controller?'

'Mike Dimmock; he went on the Cathay Pacific non-stop flight and Tim was on the MAS flight which got in 2½ hours later.'

'Will Mr Dimmock be working from our place in Queen's Road East?' the Deputy would only use a first name if he knew the person well. Gunn had only spoken to him once before and judged that that obviously did not place him on first name terms as he listened to the arrangements which had been set in hand since his report the night before. There was a squeak from a small speaker on the Deputy's console.

'Yes,' was all he said.

'Angela, Sir; I've a flash signal from the Embassy in Beijing.'

'Thank you, please bring it in,' and he pressed the door release button and switched off the recorder. The Deputy's PA came in, handed over the signal and left the room. Gunn reflected that he had never seen an unattractive woman in Kingsroad House and certainly the Deputy's PA was no exception. Miles Thompson read the signal in silence and then looked up. 'It seems that we won't be hearing from our man at the Embassy; what's left of him has just been found on the tracks of a goods yard on the southern side of Beijing. He appears to have been run over by a shunting engine. Would it make sense to get Driscoll up to Beijing?' The question was addressed to Simon Peters.

'He was going there anyway, Sir, to be briefed by the First Secretary Political and to get in touch with his contacts. The First Secretary's now dead, but he may well have left some information for Tim. He knew, of course, that Tim was coming.'

'Isn't Driscoll's mother Chinese?' the Deputy asked.

'Yes she is,' confirmed Simon. 'His father's British and both live in Hong Kong.'

'Right, leave the arrangements as they are, but see that Driscoll is briefed about the situation in Beijing.'

'Both he and Mike Dimmock will get a signal immediately I leave this briefing,' Simon said, glancing at his watch.

'Good; now just let me summarise what we have as I have to be at Number Ten by 6.30 to brief the PM,' and for a couple of seconds the Deputy Director closed his eyes whilst his computer-like brain shuffled the facts and he then spoke without a single 'um, er or ah' while it was all recorded by the tape recorder which had been switched on again as his PA left. 'There can be little doubt that Celia Harris saw ten SS20 missiles being transported to Beijing from Moscow which is in direct contravention of the Intermediate Nuclear Forces Treaty. We send a man to investigate this and he's killed. It seems that these missiles might be destined for the Middle East, but we have no proof that that is their destination. It would seem that Hassan Hussein was interested enough in an article about a submersible cargo ship to cut out the article and file it. Are the two incidents connected? Well, Hassan has the sort of money to buy ten nuclear missiles with multiple independently-targeted warheads, or MIRVS, as I believe they're called. He has a suitable place to keep this ship and, as we've known for some time, Saddam Hussein is prepared to pay almost any price to get his hands on a nuclear weapon and a delivery means; he therefore has a buyer. So, as

Agatha Christie's Poirot might have said, Hassan has the motive, he could now have the means and all he awaits is the opportunity. If all the intelligence reports reaching us from Riyadh are accurate, then the opportunity will not be long in coming, which is what Sir Jeremy is discussing with his opposite number, John Dempster of the CIA. My gut feeling is that the missiles are on their way to Hassan, but why is the President Putin committed to such a suicidal course of action, or is it someone else? Is this breach of the INF Treaty being engineered to discredit him by the many die-hard communists of the 'ancien regime' whom we know are committed to such a course of action. James, I can see you are itching to speak, so let's hear your assessment'.

'Thank you, Sir; I can't add a great deal to that summary except that our sources in Moscow - and in particular, the two we have in the KGB - would confirm that Putin is known to be briefing certain GRU operatives in person. I cannot accept that he is deliberately breaching the INF Treaty and therefore the removal of the missiles must be a plot to discredit him.'

'Thank you, James; Donald, I would like to hear from you after Richard has added anything. So Richard, I know this operation skirts around the periphery of your area, but I would like to hear your assessment.'

'You rightly say, Sir, that this is not my area, but from what I've heard I believe we might be putting two and two together and coming up with five. How much would an arms dealer pay for an SS20? I don't know - £½ million? £1million? £5million? - even ten times ten million pounds in hard currency isn't going to solve Russia's economic doldrums. No, my guess is that this is being done for private financial gain. Who is in need of these missiles? The Israelis destroyed Saddam Husseins's potential nuclear capability and his attempt to build a nuclear gun was thwarted by us. He would be top of my list with Iran a close second; there are other crackpots who would like to get their hands on something like that, but none of them have the ready cash. I think I would target my search onto those men in Russia who were chucked on the scrap heap by Yeltsin and Gorbachev - what about that Air Defence General who was dismissed after that German youth flew his plane into Red Square; what was his name?'

'Sokolovsky,' was provided by James Rayner.

'That's the man; what's happened to him?'

'The last we heard of him was that he'd turned into a penniless alcoholic, but really, Richard, you can't be serious... I mean'…

'How many others are there, like him, who would have known where the missiles were kept and how Soviet-supplied arms deals were set up?'

'Quite a large number, but'....

'Gentlemen,' interrupted the Deputy Director, quietly but firmly, 'James, Richard has a point, which I would like followed up. Will you please find out how many of these disgraced persons there are and what they're up to - have any dropped out of sight recently and so on. Now, Donald, your assessment please.'

Donald Hastings had left the Army as a highly frustrated Brigadier. He had been one of the youngest promoted Brigadiers since the end of the Second World War, had jumped straight from Lt Colonel to Brigadier at the age of 41 and had then done four appointments in that rank before retiring early. He had served in Aden in the troubles and then as a company commander on secondment in Oman. He had gone to the Staff College at Quetta in Pakistan and then an Assistant Defence Attaché's appointment in Riyadh before Commanding the Muscat Regiment at the age of 37. He spoke fluent Arabic and Urdu and many patois versions of both. He had been everywhere in the Gulf Region and most of that on foot or on the back of a camel.

'Thank you Miles; we all know that there's trouble brewing in the Gulf and, as usual, Saddam Hussein is at the bottom of it. He possesses armed forces which are completely out of proportion to a defensive role - in fact the fourth largest army in the world - and so its logical to assume that they are required for an offensive role. He failed to acquire any advantage after eight years of war with Iran and a humiliating defeat in Desert Storm in '91. Richard mentioned that the Israelis destroyed his plant for producing enriched uranium and he's still smarting from the nuclear gun fiasco and the further humiliation of UN Resolution 1441 and the presence of UN Inspection Teams. Saddam's the trouble maker and the only way he'll stop US/UK military intervention in Iraq is with a nuclear capability. He's got Scud Missiles, but no nuclear warheads. It wouldn't be too difficult to modify the SS20 warhead to fit the Scud and he's mad enough to use them, on Israel, in particular, if he's threatened by the USA.'

'My money's on Iraq as the destination of those missiles and I suggest that our cypher crackers start by seeing if those figures John turned up fit some form of grid reference or position identified by latitude and longitude in the Gulf area. On second thoughts, as it was connected with a ship, forget the grid reference, but look for a position at sea. I go for your gut feeling, Miles. Those missiles are on their way to the Middle East, but I also think that Richard has something with the money angle in Russia. Whatever Hassan is paying for the missiles you can bet your last penny that he's making a huge profit; as Miles said, Saddam will pay any price. I can't make up my mind; I smell a double cross.'

'Thank you Donald and all of you for your information and views. I'm going to have a word with my opposite number at Langley after I've spoken with Sir Jeremy. I had been considering sending you to Hong Kong, John' - the use of the first name meant that he was now 'accepted' and Gunn smiled inwardly - 'but I don't want you and Tim Driscoll treading on each other's toes. I believe that you told us that Peter de Havilland was thinking of visiting Sardrière Island during this cruise he was on?'

'So he said yesterday evening,' Gunn confirmed.

'Right, I'd like you to rejoin the boat and make sure he does visit Sardrière, but you mustn't put the de Havillands or any of the other guests at risk - the Director would never forgive me,' he added as an aside. 'Simon and Donald, I would like you to work together on this one and let me know who's to be John's controller and from where he'll operate. Donald, I know you've a lot on your plate at the moment and I expect it will get much busier even if you are only half right in your prediction of what's going to happen in the Gulf. I've already spoken to Admin and they are drafting in two more PAs and the Director has confirmed that you may recruit those two additional agents to be moved in-country. The Commanding Officer of 22 SAS Regiment has already confirmed that the four teams which we requested are also in-country. Any questions, gentlemen?' There were none. 'Very well; Simon, please see that I'm informed as soon as you hear anything from Driscoll.' They all left the conference room and Gunn rode down in the lift with Simon and Donald to the floor below.

'We'll do your preparatory brief in my office, as Donald and I arranged before the meeting. Alan Paxton...ah!' Simon stopped and he opened his office door where a well-tanned man rose to his feet. 'John, I want you to meet Alan Paxton who will be your controller for this operation. We believe this operation may well take you to the Gulf or the Far East. The latter you know as well as anyone, but the Gulf is Alan's stamping ground.' Alan Paxton was only a shade below John's height and clearly had Arab blood in his ancestry, which was confirmed seconds later by Simon Peters. 'Alan's from Saudi Arabia, but decided to throw in his lot with us and has changed his name. Now, grab a seat everyone and let's get John briefed.' For the next hour, the four men discussed communications, codes, drops, back-up procedures and finished with equipment. 'Is there anything you want from the equipment boys?' Simon asked.

'No thanks; the only thing would have been scuba gear and Peter de Havilland has four sets of the very latest stuff on his yacht, including one of those aqua-scooters which you hang on to. You might have to reimburse him if I break or lose any of his kit, but otherwise I can shout for anything through Alan.'

'Are you still carrying that bloody great blunderbuss?'

'No, I'm not.'

'Hurray! What've you got now?'

'An even bigger one!'

'Dear God! What?'

'Something the Armourer found for me; he knows I like big guns and so he found me one, much the same size as the Browning, but with an even greater stopping power.'

'What's he given you?' Donald asked.

'It's a Polish Radom.'

'A what?'

'A Polish Radom Vis 35; it's very similar to the Browning, but it has a couple of advantages. It has a higher muzzle velocity - nearly 200 foot seconds higher - and has a cunning arrangement for doing away with the safety catch.'

'Sounds highly dangerous,' Simon remarked.

'No, not really. It has a device for retracting the firing pin, which you can reset in a split second as you cock back the hammer.'

'Is it effective?' this came from Alan Paxton.

'The Armourer swears that it'll stop a charging bull at 30 metres, but I haven't put it to the test yet.'

'Oh, very well; please leave the building by route 3 and you'll find a taxi waiting for you there. He'll take you to the heliport where you'll go by charter helicopter to Southampton Airport at Eastleigh. You'll be in plenty of time for the BIA flight to Guernsey. As we've already discussed, Alan will base himself in St Peter Port.'

'Many thanks, 'bye,' and Gunn left Simon's office and took the lift to the basement. There, he was checked out through a similar steel door to the one through which he had entered the building and once more found himself in a well-lit, reinforced concrete corridor. This was the longest of the exit routes from Kingsroad House and after a 200 yard walk he stopped in front of a door which required a scan of John's palm before it opened. He was now in a small maintenance area on the basement level of Peter Jones' Department Store. John Gunn walked through into the busy store, full of weekend shoppers and tourists and took the lift up to the first floor, walked through the china and silverware department to the Symons Street exit and out into the street. There was only one taxi there and the driver was tightening the wheel nuts on the front nearside wheel. He was wearing trainers and sure enough, the brand trademark of the sportswear company was only on one heel and not on the other. 'Battersea Heliport?' Gunn enquired.

'Half a tick, mate; nearly finished,' and with that the driver replaced the wheel brace in the front of the cab and got into the driver's seat. 'Got a slight problem, Sir,' the driver's voice came through on the intercom between the driver's and passenger's compartment. 'I think I've picked up a tail an' I don't want him around when I drop you. Please sit well back in the seat,' and the intercom was switched off. The driver then picked up a small microphone and spoke into it. The taxi made its way east and then north up Warwick Road, turned right into Trebovir Road and then right again into Earls Court Road. The SAAB 9000 Turbo was three cars behind the taxi and stuck with it throughout these manoeuvres. The taxi increased speed to create a wider separation between itself and the cars behind and then a number of things happened in quick succession.

The taxi had just passed a mews entrance in Redcliffe Gardens when a large removal lorry was beckoned out into the road by an overalled driver's mate on the right of the road. The car behind the taxi squeaked through the narrowing gap, but the car behind that could not make the gap and nor could its brakes prevent the collision with the lorry. The SAAB's breaks were much better and it slewed hard to one side and pulled up with no damage. Redcliffe Gardens is a one way southbound street and the traffic quickly piled up behind the obstruction in the road effectively sealing off the SAAB from any further activity. As soon as the taxi was out of sight of the SAAB, the driver took another right and a right and headed north up Warwick road again and then through South Kensington to Chelsea Bridge. The intercom hummed; 'he'll probably have a second car tailing in parallel, but that seems to have left us clear,' his driver announced.

'Hasn't that compromised the Peter Jones' route?' John asked.

'No; that guy in the SAAB is from the Russian Embassy. It's all part of the game; I followed him two nights ago and he got my number so he's now trying to find out who I work for. I'll be changing this car as soon as I've dropped you and then the poor sod who drives this machine for the leasing firm will have a Ruskie escort until they realise what's happened.' They were now approaching the inevitable traffic jam at Clapham Junction Road on the south of the river.

'How long have you been doing this?'

'I was a driver with the Met before this; this job's better paid and more exciting. Right mate, time for you to change; your transport's coming up on the right hand side; best of luck and kill a few of the bastards for me!' The motorbike pulled alongside the taxi and Gunn was out, onto it with helmet on and away, weaving through the jammed traffic in seconds, wondering who it was that the taxi driver wanted killed. They reached the heliport in less than five minutes and Gunn removed the helmet and returned it to its owner. After checking at the information desk at the Heliport, Gunn was shown where the helicopter was waiting. It was a diminutive but fast Robinson Beta, two-seater and as soon as he was strapped in beside the pilot, the single turbine was run up and with the acceleration of an express lift, the helicopter shot into the air, banked to starboard and then headed south-west out of London. Without turning his head, the pilot spoke into the boom mike in front of his mouth.

'Business trip, Sir?' Gunn didn't miss the slight emphasis on the 'sir' which was meant to convey the pilot's disapproval of the misuse of his skills to ferry what appeared to be a down-market passenger. His clientele were usually businessmen or pop and film stars.

'No, it's my chauffeur's day off so I thought I would borrow someone else's.' The retort ensured that the rest of the flight was completed in silence and gave Gunn a chance to collect his thoughts about the course of action, which had been discussed at Kingsroad House. His was the task of getting a close look at Sardrière Island. It had been a really hot summer and that Saturday, at the end of July, was no exception. He must have dozed off because the change in the note of the turbine startled him as he realised that the helicopter was descending fast onto the helipad at Eastleigh Airport. As soon as the machine touched down, the pilot nodded and Gunn opened the door, closed it firmly behind him and ducked down as he walked away from the helicopter towards the airport buildings.

He only had a half-hour wait for the BIA flight and after a thirty minute flight, he arrived in Guernsey at a couple of minutes before six in the evening. He had no luggage so was the first passenger to reach the taxis and was on his way to St Peter Port within minutes of landing. 'Where to, Sir?' he was asked by the taxi driver.

'Drop me by the harbour please.'

'Anywhere in particular, Sir?'

'Oh, yes; the Ship'll do fine.'

'Right you are, Sir.' Gunn judged that it would be at least another two hours before Osprey reached the north marina in St Peter Port and he also realised that he hadn't eaten since breakfast that morning.

The Ship was a cosy pub and served some of the best beers and food in St Peter Port. The town and particularly the area around the harbour and marinas would be packed as it was nearly the peak of the tourist season. The one haven from the crush of tourists was the Ship, which catered to a regular clientele. It was a free house and the story went that its owner and landlord, Tom to everyone, ran the place as a hobby and was little interested in returning a profit. No electronic game, gambling machine or juke box was allowed and he boasted a fine selection of home-made ales and wines. His daughter did the cooking and nothing appeared in front of a customer, which had seen the inside of a freezer.

Gunn paid off the taxi outside the pub and went in and ordered a cool lager and steak and kidney pie with new potatoes and peas. When he had finished his early supper, he took his beer over to the bar and chatted to the landlord. 'Aye, it's a weird old place is Sardrière Castle,' he confirmed as he polished glasses before hanging them up in the racks above the bar. The comment had been prompted by Gunn's inquiry about the place and whether it was worth a visit. 'Mind you, it certainly attracts the tourists and I'm told you get real value for money on a tour round the place. It's been built to a completely authentic plan of a medieval Crusader's castle, so I'm told.'

'How long's it been there, Tom?'

'Let's see; must be nearly fifteen years; only took him two years to build it; must've cost a fortune.'

'Since it's been there, have any fishing boats - or any other sort of boats - been lost in that area?

'There was a sad business, oh, now let's see...must've been last November...yes, that'd be it, end of November. Just coming, Sir!' and Tom moved along the bar to serve a customer and then returned.

'You were saying that something happened last November.'

'Yes, that's right; it was Carteret's boat.'

'What happened to it?'

'It just disappeared.'

'Sounds as though there's a good story there.'

'Oh, aye; there's a story alright,' Tom muttered as he poured himself the beer which Gunn had bought for him. 'Jean Carteret has always taken his boat to the waters around Sardrière. Not many others go because of the overfalls and tide rips, but old Cartaret always came back with a good catch. Excuse me,' and he went to serve another customer. Gunn looked at his watch; nearly half-past seven. He would walk along to the north marina in half-an-hour and check if there was any sign of Osprey. Tom returned; 'now where was I?'

'Cartaret fishing around Sardrière Island.'

'Right; well he often goes out with his daughter, very pretty lass, but not that night. He was on his own....' he paused and John turned to see what had distracted him. A tall girl had just come into the pub with her boyfriend. She had a mane of tawny blonde hair and her looks had attracted a number of glances from around the bar. 'Sorry...his boat just vanished. He was never seen again and not a scrap of his boat has reappeared anywhere. Real mystery that; tidal streams hereabouts always throw up stuff eventually, but not a scrap of Cartaret's boat. Near broke his daughter's heart it did. She lost all her savings by putting together a salvage team and a boat, but they all quit because they were scared shitless - pardon the expression - by that Arab and his weird mob. Now she can't get anyone to help her.'

'Poor girl; does she live near the harbour?'

'Oh, not far; round towards the light on St Martin's Point.'

'Right, thanks for the beer and food; I'd better see if my boat's arrived.'

'Pleasure, Sir; see you soon.'

'You will indeed, Tom; I might drop in and see Cartaret's daughter.'

'Won't have to.'

'Sorry, what's that?'

'Won't have to go and visit her.'

'Why not?'

'She's sitting over there; you saw her when she came into the pub.'

CHAPTER 8

Simeon Bukharin awoke to find a cabin steward by his bed. In the same way as the night before, nothing was said and the steward placed a small tray with tea and biscuits on the bedside table and then left the cabin. Despite his feeling of foreboding the night before, Simeon had had a dreamless sleep and felt considerably more cheerful as he showered and then dressed in clean clothes. At exactly 7.45, his cabin door opened and his steward stood there waiting to escort him to breakfast. He was not familiar with ships, but even so he found that his surroundings were more cramped and claustrophobic than he had imagined they would be. His guide led him to a small wardroom, which, like his cabin, was comfortable, but also like his cabin had no portholes. No one else was in the room except for a steward who took his order and then vanished through a swing door, presumably into some sort of servery, Simeon guessed.

There were newspapers and magazines - all in English, but that was an advantage as all of them spoke it well and wanted to get used to it in preparation for their new life. He went over to the small sideboard and helped himself to cereal and coffee. The steward returned with his order at exactly the correct time and as soon as his breakfast was finished, his cabin steward appeared and escorted him out of the wardroom. He was expecting to be taken straight back to his cabin, but he was led in a different direction and he was shown into a room which had a small library, comfortable chairs, more newspapers and magazines and, at last, two portholes; he sighed with relief.

As soon as his escort had gone, he walked over to one of the portholes. It was like an aircraft window with two layers of glass or plastic,which must have been at least an inch thick. This consequently gave a somewhat distorted view of the world outside, but it was a view and from what he could see and the shadows cast by the ship, he guessed that he was looking towards Discovery Bay on Lantau Island. Yes, things had definitely improved and when Simeon discovered that there was a coffee percolator on another small sideboard, he collected that day's edition of the South China Morning Post, filled a cup with hot, black coffee and settled down in a comfortable armchair.

*

The four men watched as the crane in the Guangzhou dockyard lifted the crated missile cases concealed by tree trunks off the rail flats and swung them high over the docks towards the gaping cargo hold of the grey and green painted Chinese cargo ship.

'If they drop...' started Peter Milynkov.

'Shut up!' he was silenced by Rokossovsky. The last of the ten missiles disappeared inside the hold and there was an audible sigh of relief and pent up tension amongst the four men.

'Where's Volkonoff?' asked Boris Samsonov.

'He said he'd join us here just before the ship sailed tonight,' Rokossovsky replied, still watching the crane.

'How many more mess-ups is he going to make? What was that man from the British Embassy doing, snooping around the goods yard in Beijing. Why did Volkonoff have to kill him? I...'

'Oh, do shut up,' Ivan Voznesensky cut him off. If we had the answers to those questions, we'd have thrashed this all out ages ago. In the circumstances, Volkonoff did the only thing he could; the man was poking around the rail flats with the missiles and it would only have been a matter of time before he discovered what was hidden amongst the tree trunks. What would you have done? Wandered over to him and asked him for the time? You seem to have forgotten, Boris, that we've probably committed the crime of the century and will be hunted down by every nation in the world if our identities are ever discovered. Look, the missiles are on board and we're due to sail,' and here he glanced at his watch, 'in about 2½ hours time. Having discovered from the contents of his wallet that the man was from the British Embassy, Yuri has quite rightly, in my opinion, stayed behind to ensure that no information about our cargo is known by the British. Now that we've seen the cargo loaded, I, for one, am going aboard and when I've found the wardroom, am going to have a drink.'

'You'll be lucky to find anything on this rust bucket and if there's any drink at all it'll be Chinese wine or beer, both of which taste like cat's piss,' Boris muttered

'Ivan's right, we're conspicuous standing around here. Come on everyone, let's find our cabins, however awful they might be and if you're right about the booze - which I expect you are Boris - then I've got three bottles of vodka which are burning a hole in my suitcase. I promise you, once we're on the ship in Hong Kong, everything will appear in a better light,' and Rokossovsky made his way over the dockside litter to the gangway leading up to the ship's deck.

Yuri Volkonoff's training had taught him that coincidences didn't happen in the world of espionage. Somehow the British had got wind of what was happening and had told their MI6 agent in the embassy to go and investigate. That direction to the embassy probably came on a signal which would have been passed directly to the Secret Intelligence Service desk. He had told the other four men that he had discovered the identity of the man from the bits and pieces in his wallet. This was untrue as the man hadn't even had a wallet on him. He had used his usual persuasive techniques which had left the man with nearly every bone in his body broken and minus most of his finger and toenails. When Volkonoff considered that there was nothing else left to glean from the man writhing in agony on the ground, he had dragged him over to where the clatter and crash of wagons indicated that shunting was in progress. He draped the body over the rails and death came as a merciful relief to the tortured body as the wheels of the shunting engine decapitated and dismembered it.

Volkonoff took a taxi from the goods yard at Guang'anmen Station to the area where all the embassies were located; all, that is except for the Russian Embassy, which strongly resembled a fortress and was isolated in Dongzhimen Beizhong Jie. When the taxi reached the Friendship Store, Volkonoff paid the driver and walked to the Jianguo Hotel, where, posing as a guest, he hired a car which was immediately available from a rank of them which were permanently parked outside the hotel. He paid the girl at the desk for a day's hire of a Toyota and looked at his watch; 12.15.

If the silly woman at the car hire desk would only get a move on with his change, he would be able to catch the lunch time exodus from the British Embassy. Hiding his impatience with the desperately slow process of getting his change and receipt, he controlled his desire to grab the woman by the neck and shake some urgency into her. The change and receipt arrived and forcing himself not to hurry, he left the foyer of the hotel and skirted the ornamental pool to claim his car.

Driving out of the forecourt of the hotel, Volkonoff turned right onto the dual carriageway of Jianguomenwai Dajie and at the first set of traffic lights he turned right again into Dongdaqiao Lu which led towards the diplomatic enclave of Beijing. A sea of bicycles flowed all round him which made him drive with great care as he had no wish to be involved in an accident or come to the notice of the Chinese police militia. He eased over to the left lane of the dual carriageway and at the first intersection, which was controlled by a militia policeman, he turned left into Guaghua Lu.

The British Embassy was no more than 200 yards along the road on the right and at exactly 12.29 he parked his car in a space which gave him a good view of the paved forecourt in front of the embassy. The building was two storeys high, constructed in a greyish sandstone coloured brick and very vaguely Georgian in style. To the left of the building and bordering the Ritan Park was the British Ambassador's residence and to the right were a small clubhouse and tennis courts. The forecourt was sealed off from the Chinese public by a high wall and equally high wrought iron gates. To the left of the main gates was a smaller gate guarded by a soldier of the Peoples Liberation Army. It was through this smaller gate that the staff of the Embassy were just starting to appear as they left for their lunch break.

Volkonoff had spent three years in Beijing as a cultural attaché on the staff of the Soviet Embassy. The Soviet Embassy had possessed rudimentary plans of all the embassies and Volkonoff had committed all of them to memory. It wasn't long before he saw a suitable target; four, young people emerged from the embassy and walked slowly towards the gate chatting. At first, they were too far away for Volkonoff to hear what was being said and he had none of the sophisticated electronic equipment that he would have had if he had still been working for the KGB. As they came within hearing range, he realised that they were arranging to play tennis that evening. Very conveniently, they paused at the gate to conclude their arrangements. Their voices drifted across the rather thick and humid July air, instantly identifiable from the raucous chatter of Mandarin Chinese.

'Look, I'll give Jane a lift home to her flat now so she can collect her tennis things and then we'll see you in the club for a drink and a bite to eat, OK?'

'That's fine. Jeremy and I'll have a drink at the club and we'll see you later. Don't feel you have to come back here for lunch, Jane. Get David to take you somewhere interesting!'

'Fine, we might just do that!'

'See you this evening, if not before.'

'Yes, sure; bye!'

'Bye!' and Jane and David, so clearly introduced to Volkonoff, emerged from the small gate. They were both chatting and laughing as they climbed into a lime, green Citroen DCV. The small car pulled out into the lunchtime traffic and headed towards the area behind the Friendship Store where all the diplomatic compounds were located.

The British compound had a wire fence all round it and another PLA soldier at the entrance who was taking a great interest in picking his nose and paid not the slightest interest as both cars went through the gate.

Volkonoff parked close to the Citroen and followed the young couple into one of four, large apartment blocks. Neither David nor Jane took any notice of Volkonoff and only acknowledged his existence with polite smiles as he joined them at the lifts. The three of them entered the lift and Jane pressed the button for the fourth floor, hardly pausing in her light-hearted chatter with David. Had the evolution of the so-called civilized world not deprived humans of their sense of instinct, Jane and David might have sensed their proximity to danger and possibly the most ruthless, psychopathic killer ever trained by the KGB. With uncanny precision, Volkonoff had identified the ideal target.

Jane was a new arrival to the diplomatic staff of the British Embassy; she was what the Foreign and Commonwealth Office described as a 'floater' - temporary staff sent out from the UK to fill-in while a permanent member of the staff took annual leave. She was a pretty and vivacious girl and David was determined to stake his claim before another male attempted to impress her with his charm. Neither of them even noticed that Volkonoff hadn't pressed any button in the lift; there were only two flats on each floor and both David and Jane knew the occupant of the other flat. Volkonoff followed them both out of the lift on the fourth floor and as Jane put her key into the lock of apartment 4B, he made his move. They both had their backs to him and still suspected nothing.

'Both of you stand quite still, please,' Volkonoff ordered. They didn't and swung round to find themselves staring into the barrel of a large automatic fitted with a bulbous silencer.

'What do you want?' David asked, quickly clearing his throat as his voice broke into a piping falsetto.

'Please go into the apartment - both of you,' the latter was added as David hesitated. They did and Volkonoff removed the keys from the lock and placed them in his pocket. 'Now, young lady, you will sit in that chair,' and he indicated a G-Plan armchair with a bilious yellow stretch cover, 'and you will sit in that one,' and the equally awful twin armchair was indicated.

'Now, wait a min'... but David got no further. The bullet from the automatic imbedded itself in the wall, just a fraction of an inch to the right of David's head. He fell, rather than sat in the chair.

'Both of you listen very carefully to the instructions which I am about to give you. Failure to do so could cost you your life or the life

110

of the other one. I will not repeat what I say and if you get this wrong,' and he turned to David, 'this young lady will die. Have I now made myself quite clear to you both?' David nodded his head and Jane started to cry.

'You, young man,' and David immediately looked at Volkonoff, 'will return to the British Embassy and by whatever means necessary you will go through every classified communication, whether that is a signal, facsimile, email or recorded secure telephone message to find out why your first secretary political - a member of the British Secret Intelligence Service - should want to go and look at the goods yard at Guang'amen Station. Mr Trevor Baker, your first secretary, is dead. I killed him after extracting a considerable amount of information from him. So be warned; if you try to bluff me or warn anyone what is happening, you sign this lady's death warrant.' These instructions were interrupted by loud sobs from Jane who was near a state of collapse. Volkonoff paid no attention. 'As soon as you leave here, I will remove the girl. I will phone the Embassy in exactly one hour at...13.45, when I will give you instructions where to meet me, give me the information which I require and collect the girl. I worked in an embassy for three years, so please answer these questions correctly.

What's your name?'

'David Price.'

'What's your position in the embassy?'

'Third secretary.'

'What specialisation? Stop wasting time Mr Price or I will make sure that this lady is kept fully occupied while you are away. Now; chancery, consular, commerce, aid or what?'

'Chancery.'

'How long have you been in the embassy?'

'Eighteen months.'

'Right; that's quite long enough for you to know all the procedures for gaining access to information. What's her job?'

'She worked for'....the mistake was made and David realised it too late. He had used the past tense and now he was committed.

'Go on Mr Price.'

'She worked for Mr Baker.'

'Now that is a stroke of luck. Very well, Mr Price, are my instructions quite clear?'

'Yes, quite clear.'

'Remember, the slightest hint that you have informed anyone of what has happened in this apartment and she dies.' The sobs were now nearly hysterical. 'What's her name?'

'Jane Marshal.'

'Very well; go and do as you have been instructed. Move!' The last word was shouted to snap David out of his disbelief of what was happening to him. He staggered from the room and Volkonoff watched him from the window as he climbed into the Citroen and drove out of the compound.

'Right Miss Marshal, on your feet; you're coming with me.' There was no response except for intensified sobbing. A stinging slap sent her sprawling over the left arm of the chair, but the sobbing stopped and she immediately got to her feet, collected her handbag and moved towards the door. 'You will now go down to the car park. If you make one mistake I will kill you as it matters little to me whether you live or die; understood?'

'Yes,' was just audible. They met no one on the way to the car. Volkonoff made Jane get in first on the right and then he went round and got into the driver's seat. The Toyota was an automatic and specifically selected because of that. Volkonoff put the gun on the floor on his left and reversed out of the parking space. He then drove out of the compound without anyone noticing his arrival or departure. The PLA soldier was asleep in his sentry box.

*

David Price drove the half mile back to the Embassy in a complete trance. He couldn't believe that all this was really happening to him. It was all a ghastly nightmare, a joke in very bad taste or perhaps even some sort of test which he had to pass to prove his competence in a difficult situation. In the past, he had heard that this sort of thing had happened to embassy staff, but that had all seemed to belong to the world of fiction and spy stories. Perhaps when he arrived at the embassy, they would all be waiting there to have a good laugh at his expense. 'Oh God, let it be a joke or a mistake.. or something, please,' he pleaded aloud in the car.

There was no laughing reception at the embassy when he reached it and the retired sergeant-major on the reception desk greeted him cheerfully. 'Didn't expect to see you back so soon, Mr Price,' he smiled, with an overdone theatrical wink. David muttered something inaudible noting, as he crossed the reception area, that time was ticking away quickly. He went to the far right end of the reception area and let himself through the door into the secure area of the embassy after tapping out the code on the combination-locked door. He was moving like an automaton and his brain just would not function properly or grasp the seriousness of the situation in which he now found himself. It was as if David Price was a different character and he was watching all this happen on the TV.

'Damn, damn, damn,' he cursed to himself; 'think! you bloody idiot. What am I going to do? I must tell Head of Chancery. She'll know what to do. What happens if that monster realises that I've spoken tò someone?.. He'll kill Jane and me as well.. What's he doing to her now? Why me? Why did this have to happen to me?' All of these incoherent thoughts raced through David's mind as he made his way through two more combination-locked doors up to the registry beyond which lay the sanctum in which Trevor Baker and Jane worked.

Just before he went into the registry, he looked at his watch... only 38 minutes before the phone call from that man. He went through the door and stood in front of the counter, which barred any further access into the room and the large walk-in safe in which all the material graded CONFIDENTIAL up to COSMIC TOP SECRET UK EYES ONLY was safeguarded. It really wasn't David's day; there were two girls on duty in the registry and one of them was the very last person he wanted to meet at that moment. He had been having an affair with her and ever since Jane's arrival, he'd been trying to cool off their relationship. Samantha looked up as he came in.

'Hello David, what're you doing in the building? Rumour control announced that you were last seen sneaking out of the building with that new bit of skirt who's working for Trevor,' was the cheery, but barbed greeting.

'Hello Sammy; yes I was. Jeremy and Liz asked us to make up a mixed double for tennis this evening, so I took Jane back to the compound to collect her tennis things.'

'And look at her etchings, no doubt; don't tell me that you pushed your luck and the little virgin threw you out so you've rushed back to your old flame to beg forgiveness. Come on David, even in your worse moments you could do better than that. You must've been reading some sloppy, romantic paperbacks which have emasculated you.' The irony and biting sarcasm were unrelenting and would be bitterly regretted by Samantha before the end of that day. David hardly heard a word of what she had said as his mind was now made up. Priority one was to see that no harm came to Jane. That meant going along with this awful man's instructions. His mind made up, David's brain raced to produce a plausible excuse to gain access to the information he needed.

'Donald rang me and asked me to come in and check some signals. It seems that there's something going on which he wishes to discuss with the Defence Attaché and Trevor. You know, usual military stuff, if they can turn normality into a crisis they will.'

'No, I can't say I agree with that. If there's ever a crisis around here, it invariably comes from Chancery, not from the DA's office. However, that's beside the point. What's it you're after?'

'He said that there'd been a couple of signals which had been received in the last 48 hours which would probably be on the float file for strictly limited access. He wants me to read them and then come up and discuss them ASP. Can you help me please?' His final plea for help stopped the sharp remark, which Samantha had been about to deliver.

'There've been about twenty signals in the last 48 hours; what's the subject?'

'He was particularly vague about that... probably because he was speaking on an open line. He did mention that it might have something to do with railways, stations or goods yards.'

'Railways?'

'Yes.. something like that.'

'Yes, I think I know what you're after. Are you quite sure that you need to have access to this information, David.'

'Yes, I suppose so, otherwise I can't discuss it with Donald.'

'Yes, you've said that once already, but why would the Second Secretary Chancery want to discuss that subject with you. It's got nothing to do with him or you. Are you sure that you heard him correctly on the phone?'

'Oh, for heavens sake, yes; now please may I see those signals?' David had glanced at his watch; 25 minutes to the phone call.

'Alright, alright; you've certainly lost your manners and charm since you took up with your new bit of skirt. Please sign these forms in triplicate,' and she pushed them across the counter towards him, 'while I go and dig out those signals.

'Yes of course, but please be quick. Donald seemed to be in quite a hurry.'

'Are you sure that it's Donald who's in a hurry and not just you panting to get back to your mixed doubles at 4B?' came from inside the safe as Samantha looked for the relevant file.

'No, I pro....'

'Oh, come on, I'm only joking; here,' as she reappeared from the safe, 'these are the signals which you need to see. Folios four and five,' and Samantha placed a beige file, marked with a red cross and stamped TOP SECRET - UK EYES ONLY. She had opened the file and turned it towards David so that he could read folio four. It was a FLASH Precedence signal addressed to Trevor Baker. It asked him to take a close look at a particular consignment of timber, which was due to pass through Guang'anmen goods yard in the next 24 hours. It was suspected that there might be Russian military equipment concealed amongst the timber. The second signal was again addressed to Trevor Baker and informed him that he would be contacted by someone arriving from Hong Kong who would follow up anything which he discovered in the goods yard. The rest of the signal related to communications and cyphers, which meant nothing to David. He scanned them both again, thanked Samantha and left the registry. She waited until the door closed and then punched out a number on her telephone as she knew that the Assistant Defence Attaché was in his office over lunch.

'Commander Watson.'

'John, it's Sammy from registry.'

'Yes Sammy, what can I do for you?' Commander John Watson wasn't the security officer for the embassy, but Samantha, like many of the younger single members of the embassy, found the man who filled that appointment to be cynical and scathing when approached by the junior staff and younger generation. Besides, John Watson was rather good looking and rumour had it that he and his wife were about to separate. Samantha explained what had just happened in the registry.

'Were's he now?'

'On his way out of the embassy, I should think.'

'Any idea where he's going?'

'Well, he certainly isn't doing to see Donald, because what David doesn't know is that we received a signal just over an hour ago to say that Donald's father was dying and at this very minute Donald's on his way to the airport.'

'Well done, thanks; I'm on my way,' and the connection was broken.

*

As David reached the reception area, he heard the phone ringing at the desk. The receptionist in front of the console flicked a switch on the exchange and glancing up, saw David. 'Oh! That's saved me paging you, David; there's a call for you. I'll put it through to the phone over there for you.'

'Thank you, Sonia,' and he picked up the phone. 'David Price.'

'Listen carefully Mr Price,' it wasn't a dream; when would this ghastly nightmare end? David tried to concentrate. 'You will drive to the Forbidden City in Tiananmen Square; you know it, of course,'

'Yes, I know it.'

115

'Good; go to the Imperial Palace and once you are there, go through the emperor's private apartment to the ornamental garden. Do you know it?'

'I do.'

'In that garden is a 600 year old fig tree; did you know that?'

'No I didn't. How do I find it?'

'Ask someone or look at the diagram at the entrance to the garden. You will meet me at that tree.'

'What about Ja... Miss Marshall? Will she be there?'

'Oh yes, Mr Price, she'll be there. You supply me with the right information and you will both be together again.'

'When do I meet you?'

'In twenty minutes... that will be at 14.05 exactly. Good bye,' and the connection was broken. David replaced the phone and walked out of the embassy.

*

The door into the reception area of the embassy burst open and Commander Watson hurried over to the receptionist. 'Sonia, have you seen Mr Price?'

'Yes, Commander, he left here less than two minutes ago after I put a call through to him... on that phone over there,' and she nodded towards the phone on the table. Anything wrong?'

'I'm not sure. Any idea which way he went?'

'No, sorry, I can't see from here, but Bill must've seen him.'

'Thanks,' and the Naval Commander hurried out of the building checking that he had his car keys. 'Bill!'

'Yes Sir.'

'Have you seen Mr Price?'

'Yes sir, there he is now; he's just off in that little French car of his. Is...' but the Assistant Defence Attaché was already on his way with a parting 'thanks' thrown over his shoulder towards the retired sergeant-major.

The little green Citroen had pulled out from its parking slot and had done a U-turn heading left towards the dual carriageway of Dongdaqiao Lu. John Watson knew that if he didn't see which way David turned at the intersection, he would never find him. Keeping an eye on the car, he dashed towards his Range Rover. The Citroen had reached the intersection and was over on the right side - he would either turn right or go straight on. The lights changed to green and the Citroen turned right.

John Watson turned out of his parking space and did a U-turn creating a slight increase in the ambient level of cacophony in Beijing as cars braked, horns blared and a cyclist was unseated into the road,

116

but the Range Rover reached the lights as they were changing and swung right despite the strident blasts from the policeman's whistle. The Citroen was just crossing the next intersection into East Quianmen Street, which led to Tiananmen Square. John Watson floored the accelerator and dicing with weaving bicycles and handcarts, just made the intersection four cars behind the Citroen.

*

David Price parked his car some 200 yards from the entrance to the Forbidden City and hurried across Tiananmen Square to join the crowd of tourists queueing at the Gate of Heavenly Peace. He was in no mood to wonder at the splendour of the walled city or the eccentricity of the culture, which had created the vast 'prison' to house the dynasties of emperors who had ruled feudal China.

Each courtyard, some 100 yards or so wide, rose like a series of giant steps climbing towards the Imperial Palace and the emperor's apartments. Between each courtyard was a throne room, each successive one more splendid than its predecessor. A visiting dignitary would have been met by the emperor in the throne room befitting his visitor's status. An unimportant visitor would be made to walk the entire distance to the furthermost throne room, becoming progressively more tired and more overawed by the splendour of the surroundings. For an important visitor, the emperor would come all the way down to meet him at the first throne room.

How many times David had explained all this to various visitors, including his parents, he couldn't remember, but that was all in another world, far removed from the appalling train of events which had started less than an hour and a half ago. For the hundredth time it seemed, he looked at his watch as he ran across one courtyard after another as precious seconds ticked away. He swore aloud in exasperation as he realised that he only had two minutes left to get to the meeting in the Ornamental Garden.

Almost in tears of frustration, he dashed across the final courtyard, bumping into several startled Japanese tourists, festooned with cameras and camcorders. He hurried through the diminutive apartments, saw the diagram of the garden with the ancient fig tree marked on it and then pushed through a small knot of ghoulish tourists who were staring into the well where one emperor had drowned his empress so that he could make his relationship with one of the many concubines more permanent. He made his way round ornamental ponds, plants and trees until, in the far right corner of the garden, he saw the aged tree with a trellis-work of poles supporting its branches. Standing under the tree was the huge man who had

117

forced his way into Jane's apartment. With relief, David slowed to a walk as he gathered his breath. 'Where's Jane?'

'She's here, in these gardens.'

'Where?'

'You will be told that when I have the information.'

'How do I...'

'The information please, Mr Price or I will kill the girl and then you as well.'

'British Intelligence believes that there's some Russian military equipment amongst a consignment of timber on its way to Guangzhou by rail. Mr Baker was asked to check this information while someone was on their way out from London. That person arrives in Hong Kong today. That's it; there were only two signals; the first was about the equipment and the second about the man coming from London. That's all I could find out in the time and by now it will have been discovered that I've had access to information for which I'm not cleared. Now where's Jane? I wan.....' It was mercifully quick. David never even heard the silenced report of the gun. The bullet slammed into his heart, killing him instantly. Volkonoff had his arm round him even before his knees sagged and, rather like a concerned father, carried him over to a stone bench at the foot of a gnarled and twisted old pine tree in the centre of the garden.

*

Panting and cursing at his lack of fitness, John Watson went from one courtyard to another looking for David. He had been able to park quite close to the Citroen and had only been about 100 yards behind David as he went through the Gate of Heavenly Peace, but when he eventually got through the turnstiles, David had vanished. There was still no sign of him by the time the Commander reached the final courtyard, so he went through the emperor's apartments and out into the ornamental garden.

There wasn't a sign of David anywhere. Exhausted and sweating profusely, he walked round the garden trying to get his breath back. There were very few people in the garden, which was explained by the presence of three guided tours which were all vying with each other to hold the attention of the tourists. Two guides were speaking in Cantonese and one in English, delivered in a high-pitched American accent. Amidst all this noise, the scream from the centre of the garden, almost went unheard.

The Commander turned to see a Japanese couple by an old pine tree in the centre of the garden. The man was supporting the woman

118

who appeared to have fainted. He walked over to them and discovered that the cause of the woman's exclamation was a young couple seated on the bench at the base of the tree. Well aware of the oriental disapproval of public displays of affection between opposite sexes, he was about to continue his search, when he caught a glimpse of the girl's face over the man's shoulder. It was Jane Marshal. Other people had now gathered and John Watson had to push his way through them. David and Jane sat clasped in each other's arms. Both of them were dead.

*

Ten minutes before the ship was due to sail, Volkonoff appeared at the stern where the four men had broached one of Rokossovsky's bottles of vodka. 'Ah, comrade!' greeted Rokossovsky, 'is all well?'

'No comrade, all is very far from well. British Intelligence knows that there is some form of Russian military equipment in this cargo. Not only that, but they knew where to look for it as it went through Beijing and one of their agents is on his way to investigate. That is just how well everything is and while we're talking about things going wrong, I decided to do some of my own checks to make sure that my share of our pension fund was safe and you'd be amazed at what I discovered.'

'What the hell are you talking about!' blurted Samsonov. 'Everything's gone like clockwork.. that is... until we got to Beijing.'

'I couldn't agree more with you, comrade Samsonov, but gone like clockwork for whom?

'What do you mean, comrade?' demanded Rokossovsky.

'If I hadn't done my checks, we would be the proud owners of ten, worthless metal tubes in the hold below us.'

'Just what are you insinuating,' came the menacing response from Samsonov, who had masterminded the acquisition of the missiles.

'The Commandant of the Kalinin Arsenal had ten missiles specially prepared for us. They had been prepared by Moscow long before you went through all that rigmarole with that woman of yours to blackmail him. What neither you nor anyone else knows is that I made some alternative arrangements and we do now possess ten, genuine ballistic nuclear missiles and I have all the warhead-arming codes. You can imagine how overjoyed the arms dealer who is buying the missiles would have been if we had delivered what we were meant to deliver. Our life expectancy would be measured in seconds, I imagine. Now, would someone care to tell me what this is all about, or do I have to shoot you one by one until I get the truth.' Volkonoff was now holding the silenced automatic. The only answer he received was the mournful blast from the horn on the funnel above them as the warps were cast off and the ship eased its way out into the Pearl River.

CHAPTER 9

Colonel Gregorei Malinovsky looked up from the file which he was reading, mildly irritated by his Adjutant's abrupt entry into his office after only a peremptory knock. 'Yes, what is it, Peter?'

'I've just returned from Major Karpinsky's quarter, Colonel.'

'So Peter, what's so unusual about that? Why do you have to barge into my office to tell me that you have been to visit one of my missile commanders? Anyway, he's on sick leave as I understand it.'

'Yes Colonel, that's what I thought. I had to go round to see him to make arrangements for the next batch of missiles, which are to be destroyed.'

'And....' prompted Malinovsky, as his Adjutant seemed to be having trouble getting his breath and develop a coherent explanation.

'Well Colonel, I...'

'Oh, do get on with it man and leave out all the 'colonels' please.'

'Yes, of course Col...er, well I couldn't get into his house so I got the Quartermaster to get a spare set of keys and we both went into his quarter together. He's dead com...Col.. and so's his wife and their housemaid.' The young captain was almost in tears.

'Sit down Peter; now who else knows about this?'

'Only the Quartermaster, Col...'

'Yes, alright; no one else is to be told, understood? Get hold of the Quartermaster and make sure that he understands that; have you got all that?'

'Yes Col..'

'When you've done that , I want you to return here and we will both go out to the SS20 bunker. Understood?'

'Very good, Colonel.' There was a tight knot developing in Gregorei Malinovsky's stomach. He had issued such careful and explicit instructions to everyone about the SS20 missiles. Twenty minutes later, his Adjutant met him back at the Headquarters and they both climbed into the Colonel's jeep; the Adjutant had wisely dismissed the driver to limit the number of people involved in the investigation and now drove the Commanding Officer himself to Bunker 10 at the far side of the arsenal. The whole arsenal was surrounded by a pine forest and covered an area of almost 25 square miles.

They drove down a long ride in the forest, which looked exactly like all the other rides. The road started to incline downwards between steep-sided, sand embankments until they were some 60 feet below the natural ground level. The jeep slowed as they came level with the large steel doors of Bunker 10. They were met by the Bunker Commander who had been warned that the Commandant was coming. All passes were carefully checked, but the offer of an escort to the SS20s was refused.

'You lead the way, Peter. You know where I want to go first.' They put on the special clothing and footwear and the radio-active monitoring badges and then went over to a small electric vehicle and the Adjutant climbed behind the wheel. The electric transporter moved off with a high-pitched whine down a long and brightly-lit tunnel. Each storage compartment of the bunker was protected by massively thick steel doors and a guard outside each one. They stopped at the furthest compartment and once the Commandant had got off the transporter, the Adjutant parked it to one side of the tunnel. Once again, their passes were checked and then they were allowed into the missile storage compartment.

Gregorei Malinovsky walked directly to the rows of gleaming missiles and in less than two minutes his worst fears were confirmed. The ten fake missiles which had been prepared for the conspirators were all still there. Three times he checked all the serial numbers willing them to be different. Somehow, they had succeeded in doing a double switch and now ten, multiple-warhead nuclear missiles were somewhere in China. The enormity of the catastrophe to international relations and the potential for a nuclear holocaust if the missiles reached the Middle East made Gregorei feel sick with apprehension as he walked slowly out of the storage compartment and climbed back onto the transporter without saying a word.

*

'Major, please press your scrambler button now.'
'Colonel Malinovsky?'
'We have a very serious problem. The missiles were switched. Samsonov and his friends have ten genuine SS20 missiles.'
'You're sure of this?'
'Unfortunately, yes; there can be no doubt.'
'How did this happen?'
'I can only guess at the moment, as the discovery of the switch has only just come to light. The major in charge of that bunker has been murdered, as has his wife and their housemaid - very brutally and unpleasantly.'

'Volkonoff?'

'It has all the indications of his handiwork.'

'Why has it taken so long to discover this?'

'Major Karpinsky - he's the bunker commander - was on sick leave. He was not expected back until Monday and it was only by chance that the Adjutant had to go round to his house. He couldn't get any response, so he and the Quartermaster opened the door with a spare set of keys.'

'We should have been prepared for this, as soon as we knew that they had brought Volkonoff into the conspiracy.'

'I agree and I accept the blame for failing to do so.'

'That's what I'd expect an officer of your reputation to say, but there are more urgent and important things to be done than aportion blame. I will contact you as soon as I have spoken with the President.'

*

'I'll see Major Petrovsky now.'

'Very good, Sir.'

'Come in Major Petrovsky; this unscheduled meeting can only mean bad news, so please come and sit down and tell me. Am I right?'

'I'm afraid so, Sir.'

'Right, let's hear the worst.'

'The conspirators managed to do a double switch and are now in possession of ten genuine SS20 missiles.'

'How was this achieved?'

'The KGB man, Volkonoff, got hold of the commander of the bunker and tortured his wife until he agreed to co-operate; he then murdered both of them and their housemaid. That is our interpretation of the evidence available.'

'That sounds like Volkonoff. How long since the missiles were removed?'

'Eleven days.'

'Where are they now?'

'They are due in Hong Kong later tonight. The Chinese cargo vessel left Guangzhou at 1830 hours.'

'Nothing can be done there without causing an international incident. No, we'll have to deal with this problem when the ship is well out of sight of land in international waters. What's the name of the ship?'

'Spirit of the Sea.'

'No, that's the Chinese ship; the other one, which is shipping the missiles and conspirators to the Gulf.'

'Al Samak.'

'What's that... Arabic?'

'Yes, Sir; it means 'The Fish'.'

'Is my Chief of Naval Staff waiting outside, Major?'

'Yes, Sir...I'm afraid there's more bad news.'

'I'm sorry Major Petrovsky, please continue.

'Somehow, British Intelligence discovered that the missiles were being moved by train from Moscow to Beijing. A member of their Secret Intelligence Service at the British Embassy in Beijing went to investigate as the train was being shunted to get it on the southern network to Guangzhou. Volkonoff killed him and subsequently two other members of the British Embassy.'

'What a monster that man is. Time for the red telephone again?'

'Yes, Sir.'

'I agree,' and he picked it up. 'Please get me the President of the USA and after I've spoken to him, the British Prime Minister.'

*

Fifty-eight, Queen's Road East was a drab, six storey office block above a metal workshop on the south side of the street at the junction of Central and Wanchai on Hong Kong Island. The metal workshop was stacked with every gauge of sheet, tubular and box-sectioned metal and at the front was a workbench at which three young Chinese men constantly hammered, cut and riveted pieces of metal while a fourth, whose work area extended onto the pavement, wielded a gas welding torch with casual abandon which showered sparks at frequent intervals onto the legs of passing pedestrians.

The door to the right of the workshop gave access to a miniscule lobby up a flight of three stairs. At the back of this lobby, was an equally small lift, which could just take four Asians or two Caucasians at an over-friendly pinch. On the left of the lift was a pegboard which showed which businesses rented the rather down-market property. In fact, the entire building was owned by the British Intelligence Directorate, but that ownership was so well concealed by aliases and cut-outs that any investigation would have eventually ground to a fruitless halt amidst the labrynth of the Hong Kong judiciary system.

Any bona fide client who wished to visit the investment company, the insurance brokers, the gemstone exporters or the printers would find exactly what was printed on the board in the lobby. The insurance brokers arranged policies on anything from a second hand bicycle to a 50,000 ton oil tanker and together with the other companies - like the head office in London - made the British intelligence effort in Hong Kong almost self-financing.

The metal workshop and those who worked in it provided the security of the building. There were eight other men and the twelve of them were divided into a three-shift roster, which protected the building for 24 hours a day. All of them were genuinely qualified metal-workers, but had many other qualifications which had been taught at the Directorate's training centre at Maidenhead. The shop had become increasingly popular amongst the expatriate community for its wrought iron balcony furniture.

The shop itself had a number of concealed security devices to prevent unauthorised access to the building, one of the most effective and simplest of which was the gas-welder's torch; the basement of the building contained a large tank of pressurised fluid napalm. This was fed to the torch through armoured pipes and at the twist of a knob, the 2½inch oxy- acetylene flame could be turned into a thirty foot jet of searing, flesh burning incendiary napalm. If requested, the four men would produce for a customer a wrought-iron and glass-topped coffee table within an hour for HK$250. It was a coffee table that they were working on that afternoon. The customer was a Chinese male in his thirties, dressed in stone-washed denim jeans, trainers and T-shirt - like two or three million other ethnic Chinese males in Hong Kong - and like them also, with the earphones of a DVD player firmly plugged into his brain.

The man was Tim Driscoll and in the DVD in the player was all the relevant local information which he required, including an update on the deaths at the British Embassy in Beijing. He was also given a start list of possible ships, which might be carrying the missiles to the Middle East and the position of each in the various anchorages. He was told that his invoice for the coffee table would have all this information written on it. At the conclusion of the up-date, he pressed the eject button and removed the CD. The coffee table was finished and he elected to have it delivered. He paid and was given a grubby receipt. The CD had been dropped, unseen, amongst a pile of empty San Miguel bottles and tea making paraphernalia. Tim Driscoll screwed up the receipt, shoved it into his jeans and joined the melée of pedestrians on Queen's Road East.

*

The Chinese cargo vessel, Spirit of the Sea, slipped unobtrusively into Hong Kong's Western Anchorage at 2.30 in the morning. Already waiting for her where four, blunt-bowed lighters and two tugs to unload and transfer cargo. Loading and unloading of cargoes continued 24 hours a day - and night. - each ship spending the least time possible in harbour so that harbour dues were minimised against cargo profit. The harbour turned round nearly a hundred ships every 24 hours and with the extension of the Kwei Chung Container Terminal out to Stonecutters Island had overtaken Rotterdam as the world's largest container port.

Anchored two cables to the north of Spirit of the Sea was another ship. It only displayed the mandatory anchor light, but no other light was visible. The ten wooden crates were removed first and lowered down by the derricks onto the lighters, which were towed to the other ship. As the tug approached the other ship, spot lights came on to assist with the task of lifting the crates from the lighter into the ship's hold.

Four men stood by the port rail watching the cargo being transferred. 'Where's Volkonoff?' asked Voznesensky.

'Yes, where is he?' added Samsonov.

'He left the ship as soon as it anchored,' they were told by Rokossovsky who continued. 'Just bear in mind that if it hadn't been for him we'd be sitting on top of a useless load of junk which would have been our death warrants as soon as the arms dealer inspected the missiles.'

'I accept that, but I would feel considerably more at ease if he wasn't a part of our plan,' was volunteered by a rather apprehensive Peter Milynkov. 'I thought he was going to kill all of us last night.'

'He would've done if he had believed for one moment that any of us had double-crossed him,' Rokossovsky muttered as they watched the second of the missiles lifted from the lighter onto the ship.

'Where is he now?' asked Samsonov.

'He left the ship as soon as we anchored; he's gone to dig out an old informer of his to see if he can find this agent who the British have sent out and to see if there are any whispers - as he put it - about the missiles.'

'I suppose that'll mean another bloodbath and a handful of dead people. When's he returning to the ship?'

'He isn't.'

'What! When was all this decided?'

'He told me last night that there were far too many loose ends and that he wanted to tie them all quickly before there were any more leaks. He is determined to find who amongst us has leaked information about the plan. He will follow us by catching the flight to Dubai and then coming out to meet us on the helicopter that is due to lift us off that ship. He says that by then he will know who has double-crossed us and that man will be executed immediately.'

This information from Rokossovsky was received in silence and all that could be heard was the clatter of the diesel winches as the missiles were transferred from one ship to another. 'Come on, the boat's waiting at the bottom of the companionway on the other side of the ship. Let's get ourselves and our cases over to the other ship and see what Simeon has to say.' They all followed Rokossovsky to the companionway and down to the motor launch, which was tied up to the foot of the steps.

Once they were all aboard, it was cast off and ferried them through the black, lumpy sea to a similar companionway which had been lowered by the other ship. No one offered to help them with their cases and the thick humidity and heat did nothing to improve their spirits. All four of them reached the deck soaked in sweat and feeling less than well-disposed towards their new hosts. They were watched by a silent steward who guided them towards the stern of the ship as soon as all four men and the cases had reached the deck. He led them into the saloon where they were warmly greeted by Simeon. There was coffee and tea on the sideboard and the steward then spoke for the first time. They were told that they had the use of the saloon, the wardroom for their meals and their cabins; they were to go nowhere else. He then handed a brown envelope to Rokossovsky and left the saloon.

Rokossovsky opened the envelope and shook out six smaller envelopes, which he handed round after reading the name on each one. Inside each envelope was a bank credit note from their selected Swiss bank which showed that two payments of $1 million had been paid into each of their accounts. 'We're rich!' exclaimed Samsonov heading for a tray of bottles, which included vodka.

'I wonder if we'll ever live to spend any of it?' came from a less enthusiastic Peter Milynkov.

*

Sir Jeremy Hammond, the Head of the British Intelligence Directorate, and his counterpart in the CIA, John Dempster, were being briefed in the main conference room at the CIA headquarters at Langley. The reason for the cancellation of his holiday with Susan and his life-long friend, Peter de Havilland, had been the increasingly aggressive rhetoric from Saddam Hussein, although he had accepted the return of the UN Inspection Teams, which he had thrown out of Iraq the previous year. At the moment that there was a discreet buzz from the telephone beside the head of the CIA, they were being shown photos of three satellite passes over the Gulf. These blown-up photos, projected onto a large screen, gave convincing proof of Iraq's

127

preparation for war, although there was still no evidence from the Inspection Teams of any 'smoking gun' of WMDs or the ability to deploy such weapons. George Bush had discussed the situation with Tony Blair and this had been immediately followed by Sir Jeremy's flight to Washington for the two intelligence agencies to compare information.

John Dempster picked up the phone and listened and after about twenty seconds said, 'Yes Mr President, we'll be there in fifteen minutes.' He replaced the phone and turned to his Director of Operations. 'Max, please have the helicopter ready to leave immediately. Sir Jeremy and I are going to the White House. Reconvene this meeting on my direction when I know what time we'll be back.'

'Very good, Sir,' the message had already been sent for the helicopter to start up. John Dempster and Sir Jeremy Hammond left the conference room together and went down in the lift to the ground floor.

'Problems?' Sir Jeremy asked.

'I think so; he wouldn't say. We'll soon know,' and the two men climbed aboard the Bell 412 helicopter. The four bladed rotor was immediately clutched in and the revolutions quickly built up. The helicopter landed at the White House eleven minutes later and the two men were shown into the President three minutes after that. All three men had met on many previous occasions.

'John,' President Bush started, 'there's a serious complication to the situation in the Gulf. President Putin has just been on the line to me and he's speaking to Blair right now. You are fully briefed on the plan that he conceived to identify those men who were behind the plot to bring about his downfall by proving that Russia had reneged on the controls of the INF Treaty.'

'Yes, Sir.'

'It's all gone wrong. The conspirators have apparently outwitted those who were implementing the Putin's plan and have got their hands on ten MIRV SS20s. These ten nuclear missiles are now on their way to Saddam Hussein. Their last known location was Hong Kong where they were loaded onto a cargo ship registered in the Cayman Islands as Al Samak - and I'm told that means 'The Fish' in Arabic. It would seem that Saddam is poised to get his hands on some very real WMDs, helpfully supplied complete with delivery means. If Saddam gets his hands on those nuclear missiles we know he'll use them, either against Israel or us if we move against him.'

'Did the Putin suggest how he was going to try and prevent these nuclear missiles from reaching the Gulf?' the head of the CIA asked.

President Bush had taken a drink from a glass of mineral water on a small tray on the desk.

'He said that two of their Sierra Class attack submarines have been re-deployed from the task force shadowing our 7th Fleet and another two from the Soviet Southern Fleet in the Indian Ocean. The intention is to destroy the ship and its contents once it's in international waters. Putin has asked us to stand aside and let them clear up their own mess - his words, not mine - and I have agreed to that. Can we monitor what's happening with the Vigilent satellite over Hong Kong?'

'Yes Sir, but that's fallible to cloud cover and darkness just like any other satellite. The heat sensing cameras do a good job, but I would be happier with something of our own on the scene to see this ship go to the bottom.'

'I thought that's what you'd say, John, so I told the Putin that we wanted one of our subs to monitor the destruction of 'The Fish'. I've already spoken to Admiral Sorensen and General Rasmussen, both of whom are on their way to join your briefing at Langley. Sir Jeremy,' and here Bush turned to the Head of BID. 'Tony Blair has told me that the Joint Chiefs of Staff have provisionally committed an armoured division with all the necessary logistic back-up plus five squadrons of Tornado and Jaguar and a threefold increase to the Royal Navy's presence in the Gulf for an invasion of Iraq from the holding area in Kuwait. But this depends on the resolve of the Security Council of the UN and how much we're hampered by France, Germany and China.'

'That is what I understood, Mr President. There's just a possibility that my Directorate can shed a little more light on these missiles. Even before you were briefed by the President Putin on this plan of his, we had told the CIA of the discovery of the missiles on their way to Hong Kong - I hasten to add that that was purely fortuitous. You have just told us that the ship in Hong Kong is called 'The Fish'.'

'That's what I was told by Putin, Sir Jeremy.'

'That is also the name of a large private motorboat, which belongs to an arms dealer by the name of Hassan Hussein - you will know of him, John,' and here Sir Jeremy turned to John Dempster who nodded. That boat was last seen on the south coast of England yesterday and Hassan was on it - I have that information from one of my own agents who went aboard it.' The last part was added as John Dempster made to interrupt.

'Did he actually see Hassan, Jeremy?'

'He did; that agent has been briefed to keep an eye on Hassan and we have another agent in Hong Kong trying to find the identity of the ship which has the missiles. We can tell him that now and I can direct him to liaise with the CIA house in Kennedy Town.'

'Sir Jeremy, John, thank you for coming over; please keep me briefed on that ship. I must now try and catch up with my programme.' Just as the two men were leaving, President Bush stopped them. 'There was one other thing Putin said which I nearly forgot. He said that there's an ex-KGB agent who's a member of the conspiracy; his name,' and here President Bush picked up his reading glasses to see what he had written, 'Yuri Volkonoff.' The two intelligence chiefs left the Oval Office and returned to the waiting helicopter, which took them back to Langley.

*

Volkonoff paid the owner of the sampan, which had met him at the anchorage, a meeting he had arranged from Beijing, and climbed up the steps of the typhoon shelter in Yau Ma Tei. Despite the fact that it was twenty to four in the morning, he had no difficulty in finding a taxi which he paid up front with a large tip to take him through the Cross-Harbour Tunnel and then to the west of the Island. His first stop was a literage company at the Shek Tong Tsui cargo handling basin whose company logo he had recognised painted on the aft superstructure of the six lighters which had been waiting for Spirit of the Sea when it had anchored that morning.

He had phoned his contact from Beijing and had given very explicit instructions. Once he was satisfied that those instructions had been obeyed to the letter he handed over the dollar banker's draft and returned to Connaught Road West where he flagged down another taxi. He gave the driver an address and then sat back as it wound its way up through the Mid-levels to Magazine Gap and Bowen Road. There was a block of flats next door to the Nicaraguan Consulate, which was his destination.

On the third floor of the block of flats was a Rumanian who was living under the alias of a West German shipping agent; he had been a senior officer in Ceaucesceau's Securitatet Police and had escaped, with only seconds to spare, through the labrynth of tunnels under the presidential palace. Like Volkonoff, he was a member of the old school of KGB espionage where the most important qualification was to be a psychopathic killer.

The front door of the flat had a spyglass aperture and Volkonoff didn't want the occupant to have any warning of his visit. He walked to the door and without a pause, raised his leg and drove it forward

130

to strike the solid wood by the lock. The door burst open, ripping the safety chain out of the woodwork. Volkonoff strode through the apartment to the bedroom and then dragged the occupant out of the bed into the living room where he attempted to break free and struggled to open a draw in a glass-fronted display cabinet. 'You won't be needing that, Alexei. What a way to greet an old comrade. Now come and sit down, here,' and he pointed to the middle of the sofa.

'I was told that you had been executed,' came the terrified response from the Rumanian.

'You were deceived, my old friend. Now, I know that you have been up to your old tricks while you've been out here and I'm told that for the right price you will sell information on anything and everything that is happening in Hong Kong. Am I right?'

'No, I...'

'Good, now I'm prepared to pay top price for information and what I want to know is the movements and whereabouts of a British SIS agent who arrived in Hong Kong on the Friday night MAS flight.'

'I told you...' the back-handed blow from Volkonoff knocked the stout little Rumanian over the back of the sofa where he rashly made another attempt to get whatever it was from the display cabinet draw. The bullet from Volkonoff's gun slammed into his thigh, knocking him to the ground. Volkonoff walked round the sofa and dragged the screaming Rumanian by his wounded leg back to the area in front of the sofa. 'I said I was prepared to pay for this information, but if you want to play hard to get then that's fine by me. I've got all the time in the world and if you resist any longer then it will be two days of agony before I allow you to die. Now, are you going to co-operate?' He did and was then shot through the head before Volkonoff left the flat closing the door carefully behind him.

*

Simon Peters picked up the phone, it was the Deputy Director. 'I've just finished speaking with the Director in Langley and we must all meet again quickly, but before you come to the conference room, will you get a message to Hong Kong. Tim Driscoll must be contacted immediately and told that one of the conspirators is Yuri Volkonoff,' Simon groaned inwardly as he heard the name, 'who's in Hong Kong now, knows that Driscoll is there and will be looking for him. Driscoll must be alerted. Got that?'

'Yes Sir; when's the meeting?

'Come to the conference room as soon as you've got that message to Hong Kong.'

'Very well, Sir,' and he broke the connection. 'Louise,' he spoke into the intercom, 'get Communications and warn them that I want an immediate link to Hong Kong; I'm on my way up to them now.'

'Yes Simon.' He went up to Communications where he found them waiting with the connection made. As soon as his message had been passed, the third shift in the metal workshop at 58, Queen's Road East was briefed and the four men disappeared into the streets of Hong Kong in a desperate race to find Tim Driscoll before Volkonoff did.

*

Tim Driscoll knew every nook and cranny of Hong Kong and he had contacts, sources and informers in every part of the city and the New Territories. After leaving the workshop on Queen's Road East he had made his way over to Kwai Chung where he had a long talk with a colleague of his who worked in the Container Terminal. That conversation led him back to the cargo handling basin by Kellet Island and the Royal Hong Kong Yacht Club. He had a boyhood friend who not only owned his own lighter and tug, but leased out three other lighters to various shipping agents. He walked from one lighter to another until he found his friend and then over a bottle of San Miguel beer, another piece of the jigsaw was slotted into place.

His next port of call was the cargo-handling basin at Shek Tong Tsui where he eventually found his friend's cousin who supplied another snippet of information. One of his best informers worked in the Stock Exchange Building and ran an unofficial information service on almost everything, which happened in Hong Kong. When he was contacted by Tim, he asked Tim to meet him in the Hong Kong and Shanghai Bank Building at 1, Queen's Road in Central. The bank building was probably one of the most spectacular and controversial buildings in Hong Kong. It was state of the art engineering and architecture and despite the construction of the 70-floor, Bank of China, almost next door to it, it still attracted more attention than any other building.

Tim rode up to the 20th floor in the glass elevator, from where you could look down on the open plan construction all the way to the first floor. His contact was at the personal investment counter and as Tim stood beside him he saw a note scribbled on the back of a paying-in slip. It read, 'The Fish - written in Arabic - flying Cayman Islands flag - Western Anchorage - left Hong Kong at 0530 hrs this morning.' His contact finished his enquiry and without ever looking in Tim's direction, walked to the elevator. Tim screwed up the note and dropped it into a black and chrome litter bin. He turned towards the elevators just as the cellphone in his duffle bag started to ring. He walked away from the counter and removed the phone from the bag.

As Tim's contact left the elevator on the first floor, there were people running in every direction and a crowd already converging on the tiled entrance area below the first floor of the Bank. Out of curiosity, he wandered over to the central well of the building where he saw the shattered glass and below it on the tiles a thick knot of police hiding what was there. He asked what had happened and was told that someone had jumped from the 20th floor. He went down the escalator to ground level where the police had already cordoned off a route in and out of the Bank to keep the ghouls away from the body on the pavement. Wailing sirens preceded the ambulance and uniformed ambulance paramedics rushed past with a stretcher. The body was lifted onto the stretcher while the police held the crowd back. The contact turned away and headed for the Stock Exchange Building. The man he had spoken to on the phone less than an hour earlier had just been pushed past him on a stretcher, smashed like a broken rag doll. The warning had reached Tim Driscoll too late.

CHAPTER 10

'Thanks for that, Tom; perhaps I will have another beer,' and when it had been pulled, Tom placed the beer on the bar close to the table where the girl was sitting. Gunn moved round the bar and picked up his beer, which was acknowledged by a large wink from the landlord.

'Claudine Carteret? please forgive me for interrupting, but....'

'Shove off!' was the hospitable response from the girl's self-styled minder. Gunn paused and placed his beer on their table and turned towards the minder. Not only could this girl be helpful with information about the disappearance of her father's boat, but diving in the area of Sardrière Island with the excuse for looking for her father. It was the ideal cover to get a close look at what went on under the sea in that area. The boyfriend or minder was an encumbrance which would involve a great deal of wasted time; time that Gunn didn't have to spare at that moment with Peter's yacht either in or due in any moment. Gunn judged that it was probably better to get this confrontation over quickly and surgically.

'I have many failings, sonny, but one of them certainly isn't crossed eyes. When I want to speak to you, which is unlikely, I will address my remarks to you in words of one or two syllables so that there's a chance of you understanding them. In the mean time, belt up! you sawn-off little runt!' The insult produced exactly the effect that Gunn wanted. The young man, at a disadvantage sitting down, started to get to his feet. Gunn waited until he was half way to his feet and off balance and then hit him, once, very hard. He crashed back over the chair and lay quite still. There was complete silence in the pub; all the clientele had heard the exchange between the two men. Gunn bent down and picked up the youth and carried him through the bar flap, which Tom had lifted.

'Alright folks,' Tom addressed his clientele, 'the entertainment's over. Drinks on the house - come on, Sir, I'll take him,' and he removed the youth from Gunn and carried him through a door into the back of the pub like a rag doll.

'He's a pain, but you didn't have to hit him that hard, did you?' The girl was standing, having watched the removal of her minder.

'I'm short of time Miss Carteret and..'

'Claudine'll do fine.'

'Claudine; I really haven't the time to muck about with young Sir Galahad. I want to talk to you about salvaging your father's boat. I've got the use of a boat with all the latest Scuba gear to do a preliminary dive. Incidentally, I would have introduced myself, but your friend prevented that; my name's John, John Gunn.'

'You know mine; yes, of course I'm interested, but what's your interest? There's no treasure or drugs in the boat.'

'Would you come with me now and meet the people who own the boat? and I can then explain my interest in slightly less public surroundings.'

'Should I trust you?'

'I really can't think why you should, but Tom, here, will vouch for me.'

'Aye, I will,' confirmed the landlord.

'That's good enough for me. Come on then, let's go. I've finished my drink.' She paused while Gunn finished his beer and then the two of them left the pub.

They both came out from the Ship into the warm evening sun. The whole area of the harbour and the old and new marinas were swarming with tourists and every café and pub was doing a roaring trade in the longest period without rain in however many years it was - another meteorological record announced by the media to satisfy the British preoccupation with the weather.

'Where's your boat?'

'In the north marina, if it's arrived, but it's not mine. It's owned by a man called Peter de Havilland who..'

'De Havilland Boats?'

'Yes, that's right. How did you know?'

'If you'd been brought up in a family that's lived with boats for generations, you'd also know the majority of major boatyards and naval architects. De Havilland Boats is right at the top end of the market of British boatbuilders, like Oyster, Camper and Nicholsons and a handful of others. You're going to have quite a problem finding his boat unless you know the number of the pontoon and berth.' They were still some way from the marina, but all that could be seen was a forest of masts.

'Peter has booked Osprey into visitor's berth 162, but I'll just go and check with the marina office as I'm not as familiar with this marina as the old one.'

'So what's your interest in my Dad's boat?'

'You make that sound as though you believe he's still alive.'

'I'm certain of it,' and there were tears very close to the surface which were being held in check. 'Dad and I were very close. I'm the only child and my mother died producing me. My father never remarried. He brought me up all by himself and a large part of that upbringing was on his boat. I've no idea whether it's a sixth sense, instinct or whatever, but something in me says he's not dead. So where can he be? I know that I can't accept his death until at least some remnants of his boat are found. I've already spent all our savings on hiring boats and equipment and until you walked into the pub, I've had no luck in getting anyone to lend me money. So why are you offering to help?'

'I want an excuse to dive in the area of Sardrière Island because there's something I'm looking for; it's not your father's boat, but the disappearance of your father's boat is connected with what I want to investigate. I'm sorry that I'm being so vague, but I'm loathe to involve you too deeply in anything other than, hopefully, an explanation for your father's disappearance.'

'Thank you for being kind enough not to say death. Most of my friends think that my father's disappearance has sent me round the bend. They point to the fact that it was all some time ago and therefore he must be dead. They're very kind and poor Stan - the man you hit this evening - follows me like a faithful dog until I could almost scream. I should be grateful for their sympathy, but instead it drives me into a rage of frustration because I can't do anything positive. That's why I've clutched the straw of your offer. You don't have to humour me, John; just give me the chance to know what happened that night and live in peace with myself.' They were now nearly at the marina office and Gunn paused before going in.

'I have no intention of raising false hopes. As I see it there are three explanations for your father's disappearance; the first and most callous one is that he's dead and some freak current has carried the remains of the boat out to sea. The second is that there was an accident that night which he may have survived, but is suffering from loss of memory - that could explain your instinct about him still being alive. The third explanation is what I'm going to Sardrière to find. I won't be a second,' and Gunn disappeared into the office.

'She is on berth 162 at the end of pontoon 'L'. It's an end berth which Osprey's got all to herself, because of her size I expect, and she arrived ten minutes ago.' They walked down the ramp to the pontoons and then followed the lettered piles until they found 'L'. Gunn could see Osprey right at the end of the pontoon and pointed her out to Claudine. Peter, Tricia, Celia and Susan were all sitting in the cockpit having a drink and saw him when he waved.

'You're a dark horse, John,' Peter greeted him. 'Woman in every port?'

'No such luck; let me do the introductions,' and he introduced Claudine to the four of them.

'Now, what can I get you to drink, Claudine?' Peter offered.

'I'd love a Dubonnet and ice, if you have it.'

'Dubonnet and ice it is; John?'

'A glass of red wine, please.' When everyone had a drink, Gunn suggested that Claudine tell them how her father and his boat had disappeared.

She explained that the reason that he liked to fish in the waters to the south of Sardrière Island was because the combined effects of the deep water and strong currents produced a remarkable variety of fish and in considerable quantity. She went on to explain that the area was surrounded by heavy overfalls caused by the island's position at the confluence of tidal sets and currents and the very deep waters to the south which tended to 'pile up' the sea on the shelf of rock which supported Sardrière Island. In conditions of wind against tide, coinciding with a tidal surge, the overfalls were more than capable of swamping a forty foot fishing boat and sending it straight to the bottom.

'Was your father braver than the other fishermen, a better seaman or was he prepared to take more risks than the others?' Peter asked which touched a raw nerve.

'Mr de Havilland...'

'Peter.'

'My father was accused of taking unnecessary risks by the other fishermen because they were envious of his catches. He never, ever took risks. Purely through his perseverance and knowledge of the seas around Guernsey, he discovered two calm passages into the fishing grounds to the south of the island. These passages avoided the overfalls, but they only occurred for a few minutes either side of high and low water Springs, never during Neaps.'

'Was this channel into the fishing grounds always in the same place,' Gunn asked.

'Oh yes; exactly the same spot. Dad only fished there at night so that he wouldn't give away the exact location of the channel. I have to admit that he... we were both guilty of unseaman-like behaviour because we used to turn off our nav' lights so that the other boats couldn't see where we were waiting for the calm channel to appear.'

'Nothing unusual about that,' Peter remarked. 'Plenty of fishermen do that all over the world to protect their favourite fishing grounds.'

'How did you know where to find this channel?' Tricia asked.

'Do you know the Islands well Mrs... sorry, Tricia?'

'Not as well as Peter, but fairly well.'

'The position is found by taking bearings to five lights; St Martins and Pleinmont on Guernsey, Corbière and Grosnez on Jersey and in the south, the Roches Douvres.'

'Did you always go with your father when he went to these secret fishing grounds?' Gunn asked.

'No, never; Dad wouldn't let me go with him for two reasons; the first was the element of risk and the second was a thoroughly practical one. If something did go wrong and he needed help, he wanted someone ashore whom he could trust to call out the rescue services and point them in exactly the right direction. We had a system of communications on the locally allocated frequency, which kept us in contact every ten minutes that he was in the 'special area'. If he missed one contact schedule, my instructions were to call out the lifeboat. There was an alarm system on the boat to make sure he never forgot a contact schedule.

'It must have been very tiring for you because, presumably, he had to stay in the area for six hours until the next high or low water,' Peter commented.

'Yes it was, but it wasn't as though he went there all the time. During Spring tides, he might go a couple of times and then, of course, only if I was at home.'

'So what happened on the night he disappeared?' Gunn asked.

'Before I tell you that, I would like to know a little more about your interest in all this. I get the feeling that you've got something to do with the Government, Customs and Excise or perhaps the Services. The trouble is that there are so many crooked politicians and bent government officials these days that to find anyone straight is close to a miracle. I know of you,' and here she turned to Peter, 'because I've seen pictures of you in the yachting magazines that are stacked all round our house,' but who do you work for, John?' At that moment, Gunn's phone rang in the wheelhouse.

'I'm sorry John, that thing rang a couple of minutes before you got here and someone said he would ring again when I said you hadn't turned up yet.'

'I'll only be a couple of minutes,' and Gunn went into the wheelhouse. It was Simon Peters.

'A lot's happened since you left the office, so I must bring you up to date quickly. Most of this has come from the Director, who, as you know, is with his opposite number at Langley to discuss the crisis developing in the Gulf. Putin has made two calls to the Bush; the first was to tell him of a scheme which he had devised to identify those in the old Soviet hierarchy who wish to remove him and any form of democracy and return to the bad old days. This scheme involved the sale of some SS20s to an Arab arms dealer. The export route was via the Trans-Siberian Railway...'

'Ah hah!'

'Yes, your Mrs Harris was spot-on and provided our Director with a considerable amount of kudos as he knew about this. He thinks the CIA know more about Putin's scheme than they are telling us at the moment. He says he can't put a finger on it, but it was almost as though the 'phone call from Putin was expected. However, that's another matter at the moment; now where was I... right; they - the missiles - went by rail to Beijing, then to Guangzhou and then by ship to Hong Kong. Special fake missiles had been prepared for the conspirators which, when they reached the arms dealer with all the conspirators, would result in the death of the latter at the hands of the former - if you see what I mean.'

'Got it.'

'The plan worked extremely well - from the Putin's point of view - uncovering a small swarm of disaffected, hard-line communists, in addition to the six key conspirators. The latter travelled with the missiles, but all the other people have been identified for further action if necessary.'

'So what went wrong?'

'They got hold of real nuclear missiles instead of the fakes..'

'Jesus Chris....'

'And that's not all; one of the conspirators is Yuri Volkonoff...yes I know,' as Gunn made to interrupt, 'we thought he was dead. So did the Russians, incidentally. Somehow bodies were switched and the man who was incinerated in a contrived accident at the Zaporozhstal steel foundry evidently wasn't Volkonoff. After you had briefed us on Mrs Harris' discovery, we told our man at the Embassy in Beijing - incidentally he was SIS and had failed to meet our criteria for BID; we were about to replace him - to investigate the train as it was switched through various sidings onto the southern line to Guangzhou. He was brutally tortured and then killed..'

'Volkonoff?'

'Who else, as were two young diplomatic staff at the Embassy. Volkonoff managed to find out that we were sending Driscoll to Hong Kong.'

'Does Tim know all this?

'We've spoken to our place in Hong Kong and they've got four of their operatives out looking for him, but it's only 5 am there and you

139

know what Tim's like once he gets lost in the maze of intrigue in Hong Kong.'

'Let's pray that they find him before Volkonoff does. Are my orders altered in any way?'

'No; you are fully up to date now. Please use your own judgement on the use of Peter de Havilland's boat. It may not surprise you to hear that Alan Paxton's already chartered a diving-cum-salvage launch so it's it'll be ready if you shout for it.'

'Fine, thanks for all that. I'll be in touch, bye,' and he replaced the phone and went out to the cockpit.

'Hello John, I've been fighting a losing battle trying to avoid telling Claudine for whom it is that you work. I've explained that you work for the Government.'

'That's right, Claudine; I work for MI6 - sometimes known as the Secret Intelligence Service.' This comment was followed by an embarrassed silence filled with the noise of frapping rigging and screeching gulls.

'If I asked you to prove it, would you?'

'No.'

'Right; this is what happened on the night of 26th November last year. It was mid-Springs and high water at St Peter Port was 0125 hours on 27th November. There was a high pressure system over the southern part of England and the Channel Islands and little or no wind with fog was forecast. These were exactly the conditions that Dad liked for his visits to the Sardrière fishing grounds, so it came as no surprise to me when he asked me if I would stand by on the radio.'

'Surely, if there was fog, he wouldn't be able to see those lights you were talking about,' from Celia who was following every word which Claudine said. After the success of her sharp observation at Erlian, Celia was fired with enthusiasm to see this investigation through to its conclusion. Claudine smiled.

'All of those lighthouses transmit a radio signal - these are all listed in the current nautical almanac for the year and until last year, Dad had used the radio bearings to fix his position. Last year, he treated himself to a GPS navigator and then only had to follow the way points which he'd entered into the machine until it told him that he was over the correct spot. The boat was fitted with radar and he used this with the alarm set to the 3 mile range scan to warn him of the approach of any other boats, as he was carrying no lights. It was the radar that warned him that something unusual was happening.'

'How do you know this?' I mean....' Tricia started and then hesitated.

'Bear with me a little longer and you will see how I know all this. It's very rare for large ships to come anywhere near Sardrière Island. The inter-island ferries go well to the north of the island and those heading for St Malo are well to the east. It was just after two in the morning and a real pea-souper of a fog. My Dad was in the middle of his routine radio check with me, when the radar alarm sounded; I could hear it buzzing during my father's transmission. He finished his transmission, saying that he was going to check the VDU of the radar.'

'It was only about five minutes later that he was back on the radio to say that a very large ship was approaching him on a collision course and that he was about to cut his nets adrift so that he could manoeuvre clear of its course. He finished his transmission and I can only assume that he went to cast the nets adrift. Then came his last transmission,' and the tears were, once again, very close. 'He came back on the radio to say that he couldn't understand what was happening, but the ship had just vanished off the radar picture and the whole incident must have been a fault on his radar so he hadn't cast off his nets.

There was a pause for a couple of seconds and then the most awful noise of things breaking and crashing and I heard my father say "God help me!" and then the transmission was cut off. I called out the lifeboat, which reached the spot in fifty minutes, but there was nothing. Nothing has been seen of him or the boat since. I've made two attempts to dive in that area, but both were aborted after near fatal accidents to the divers, after which no one was prepared to dive and anyway I'd run out of money.'

'What sort of accidents?' Gunn asked.

'One of the divers was knocked unconscious when the current drove him into an undersea ledge of rock - that was his account of the incident - and another was attacked by a huge octopus which ripped his aqualung off. We were lucky to save him. That's it, really. Am I allowed to ask why you want to dive in that area?'

'Yes, of course, since I expect you'll be coming with us, if that's alright with the owner and skipper of Osprey?'

'Sure,' Peter agreed.

'Very quickly then, Claudine; some time ago a ship was stolen from a German shipbuilder in Hamburg. It vanished without trace. It was being built for the South African Government and we believe that it was a submersible cargo vessel designed for sanction busting.'

'That's why it disappeared off....' Claudine gasped and Gunn held up his hand to prevent any further speculation.

141

'There is a connection between the theft of that ship and the man who owns Sardrière Island. He is an arms dealer and we believe that the ship was stolen to transport a very special cargo - nuclear missiles - from Hong Kong to the Middle East. When I arrived here, I asked if there had been any incidents of boats disappearing just in case there had been accidents like those fishing boats lost in the Irish Sea when they've been sunk by submarines leaving or returning to their base at Faslane. It was Tom, the landlord of the Ship, who told me about your father and he then pointed you out in the bar when I said I intended to visit you. There, that brings all of you up to date except for the briefing I had in London and the phone call I've just had from the same place.'

'Can I top up that glass, John?' Peter offered and then refilled everyone's drink.

'Before I tell you all that, I must again say that this has gone well past an intriguing riddle and is now very serious and dangerous. I am certain that neither Sir Jeremy nor Robin would want their wives to be involved any further in this and I believe that if Osprey is used, there is every possibility of her being damaged. I am assured that any damage will be fully compensated by the Directorate, but I've also been advised to charter a proper diving and salvage vessel. I must also put all my cards on the table and say that whatever decision is made, Susan must certainly play no further part in this and I don't believe I need elaborate any further on the reasons for that.'

'May I add just one factor of which you won't be aware,' Peter chipped in, 'I'm not taking Osprey on spec' to look at Sardrière. I have Hassan's permission, not only to sail all round his Island - I'm not sure that's in his gift to grant - but he has said that Osprey will be welcome in his private harbour. The arrival of Osprey off Sardrière should raise no suspicions, but a salvage vessel is bound to. There! I've said my piece. Osprey is still volunteered for the job and I will skipper her.'

'If you get rid of all the women and use Osprey, Hassan will smell a rat immediately. He knows who is on the boat - incidentally, the more I think about it the more I'm convinced that the presence of Hassan's boat next door to us at Hamble was no coincidence. Having given Peter permission to visit Sardrière Island, I'd lay more than evens that that boat came over to study who was on Osprey. If you now remove all the women, then there is no point in taking Osprey. If Osprey's used with Peter skippering her, then I come with that package,' and Tricia downed the remains of her wine and went to fill her glass.

'That goes for me too; here Trish, can you top that up, please?' and Celia held her glass out as Tricia topped it up.

'I, likewise, want to stay, but accept what John was obviously told either in that phone call or in London. I am not so naive that I don't realise how difficult it would be for Jeremy if something went wrong. Unless you're thinking of dashing off tonight, I'll stay the night and then catch the flight back tomorrow,' Susan Hammond added in a thoroughly practical manner.

'That's it then,' Gunn decided, 'thank you Susan. I'll now bring you all up to date and will spare no details. I hope it won't make you change your minds.' Gunn covered most of the detail of his brief and the 'phone call from Simon Peters and made quite sure that they understood about the deaths of the three people at the embassy in Beijing.

'How long will it be before we eat, Trish?' Peter asked when Gunn had finished.

'Oh, about an hour.'

'Why don't you dash back to your house, Claudine, and pick up whatever you need and then come back here in time for something to eat,' Peter suggested.

'Right, I'll do that.'

'Do you want any help?' Gunn offered.

'No thanks; I'll grab a taxi and will be back in no more than half an hour.' Claudine put down her glass and walked back along the pontoon to the marina office and hailed a taxi.

*

Just before he was shot by Volkonoff, the Rumanian told him that there was a young Chinese stockbroker who was an information source used by British Intelligence. For the next 24 hours, Volkonoff had followed the young stockbroker everywhere until his patience was rewarded and he saw the contact made in the Hong Kong Bank building. Death was mercifully swift for Tim Driscoll and he never knew anything. Volkonoff broke his neck, heaved him over the balustrade and then joined the throng of tourists and customers descending to the first floor.

He left the building after the body had been removed in the ambulance and walked over to the British Airways office in the Hilton Hotel to book his flight to Dubai. He got a business class seat on the flight that evening and then hailed a taxi. The driver knew the address in Wanchai well and the building in Li Chit Street was well known as the most expensive brothel in Hong Kong and catered for every taste, however warped or bizarre.

143

At the same time as Volkonoff was being welcomed in the lobby of the Wanchai brothel, a powerful 60 foot Sunseeker express motor cruiser made its way through the afternoon water traffic of Hong Kong Harbour towards Queen's Pier. At the stern flew the Stars and Stripes and on the flying bridge its owner steered the boat himself. Frank Peterson was a highly successful business entrepreneur who had a finger in almost every financial pie in Hong Kong; he was also the local director of the CIA and ran the agency from his warehouse in Kennedy Town.

He had taken his boat out to the West Lamma Channel to monitor the departure of Al Samak so that the course and speed could be passed to USS Los Angeles, a nuclear-powered attack submarine of the Seventh Fleet which had been travelling at its maximum submerged speed of 38 knots ever since the signal had been received with orders to shadow the cargo vessel until it was destroyed by the Russian submarines. The signal had contained various communication and identification procedures so that the US and Russian submarines could contact each other.

Frank Peterson had failed which was an occurrence unfamiliar to him. As the boat approached the pier, he again went over the instructions he'd given and was convinced that every angle had been covered. From a house in Discovery Bay on Lantau Island, a very powerful starlight-scope had been used to watch the departure of the cargo vessel when it had weighed anchor at 0530 hours. He had positioned a man on Mount Davis who had reported that the ship was heading slightly west of due south for the West Lamma Channel and this had been acknowledged by the man he had placed on Mount Stenhouse on Lamma Island.

The fishing junk, just to the east of Cheung Chau reported that the ship had passed neither to the north or south of the island and the man on Mount Stenhouse never saw the ship. Somewhere between Green Island and Lamma Island, the ship had vanished. Once again, Frank Peterson studied the chart having handed over the wheel to his boat boy to bring the boat alongside the pier. The ship must have doubled back on its course and gone north of Lantau Island was his only conclusion. He had the tip of the dividers resting on the information on the chart, which would have solved his riddle, but he hadn't been given enough information and when he did receive it, it was too late.

The twin points of the dividers rested on the 15 fathom sounding contour which marked a deep channel close in to the west side of Lamma Island. Al Samak's captain had brought her close in to shore in the deep channel round the north-west tip of Lamma Island which had completely hidden the ship from any eyes on Hong Kong Island. Once the lookouts had reported a completely clear sea all round, the ship had submerged to a depth of 10 fathoms which gave a clear 5 fathoms under the keel and allowed the captain to use the periscope, disguised by the funnel, to pilot the ship out of Hong Kong waters.

Frank Peterson had scoured every approach to Hong Kong since six that morning, using the Sunseeker's powerful engines to drive the motor cruiser at maximum speed. He was returning with almost no fuel left in his tanks and not the faintest idea where the ship had gone. By the time John Gunn had spoken to Simon Peters, recounting Claudine's account of the loss of her father's boat and that had been passed to Langley and then Hong Kong, it was too late. Just as the motor cruiser passed the Star Ferry terminal, Frank Peterson's secure telephone buzzed. He picked it up and listened. He swore loudly and drove the dividers a full half inch into the teak chart table.

*

Gunn replaced the phone in its cradle, picked up his glass of wine and glanced at his watch. There was a very savoury aroma coming from the galley, where he could hear the three women chatting. Peter walked into the wheelhouse. 'Claudine's been gone nearly an hour hasn't she, John?'

'Yes, the same thought had crossed my mind. Shall I see if there's any sign of her. I don't want Tricia's meal to spoil.'

'Yes, why not.' Gunn left the wheelhouse and jumped down onto the pontoon. When he reached the marina office, there was still no sign of Claudine. There was a line of taxis waiting. Gunn walked to the front one and gave the address at St Martin's Point. He looked out for taxis coming in the other direction with Claudine, but there was no sign of her. It only took the taxi just over ten minutes to get to the house and with a slight relaxing of the tightness which had gripped Gunn, he saw that there was indeed a taxi parked outside the small bungalow.

He asked the driver to wait and got out. There was no sign of the taxi driver and he assumed that he had gone into the house to help Claudine with whatever she was bringing for her stay on Osprey. The door of the bungalow was open. The taxi driver was sitting in one of the armchairs in the small sitting room. He certainly wouldn't be driving taxis or anything else again. He had been shot through the head. Gunn supressed the urge to dash from room to room looking for Claudine. He bent down and removed the 9mm Radom from its

145

ankle holster and pushed back the door of a bedroom; no one; an empty room.

He moved along the small corridor to the next room and opened the door. It was Claudine's room. There was an open sailing bag on the bed, half-filled with clothes; no sign of Claudine and no sign of a struggle. The same went for the rest of the bungalow. She had vanished. Gunn went out through the front door and closed it behind him. He climbed into the taxi and asked the driver to take him back to the marina. As the taxi drove along the high cliff road back to St Peter Port, Gunn looked out across the sea. It was a perfect evening with a deep red sunset promising another warm day to follow. Across the blood-red reflection of the sun on the sea, was the broad pink-tinged wake of a big motor boat, pointing like an arrow towards Sardrière Island.

CHAPTER 11

Madam Butterfly had been nick-named as such by her regular clients, because anything less like a butterfly would be hard to imagine. She weighed-in at something close to 350 pounds, but it was impossible to know for sure as no one had seen her on a set of scales and there were very few scales that were designed to withstand that sort of weight. She catered for only the wealthiest of clients and since the advent of Aids, no servicemen - and particularly no American servicemen - got past the screening and security at the front door of the brothel on Li Chit Street. A handful of high-ranking men in the Hong Kong Government and its Disciplined Services were provided with women who would meet them at one of the flats which Madam Butterfly owned; they obviously couldn't be seen going into the premises on Li Chit Street.

Madam Butterfly was sitting in her office in the lobby where she not only kept a strict eye on the receipts, but also the time for which each client had paid. There was a clock for each client and this was started as soon as the door closed on the client and for however many women – gays were not catered for - he had paid. It was now 8.20 in the evening and the Russian was nearly forty minutes overtime, even if he had paid over the rate to ensure that he was not disturbed. Over the rate or not, business was business and Madam Butterfly heaved her weight off a massively-carved teak chair - her girls joked amongst themselves, never in front of Madame! that it would take the weight of an elephant - and waddled over to a lift.

She went up to the second floor and then along the plush corridor to Room 22. With difficulty, the large woman put her ear to the keyhole and listened; not a sound came from inside. Her pass key went into the lock and she quietly opened the door. Madam Butterfly staggered away from the open door trying to hold back the bitter vomit in her throat, but was unable to control it until she reached the toilet and was violently sick in the corridor, having just managed to press the alarm which alerted her minders who were kept out of sight in the lobby. They arrived within seconds and still unable to control her vast, heaving gut, Madam Butterfly pointed to the room. The men walked into the room and stopped dead.

The Russian had paid for three women all of whom were now dead. There was hardly anything in the room, which wasn't saturated in blood. What had happened in that room would have beggared the vilest imagination of the warped minds which produced 'video nasties'. It was certainly too much for one of the minders and he bolted out of the door and just succeeded in reaching the toilet before he was sick. Of the Russian, there was not a sign.

*

'Drink Sir?'
　'Vodka.'
'Ice?'
'I asked for vodka, not ice.'
'Very good, Sir, I'… The British Airways stewardess was about to make a mildly smart reply to the ill-mannered man she was serving in Club World Class, but a glance at the expression on his face turned her blood cold and she shuddered as though someone had walked over her grave.

'Here you are, Sir,' and she held out the small, silver tray with the drink, a linen mat and a packet of nuts. A huge hand reached up to take the drink and the stewardess saw what looked like a small bloodstain on the cuff of his white shirt. 'Can I get you a hot damp cloth, Sir, to remove that stain on your cuff?' He looked at it once he had placed the drink on his tray. To her amazement the coarse and brutal face broke into a lop-sided smile and the head was shaken. Yuri Volkonoff was recalling with something akin to post-coital sexual satisfaction, the carnage in Room 22.

*

'Feels as though we're under way,' Simeon had been unable to get back to sleep after the other four men had arrived on board. He had been reading a book, which he closed and then got out of bed. He put on a dressing gown and opened his door; now that they had been given freedom of movement between their cabins, the wardroom and the saloon, the doors to those rooms were no longer locked. He looked at his watch. It was a couple of minutes after 5.30. He went into the saloon and looked out of the port scuttles; the ship was turning. He went over to the starboard scuttles and looked out.

A thin, pale line above the hills of the New Territories indicated that the first light of dawn was only a half-hour or so away. Simeon saw that there was still half a pot of stewed coffee in the percolator and poured some into a used cup and then watched as the ship moved on a southerly course away from Hong Kong. He had no idea of the names of all the islands, which he could see, but he did recognise the western end of Hong Kong Island, which he could now see through the port scuttles. Slowly, the dawn gave shape and form to the blackness of the islands and the lights lost their sharpness and sparkle.

The door opened and Rokossovsky appeared. 'You couldn't sleep either,' and he saw the cup, which Simeon was holding. 'Any more of that coffee?'

'Yes, plenty, if you don't mind it stewed and in a dirty cup.'

'Oh, I think I'm prepared to overlook that,' and he poured himself a cup. 'Where are we?'

'Well, we've only been under way for half-an-hour and we're travelling south. That island you can see out of that side of the saloon is just to the west of Hong Kong, but I can't remember its name. We seem to be passing quite close to it,' he added. The engine note altered and the ship seemed to slow.

'I wonder what's happening now,' but when he saw what was happening, Simeon refused to believe it. 'We're sinking, Andrey!' he gasped in a strangled tone as he saw the seas break over the side of the ship in the limited field of view which the thick glass of the scuttle allowed. Rokossovsky rushed to the scuttles on the other side of the saloon as a turbulent mass of water boiled past the armoured glass only inches from his face.

'Quick, there must be an alarm, somewhere!' Rokossovsky shouted in desperation and then added, 'we must wake the others, quickly!' he almost screamed and rushed for the door, which was opened by their steward as he reached it. 'We're sinking!' he shouted at the steward as he made to push past him on his way to alert the other two men.

'We are not sinking, Sir,' it was the first time that the steward had spoken and Rokossovsky had gone past him before the statement registered.

'What do you mean, man, look!' and Rokossovsky pointed to the scuttles through which nothing could now be seen except water.

'The ship is now travelling submerged and will remain that way for most of the duration of this voyage. Would you gentlemen care for breakfast now or would you prefer it at 7.30 as usual,' was the steward's response to Rokossovsky's outburst. The two Russians looked at each other and it was Simeon who broke the brief silence.

'I think we'll have breakfast now... please,' and then both Russians burst into laughter as the steward replied, 'very good, gentlemen,' and left the saloon.

The USS Los Angeles had covered 1000 miles since receipt of the signal giving the submarine new deployment orders to Hong Kong to shadow the ship Al Samak. Commander George Gresham brought his nuclear-powered attack submarine to periscope depth with 45 seconds to spare before the pre-arranged contact time. He had no wish to stay at that depth for any longer than necessary and once he knew the ship's position speed and course, the shadowing of the ship would be done entirely by sonar. The noise print of the ship's propellers would be automatically fed into the sonar computer and from there to the inertial navigation computer.

The milli-second, burst transmission was received and the submarine dived to 250 feet just above a cooler layer of water, which flowed south from the East China Sea. Once the ship had been identified, the Los Angeles would slip below the cooler layer of water to mask her presence in the area. The radio officer appeared looking slightly puzzled.

'What's the problem, Hal?' Commander Gresham asked.

'If this wasn't for real, sir, I would say that someone is having a good laugh at our expense,' replied Lt Commander Harry Tudor.

'Didn't we get the ship's position and course?'

'No sir; the ship was last seen 5000 metres sou-sou-west of Hong Kong Island at 22°15' North, 114° 06' East, on a course of 182° true at 0604 hours this morning; speed estimated at 22 knots. Between that position and a 'guesstimated' position 2000 metres due south, the ship submerged.' There was a smothered snort from the navigating officer.

'It did what, Hal?'

'It submerged, Sir.'

'Who said so?'

'The CIA, Sir; look there's a lot more in the signal, but I'd like to discuss it in your cabin if I may Sir.'

'Very well; what's the tonnage of this ship?'

'20,000 tons.'

'Screws?'

'Two, Sir.'

'Right,' and the Captain unclipped the PA mike and switched it so that he was addressing everyone in the main control centre of the submarine, 'now hear this. We are searching for a twenty thousand ton cargo ship which is proceeding submerged, I repeat submerged, on a course of 182 degrees true at 22 knots. Last known position at 0604 hours was 22°15' North, 14° 06' East. This ship is heading for the

Persian Gulf and we are co-operating with the Ruskies to stop it and sink it. It is carrying a cargo of ten nuclear missiles, which are destined for sale to Iraq. The Ruskies have deployed the Sierra Class subs from their Southern Fleet; two to the Malacca Straits and the other two to block the passage through the Selat Sunda between Sumatra and Java. For the man who correctly predicts this ship's positon and course and the sonar operator who identifies it, the beers are on me!' and the Captain and his radio officer left the control room.

*

Simon Peters was woken by the persistent buzzing of the phone beside his bed. He struggled out of a deep sleep having only gone to bed at 2.15 in the morning. He looked through screwed-up eyes at his watch; 5.20. Beside him, his wife slept on undisturbed by the phone; fifteen years of married life with Simon being called out at all hours of the night had resulted in a thoroughly practical solution and the earplugs firmly wedged in her ears assured that at least one member of the family achieved a reasonable night's sleep. He acknowledged the summons to the office and replaced the phone. Simon went past the rooms in which his son and daughter slept undisturbed and then down the stairs to the kitchen where he made a cup of instant coffee, before he went through the door into the double garage of their detached house on a private estate on the outskirts of Esher in Surrey.

It was yet another lovely day with the sun already bright in a cloudless sky. He joined the A3 and had a completely clear run on the Kingston by-pass and even Putney and Fulham were clear, so within 25 minutes he was in his office in Kingsroad House. Louise was already in the office and waiting on his desk was a small tray with a percolator of coffee, some fresh croissants and peach jam which she had bought on her way to the office from her flat in Gledhow Gardens. She came into his office after a couple of minutes and placed a slim red file on his desk with all the documents, which he would require for the Director's briefing. 'Any news from the Gulf, Louise?'

'Yes, Simon; Donald Hastings was here all night. The Iraqis have now got more than 200,000 troops deployed for the defence of Baghdad and Basra against any US/Brit invasion. Donald's agents in Baghdad are saying that the invasion's a foregone conclusion and the atmosphere in the city is one of euphoria and passionate nationalism for the defence of the mother country. As Donald put it, 'there are more media journalists than fleas on a pye dog's anus'. I'm afraid it's bad news from Hong Kong.'

'What's happened?

'Tim Driscoll's dead and the CIA has lost Al Samak. The Director got in from Washington only an hour and a half ago and Melanie, his PA, says he's furious about something. He will be asking you for a minute by minute account of how long you possessed that information about Hassan's submerging cargo vessel and Volkonoff's presence in Hong Kong before it was passed on to those who needed it. In that file, I've typed out the exact sequence of events with all the timings. I'm afraid you could be in for a rough ride. Look, only a couple of minutes to go; you'd better be on your way,' and Louise removed the tray from his desk. Simon Peters picked up the file and walked out of the office, but then stuck his head back round the door,

'Thanks for the breakfast, Louise, and this,' and he held up the red file before leaving the room and closing the door.

*

Gunn paid off the taxi driver in the car park by the marina office and walked along the pontoon to Osprey's berth. Peter de Havilland and the three women were in the wheelhouse and as soon as John came aboard he apologised to Tricia for delaying the evening meal. 'What's happened to Claudine?' Peter asked.

'I think she's been abducted by Hassan's men, Peter...'

'Oh no!' gasped Susan Hammond.

'She must've been followed to the house because she had started to put some things into a bag and the taxi driver was sitting in a chair in the sitting room, so presumably she had asked him to wait there while she packed.'

'Didn't the driver hear anything?' Tricia asked.

'He had been shot through the head.'

'What happens now?' Peter asked quietly.

'It may only be wishful thinking on my part, but as I was driving back from St Martin's Point, I saw a large motorboat, which looked a lot like Hassan's Al Samak, heading, at what looked like maximum speed, in the direction of Sardrière Island. I'll just have a quick word with the office in London and get them to speak direct to the Chief Constable here so that the poor taxi driver can be removed. If the meal isn't ruined, Tricia, I suggest that we all have supper and work on a plan for tomorrow. Frustrating as it is, there is no point in making a bad situation worse by rushing off into the night to try and rescue Claudine.' Gunn made his call and then they all had supper, during which a plan was made for the visit to Sardrière Island.

*

Sir Jeremy Hammond was angry. He demanded to know exactly when the information that Hassan might have possessed a submersible cargo ship was known, firstly by the field agent and secondly by the controller or Kingsroad House. He also wanted to know how long it had taken for the information about Volkonoff to be despatched to Hong Kong after he had passed it to London from Washington. This last piece of information, he was told, had gone immediately it was received; the delay had occurred because the Hong Kong office had been unable to find Driscoll in time. This did nothing to cool the Director's anger.

'This is exactly the point I made when this Directorate was set up. MI5 and the SIS consistently failed to produce timely intelligence because everyone worked in watertight compartments spending more time guarding their information from each other than the enemy - who, in many cases had better access to British Intelligence than the British agencies which required it. Secure and timely communication of intelligence, so that it can be collated centrally is the key to an effective intelligence organisation. I can't remember how many times I've said that to you all. You are not employed by her Majesty's Government as collector's and hoarders of intelligence.'

'We are only doing our job properly if intelligence is provided to those who need it - our Prime Minister, our Government, our allies, our Service Commanders and our agents - so that it can be used effectively either defensively, as was the case with Driscoll or offensively, as was the case with the cargo ship carrying the nuclear missiles. The British Intelligence Directorate failed in both instances and because of that failure, one of my men is dead and the US Navy has lost the ship with a cargo, which could be the cause of Armageddon in the Middle East. Miles,' and here the Director turned to his Deputy, 'please see that I have a report within 24 hours - no more than one side of paper - which lays out clear steps to ensure that this failure to communicate intelligence never happens again. That concludes this meeting, gentlemen, as I must be at 10 Downing Street in half an hour. Donald, I would like a full brief from your Section as soon as I return which is likely to be between 9.30 and 10.00. Thank you all for getting here so promptly,' and the Director stood up and left the conference room.

*

Just like Esher in Surrey, the morning also dawned bright and clear over the Channel Islands which slightly cheered the rather preoccupied mood of the five people on Osprey. In Peter's original plan, he had told Hassan that he would be in the area of Sardrière

153

Island between eleven and twelve. Gunn had agreed that it was most important that they stuck to these timings to allay any suspicions which might have been aroused at the marina in Hamble. There was a fresh easterly breeze and it was only ten miles to the island so they had decided to leave at ten o'clock.

They had a leisurely breakfast at 8.30 and then the three women went ashore to do some shopping while Gunn and Peter checked over all the scuba gear, which had been laid out in the cockpit. In the middle of doing this, the phone in the wheelhouse rang and Gunn picked it up. 'Hello John, it's Simon. I must bring you up-to-date quickly before you set off for Sardrière Island. All Heads of Sections, and I in particular, have just been given a right bollocking from the Director, who's back from the States, about passing on information quickly to our agents in the field. He blamed this failure for the death of Driscoll...'

'Damn!'

'Yes, I'm afraid so, and the loss of Hassan's ship because the Americans weren't told, until it was too late, of our suspicions about it being able to submerge. So I'm trying to make amends by keeping you right up to date. Alan Paxton passed on all your information last night and I spoke to him just before ringing you. The Chief Constable of Guernsey has been told - in broad outline - what's happening and his men have removed the taxi driver from Miss Carteret's house. Now, any more developments your end?'

'No, none; we'll be on our way shortly. Was it Volkonoff?'

'Yes, it was, but for God's sake don't let this develop into a personal vendetta otherwise you'll lose all your objectivity if you allow yourself to become emotionally involved.' Gunn ignored Simon's caution.

'Do we know where Volkonoff is?'

'Not yet; Hong Kong's working on that now. He was traced to Madam Butterfly's brothel in Li Chit Streeet, d'you...'

'Yes, I know it. What butchery did he get up to there?'

'You're obviously way ahead of the game; he carved up three young tarts until they were barely recognisable as humans.'

'What happened to Tim?'

'He was killed instantly without knowing anything.'

'How do you know that?'

'His neck was broken and then he was thrown over the balustrade of the twentieth floor of the Hong Kong Bank.'

'Anything more for me?

'No; pl...' but the connection had been broken.

At twenty to ten the women returned and Gunn gave Susan a hand with her bag up to the marina office where he put her in a taxi. She was booked on the 11.30 flight to Southampton and a phone call to London had ensured that a car would be waiting for her at the airport. Gunn returned to Osprey and gave Peter a hand in preparing the ketch for sea. Having checked all the scuba gear, it had all been put out of sight in the wheelhouse and the aqua-scooter was covered with a tarpaulin on the foredeck.

Gunn and Celia slipped the moorings a couple of minutes after ten and Peter steered his yacht towards the marina entrance. Osprey was heading into the wind on her engines so by the time she had reached the Little Russel Channel outside the marina, all the sails were set. Peter held her into the wind to achieve a reasonable offing to clear the shallow water due south of the harbour and once he was able to set a course of 195°, he swung the wheel clockwise until the binnacle compass read that bearing. The easterly wind was a fraction abaft the port beam of the yacht; the engines were stopped and on a broad reach, Osprey's speed rose rapidly to 9 knots.

'He has three patrol boats on duty all the time, John, and one of them is bound to come out to inspect Osprey as we approach. He has imposed an exclusion zone of a mile all round the island and any boat, other than the regular tourist one, is always stopped and inspected. As it's a Sunday, there'll be no tourists, so we'll be the only boat approaching the island. You must be off the boat before that inspection and there mustn't be a sign of any diving gear. As we agreed last night, we will then go into the harbour and I have no doubt that some sort of conducted tour round the castle will take place. You are taking a very dangerous risk by diving on your own in an area of such violent currents, but I said all that last night. The two spare sets of tanks you're taking should give you enough air for a thorough look round, decompression and a safe margin spare for emergencies. Now you'd better get ready as we'll be there in less than thirty minutes at this speed.'

Gunn changed into the full wet suit and then brought the aqua-scooter aft to the starboard side of the wheelhouse where he attached the two sets of spare tanks to it. He strapped on the diving knife, compass and lead-weighted belt, cleaned the glass of his goggles and put on the flippers. Osprey's course had brought her round to the southern side of the island. 'We're less than a mile from the island now, John,' and no sooner were the words out of Peter's mouth than the patrol boat appeared from the direction of the harbour on the south-east tip of the island. 'He'll be alongside in three or four minutes, so you'd better be off, John.' Gunn pushed the aqua-scooter

155

over the starboard side of the yacht and followed it into the water, disappearing beneath the surface immediately.

The patrol boat swept round Osprey's stern and came to within hailing distance. Peter was asked to start his engines and take off the sails. With Tricia and Celia helping, this was achieved in a couple of minutes and once the fenders were in place the motorboat came alongside and a very nautical-looking deeply sun-tanned skipper, complete with cap and yachting shoes, jumped nimbly aboard Osprey. 'Welcome aboard!' Peter greeted him, without leaving the wheel. The motorboat veered away from the yacht and took up station astern and slightly to the starboard side.

'Captain Rashid, Mr de Havilland. I'm responsible for the security of Mr Hussein's property.'

'Nice to meet you Captain Rashid. Allow me to introduce you to my wife, Tricia, and our guest for this cruise, Mrs Harris. Can I offer you a drink?'

'Thank you, but I won't. May I have a look round your boat, Mr de Havilland. Mr Hussein insists that every boat is inspected before it comes into the harbour.'

'Yes, of course; Tricia will show you around. Please go anywhere you wish.'

'Thank you,' and Captain Rashid followed Tricia into the wheelhouse and then down into the saloon. The two of them reappeared some minutes later and as Rashid came out of the wheelhouse he spoke to Peter. 'Have you had anyone else on board this cruise, Mr de Havilland?'

'Yes, indeed we have, Captain. I've had two guests who left us in Guernsey. One was the wife of someone I've known ever since I was in the Navy and the other was a fellow yachtsman friend who came along to help me with the Channel crossing, but then had to go back as he's working tomorrow.' All Gunn's clothes had been put with his in the fitted wardrobe in the aft cabin and the small starboard cabin was empty.

'Thank you, Mr de Havilland. Please follow us into the harbour and tie up beside the steps on the jetty.' Rashid waved to the motorboat and when it came alongside he jumped aboard and climbed up to the flying bridge. The water boiled under the stern of the boat as Rashid took the wheel and it surged ahead of Osprey as the two boats headed for the harbour entrance. Peter had been watching Rashid closely and hadn't missed the almost imperceptible negative shake of the Captain's head as he rejoined the patrol boat. John reckoned that he'd seen Al Samak leaving St Peter Port the previous night. One of the crew had seen John after the search of

Hassan's boat in the yachtclub marina. It must be assumed that they had been watched, so Susan and John would have been noted at the yacht club marina and Claudine's arrival on board last night would have been seen. She would have been followed to her house from the marina.

Peter continued to try and analyse how much was known by Hassan's men and in how much danger Tricia, Celia and he were, as he steered Osprey into the harbour. He spotted the stone steps on the jetty and slowed Osprey right down as he prepared to bring her alongside. Tricia and Celia had the bow and stern warps all ready and having indicated that he was going to put the port side against the jetty, all the fenders were out on that side. They would assume that Claudine had told them about the disappearance of her father and their interpretation of seeing her pack a bag was that she had been offered a lift over to the island to see if she could find out anymore about her father or his boat. Both Celia and Tricia threw their warps extremely competently and they were caught by two of Hassan's men who made them fast to two, large iron bollards.

Peter decompressed both the engines and saw that Captain Rashid was already at the top of the steps on the stone jetty. Was his reasoning wishful thinking? No, Peter thought not. He had booked this visit months ago; no one had seen John on Al Samak. Hassan's men had left St Peter Port immediately after abducting Claudine. Or had they? Did they leave someone behind to watch Osprey? If they had and he, she or they had seen John on the boat as it departed, then they were in trouble. Peter shrugged; the die was cast and so that was that, but he had to warn Tricia and Celia that it was possible that they had just walked - or sailed - straight into the lion's den.

*

Hassan Hussein watched the graceful yacht berth alongside the stone jetty in his harbour and then all three people go below to get ready for the lunch invitation, which Captain Rashid had delivered. He had spoken with Rashid on the cell phone after his inspection of the yacht. There had been no sign of the man who was with the boat in Guernsey and no sign of his belongings on the boat. The Carteret girl had been spotted on the boat, but then she had become a nuisance as she had been seen on many boats trying to persuade owners to take her to the island or help her look for her father's boat and so that irritation had been dealt with last night.

It was unusual for his affairs to have had so many things go wrong in such a short time. One of his men killed - very efficiently and with a most unusual blow - and the other two to be deported

157

when they were discharged from the hospital where both still had residual concussion from their fractured skulls. A break-in to his yacht which almost succeeded in by-passing his security alarm system and the man responsible for fitting that system had been moored in the yacht for'ard of Al Samak. Nothing had been taken, but then what had the person been looking for? There wasn't a single incriminating document aboard his boat.

He had received a phone call from Rokossovsky in Hong Kong, which had been made from his ship, to warn him that British, and probably American intelligence agencies, were now aware of the theft of the missiles, the mode of transport and the probable destination. He had accepted Rokossovsky's advice on the transport of the missiles and they were now all loaded. The wretched man Volkonoff had chosen to stay in Hong Kong and fly direct to Dubai, which had required a rearrangement of his plans and instructions had already been sent to his agent in Dubai who had assured him that Volkonoff would receive every possible assistance to join his five colleagues.

No, Hassan decided, the plan was still running like clockwork and that fool Saddam would be desperate for his missiles now that the US and UK were committed to an invasion or a very demeaning climb-down. Hassan laughed; the noise which emerged wasn't like a human laugh, but more of a robotic screech as the synthesizer strapped to his side tried to convert the electronic impulses from the electrodes implanted in his neck into a noise which its computer memory told it was a human laugh. What price would Saddam be prepared to pay now for the missiles? Oh yes, and another screech echoed around the stone columns of the banqueting hall as Hassan turned away from the window and slowly climbed the stone stairs to his private suite of rooms.

Oh yes, Saddam would get his missiles, but not for the price he was expecting to pay. The minor irritation caused by the de Havilland yacht and any of its guests had been temporarily dismissed by Hassan in his euphoria of the anticipated invasion of Iraq. The Americans and British, under the guise of the UN, would have to proceed with their invasion plans, but what a shock they were due to get. After all the farce and spin about non-existent WMDs, the coalition forces would suddenly find themselves threatened with the real thing and in the hands of a complete madman. Who would save them? He, Hassan would, when his plan came to fruition. What a perfect opportunity that now provided for his cataclysmic revenge.

*

In an office on the fifth floor of Kingsroad House, Miles Thompson had just returned with the Director from briefing the Prime Minister on the situation in the Gulf and the efforts being made by the Russians and Americans to destroy the SS20 missiles. If all the Heads of Sections had been chastised by Sir Jeremy Hammond for any responsibility in the failure to pass on information quikly, it was nothing compared to the tongue-lashing which the Director received, in private, after the Prime Minister had been briefed. In the car coming back to Kingsroad House, he had told his Deputy that he had been warned that if the missiles got into Saddam Hussein's hands, he could start looking for another job - without references!

Miles Thompson looked at the large stack of files, which had collected in his 'in' tray while he had been out at 10 Downing Street. He looked at his watch; it was 12.21 and the day had started at six that morning. It was going to be another full working Sunday, but he was determined to get away from the office for some lunch. He called in his PA and told her that he was going for an early lunch. He left the building by Route 2 and hailed a cab. He was particularly fond of Italian cuisine and had a favourite restaurant in Villiers Street by Charing Cross Station. He had decided to treat himself and gave the address to the taxi driver. It was extremely hot in London that day and he removed his jacket and tie before sitting back in the seat of the taxi. What was Hassan up to? Miles Thompson recalled his summary at the briefing the day before. He had imitated Agatha Christie's Poirot by saying that Hassan had the motive and the means, all he needed was the opportunity. Saddam Hussein was just about to give him that opportunity. So what was Hassan's game?

CHAPTER 12

The aqua-scooter was nothing more than a truncated torpedo with a powerful light at the front, scooter-like handlebars with a twist-grip throttle on the right and a similar twist-grip on the left which controlled the angle of dive or surface on the stabilising planes. There was a seat and the double, contra-rotating propellers were encased in a metal drum to prevent arms and legs from being mangled in the blades. At the rear of the drum were two rudders which gave lateral control to the scooter when the handlebars were moved left or right.

In the centre of the handlebars was a large compass with compensating magnets which Gunn had swung and zeroed during the preparation of the diving gear; beside the compass was a depth gauge. Just in front of the seat was a small odds and ends compartment, which contained a torch and a diving knife. The two additional, double-tank harnesses strapped to the scooter made it cumbersome to handle and Peter had wisely insisted on a safety line which attached Gunn to the scooter.

Gunn and his scooter had gone over the side of Osprey just over half a mile from the island. He had dived to thirty feet to get clear of the approaching motorboat and then levelled off and turned the throttle to maximum to get out of the strong, off-shore current as quickly as possible. There was still a reasonable amount of light at 30 feet and it was only two or three minutes before he could distinguish the rock face of the island. As far as he could judge, he was on the approach line where Carteret's boat had been when it had been dragged under the surface.

Within a 100 metres of the island, there was virtually no current; Gunn set the diving planes to maximum angle and twisted the handlebars over to the right so that he immediately started to descend in a tight corkscrew motion. At sixty feet, all the ambient light from the surface faded and he switched on the powerful spotlight. The depth gauge went past 100 feet and he was now in Stygian darkness with just a glimpse, every now and then, of a startled fish caught in the beam of the light. The depth gauge showed 150 feet and Gunn eased the angle of dive and the speed of the scooter. The chart had showed that the depth should be 170 feet, which meant that the scooter should be approaching the seabed.

The spotlight momentarily picked out something directly in the path of the scooter and then Gunn was thrown from his seat and the mask ripped from his face. He bumped into something very hard as he groped for his mask, which was over the back of his head, the strap still threaded through the loop on the rubber head cowl. Gunn pulled the mask over his face and then used the air from his demand valve to purge the water. He felt down to his waist to the safety line and then pulled himself towards the scooter. If it hadn't been for the bubbles from his demand valve, Gunn would have had no idea of what was up or down. He could only see his hand when he placed it over the glass of his mask. His hands found the scooter and in front of the seat was the small twist handle.

Very carefully, he opened the lid and slid his hand inside where he felt the comforting shape of the torch. There was a lanyard on the base of the torch and this he pulled out first and placed over his wrist. He switched on the torch. The scooter was relatively undamaged, except for the spotlight on the front, which was broken. He shone the torch along his safety line and saw that it was looped around something. He swam along the line until he came to a huge metal girder. It had an 'I' cross-section and was large enough for him to fit in between the top and bottom flange of the girder. It was of the size and strength of the girders used to construct oil rigs and it was in pristine condition, coated in some form of anti-fouling paint.

The scooter had a slightly negative buoyancy and he allowed it to pull him down the girder until he reached the base of the contraption; his depth gauge read 190 feet. It was painstakingly difficult to grasp the size of the construction with which he had collided as his torch only illuminated a minute area with its slim beam. The base of the girder sat on a set of bogie wheels, which in its turn ran on a rail set into the seabed. Gunn realised that what he was looking at was an enormous cradle mounted on rail-type bogies which was identical to those used by boatyards all over the world to haul boats out of the water. This one was designed to drag a 20,000 ton cargo ship along the seabed. Drag it where? Almost as though someone had responded to his query, rows of spotlights mounted on the cradle flooded it in light. All the lights were directed onto the cradle itself and were apparently used, just like landing lights, to guide the ship into the cradle.

Gunn felt the cradle move and then stop; he looked down. The scooter had been lying across the rail and one of the huge iron wheels was trying to cut it in half. The wheel eased back and Gunn pulled the disabled scooter clear of the rail. At that point, the rails for the cradle ran in a cutting, which must have been blasted out of the rock. Gunn swam with the scooter over the lip of the cutting and detached the two sets of air-tanks from it.

Three streams of air bubbles, in the distance, gave warning of the approach of an inspection team to find out what was blocking the movement of the cradle. They would find nothing, which would seem odd. Gunn pushed some rocks over the edge of the cutting and then swam down and jammed them in front of the wheels before retreating hastily into the impenetrable blackness of the sea beyond the illuminated area of the spotlights.

The three divers were astride a scaled-up version of Gunn's aqua-scooter and headed straight for the offending bogie which meant that there must be sensors all over the cradle to indicate the area of a fault. All three divers had orange helmets and Gunn could see lines from each of these connecting the divers so that they could speak to each other. One of the divers was armed with a compressed-air bolt gun whilst the other two carried long metal levers. It seemed that rock falls were not an unusual occurrence.

Once the obstruction was cleared, the guard diver with the compressed-air gun swam to the foot of the cradle, unplugged his lead from one of the other divers and plugged it into a socket on the bogie. This presumably allowed him to speak to whomever controlled this contraption which was proved correct as the cradle started to move away from him. The guard diver rejoined the other two and the scooter set off on its return journey.

Gunn emerged from his hiding place and swam with the extra set of tanks to the girder. Once there, he strapped the tanks inside the flanges of the girder, using his safety line, and then clung inside the flanges himself, noticing with relief that the bubbles from his demand valve rose up the channel provided by the flanges.

Gunn looked at his watch; he had been down for twenty minutes. The luminous hand was only ten minutes away from the first mandatory decompression halt if he was going to rely on just the one set of tanks on his back. He reset the outer ring of his watch, which meant that he would now have to change tanks. Gradually the vertical rockface of the island came into view and as it did so, Gunn saw that the face was split apart by a fissure which must have been quite a 100 metres wide at the base and narrowed as it disappeared towards the surface. As the front of the docking cradle entered the fissure, all the spotlights went out making the sea blacker than ever before, but a matter of seconds later, the enormous size of the subterranean cavern was revealed as bank after bank of lights came on.

The scale of the engineering feat which had gone into the construction of this underwater harbour was staggering. It was little wonder that Hassan had needed to find an outlet for the thousands of tons of rock, which must have been excavated. What better use than to build a castle for the benefit of tourists? To his left, Gunn saw the inspection team take their scooter into a rectangular-shaped compartment which had been hewn out of the rock. Below this was a piece of equipment which looked exactly like the covered walkways which reached out to aircraft from airport terminals. Not even the banks of floodlights could illuminate the full extent of the cavern, but the riddle of the disappearance of Carteret's boat was solved. On the right side of the cavern was the fishing boat in near-perfect condition, held to the seabed rock by two large chains.

*

Alan Paxton watched the departure of Osprey from the marina and then returned to his car and drove out to St Martin's point where he had been asked to meet the Chief Constable and explain in outline who was responsible for the death of the taxi driver. This was a fairly laborious process and by the time it was all satisfactorily settled, it was nearly mid-day. Simon Peters had told him that the entire Directorate had been chastised for the errors that had resulted in the death of Driscoll and the loss of the cargo ship. He had been told that any other errors of this nature would result in all of them looking for alternative employment.

As he drove back along the coast road, Alan had an uneasy feeling that Gunn and the de Havilland boat were too inaccessible out at Sardrière. By the time he had reached the marina, his mind was made up. The salvage boat, which he had chartered would not be suitable for the course of action which he had in mind, so an alternative solution had to be found. He went into the marina office and after making an enquiry, was directed to another adjacent office, which dealt with boat charters.

In between leaving the marina office and entering the boat charter office, Alan Paxton became Prince Mahama Alhaji Fahyed - a well-prepared alias, and as such approached the receptionist in the charter office, who, sensing a lucrative charter, immediately showed the Prince into her manager. In less than ten minutes, the charter company's largest motor cruiser had been chartered for a week's fees in advance and in less than an hour, having been back to his small, rented flat in St Peter Port, Prince Fahyed, in full Saudi Arabian royal garb, boarded his 50 foot motorboat and directed the charter skipper to Sardrière Island.

*

Commander Gresham returned to the control room followed by his radio officer. He went over to the chart table where the navigating officer had a chart clamped to the table covering the whole of the Western Pacific, South China Sea and part of the Eastern Indian Ocean. As the Captain reappeared in the control room, the last of the duty hands monitoring all the equipment in the control room, returned to his position. Each had had an opportunity to study the chart and make his guess as to the course of the lost cargo ship.

Word had quickly spread to the various messes and wardrooms and sweepstakes were organised to see who could guess the course of the cargo ship. In the control room, it appeared that there were four choices; Straits of Malacca, Selat Sunda, Bali or some other route. As the first two were the most commonly used routes by shipping heading west towards the Gulf or Suez, these had the least number of supporters. The route east or west of Bali was the most popular and there was one marked 'other' against the name of Leading Seaman Murphy. Murphy was a black sonar operator in the compartment for'ard of the control room.

'Right Pete, you're my navigating officer so you get first shot at telling me where you reckon this sonofabitch has gone.' Lieutenant Peter Baker pointed to a neatly marked estimated position on the chart.

'My guess is that he'll go for the double bluff and head for the most obvious route while we and the Soviet – sorry! Russian subs are chasing our tails all over the South China Sea. That's the course I think he'll take and that's our intercept position,' and the Lieutenant pointed to the ringed pencil mark on the chart.

'Thank you, Pete; now let's see. There are two of you who think he'll go south of Sumatra through the Selat Sunda and five who've gone for the Bali route,' George Gresham looked round his control room. 'I suppose you think you're going to persuade me to stop offshore while you all get acquainted with the dusky maidens,' and laughter greeted this reasonably accurate assessment, but he continued, 'I'll give you all some free advice about Bali. You'd all do better to fornicate with a female Great White than screw around with the ladies on that island. We, the Australians, Europeans and particularly the Scandanavians have ruined the place. You'd be lucky to get away with nothing worse than a very pernicious form of syphillis. Having said all that, I have to say that that was the course, which I think I would have put my money on. Now what's this 'other' against Murphy's name?'

'I'll get him to come and explain his theory, Sir,' and the Lieutenant signalled to the petty officer in charge of the sonar station who sent Murphy into the control room while he took his place.

'Ah! Murphy; right son, now you tell me what you think this ship is going to do.'

'Does the captain of the ship know that we're looking for him, Sir?'

'We have to assume he does.'

'Would it be a reasonable assumption, Sir, that the man who owns this submersible ship would have hired an ex-submarine captain to drive it?'

'Yes, that's a reasonable assumption; what are you getting at?'

'Very simple, Sir; sub captains and navigators look at charts in a completely different way to captains of surface vessels. Sure, soundings are very important to them, but you will know, Sir, that you were taught to visualise the shape of the seabed - like a landscape - not just a series of depth contours.'

'Go on.'

'It's like this, Sir; if I'd been that captain and I was told that I had to get to some place in the Gulf, that it was likely that there would be subs out looking for me, that the usual routes would be watched and - I presume - that I'm not allowed to go east about to my destination, then this is the route I'd choose,' and he picked up the dividers from the chart. 'From Hong Kong, I'd go east - south-east to be more accurate - for two reasons; the first is because everyone would be looking in the opposite direction - which is exactly what everyone is doing, incidentally - and secondly because I would want to get to the eastern side of the Philippines. I would hug that eastern coastline all the way south through the islands,' and Murphy traced the course with the tip of the dividers, 'until I reached the Philippine Trench. A sub would then go deep - it's,' and he paused as he bent closer to the chart, 'over 30,000 feet deep in places. Now I don't suppose that this ship can go to a fraction of that depth, but he would still be a bitch to find.'

'And then where?' his captain asked.

'Straight on south, weaving through the Moluccan Islands, to the south of the island of Timor and out into the Timor Sea. Once he's out into the Indian Ocean, it would be easier to find a needle in a hundred haystacks than to find him in the vast expanse of the Southern Indian Ocean'

'So where would you go for an intercept?'

165

'Here, Sir: off the north-east tip of East Timor where he leaves the Banda Sea,' and Murphy had the point of his dividers at the intercept point.

*

At the top of the steps in the jetty, Captain Rashid was waiting beside a machine, which looked like, and probably was, a derivative of a golf buggy. Once ashore from their boat, it ensured that tourists had no cause to exercise their limbs as half a dozen of these machines took them up to the castle; it also ensured that none of them saw anything that they were not required to see. Peter, Tricia and Celia got onto the buggy and Captain Rashid drove them up to the castle. They went over the drawbridge spanning a natural chasm some fifty feet down to the sea between one part of the island on which the harbour had been built and a rocky outcrop on which the castle had been built. Expert advice had been sought and paid for handsomely to ensure that the castle was authentic in every detail - every detail that is, except modern plumbing, heating and many other assets of the 20th century which were denied to those who had lived between the 5th and 15th century.

It was a very warm day, but once they were in the castle, the thick walls kept the weather at bay and they were able to have their conducted tour in comfort. Their guide, Rashid, had made himself an expert on the architecture, customs, traditions and history of the Middle Ages and kept up a constant guide's chatter of both facts and anecdotes as they went from room to room and finally the dungeons which were evidently the most popular part for the tourists. Here, as in many other parts of the castle, there was an imitation of the wax models of Madame Tussauds. Every room in the castle had people dressed in the costumes of the era and in the dungeons, the wax models depicted the horrific death and maiming inflicted by the nightmare machines of torture which that age had developed with almost the same finesse as had their descendants in the 21st Century with weapons of mass destruction.

Hassan was following the progress of his guests as it was relayed to him by the closed circuit TV, when his phone rang; it was the deputy head of security who was in charge while Rashid was doing his tourist guide duties. He was speaking from one of the patrol boats. Hassan was told that a large private motorboat, owned by Prince Fahyed of Saudi Arabia was now inside the exclusion zone and the Prince had requested a most urgent meeting with Mr Hussein. 'I bet it's urgent,' Hassan smiled, 'now that he's got that madman slavering on his doorstep. Ask him which Prince Fahyed he is,' Hassan replied. There was a pause for a couple of minutes and then the information was passed, Prince Mahama Alhaji Fahyed. Hassan buzzed his PA who answered immediately. Hassan told him to get verification on the whereabouts, background and any other information he could on the Prince and contact him immediately the information was available. 'Please make sure that I have the exact stock state of our merchandise on the computer. Invite him to join me and don't forget to say how honoured I am with his visit. No one else is to leave his boat. The meeting will take place in the usual room. I will speak to him from here.'

*

The three divers on the inspection team went through a watertight door at the back of the aperture in the rock and then the whole world was plunged into total darkness as the floodlighting was switched off. Gunn switched on his torch and swam in the direction of the aperture. He slightly misjudged this and had to swim up the rock face and over the edge of aperture. He swam round the area which had been cut from the rock and his careful and tedious inspection revealed a waterproof switch which, when pressed, lit the area.

On the right of the watertight door was a bank of levers connected to pushrods which disappeared through seals in the metal wall at the back of the man-made cave. Three scooters were parked to one side and there was a heap of rubbery material on the opposite side of the cave. Gunn swam over to examine it; another mystery was solved as he unfolded an enormous rubber octopus. He pulled one of the levers and a bank of floodlights came on. He switched that off and by a process of trial and error found the bank, which provided illumination of Carteret's fishing boat. He swam across the huge cavern and down to the boat, which he inspected from bow to stern, but there was no sign of Claudine's father. He swam across the deck into the wheelhouse, but there was nothing there to help him. He brushed some sand off the chart table and a pair of dividers slid off the table and fell slowly to the floor of the wheelhouse. He bent down to retrieve them, which saved his life. The bolt from the compressed air gun hissed over his shoulder and the explosive head detonated as it struck the side of the wheelhouse.

There were two divers and there must have been some warning light or system that had alerted them when he switched on the lights. He went straight down inside the boat, through the saloon into the heads and heaved off the tanks from his back. He took a deep breath from his demand valve and then unscrewed the valve so that a steady stream of bubbles came from it. He swam back into the saloon and

167

behind the door as the first diver appeared, preceded by his compressed-air gun. The diver spotted the bubbles and swam forward slowly.

Gunn's knife sliced cleanly through his airline and continued in the same movement into his throat. He wrenched the gun from the diver's hands and swung towards the second diver, but a swirl of blood-tinged water showed that he had swum up to the wheelhouse again. With lungs bursting, Gunn returned to the heads and dragged the demand valve towards his mouth. He paused while he got his breathing under control and he studied the interior of the boat in the dim light filtering through the portholes from the floodlighting.

He slipped the harness of the tanks over his shoulders and armed with the compressed-air gun, swam cautiously towards the steps leading up to the wheelhouse. There was no sign of the other diver. Gunn swam back into the saloon and tried the door beside the heads. It opened towards him and led into the engine room. There had to be an exit from the engine room to the deck and sure enough, right at the stern was a set of steps to a hatch in the deckhead. He undid the securing clips. This had all only lasted three or four minutes and throughout that time, the bubbles from Gunn's demand valve had collected into an air pocket on the deckhead of the boat. As soon as he opened the engine room hatch, the bubbles would escape and immediately give away his position to the diver who was either waiting to deal with him as he appeared or had gone off for reinforcements.

Once again, he took a beep breath, switched off the valve and gently eased up the hatch. He put his head out and the bubbles of the other diver immediately identified his position. He was waiting below the starboard gun'le to one side of the door through which he had to emerge if he had gone out that way. He closed the hatch, slipped over the side of the boat and swam fast round the port side of the boat until he reached the bow. Here, he risked exhaling his breath slowly and opened the demand valve again. He checked the compressed-air gun and saw that the safety catch had been on 'fire' the whole time. He had only used harpoon guns before, but these weapons had been designed to hunt shark. The harpoon had been replaced by a steel bolt, which had an explosive charge in the tip which was detonated on impact.

Gunn swam slowly along the curve of the hull down the starboard side of the boat from the bow towards the wheelhouse. The other diver saw him and swung round as Gunn pulled the trigger. The bolt struck the diver in the centre of the chest and the man's body disintegrated in an expanding cloud of blood. The diver's harpoon gun fell to the seabed and Gunn removed a yellow plastic cylinder from what was left of the trunk of the body and found that it contained three more bolts. He let his harpoon gun fall to the seabed, retrieved the one which was still loaded and then swam towards the rectangular cave, collecting the spare tanks on the way which he placed beside the watertight door.

The door opened into a small compartment like an elevator and Gunn closed and sealed the door behind him after lifting in the two spare harnesses. The instructions for pumping out the water were written in English on the steel wall and he did as directed. Once the flooding compartment was empty, a green light told him that he could open the inner door. He held the compressed-air gun ready after spinning the wheel anti-clockwise, but there was no one on the other side; he was now in a decompression chamber. On the curved walls of the chamber were all the instructions and the decompression times for various depths and the time spent at those depths. All he had to do was punch all the information into a display unit and then press 'enter' and wait while the tedious process of decompression took place.

There was an amplified 'click' in the chamber. 'I'm sorry that you felt you were unable to use the front door as you could have joined your friends, the de Havillands, for lunch. I think that I can presume that you have disposed of two of my men and I suspect that I might be talking to the person who disposed of another of my men in Hamble and who came uninvited aboard my boat. Well, whoever you are, whilst I can't reverse the process of your decompression, I think that you will find that to do it with nothing else to breathe other than nitrogen dioxide will kill you as effectively as you have so effectively killed three of my men,' and the loudspeaker clicked off.

*

Simon Peters' phone buzzed; he pressed the button and answered, 'yes, Louise?'

'Simon, it's David Pettigrew from Cyphers and Codes on the internal line.'

'Thanks, put him through, please.'

'Your're through David, Simon's on the line.'

'Simon, David here; look, we're having very little joy with that telephone number you gave us. That number belongs to an animal rescue centre in Bexhill - which is on the south coast of Sussex near Hast....'

'Yes, alright David, I know where Bexhill is,' Simon laughed.

'Other than that, you could make that number into almost anything you want. Without any hint as to the key, a birth date or something like that, we really don't have a chance. I know that you were thinking that it might be a position measured in latitude and longitude, but again, if numbers have been added or subtracted, it could be anywhere.'

'David, come down to my office and see if I can shed any more light on the matter.'

'Thanks, on my way.' Three minutes later, he appeared in Simon's office. Louise was pinning a map to a piece of softboard. The map covered the Middle East and Southern Asia. Simon got up from his desk and came round to the small conference table where Louise had positioned the board and map.

'Coffee, gentlemen?'

'Yes please, Louise, and then come and join us; the more ideas and theories, the better. This is what we know,' Simon spoke to David Pettigrew as he stood, looking down at the map. 'There are ten, SS20 missiles on their way from Hong Kong to the Middle East in a ship which can travel submerged and which has unlimited range because of its nuclear propulsion. It seems that these missiles are destined for Iraq. The arms dealer is Hassan Hussein.....' Simon paused as David drew in his breath.

'I thought that Saddam and Hassan were sworn enemies apart from the fact that they come from different Muslim sects; one's a Kurd and a Shi'ite fundamentalist and the other's a member of the Ba'ath Party which makes him some sort of socialist/fascist. Saddam's security police - which is little more or less than the German Gestapo - have either killed or driven out of Iraq the leaders of the country's Shia Muslims who occupy the majority of the south part of the country. Then there's that business of the poison gas attacks on the Kurds instigated by Saddam; Hassan was supposed to have been one of the few survivors of that purge. Why would he sell weapons to Saddam?'

'Money?'

'No, doesn't sound right. Hassan's wealthier than even Adnan Kashoggi was at the peak of his arms dealing. He doesn't need the money,' David was almost talking to himself as he scanned the map. 'What's the range of these SS20s, Simon?'

'2,500 miles.'

'Got some dividers or a piece of string? That'll do,' as Simon offered him a piece of ribbon, which had bound an over-thick file. He searched for the scale on the map, then took one of the map pins, tied the ribbon to it and measured off the scale. He tied a knot in the ribbon at the point, which marked 2,500 miles and then buried the point of the pin in Baghdad. David reached into his jacket pocket and produced a pencil, placed the tip against the knot and drew an arc which swept across the Arabian Sea from the southern tip of India in the east to the port of Mombassa in Kenya at the western extremity of the arc. 'Could he fire one of these SS20 things from this boat of his?' David asked, looking at his handiwork.

'Impossible; without completely rebuilding the missile; the SS20 has to be fired either from the ground, using a launch gantry or from underground, using a silo.' Louise reappeared with the coffee and some biscuits, which she placed on Simon's desk. She carried the mugs over to the conference table and handed one to Simon and the other to David.

'So that means we're looking for dry land from which to launch within that arc, right,' David was muttering to himself as he held his mug in one hand and, with the pencil in the other, was putting crosses against national landmasses that lay within the arc.'

'What are the crosses for?' Louise asked.

'It's most unlikely that Hassan is stupid enough to fire his missiles from another country. Somewhere inside this arc, which covers thousands of square miles of the Arabian Sea, is an island which Hassan has acquired - just like Sardrière. It's possible that the telephone number will identify the location of that island, but we still need more information. Just take a look for yourselves at the myriad of possibilities. Start over here on the west of the arc; there must be something like two or three hundred islands in the Red Sea, dozens more along the coast of Southern Yemen and Oman and hundreds more on the east side of the arc off the coast of India - even the northern islands of the Maldives are just in range of Baghdad. What we'll do now is to use the large scale 1:250,000 MOD maps of the area and the Hydrographic charts to put the latitude and longitude of every island in that arc into the computer.'

'Thank you, David. I feel we might have made some progress. Please let me know if you have a sudden flash of inspiration or if the computer throws up anything.'

'Pleasure; I'll be in touch,' and David left the office.

'Any ideas, Louise?'

'It's dreadful how large the gaps are in my knowledge of the geography of this part of the world.'

'That's hardly surprising, as these countries change their names every time there's a coup. What are you so engrossed in?' Simon asked as he saw that Louise had her nose only inches from the map.

'Have you ever heard of the Lakshadweep Islands, Simon?'

171

'Can't say I have. Where are they?' and he came out from behind his desk and walked over to the map.

'Here,' and Louise placed a slim, neatly painted nail on a chain of minute islands which stretched for nearly 450 miles along the west coast of India.

'There must be hundreds of them,' Simon muttered. 'Why don't you pop along the corridor and have a word with your opposite number who works for Richard Preston. See if you can dig anything up about the Lakshadweep Islands.'

CHAPTER 13

The process of decompression after a dive below 60 feet allowed the oxygen absorbed by the blood, at greatly increased pressure, to escape as the pressure reduced. A pause at every 30 feet of ascent allowed this process to occur naturally, but, of course, meant that a diver had to have adequate surplus air to cater for the decompression halts. If a diver was brought straight to the surface from a depth of 60 feet or deeper, bubbles of air formed in the blood, collecting in the joints which were then locked solid - hence the term 'bends'.

The super-aerated blood also did a very efficient job of scrambling the diver's brains. The only cure, if a diver had to be rushed to the surface, was to place the person in a decompression chamber where the pressure at the depth the diver had been working could be restored and then gradually reduced, allowing the oxygen and nitrogen to escape from the blood. Gunn knew that to pressurize the chamber with Nitrogen Dioxide would suffocate him as effectively as rapid decompression would have turned him into a vegetable.

He had identified the two TV cameras which had allowed Hassan to see him enter the decompression chamber. Both of the cameras were fixed and did not appear to have wide-angle lenses, so various parts of the chamber would be invisible to whomever was watching him on the two TV screens. The two spare harnesses and tanks were on the steel floor of the chamber, half under one of the four couches which had been provided for the divers to rest during the tedious decompression process. Using his foot, he pushed them further under the couch. He was already finding it difficult to breathe, so to imitate the onset of asphyxiation was not difficult and he sank to the floor clasping his throat. Once on the floor and with his head under the couch, he pulled the mouthpiece of one of the spare harnesses towards him and turned the valve anti-clockwise; he was rewarded with clean compressed air and remained motionless to wait out the forty minutes which it would take to decompress.

Gunn guessed that at least two men would be sent to remove his body and anything which he did in the chamber would be monitored by the cameras. He saw little point in smashing or covering the lenses because if they thought he was dead and saw his body on the floor, it would be to his advantage. Eventually, after what seemed like hours, but which his watch told him was only 45 minutes, he saw the locking wheel rotate. He took one last breath of the compressed air and then pushed the mouthpiece under the couch.

The circular door swung open and two men came into the chamber and carried him out where he was unceremoniously dumped on the concrete floor. There was a third man who went into the chamber and reappeared with the compressed-air gun and quiver of bolts which were thoughtlessly, but conveniently, placed on the ground beside Gunn. The third man went back into the chamber and this time he would inevitably find the extra tanks.

Time had run out. Gunn sat up, grabbed the gun and fired it at point-blank range at the nearest man and at the same time launched himself towards the chamber, ramming his diving knife up to the hilt under the second man's breastbone. As Gunn reached the circular door of the decompression chamber, the third man turned, holding one of the spare sets with a puzzled expression on his face. John slammed the door and spun the wheel. The first two men had been unarmed and had been caught totally by surprise. The compressed-air bolt had blown the man apart and the second man had died before he hit the ground. The third man was looking at one of the cameras and the soundless movement of his mouth meant that he was explaining to the men monitoring the chamber what had happened.

Gunn inserted another bolt into the gun from the small yellow quiver. He spun the wheel on the chamber door and opened it. The man inside swung towards him reaching for an automatic which he'd placed on the couch. Gunn quickly closed the door on the indescribly bloody mess as the exploding head of the bolt spread the man all over the inside of the chamber.

There was a bank of three wide-doored lifts and, apparently, no other means of reaching or leaving the place. Gunn pressed the button and the doors on the right-hand lift opened immediately as it had been waiting on that floor. The indicator panel inside the lift told him that he was on the 12th floor and that there was a total of 15 floors. He pressed the button opposite 15; the doors closed and the lift descended.

The doors opened onto what appeared to be a loading area. There were empty pallets, fork-lift trucks and at the far side was a short ramp which led to two, very thick steel watertight doors. Gunn assumed that the doors led into the connecting tunnel which he had seen by the docking area in the submarine cavern. He turned as he heard noises from the centre lift. He stepped back and pressed the button for the 11th floor. His lift started to move just as the door of the centre one slid open and eight men, armed with sub-machine guns, burst out of it. Two of the men turned to the left and fired immediately, sending a couple of bullets ricochetting into his lift before the doors had closed.

Gunn assumed that the men would wait to see at which floor his lift had stopped before they all rushed back into their lift and gave chase. His lift stopped at the 11th floor; he waited for ten seconds to let them all get into the lift on the 15th floor and then he pressed the button for the 7th floor. Just before the lift stopped, he pressed the button which indicated the ground floor; as soon as he got out, the doors closed and the lift went up.

He was in an underground warehouse, which was crammed from floor to ceiling with every conceivable form of explosive. By the lifts were pegs on which hung overalls and soft-soled overboots. There was a large red box with English and Arabic demanding that cigarettes, lighters and matches must be left in the box. The storing and distribution of the stock was state of the art store-keeping technology. Gunn had been wrong in thinking that the stores were loaded into the lifts to be taken down to the 15th floor. There appeared to be at least three shafts, which connected all the warehouse floors with the loading bay and down through these ran a hoist. This hoist was automatically fed by robot machines which went to each pallet of stores required and placed it on the hoist.

The entire system would be computer driven and every time an item was removed the computer would immediately register the need to replace the stock. A stock check would take a matter of milli-seconds for the computer to register what was being held. Gunn reckoned that there must be somewhere in the region of 1,000 tons of explosive stored on the 7th floor. To his right was a steel door with a sign above it announcing that detonators, fuses and cordtex had to be stored in that area only.

Gunn opened the door and walked past the wooden shelving until he found the fulminate time pencils. He removed a handful of these and walked back into the main warehouse. It only took a matter of seconds to find where the Semtex was stored. Gunn used his diver's knife to open the 500 gramme packages and then insert the time pencils. He replaced each package, well hidden amongst unopened packages and returned to the lifts. There was still no sign of Hassan's men who would now be searching every floor to find him. The time pencils only gave him an hour to find Claudine - if she was still alive - and to get the de Havillands out of the castle.

Peter de Havilland had told him that there would be no tourists. All three lifts would be watched and the moment he pressed the button he would announce which floor he had been on. Gunn walked over to the hoist shaft; it disappeared into the distance both up and down. Gunn stripped off the wet suit, which was now clammy and constricting and dropped it down the hoist shaft. At the side of the hoist shaft was a steel maintenance ladder. Now dressed only in his swimming trunks, Gunn stepped out onto the ladder and started to climb.

Hassan's men had reached the 6th floor and Gunn very nearly gave himself away as his head appeared above the floor. Two of the lifts had been stopped and the search team were taking each floor in turn. The original eight or nine, which he had quickly counted on the 15th floor had increased to twenty or more. There was a man standing only a few feet from Gunn looking down one of the many aisles in the racked stores. The search was being undertaken systematically; first sealing all the avenues of escape and then sending in a search group to winkle him out of his hiding place. Gunn's bare feet made no sound on the metal rungs of the ladder as he quietly climbed up and disappeared up to the 5th floor.

This warehouse was stacked with crate after crate of small arms, but it would have taken far too long to try and break open one of the wooden crates to arm himself with something more substantial than his diving knife. The 4th floor was ammunition; every calibre imaginable according to the black-stencilled markings on the boxes. On the third floor were mines and then the hoist shaft stopped. Beside the lifts were stairs leading to the second floor, but none leading down to the fourth floor. Gunn went up the stairs and on the second floor there was a small lobby. He opened the door a fraction and looked in; these were the offices from which Hassan's arms empire appeared to be run. Gunn shut the door and went up the stairs. The first floor was the accommodation level.

The whole atmosphere was similar to a five star hotel and Gunn could see a very well appointed reception area with corridors leading off it. There was a reception desk, but fortunately no receptionist behind it. He went through the fire door from the stairwell and over to the reception desk. The key rack indicated that there were fifty rooms, which would take an age to check. Would Claudine have been brought here? Always presuming that she hadn't been dumped over the side of the boat on the return journey from Guernsey. If one or two rooms had been set aside for uninvited guests, where would they be? Close to the reception area or elsewhere? Gunn walked quietly behind the reception desk on the thick carpet and over to the door into the reception office, which was ajar.

The absence of the receptionist was explained. Her receptionist duties seemed to include the provision of sex for certainly one occupant of the accommodation floor who was seated on her swivel typing chair with his trousers and pants round his ankles. That is all Gunn could see of him because the rest was hidden by the almost naked receptionist who had straddled him and whose clothes were scattered across the desk and floor. On the belt of the trousers round the man's ankles was a holster with a pistol butt sticking out of it and on the desk, draped in the girl's thong was an Italian Franchi automatic shotgun. Gunn crawled into the office and removed the automatic from the holster first, to the accompaniment of gasps and moans of sexual ecstasy above him. Backing out slowly, he reached up and removed the auto-pump-action gun, which came complete with the receptionist's thong. Once back through the door, he put his hand round and removed the key and then locked the fornicating couple into the office.

'Sad about the thong,' Gunn muttered, 'but then I don't suppose she'll miss it for the next ten minutes or so.'

It seemed that in addition to their current activity, it was probably a reasonable guess that the man was the guard for visitors undergoing a forced stay in Hassan's castle. This raised Gunn's hopes. There were four rooms, numbered one to four, all in view of the reception desk. All four keys were of the electronic card type and were hanging on the keyboard. Gunn removed them all and started at one. He pushed the card into the slot, turned the handle and went in, ducking only just in time to avoid a haymaking punch that would have felled him for a week. The man who had thrown the punch was completely off balance and Gunn pushed him back into the room. He was of medium height and had a thick beard.

'Cartaret?'

'Who the hell are you?'

'This isn't the time or place for introductions, but my name's John Gunn and we've got less than,' and he glanced at his watch, '45 minutes before this whole place is blown sky high. First I've got to find Claudine. Do you know how to use one of these?' and John Gunn held out the shot gun.

'Yes, I can use one of those. Sorry about the punch, but I heard a lot of commotion going on and I thought that I might be able to get away. Are you the cause of the commotion?'

'I expect so, come on,' Gunn urged the rather bewildered fisherman to leave the room, which had been his prison since the wrecking of his boat. He tried the card in room two, but that was empty and so was three. Room four resulted in a tearful reunion of

177

father and daughter, which Gunn had to break up. 'Come on both of you, we're a little short of time,' and he led them to the right of the reception area where he'd seen some glass swing doors leading into a corridor. As they went past the reception desk, there was furious hammering on the office door. 'I think the young lady wants her thong' but Gunn's remark was lost on Claudine and her father. At the end of the corridor were two sets of escalators; one going down and the other coming up. They all stepped on the down escalator which appeared to take them down about thirty or forty feet to another corridor which led under the 'moat' to the harbour.

Peter de Havilland had told Gunn that there were three fast patrol boats. Two of them were in the harbour in addition to Hassan's boat and another large motor boat, which was flying a red Ensign at the stern. The only people in the harbour were on this large motorboat which identified itself as registered in St Peter Port. 'Go aboard the ketch and stay there until I get back or Peter de Havilland arrives and then leave with him. Don't touch that boat with the red Ensign, but if you get the chance to go aboard the others and immobilise them, it would be a great help. Don't hesitate to use that,' and he pointed at the pump-action gun.

'Where are you going?' Claudine asked.

'To try and find Peter, Tricia and Celia who are somewhere in there,' and he ran back up the corridor to the castle.

*

The 747 touched down at Dubai and once it had come to a halt in front of the gleaming, white marble terminal, the passengers were ferried the 100 yards from the aircraft to the air-conditioned comfort of the building in the airport's squat, wide bodied buses. Inside the terminal, all the passengers headed for the duty free shops which were not only the cheapest in the world, but were the only ones that were genuinely duty free.

All the passengers that is, except one; Volkonoff went into the transit area and went to the Iraqi Airways desk; it was easy to identify because it was being shunned by all the other people in the terminal. There was a connecting flight to Baghdad leaving in less than half an hour, which was almost empty, provided he only had hand baggage. He confirmed that he only had hand baggage as the suitcase, which would eventually be off-loaded from the 747 was of little further use to him. He was ticketed and told to go to Gate 8 in the departure lounge. In the departure lounge, he stopped at one of the telephones and put through a call to Baghdad after which he joined the passengers boarding the bus out to the Iraqi Airways 727.

It was only an hour and a half's flight to Baghdad where he arrived just before 10.30 at night. The five hour time difference between Dubai and Hong Kong was only a couple of hours less than the time it took to fly from one to the other and so Volkonoff arrived in Dubai only two hours local time after he had taken off from Hong Kong. The immediate connection to Baghdad made for a reasonable arrival time at the airport. He was met at the door of the aircraft and taken straight to a car. The car belonged to Saddam Hussein's security police and it was impossible to see through the windows into the interior of the car.

The car drove into Baghdad and directly to the Presidential Palace where it entered by a discreet side access and went round to the back of the building and into a garage. The door closed behind the car and then the floor of the garage sank, taking the car down some thirty feet to an underground car park. There were no handles on the inside of the doors and Volkonoff waited until his door was opened and he was escorted across to a row of four lifts. One of these lifts was for the personal use of the President and his bodyguard only. He was shown into the lift next to it and the lift descended 100 feet to the President's command bunker.

Volkonoff was taken to a comfortable lounge where there was coffee and soft drinks laid out on a side table. He was told that the President was meeting with his Revolutionary Command Council, but should be free shortly. Volkonoff was just pouring coffee from the percolator into a cup when his escort returned to say that the President wished to see him immediately. He was led along the corridor to a set of doors with a glowing red light above them. His escort pressed a bell push and the door was opened by an armed soldier. Volkonoff's escort indicated that he was to enter and as soon as he was in the room, he recognised a number of the faces around the table.

All Saddam Hussein's top military commanders were present at this meeting of the Revolutionary Command Council and he, Volkonoff, was the focus of their attention. He was not offered a seat. The President turned to Volkonoff; each of them was aware of the other's reputation. Volkonoff knew that Saddam was reputed to have executed hundreds of his enemies personally and was responsible for the slaughter of tens of thousands of dissident Kurds by shooting, poison gas and napalm. He had heard that two of his Council who had foolishly disagreed with Saddam during the the first Gulf War had been disposed of immediately; one in a bath of acid while Saddam watched the body dissolve and the other was shot dead at the conference table. Truth or rumour, Volkonoff was well aware that he was now standing in the proverbial pit of vipers.

'I am informed that the news is good; is that correct?'

'It is, your Excellency.'

'When can we expect delivery?'

'Within two weeks.'

'Where's Hassan?'

'At his castle off the coast of Britain.'

'I want him killed.'

'Very well, your Excellency.'

'You will be paid in gold - Kuwaiti gold,' this remark was greeted with laughter around the table, 'when the missiles are delivered and Hassan is dead.' That was the end of the audience and Volkonoff was shown out of the room.

*

Leading Seaman Murphy's assessment of the course which Al Samak would take had been uncannily accurate. The one factor, which had not been given to the young sonar operator was an accurate assessment of the ship's surface or submerged speed. Both of these had been assessed very much lower than the ship's actual performance. Whilst the 120,000 shaft- horsepower reactor gave the ship a surface speed of between 25 and 30 knots, this could be increased to 35 knots when it was submerged due to the most ingenious transformation of the ship's superstructure to streamline its profile. There was very little deck clutter once the derricks had been stowed and as the ship submerged, a steel plate the full width of the ship's beam and lying flush with the deck in the surface mode, rose under the power of large hydraulic rams at its aft edge.

The plate was hinged to the deck at the for'ard edge and as its aft end rose like a door in the horizontal plane, so its trailing edge extended in exactly the same manner as the flaps on a large aircraft. The trailing edge locked into the top of the bridge superstructure and then side, triangular shaped plates rose out of their housing in the deck to complete the streamlining of the vessel. Once this transformation was complete, which included the deployment of diving and stabilizing planes from the ship's hull, Al Samak looked like a submarine with a wide, aft-mounted sail.

There were other factors of which both Eastern and Western intelligence agencies were unaware which was a serious error in their intelligence evaluation process. In the period between the acquisition of Al Samak and its mission to Hong Kong, it had spent six months in the dry dock prepared for it on the remote island at the northern extremity of the Lakshadweep Islands.

The island had been bought by Hassan Hussein in 1985 from the Indian Government for $5 million and converted into his main trading base for the supply of arms worldwide. The acquisition of his two islands, one in the Arabian Sea and the other in the Channel Islands, enabled Hassan Hussein to supply the areas of maximum demand for weapons and munitions; Sardrière dealt with South America, West Africa and the terrorist factions operating in Europe, while Al Samak- as the island was named - dealt with the Middle East, North Africa, Sub-Sahara, East, Central and South Africa and South-East Asia.

Whilst in its dry dock, the ship had been equipped with submarine-launched cruise missiles, four torpedo tubes - two either side - to defend itself against over-inquisitive warships of national navies, the very latest captor mines and an active and passive sonar capability that was as sophisticated as those in use by the NATO and Russian Navies.

Captain Axel Steinbaum was in the centre of the control room in the submerged cargo ship which bore the same name as its island home - Al Samak. Beside him, stood Commander Dieter Schwendler and both men were bent over a chart covering the Western Pacific and the South China Sea; a scene very similar to that on the USS Los Angeles some hours earlier. It was nearly 1800 hours and Al Samak had been travelling at maximum speed for nearly 12 hours which placed the submerged cargo vessel just to the south of the north-east tip of the Philippines. The remainder of the crew were all of middle-east ehnic origin; either Steinbaum or Schwendler were always on duty.

Unterseebot Kapitan Axel Steinbaum and his navigating officer, Schwendler, had been dismissed from the Deutsche Bundesmarine for hazarding their Type 209 diesel-powered patrol submarine. Both officers came from the same village of Forstkirchdorf, deep in the Bavarian Tirol and well known for its neo-Nazi sympathizers and folklore. The German federal police had been called in on numerous occasions to break up demonstrations in the village where students from Munich University had clashed with skin-headed supporters of the neo-Nazi Movement during celebrations of anniversaries of key events of the Third Reich.

The Type 209 submarine had been supplied to the Argentinean Navy and shortly after the Falklands War, there had been a scandal in the Navy Department of the West German Ministry of Defence when the West German Intelligence Service narrowed down, to three or four men, a leak of classified NATO Naval documents on the British Naval deployment in the South Atlantic. Both Steinbaum and Schwendler had been among the suspects. Both men were then appointed to the same 'unterseebot' which was one of three designated by the Bundesmarine to the Standing NATO Naval Task Force.

The West German Intelligence Service had maintained its interest and surveillance of all the suspects and when two of them were appointed within weeks of each other to not only the same Fleet Command, but the same submarine, this interest was intensified and widened to identify the person or persons responsible for the appointment of the two officers. As the two men joined their new submarine, so had another young officer who had been very carefully briefed by the Geheimdeinst - German Secret Service. It had been this young officer who had successfully engineered the hazarding of the Type 209 - it had run aground on a well known shoal to the east side of the approach to Kiel Fjord doing no damage to submarine or crew.

The whole intelligence operation had succeeded in uncovering a large, influential and widely dispersed Nazi cell in the Bundesmarine, Bundeswehr and Luftwaffe. Some of the men disappeared completely, others were dismissed from the Services on contrived charges - Steinbaum and Schwendler - and others turned 'Staatzeugnis' or state evidence, giving a whole list of names involved in the conspiracy to infiltrate the armed services. Hassan Hussein had been asked to supply certain items of equipment to the neo-Nazi conspiracy and the dismissal of Steinbaum and Schwendler provided him with the captain and first officer for the boat, which he had been watching since the day its keel had been laid.

Al Samak's radio officer approached the Captain and handed him a signal. 'Buoyant cable antenna has been stowed again, Sir.'

'Thank you, Assad.' Steinbaum read the signal and then handed it back to the radio officer. He spoke to his first officer. 'That's from base confirming that the Russians are looking for us as well.' He lowered his voice so that the remainder of the duty watch was unable to hear him. 'Their orders will be to destroy us. They cannot allow this cargo to remain in the hands of Hassan. They'll put their nuclear hunter-killers onto us, so, Dieter my friend, we've got to outwit them. Now, bearing in mind that our maximum depth is 500 feet, take yourself back to those boring navigation classes at the Bundesmarine Academy in Kiel and tell me where we'll find the largest differential in sea temperature and salinity. I'll be back in a couple of minutes,' and Steinbaum crossed the control room to the sonar station to confirm that both bow and towed array sonar were operative.

They were; he smiled at the operator and patted him on the back and then went to his weapons and electrical officer where he asked for a functions test of both weapon systems. All the lights showed green. All passive measures were operative, but not necessarily operating at their most effective because of the speed of the ship. Steinbaum returned to the chart table. Open on the chart was a thick folder of graphs showing sea temperature plotted against depth. The folder was opened at the meridians, which ran north/south through the Philippines and Moluccan Islands between the longitudes of 120°and 130°East.

Schwendler had the sharp point of his pencil at a point on one of the graphs where the trace suddenly dipped in temperature as it reached the thermocline - a point where the sea temperature rapidly decreased until it eventually stabilised to a slow decrease towards the seabed.

'This is the layer in which we need to stay, Herr Kapitan,' and he was indicating the sea depth between 200 and 800 feet, where the temperature and salinity varied so rapidly that sound waves would be distorted and refracted.

'Excellent, Dieter; we'll use the thermocline and our speed to outwit the hunter and our weapons to turn hunter into hunted. Join me in my cabin; I picked up some excellent Black Label whiskey in Hong Kong,' and the two Germans left the control room and went below to the captain's cabin.

*

Commander George Gresham pressed the button on the intercom in his cabin for the radio officer.

'Yes Sir.'

'Anything on our 1800 hours schedule, Hal?'

'Yes Sir, I'll bring it straight down to your cabin.'

'No, that's OK. I'm on my way up. I'll see you in the control room.'

'Right Sir,' and the imtercom clicked off. George Gresham checked himself in the mirror and ran a brush through his short haircut before going to the control room. He was met by his radio officer as he reached it. 'Just on my way to disturb you, Sir, when you rang.'

'That's the problem with this life. Not only do all the machines in this boat get programmed, but so do our bodies. Any change to our radio schedules?'

'Yes Sir; we have to stream the antenna every hour on the half hour for only two more hours and then revert to once every four.'

'Right, let's see what's happening,' and he took the signal from the radio officer. The signal told him that the Russian Navy had deployed a task force to deal with the missile carrying cargo ship, in addition to other ships and submarines deployed from the Russian Southern Fleet. The task force was led by the aircraft carrier Novorossiysk and consisted of six other surface ships; Slava, an anti-submarine cruiser, two destroyers named after Russian Admirals - Zakharov and Kulakov, the nuclear-powered cruiser, Frunze and two missile frigates, Silnyy and Menzhinsky. There were also two additional Sierra class attack submarines on their way - from where was not disclosed in the signal - to join the task force.

The Southern Fleet was to take on the task of closing all routes to the west through the Straits of Malacca and the Selat Sunda and the task force would close any route west of Java through the Arafura and Timor Sea. The signal said that Russia was most grateful for the help provided by the US Navy, but the loss of the missiles was a serious miscalculation by Russia and it must accept the responsibility of recovering them. In order to give the Russian Navy an uncluttered task, the US Navy had been asked to withdraw from the search area for Al Samak so that no possible error could be made by any of the Russian ships and submarines now engaged in the hunt for the cargo vessel.

That was the summary of the Russian request, then came his orders. USS Los Angeles was to rejoin the Seventh Fleet and signal ETA. George Gresham sighed; so that was that. He turned to his navigating officer and gave him the change of orders and went back to his cabin.

CHAPTER 14

Hassan Hussein turned away from the TV screen monitoring the decompression chamber, dismissing the occupant from his mind as he pressed the button to indicate that his visitor from Saudi Arabia was to be shown into the guest interview room. The room was comfortable and the half-dozen CCTV cameras could study his visitor from every angle while Hassan conducted the interview from behind a bank of TV screens in his control room. He saw Prince Fahyed enter the room and sit in the chair indicated by his escort.

'Good morning, your Highness; you are a welcome guest in my house. How can I be of service?' The computer check which had been run on Prince Fahyed by Hassan's information system had given him a clean bill of health confirming that his present location was in the UK where he was acting as an envoy of the Saudi Arabian Royal Family.

'Salaam Allekum, Hassan Hussein; my thanks for receiving me in your home.' The Muslim formalities of greeting now over, coffee was served by a steward and the matter of business could be discussed. 'You will, of course, be well ahead of the news of what seems to be the inevitable invasion of Iraq by coalition forces. My country has received assurances of support from the United States of America and the US and British Navies are in the Gulf. My father has asked me to visit you to find out where your sympathies lie and to request respectfully that you consider his plea to you not to provide any new arms or spares for existing military equipment in Iraq.'

'Thank you, your Highness, for coming straight to the point. I'm sure that both of us are busy men and much of my time is wasted with guests who prevaricate before revealing the reason for their visit. You have my assurance that not one bullet will be sold to Saddam Hussein. Now, will you stay and have lunch here? I regret that I cannot join you, but I have three English guests who have been visiting my castle whom you might care to join.'

'Thank you, that is more than generous. I would like to do that.'

Hassan gave orders to his stewards and the Prince was escorted from the interview room to a small lounge with long arched windows with stone mullions and leaded lights overlooking the sparkling deep blue of the sea to the south of Sardrière. The room was richly

185

furnished in the Regency style and the four occupants turned as he was shown into the room. Alan Paxton was well aware of the identity of the de Havillands and Celia Harris and assumed that the yachting character must be one of Hassan's men, but his arrival took them all completely by surprise. Hassan's steward made the introductions and the conversation proceeded with small talk about the visit to the castle.

'You've enjoyed your visit, Mr de Havilland?'

'Very much indeed, your Highness. Is this your first visit to the castle?'

'It is, Mr de Havilland. I understand that you are the Chairman and Managing Director of de Havilland Boats?'

'Yes, that's correct, Sir. Any chance of my company getting an order from you or a member of your Family?' Peter asked with a smile.

'That's always a possibility, Mr de Havilland; do you have a card?'

'No, I'm afraid I don't...not on me, that is...er'

'Not to worry; perhaps you could write your phone number on the back of this one,' and the Prince produced a gold embossed card. 'Don't use that official number, use this one,' and he produced a slim gold biro from his richly embroidered bernous and wrote on the card, "I'm JG's controller" and handed it to Peter de Havilland. Peter didn't hesitate, showing no reaction to what was written on the card and wrote his telephone number on the card.

'There, that's my business and private number.' Hassan had been watching this exchange closely on the TV monitors, grasping for the joystick to zoom the lens of the camera which he had pointed at the card as it exchanged hands. It was all done perfectly naturally and the lens finally picked up the telephone numbers on the reverse side of the card. His attention was suddenly distracted by the monitor of the decompression chamber. He reached over and turned up the volume.

'....found these under the couch, he's just killed the other two and locked me in this chamber.' Hassan watched in disbelief as the circular door swung open and then the screen went dark red as it was sprayed with the blood of the disintegrating body. He reached for the alarm which sounded on the first and second floors below ground level and in the office of the security building by the harbour. Captain Rashid was still with the visitors and his deputy appeared on the screen.

'Get everyone available to search for that man who has now escaped from the decompression chamber. I want him killed.'

186

'Yes sir,' and the screen went blank as the deputy security officer disappeared to carry out his orders. Hassan reached for another button and pressed it. Down in the lounge, Captain Rashid's conversation with Celia was interrupted by the bleeper attached to his belt.

'Excuse me, Mrs Harris,' and he walked over to a phone and rang Hassan's control room. He was told to report to the control room immediately. Rashid made his apologies and left the room. He reached the control room less than 30 seconds later where his deformed employer was seething with rage.

'Take charge of the search for this man who has succeeded in getting through all your security measures. Your deputy is over there at the moment. I want this intruder killed without any further delay.'

'The Prince and the de Havillands, Sir?'

'This man had to come with either one or the other so they can all be killed as well. Make it look like an accident, but that's all of secondary importance. Get that man, whoever he is!' Rashid retreated hastily from the room as Hassan's voice rose to a shriek. As soon as the door shut behind him, the gnarled and twisted hand tapped out another number. The phone was answered. 'Be ready to leave in ten minutes!' and the phone was slammed back onto its cradle. Another buzzer sounded in Hassan's control room and the guard from reception on the accommodation floor appeared on the TV screen. 'Yes, what is it?'

'The two prisoners have been released, Sir, and my weapons have been taken.'

'How did he manage that, you imbecile?'

'I had no warning and was caught by surprise, Sir,' which was absolutely true, but not a full account of why he'd been caught by surprise.

'How long has this man been on the loose among the munitions?'

'I've no...' but he was pushed aside by Rashid who was now down in the accommodation area.

'From what I can gather, Sir, from the time you saw him on the 12th floor by the decompression chamber until now is some thirty minutes. No one I've spoken to has any idea either where he is now or where he's been in those thirty minutes. If he did stop on the seventh floor, then Sardrière has only minutes left to exist.'

'If nothing has been found in the next ten minutes, sound the alarm to evacuate the island.'

'Very good, Sir.' Captain Rashid switched off the camera, turned and his mouth opened to give instructions, but closed again as he faced the automatic pointed at his midriff.

'Lie down on the floor...face down,' he hesitated and the shot from the automatic ripped through his immaculate blazer at waist level. He lay face down. Gunn removed the pistol from a shoulder holster. 'Right, both of you get up,' and when Rashid was on his feet again, he saw the guard struggling to his feet. 'In there...both of you,' Gunn slammed the door and locked it again.

Of the receptionist there was no sign and this time Gunn took the key and threw it through one of the open doors of the bedrooms opposite the reception desk. Still mistrusting the lifts, he went to the stairs and ran up them until faced with a large door. The door was perfectly balanced and opened easily into the dungeons of the castle. The other side of the door was stone faced and matched perfectly the surrounding wall so that when the door shut it was impossible to see it. There was no handle on the dungeon side, but no doubt some mechanism or handle released it when required, Gunn guessed, as he made for the narrow winding stairs which appeared to lead out of the dungeons.

He found himself in the banqueting hall and then pulled back into the archway as a robed Arab figure appeared on the balcony above him. He looked at his watch for perhaps the twentieth time; 23 minutes to go and then he heard Tricia's laugh. He looked round the arch and saw his three friends and the Arab descending the stairs. He walked out into the open holding the gun on the magnificently dressed Arab, who turned as soon as he moved. 'John, for heaven's sake point that in another direction. You know I'm terrified of the things.'

'Alan!' Gunn exclaimed. 'Never recognised you in your fancy dress.'

'Thank God, you're safe, John!' That was Tricia and before there were any more greetings and expressions of gratitude at finding each other all in one piece, Gunn interrupted.

'We're on borrowed time; which is the quickest way out of here to the harbour?'

'This way!' and Alan strode towards the main door followed by the four others.

'Claudine?' Celia asked as she ran to keep up with the men.

'Alive and on your boat, I hope...with her father. Quick through here,' and Gunn pushed them round the side of the great door as a group of four guards appeared on the balcony and two bullets thumped into the four inch thick oak door. The golf buggies were parked outside on the other side of the drawbridge and as they stepped onto it, Gunn felt the movement of the bridge under his feet. He grabbed Celia and carried her to the end of the bridge, which was now a couple of feet off the ground and lowered her, jumping down afterwards. Alan and Peter had started up two of the buggies and they set off down the path to the harbour. Some wide shots followed them and then stopped.

'Thank heavens for that,' gasped Tricia.

'Sorry, it's not over yet by a long way. They're taking the underground route to the harbour, so keep your foot down Peter.' The buggies swung round the final curve onto the harbour and raced for Osprey. As they jumped out, Gunn was about to suggest that the women went on the fast motorboat and he and Peter would bring up the rear with Osprey. Tricia was not going to be separated from Peter and Celia was not leaving her friend. The charter crew on the motorboat had no idea what was happening, but picked up the sense of urgency and both powerful diesels roared into life as the moorings were pulled aboard.

Gunn rushed into Osprey's wheelhouse, having seen no sign of the Carterets. Claudine's father lay on the floor of the wheelhouse and Gunn bent down to feel the pulse at his neck and then gently turned him over. There was a dark stain on the carpet. Carteret's eyes opened and focused on Gunn.

'They've got Claudine,' he managed to whisper with difficulty.

'Who's got her?'

'Two men took me by surprise....shot me, took her,' and then the eyes closed again. Gunn pulled the sweatshirt up as gently as he could. The bullet had gone into the left shoulder; Carteret would survive if the bleeding was stopped and he was taken to hospital quickly. Gunn picked him up and carried him off the ketch and over to the motorboat. Alan helped him get Carteret into the saloon.

'Shoulder wound, Alan; stop the bleeding and I'll be with you in a second.'

'Right.' Gunn rushed back to Osprey.

'Get the hell out of here, Peter. I'll follow with Alan. In about 11 minutes there'll be an almighty explosion which could well smash the glass in this boat. Open as many scuttles and portholes as possible. Now get going,' and Gunn threw the mooring lines aboard as shouts could be heard from the underground access to the harbour.

*

Hassan Hussein walked from his control room in Sardrière Castle to the upper courtyard where the whine of the twin turbines of his

189

helicopter drowned all other form of communication except hand signals. His pilot and co-pilot were both doing the final pre-lift off checks and the Carteret girl was bound and handcuffed to the tubular frame of the rear bench seat. Beside her was Rashid with an Armalite carbine. As soon as he was spotted by the co-pilot, the latter jumped from the helicopter and opened the door to the middle row of seats; there were just two and these were identical in shape and comfort to those in first class compartments of passenger aircraft.

As soon as Hassan was strapped in, the power was increased and the helicopter rose above the surrounding turrets. Hassan was wearing his mask over which he placed the earphones and boom mike handed to him by the co-pilot. The pilot turned the machine to starboard and dipped the nose to gain speed and put as much distance as possible between the castle and the helicopter as he could. The microphone crackled as Hassan pressed the intercom switch. 'Pilot! Rashid!' the synthesized voice ordered, 'I want that man on the jetty by the motorboat killed.' The pilot pushed the collective stick forward and glanced over his shoulder quickly as Rashid slid back the rear door and flicked back the cocking handle of the Armalite.

*

Above the noise of the boats' diesels and the shouting, Gunn heard the unmistakable beat of a helicopter's rotor blades. The machine rose up above the turrets of the castle, the nose dipped and then it dived for the harbour. Gunn started to run back towards the castle in what he knew would be a forlorn attempt to find Claudine. The beat of the helicopter blades rose to a crescendo as it dived towards him, cutting him off from the shelter of the tunnel under the moat. In despair, Gunn saw Hassan's guards pour out of the tunnel entrance; he stopped and turned. The side door of the helicopter was open and he saw the barrel of some weapon pointing out of it. He raised the 9mm automatic which he'd taken from the guard and held it at arms' length. The helicopter was diving straight at him..500...400...300...200...100 yards and Gunn emptied the magazine.

*

'Low and to port of the boat,' thought the pilot, 'to give him a reasonably long burst.' The helicopter was now at maximum speed in a shallow dive pointing at the man who was now running towards the tunnel entrance to the castle. The pilot saw the man's hands come up at full stretch holding the automatic. He smiled; the chance of one in a thousand bullets hitting the chopper was negligible, he reckoned, but then he'd qualified as a pilot some years after the war in Viet

190

Nam was finished, had never flown a combat mission in his life and wasn't a student of military history. It was the first bullet which killed him; he was dead before the second and third struck him, but the involuntary straightening of his right leg and his hand falling from the cyclic stick, hurled the chopper onto its right side, jettisoning Rashid straight through the open door. The co-pilot grasped the cyclic stick on his side and rammed his left foot onto the rudder pedal, just succeeding in stabilising the machine a matter of feet above the waves. He dragged the helicopter back into the air and kept the nose pointing south towards France.

Hassan leant forward, turned the buckle at the pilot's waist, cleared away the safety straps and then pulled the man back over the seat and pushed him out of the open rear door which he then closed.

*

Gunn ran to the motorboat and jumped aboard. The stern of the boat dipped as the large propellers bit into the water and the powerful boat swung away from the stone jetty. Gunn told Alan to get his crew to open all the scuttles that could be opened and be prepared to get on the floor when told to. Osprey was already through the harbour entrance and the motorboat heeled steeply in a sharp turn as its powerful engines drove it at maximum speed in the same direction. As the helicopter had banked steeply, momentarily out of control, throwing out the guard, Gunn had caught a glimpse of blonde hair; Hassan had taken Claudine.

*

'I'll see Major Petrovsky now, please.'

'Very good, Sir.' There was a pause and then the doors opened and the Major entered the President's office. It was just after seven in the evening and the shadows cast by the trees in the formal Kremlin gardens were beginning to lengthen. The Russian President turned from the window as he heard the door close.

'Come and sit here, Major Petrovsky,' and the President indicated some comfortable chairs to one side of the large desk. When they were seated, the President leant forward to the low coffee table and poured two cups of coffee; his, he took without milk or sugar. 'We're in a spot of trouble.'

'More trouble, Sir?'

'More trouble, Major. I had badly underestimated the resourcefulness of Rokossovsky and the brutal ruthlessness of Volkonoff. The former is inoperative at the moment while he's aboard that ship, if your information is accurate..'

191

'I assure...'

'I'm not doubting you, Major, but you, like me, have to rely on information supplied by others who may not have the same motivation for painstaking accuracy which I know has been a hall mark of your work for military intelligence. Volkonoff is now in Baghdad. I do not intend to underestimate him again. He knew in Hong Kong that we, British Intelligence and subsequently, the American CIA had picked up details of the plans to ship SS20 missiles to Iraq. The ship had been identified which was carrying those missiles, but its extraordinary capabilities were not revealed until too late to prevent the cargo leaving Hong Kong.'

'Now, Major, you are Volkonoff; all your bridges are burnt and you are determined to get these missiles delivered and receive payment for them. You are going to let nothing stand in your way. We are now at the stage when you arrived in Hong Kong on the Chinese cargo ship with the ten, SS20s in the hold. It's just before two in the morning and Spirit of the Sea has anchored a short distance from Al Samak. All of this we know is correct.'

'Just after 5.50 - three or so hours later - Al Samak sailed and disappeared. At 7.30 that evening, Volkonoff caught the British Airways flight to Dubai where he connected with another flight to Baghdad. Once in Baghdad, he was followed by our man to the Presidential Palace; he was driven there in a Security Police car having had all arrival and customs formalities waived. He is now staying at the Hilton Hotel in Baghdad. Between his arrival aboard Spirit of the Sea and his departure on the British Airways flight that same evening, a known informer was found shot in his apartment, a man who might be a British intelligence agent was then thrown from the 20th floor of the Hong Kong Bank and three prostitutes were found dead, horrifically mutilated, in a high class brothel.'

'Now that sounds like the sort of bloody trail that Volkonoff always left behind him before his accidental death was arranged in a blast furnace. He outwitted us then and he's gone on outwitting us ever since. That is to stop!' The President had raised his voice for the first time.

'Yes, Sir.'

'Major Petrovsky, don't rush. Enjoy your coffee and think. Think like Volkonoff, where there are no rules except those of survival by whatever foul means necessary. What would you do, having defeated me by getting your hands on real missiles, to ensure that those missiles reached Iraq and you were paid. Remember that Volkonoff has no concern for the rest of the deadbeats in that conspiracy. Don't apply any scruples that normal humans might

192

possess. Volkonoff is neither normal nor human. Now think, Major, think and when you're ready we'll compare notes. I'm just going to walk down to the garden for some fresh air,' and the President left the office by a side door.

While the President walked across the grass to admire a bed of superb roses, Major Petrovsky paced up and down the large office, scribbling notes on a jotting pad. Just over a quarter of an hour later, the President returned quietly by the same side door and sat in the armchair once more. The Major had been standing by a large map of the world.

'I have some additional questions, Sir... if...'

'If I can answer them, I will. Go ahead.'

'Is it reasonable to assume that Volkonoff would have known that we and the Americans would use everything and anything available to destroy those missiles rather than let them fall into Saddam Hussein's hands.'

'It is.'

'Right; is Rokossovsky relevant in the equation?'

'No; not any longer.'

'Very good, Sir; this is what I would do if I was Volkonoff. I've got to ensure that I get a nuclear weapon to Iraq, not necessarily all ten, but enough to use as a threat against Israel or any invading force put together under the UN flag. The Russians, the Americans and the British know where the missiles are, the ship which will transport them and the destination. I certainly wouldn't put all my eggs in one basket. I'd try and split the missiles up into penny packets and send them by different routes to make the task of finding and destroying them a hundred times more difficult.'

'And you would do all of this in 3½ hours?'

'No; what I've just proposed would be the ideal. What I'm convinced he's done is to leave some of the missiles on Spirit of the Sea - or another ship - and the remainder are in Al Samak's hold. It's time Volkonoff was dealt with, Sir.'

'My thinking exactly; both with Volkonoff's thought process and the immediacy of his removal. Thank you Major Petrovsky, you have been a great help. You fly tonight on a circuitous route via Athens and London to Baghdad. Your mission is to kill Volkonoff.'

*

There was an air of surpressed excitement and expectancy mingled with chaos and panic in Baghdad on the night of 29th July. Crowds marched along the main streets waving Iraqi flags and pictures of Saddam Hussein. At the large international hotels and the airport, there were scenes of chaos as the foreign community started the mass exodus from the city. There wasn't a seat to be had on any flight out of Iraq. The street cafés were full of smiling Iraqis in direct contrast to the hotel reception areas which were crammed with anxious looking foreigners who would have rather been anywhere than the country in which they now found themselves temporarily stranded.

The world media was much in evidence attracted to the impending crisis like hyenas to putrefying carrion. Volkonoff's room at the Hilton had been reserved by the Security Police and no bribe from any international journalist would make a receptionist give up that room. The phone rang in his room. He turned off the shower and walked across the thickly carpeted room to the table between the twin beds where all the gadgetry, including the phone, was positioned. Volkonoff was in his early forties, but had the physique of a man ten years younger and possessed not an ounce of excess weight on his huge frame. He picked up the phone. 'Yes.'

'Meet me in the coffee room on the mezzanine floor in ten minutes.' Volkonoff didn't acknowledge the instruction, but just replaced the phone and went back to his shower. Ten minutes later, he walked into the coffee room, which was packed with people and there wasn't a spare seat anywhere. A waiter walked towards him.

'Mr Czesnak?' which was the name on Volkonoff's passport and the one he had registered at the hotel. Volkonoff nodded. 'This way Sir, please.' He was led through the crowded tables to a small, corner one where there was a man seated and the other chair was empty. Even as they approached the table, a long-haired male, sporting a multi-pocketed waistcoat, which had become the in-fashion for the pseudo-safari-reporter-photographer, was attempting to remove the empty chair. The look he received from the man seated at the table made him retreat rapidly, bumping into Volkonoff as he did so who pushed him out of the way so that he fell and sprawled across the table at which his colleagues were seated, scattering cups and plates.

'Hey! wha.....' but the words died as the colleague of 'waistcoat-pockets' saw the size of the man to whom he was talking. Volkonoff ignored him and sat down at the table and waved the waiter away.

'Will you confirm...'

'Show me proof of your identity,' Volkonoff demanded.

'You have no right to behave so imperiously in my country...'

'Show me your proof of identity or you, your President and your country can get stuffed,' and Volkonoff made to get up.

'Very well, but you will have to be careful what you say as we in the Mukhabarat of the Security Police are very powerful.'

'Look, my friend; I've got something that your President wants more than anything else in the world and if you screw it up you'll be able to count your life-expectancy in minutes. Now cut out all this bullshit and listen, but first give me that ID card.' He ripped the card out of the man's hands and studied it closely. 'Wait here,' which was an order.

Volkonoff went out to the reception area and the long line of telephones, all of which were occupied. He selected his target and went over to a booth where a woman of indeterminate age, but who was nearer forty than twenty, dressed in well-faded jeans and a sweat-stained T-shirt, dragged on a cigarette as she read something over the phone from notes held in her hand; the telephone was tucked under her chin. Volkonoff reached over and removed the phone and replaced it.

'What the fuck....' but the expletive died as Volkonoff's thumb pressed down on the nerve point and the woman crumpled to the floor. Volkonoff signalled to a member of the hotel staff and told him that the woman had just fainted and she was removed to a sofa after other people had been asked to make room for her. Volkonoff rang the same number that he had from Dubai Airport and read out the number of the ID card, which he was holding. He replaced the 'phone, which was immediately grabbed by another person and walked back into the coffee room and sat at the corner table.

'Well, are...'

'Shut up and listen. Spirit of the Sea gets into Bangkok at 1230 hours on 31st July. The warheads will have been separated from the missile propulsion section and inertial guidance system and re-crated. The crates are marked for shipment to Riyadh by a Saudia Boeing 747 freight carrier which is due to leave Bangkok on 3rd March at 1030 hours local time. The genuine Saudia 747 calls at Calcutta, landing at 0720 hours that same morning. You must ensure that it stays at Calcutta just long enough for the Iraqi 747 - painted in Saudia livery of green, black and blue and with the correct designator callsign - to overfly it and arrive at Bangkok to pick up the cargo. Got all that?'

'Yes; what will you do?'

'I will remain here until I fly with the fake 747 to Bangkok. Once the cargo is on your 747 and on its way, my job is finished and I will just tidy up some loose ends in Bangkok. Remember that all the crates have been fitted with an explosive device,which will destroy all the warheads. Once I have received full payment for the cargo, I will inform my contact by 'phone of the disarming sequence.'

'You don't trust us?'

195

'No; I now have other matters to attend to.' Volkonoff got up from the table and walked out of the coffee shop.

On the adjacent table, 'waistcoat pockets' got up and asked if he could borrow the ash tray from the small corner table. The man from the Security Police paid no attention, so it was removed, as was the minute self-adhesive microchip transmitter microphone, before it was placed on the larger table.

*

'Reduce to revolutions for 15 knots and come to six zero feet; blow main ballast, stand by to raise periscope,' having given his orders, Captain Steinbaum walked over to the sonar station in the control room of Al Samak. 'Anything to report?

'No, Sir. I have sonar prints for both Soviet and US submarines stored in the computer and there is no indication that we're being followed. We're only picking up routine commercial shipping moving north and south along the eastern seaboard of the Philippines.'

'Well done; keep up the concentration. The difficult time will come in about 36 hours and then all of us are going to rely on you and your team for our lives.'

'Very good, Sir.' Captain Steinbaum moved on round his control room. He checked the latest navigation plot, which placed Al Samak just to the north-east of Talaud Island. The ship had covered more than 1,500 miles since leaving Hong Kong.

'Six zero feet, Sir,' came from the planesman controlling the ship's depth.

'Thank you. Up periscope.' The periscope rose out of its well and Captain Steinbaum grasped it, swinging it to start his search from the bow. The streamlined funnel of the ship was now just below the surface of the sea and the periscope rose up within the funnel until it broke clear of the surface. There was absolutely nothing in sight at all points around the ship which was just as well because the sea was oily calm and the tell-tale white plume from the periscope where it broke the surface could have been spotted a long way off - by an alert lookout.

Commander Schwendler appeared in the control room to relieve the Captain. The Captain lowered the periscope, gave orders to dive to 400 feet and increase speed to 35 knots; he turned to his First Officer. 'Dieter, if you were a Russian Task Force commander with the task of hunting and destroying Al Samak, what would be your attitude of mind for the job. I'm not asking, yet, how you would go about it, but would you be keyed up, relaxed or just treating the task as a routine mission to carry out. You see, I want to get inside the mind of my enemy so that I neither under or over estimate his skill or tactics.'

'Fully understood, Kapitän. They will do the job professionally, but the adrenaline won't be there, as is the case if they were hunting a US sub or shadowing our NATO manoeuvres. They don't know that we have weapons and sonar which is as or more sophisticated than their own. That will be their first mistake. They don't know of our alternative propulsion unit, which will completely alter our sonar signature; that is likely to result in their second mistake. That mistake will be compounded by the anechoic tiles on our hull, which will absorb any active sonar used against us. Herr Kapitan, you asked me what I would be thinking if I was the commander of the Russian Fleet sent to destroy us. I think my state of mind would be similar to those days when you and I went hunting for wild boar in the Schwarzforst. Excitement, determination to achieve a good shot, a modicum of caution in case the beast was wounded and rounded on me, but little or no thought that the unthinkable might happen and the boar would suddenly appear from behind a tree and shoot at me!' Both men laughed.

'That is an excellent analogy, and I suspect is very close to their state of mind. We must use the proverbial cunning of the fox to fool the hunter and then we will turn from being a fox into a lion. Have you checked all our weapon systems?'

'Yes, Herr Kapitän. Torpedoes, missiles and mines are all armed and the APU was working perfectly. We switched to it while you were at periscope depth and it gave us a speed of 18 knots almost soundlessly. The batteries are fully charged, on which we can run indefinitely at ten knots if we recharge with the reactor or for 12 hours if we shut the reactor down for maximum silent running.'

'Thank you. I believe that the Russians have quite a surprise heading towards them.'

CHAPTER 15

As Alan Paxton's powerful charter motorboat caught up with Osprey, it throttled back and Gunn hurled across a light coiled rope he'd attached as a messenger line to a heavy warp. Peter had handed the wheel to Tricia and having caught the messenger line, he pulled it through the stem fairlead at the bow. Once the heavy warp was on board, he took a couple of turns round the drum on the anchor winch and then made the end fast round the base of the mast at the tabernacle. As soon as Gunn saw that the warp was secure, he raised his arm and the motorboat moved ahead until the line came taught. The power built up on the big turbo-charged diesels and in very little time both boats were surging through the slight swell at a shade over twenty knots.

Gunn looked at his watch. As soon as he'd set the first of the fulminate of mercury time pencils by pressing the plunger, he had twisted the time bezel on his diving watch to indicate the detonation time of that pencil. The thick luminous-painted minute hand of the watch was less than 2½ minutes from the mark on the watch bezel. Both boats were nearly three miles away from the island and Hassan's helicopter had long since disappeared, heading due south for the Brittany coast. A boat appeared round the south-east tip of the island and headed for the harbour entrance.

Gunn went up to the flying bridge on the motorboat and borrowed a pair of binoculars, again checking his watch as he did so. The boat was the third patrol boat returning to the harbour; presumably, no one had thought to pass a message to its crew of the turn of events on the island. One minute to go. Gunn signalled to Peter on Osprey who cast off the tow as the power was reduced on the motorboat's engines and the line was hauled back on board. Both boats then turned towards the island, presenting the smallest area possible to the imminent blast and shockwave. Twenty seconds; John Gunn made his last signal to Osprey and the crews of both boats lay face down on the deck, the autopilots pointing the bows of both boats at Sardrière Island.

The blinding flash of the explosion was followed milli-seconds later by the blast shockwave. The deck under Gunn seemed to lift and for a couple of seconds it was quite difficult to breathe in the partial vacuum caused by the shockwave. The sound of splintering glass came only seconds before the shattering thunder of the explosion made the boat shake from stem to stern. Gunn got to his feet, shaking off shards of glass, which had fallen out of the plexiglass screen round the coaming of the flying bridge. His first concern was for Osprey, but she appeared to be unscathed and a wave from Peter in the cockpit confirmed this.

Successive explosions shrouded Sardrière Island under a thick pall of black smoke out of which shot great gouts of vivid orange flame, hundreds of feet into the air as the munitions detonated. The skipper of the motorboat was on his feet and Gunn pointed towards the island. A steep wave with a tumbling, breaking crest was rapidly approaching the two boats. To his relief, Gunn saw that Peter had spotted this and all of them had safety harnesses on with lines attached to the boat. Just like a volcanic eruption, the explosion had torn the island asunder sending thousands of tons of rock into the sea. The displaced water was now rushing towards them in the form of a thirty foot tsunami at the speed of an express train. Both boats rode up the leading edge of the wave like cars on a roller-coaster and were then smothered by the tumbling, breaking crest. A large quantity of water poured through broken scuttles and windows, but both boats emerged the other side of the wave without any major damage.

'I think the worst's over, Alan. Could you drop me off on Osprey and then you'll need to make best speed back to St Peter Port and get old man Carteret into hospital. I dread to think of the extent of damage to all those greenhouses on Guernsey and only hope that there weren't any deaths or serious injuries.'

Alan Paxton passed the instruction on to the charter skipper who brought the motorboat alongside Osprey. Gunn jumped across to the yacht and waved to Alan. The sea burst into foam at the stern of the motorboat, which was soon up on the plane as it made best speed back to St Peter Port with Claudine's father.

'Could anyone have survived that on the island, John?'

'I very much doubt it, but if you're prepared to risk Osprey even more than you already have, we can see if there's anyone who can be rescued. I can't believe that it will be very long before the Guernsey, Sark and Jersey lifeboats are on the scene. Did Osprey take much damage?'

'Remarkably little, and considerably less than Alan's motorboat I should imagine. Osprey doesn't have anything like the expanse of glass that's on that boat. We didn't ship any water from that wave which followed the explosion and both the girls are fine... ah, speaking of whom, here they are!'

Tricia and Celia appeared with mugs of coffee, which they drank as Osprey approached the smoke-shrouded island. The brisk westerly wind was clearing the smoke and it seemed as though there was little left to explode. The reason for this became clear as the thick smoke and stench of cordite was carried away from the island. There was almost nothing left of the island above sea level. What had been the harbour was now a tumbled heap of rocks and that was almost all that protruded above the water. The castle and its rock promontory had vanished. Sardrière Island no longer existed; all that remained were some scorched rocks, jutting like a tombstone out of the sea.

*

The Kamov Helix ASW helicopters of the Russian aircraft carrier, Novorossiysk, had returned to the ship after their final mission of laying sonar buoys in all the navigable passages between the chain of islands stretching for 700 miles due east of Java towards the island of Timor. The Russian Task Force was deployed in the Arafura Sea between Timor and Bathurst Island off the coast of the Northern Territory of Australia. The Russian Pacific Fleet had been re-deployed to the Coral Sea to block any escape route south of Papua New Guinea and a further two task forces had been sent at maximum speed from Vladivostok to the Southern Phillipine Sea. The trap was now set for Al Samak.

*

In the last 24 hours, Al Samak had added another 1,000 miles to its submerged passage through the Moluccan Islands. The last satellite fix, which was accurate to within one metre, placed the submerged ship twenty miles to the west-sou-west of Leti Island which, itself, lay some twenty miles to the east of Timor Island. Captain Steinbaum had ensured that all his key operators of sonar, weapon control systems and the driving and navigation of the ship had been well rested. Once again, he and his first officer stood to one side of the central chart table where the navigating officer was updating the plot constantly from the inertial navigation system.

'Now, Dieter, there's no reason to suppose that Ivan's going to deploy his task force any differently from the many times we monitored his Spring and Summer exercises between '94 and '96 in the Norwegian Sea. Forgive me, but I'm thinking aloud so that if I'm guilty of an error of judgement, you must stop me, understood?'

'Very well, Herr Kapitän.'

'Now, he'll want to make the maximum use of the capabilities of all his ships and aircraft - both fixed and rotary wing. We don't know the composition of what's been deployed to intercept us, but it would be logical to send a task force and if that task force has come from the Southern Fleet, then I must assume that we are up against Ivan's very latest and best equipped ships.'

'I agree, Herr Kapitän.'

'Right; we must expect a Kirov class carrier, two ASW frigates, two ASW cruisers, two destroyers and at least two SSN hunter/killer subs; any additions or deletions, Dieter?'

'Not at this stage.'

'Good; now the task force commander will want to ensure that the immediate area round the carrier is sanitised of any threat, so within that inner zone will be his frigates and helicopters - probably using active sonar.'

'I agree, Herr Kapitan. That would be the routine if the task force commander was advancing towards a NATO objective, but do you really believe that he will bother with the inner and outer zones of protection when he has been told that the ship for which he's searching has no weapon system?'

'The point you make is valid, but I'm going to credit the task force commander with a high sense of professionalism and - rather more importantly - a strong sense of self-preservation! Failure to destroy Al Samak will finish his career; of that there can be little doubt. However, if we should identify any failure in his measures to provide proper protection to himself and his task force we will exploit it to the full.'

'So, outside his inner zone, we can expect to find an outer zone of aircraft and his other two classes of ships using passive sonar. Here also, I would expect to identify his hunter/killer subs and finally, deployed ahead of all that, will be his long range maritime patrol aircraft. The latter will use their magnetic anomaly detectors to identify if our movement through the sea is causing a disturbance to the Earth's natural magnetic field,' and right on cue came a report from the sonar operator.

'Aircraft dropping sonar buoys across our course, Sir.'

'So, the hunt has started. Secure all areas to action stations! Adjust to maximum cavitation!'

At the control station from where the ship was steered, trimmed and its speed controlled, a small adjustment to a switch altered the angle of the variable pitch propellers from maximum efficient forward thrust to a rough angle causing maximum cavitation and noise.

'Reduce to revolutions for 20 knots,' this was to ensure that the hunters had no idea of the ship's maximum submerged speed. Dieter Schwendler had taken his place commanding the weapons control systems. Now the plan, which the two Germans had worked on in the captain's cabin was going into operation.

Al Samak turned to the north and headed for the southern coast of Timor. The plan was simple and relied totally on the attitude of the Russian Task Force being one of efficient preparation for the unopposed destruction of a defenceless submerged ship. As Al Samak headed towards the shallower inshore waters on the coast of Timor, its noisy sound signature was recorded by the sonar buoys. Its course, speed and depth were passed to all the ships and weapons control rooms of the task force where firing solutions were immediately fed into weapon computers.

The three Sierra class attack submarines swung north from the zig-zagging patrol at the vanguard of the task force and raced at flank speed towards their quarry. The Russian Captain commanding the task force leant back in his chair on the bridge to accept his coffee. None of the ships in the task force had secured to action stations with the exception of the attack submarines.

'Stand by to discharge decoy!' Steinbaum gave this order as he paced round his control room. The decoy resembled a short, fat torpedo with a very large propeller with specifically- shaped holes drilled in the blades to cause a cavitation signature identical to that which Al Samak was producing with the rough adjustment to its propellers.

'Sir!' came from his sonar operator and Steinbaum walked quickly over to the sonar station. 'There are three of them.'

'Well done; got the sonar signature of each?'

'Yes Sir.' The Captain turned to his first officer.

'Stand by to release captor mines one thru' six, two to each sound signature five seconds delay between each.'

'Roger, all set,' was the response. Steinbaum was now holding a stopwatch in his hand.

'Stand by APU drive!'

'APU drive ready,' was confirmed. The release of the decoy and the switch to the alternate propulsion unit required perfect timing.

'Countdown for decoy commences. Five..four..three..two.. one, now!' Steinbaum wiped the sweat from his forehead, but never took his eyes off the stopwatch. 'APU... now!' and it seemed that all noise in the ship stopped. 'Commence release of captor mines...now!' and in pairs at five second intervals, the captor mines were deployed.

They were classified as mines, but were far more like highly sophisticated torpedoes. Just like the cruise missiles and smart bombs, these mines carried the sonar print of a specific submarine in their computer brains and would now lie in wait until the matching signature woke the computer brain and activated the torpedo which would then produce its own target solution and move quietly to that point.

Down below in the engine room, the reactor had been shut down and four very powerful electric motors with such superbly engineered bearings that they ran with virtually no friction and only the minimal whisper of sound, were now providing the propulsion for Al Samak. These motors were, in turn, connected to pumps and compressors, which sucked in water and ejected it at the stern of the vessel.

'Secure to silent running,' was ordered quietly by the Captain. He turned to the duty steward who was standing at the back of the control room. 'Please go down and warn our guests that if they make any noise it will cost them their lives.' He then walked over to his sonar operator. 'What've we got?'

'Even with the noise that those Sierras are making, the computer has identified seven ships. They aren't even manoeuvring to avoid a torpedo attack.'

'So I did give Ivan too much credit, well this is where he finds that he's now gone bankrupt,' Steinbaum again patted his sonar operator on the back and moved round to Schwendler, his weapons control officer. Al Samak had dived down a further fifty feet to 450 where the temperature decrease was most rapid and turned gradually to port until the submerged ship was heading straight for the Russian Task Force. Schwendler looked up as his Captain came over.

'All firing solutions computed and now on auto-update. The port salvo of homing torpedoes and two cruise missiles go for the carrier. Starboard salvo goes for the frigates. All remaining cruise missiles targeted on the other four ships. As soon as the torpedoes are reloaded, they will be fired at the cruisers and destroyers. All spare manpower is in the torpedo compartment as you ordered. Reloading will take 33 seconds.'

'Thank you. How long 'til the first mine....' but everyone in the ship heard the explosion, followed by another and then another. Steinbaum placed his hand on Schwendler's shoulder and said quietly, 'fire!'

*

The Russian Captain on Novorossiysk acknowledged the report that the submerged ship had been identified. With a bit of luck this would all be over within the hour and then he could make the signal direct to Moscow to inform the President that the task was completed.

'We have a report from Zakharov, Sir, that the sonar signature has altered slightly.'

'So wouldn't you try to get away if you had three attack submarines chasing you. Listen, my friend, when....' but he got no further with telling one of his interminable anecdotes for which he was known as 'the boring old fart of the sea'.

'That's it, Sir; report from sonar of huge explosion,' but he also stopped as sonar reported two more explosions.

'Sir! report from weapons control,' the voice of the young officer was close to hysteria.

'What is it?'

'Radar has identified two missiles in-coming.'

'Sound action stations! Engine room, revolutions for maximum speed, hard to port, come round to 15°. Launch chaff and switch Gatlings to auto-fire on acquisition,' but it was all too little, too late. While the chaos of bringing the task force to action stations began, the second salvo of torpedoes was already on its way as was the main salvo of submarine launched cruise missiles. Three Russian SSNs were on the seabed with the total loss of all their crews. The cruise missiles struck first; one exploded just below the weapon control centre of Novorossiysk and the other went straight through the angled flight deck exploding in the hangars below the deck. Both the cruisers fired their ASW torpedoes, as did the destroyers, but all were aimed at the decoy which was running on a fixed course parallel with the Timor coastline.

Novorossiysk had started to turn to face the incoming torpedoes, but the manoeuvre was too slow. Instead of striking the ship in two different places, the change in angle made both torpedoes strike in the same area, opening an enormous hole in the side of the aircraft carrier which was way beyond the capability of any damage control team. The sea engulfed the below-waterline decks and the huge warship listed over to port spilling its Kamov helicopters and Yakolev fighter/bombers into the sea. Both the frigates erupted with explosions as the cruise missiles struck. The panic on the other ships was indescribable; from where was this attack coming? Order and counter-order caused chaos, which allowed no one time to think coherently. The distress signal from Novorossiysk only served to inflame the panic further. The cruisers received the next salvo of torpedoes and missiles followed by the destroyers. Within the space of 12 minutes, the entire Russian Task Force had been destroyed.

*

'Change to main propulsion!' The hum of the reactor came back into the control room.

'Main propulsion, Sir.'

'Revolutions for maximum speed, course 278°.'

'Course 278°, Sir.'

'Secure from silent running. Well done all of you. It's not over yet by a long way, but you've just sent ten of Russia's latest warships to the bottom of the sea. First officer, please see that all weapon systems are reloaded and checked and then join me in my cabin, and with that Captain Steinbaum left the control room of Al Samak.

*

Monday 30th July was an oppressively hot day in London and Simon Peters had had an exhausting morning attending one meeting after another. The first part of the morning had been spent with Alan Paxton, who had flown from Guernsey to deliver his report on the explosion on Sardrière Island. By some freak quirk of happenstance, the worst injury sustained by anyone in Guernsey, Sark, Herm and Jethou had been superficial cuts and abrasions. Many acres of greenhouses on the southern part of Guernsey had sustained a great deal of broken glass from the blast and falling rock debris, but a guarantee of government compensation for damage to crops and for repairs had been announced on the radio and TV.

Gunn was helping the de Havillands tidy up their boat and Simon had been warned that there would be some hefty bills for both Osprey and Alan's charter boat. Simon was told that Gunn would be back later that afternoon and would give him a detailed report of everything that happened on the island. Alan Paxton reappeared in Simon's office just before 12.30 and both of them left the building with all the Express Delivery Services staff for their lunch break. 'I could murder a cold beer; what about you Alan?'

'The first one won't even touch the sides. Where shall we go? Admiral Codrington?'

'Yes, that'll do fine,' and the two men went off for their lunch.

Louise had been absent most of the morning and had stuck her head round the door when Simon had been talking with Alan to say that she was off for an early lunch unless there were any objections. When Simon returned to the office at a few minutes before two, there was still no sign of her. She was due to take her leave very shortly

205

and was flying to Kenya to stay with a girlfriend who had married a man in the tourist industry. The girlfriend's husband was currently running the Norfolk Hotel in Nairobi. There had been a number of shopping expeditions during lunchbreaks in the last month to kit herself out in the right gear for safari parks and the ex-patriate social life of Nairobi. Simon assumed that lunch that day had been another shopping excursion. He was completely wrong. Only a few minutes after he got back, a pink-faced Louise burst into his office.

'Good heavens above! Can I hope that you're about to assault me, Louise.'

'You should be so lucky, Simon,' and Louise could contain her excitement no longer, as she had obviously been bursting with the news all the way back to the office. 'Eureka! I've hit pay dirt!'

'Steady, steady old girl, come and sit down and tell me what it is you've got, unless it's catching, of course!'

'Oh, shut up! No...it's the job you gave me.' Simon mentally wracked his brains to think what Louise was talking about. 'The Lakshadweep Islands!'

'Bloody hell! you're not going to tell me that shot in the dark has paid off?'

'I am.'

'Come on then, let's have it. Should I record this?'

'No, there's no need. I got most of it photocopied.'

'Right; you get the coffee while I have a pee - two pints of beer for lunch!- and then tell me what it is you've found.' Simon Peters returned to the office to find two cups of coffee on the table. He picked up his notebook and sat down. 'Now before you tell all the detail, do you reckon that you've found Hassan's island and does it match our number?'

'The answer to the second question is, yes, I think so and to the first is that I would lay a year's salary on the odds that I'm right.'

'Last of the big time gamblers! clever girl. Right, I want it all - from the top.' Louise removed various pieces of paper from her handbag and sorted them into order before she started.

'I did as you asked, Simon, and went and saw Caroline - that's Donald's PA - but that department is up to its eyes in work, incidentally, did you know that they've no less than eight agents and controllers in Iraq?'

'Yes, I did; that's why all the extra staff have been drafted into that department, however we're off the subject.'

'So I took myself off for an early lunch today and went to the Indian High Commission - at the Aldwych. I met a very pleasant second secretary in their chancery section who was their information officer and he is the one who has given me all this,' and Louise indicated the paperwork in her lap.

'Before these islands were called the Lakshadweep Islands, which was in 1973, they were known as the Laccadives. The word Lakshadweep is the phonetic English spelling of two words of Malayalam - the language spoken on the islands and in Kerala State on the Indian mainland. The two words are 'laksha' - which means many or millions - and 'dweep' - which means gems. So the colloquial translation, according to my source at the High Commission, is a 'necklace of gems'. The name is well chosen as you will soon find out, Simon. Lakshadweep is a group of coral islands which consists of twelve atolls, a number of reefs and 36 islands of which about ten are inhabited. They lie between 8° and 14° North and 71° and 74° degrees East - you'll see how that ties in with that number which John Gunn found on Hassan's boat.'

'The islands' history dates from around the 6th or 7th Century as it's known that the inhabitants at that time were converted to the Islamic faith by an Arab missionary called Hazrat Ubaidulla. The inhabitants have led a life, which has been totally isolated from the rest of the world and have created an environment, in this idyllic setting, where crime is unknown. They live off fishing and coconuts. Tourism has only just started and foreign tourists are allowed onto only one island - Bangaram. The whole place is a tourist's mecca with crystal clear lagoons, miles of deserted beaches and coconut palms. The High Commission quoted that some 500 foreign tourists visited the Lakshadweep Islands last year. There's a lot more here which can wait, but the juiciest tit-bit I've saved until last.'

'The northernmost of the atolls consists of a large lagoon, a main island and some smaller islands dotted around the edge of the lagoon. The atoll had never been inhabited, probably because it was so isolated from the rest of the islands, and in 2001, the Indian Government put all the islands of the atoll up for sale by auction. The Indian second secretary told me that they never came to auction because an agent acting for one buyer offered to pay well over the reserve price to keep the islands out of an auction. All of the islands were bought by this one company or person. And now comes the crunch, Simon. The name of the atoll was 'Al Samak' - The Fish - named as such in honour of the Arab missionary. He was the disciple who brought the Islamic faith to the islands by being washed up on the shore of this island in a fishing net - and the position of the main island is 13°40' North, 71°42' East. Reverse the minutes and you get 0424 and add a zero to the degrees to make it look like a telephone number and you get 0424 130710 - the number which John Gunn saw on Hassan's boat.'

'What are you doing for dinner tonight?'

'Well, my fiancé was...'

'Will you and he come and have dinner with Audrey and me at an expensive restaurant.'

'Yes please, that'd be lovely.'

'Done; I'll fix it. Brilliant, absolutely bloody brilliant; I knew it was a flash of my genius to get you to investigate those islands...' Simon ducked too late and Louise's handbag caught him fair and square on the back of the head.

*

The easterly wind, which had given Osprey such a fast passage to the island, did just the same on the way back. Only two of the armoured glass panes in the wheelhouse had cracked and Osprey hadn't shipped a drop of water from the tidal wave, which followed the explosive destruction of Sardrière Island. In contrast, Alan Paxton's motorboat had lost 20% of the glass in the panes facing the explosion and had then shipped over a ton of water from the breaking crest of the tidal wave. Gunn and Alan spoke on the local shipping channel while both boats were on the way back to St Peter Port. It only took the motorboat just over a quarter of an hour to get back to Guernsey, where an ambulance was waiting to take Claudine's father to hospital. There was no need for Gunn to go to St Peter Port and the de Havillands and Celia had decided that they wanted to go back to the Hamble. It was six hours after High Water Dover and there would now be six hours of north-going tide to carry Osprey through the Great Russel Channel and the Alderney Race. The decision was made and Osprey sailed past Sark and Herm and Peter de Havilland programmed the GPS and autohelm to take Osprey back to the Needles Channel.

Gunn had phoned in a preliminary report to Simon Peters and told him that he expected to be back in London by late afternoon on the Monday. Alan Paxton's job was to square away the police on Guernsey, reassure the charter company that full compensation would be paid for the damage to the motorboat and then catch the evening flight to London. Gunn retrieved his clothing and his automatic from Peter's cupboard in the aft stateroom and Celia and Tricia set about preparing supper as the sun sank lower towards the western horizon. Peter was at the aft steering position and the other three were in the cockpit - possibly the best time of the day on a cruising yacht when everyone pauses for a drink. Tricia disappeared now and then down to the galley to tend the supper.

'All in all, that was a pretty catastrophic visit we paid to old Hassan and his island,' she remarked, returning from a visit to the galley. 'Where do you suppose he's gone now?'

'To another of his business headquarters, I should think; perhaps to a meeting with his ship,' Celia offered.

'I'm sure that's as good a guess as any; I've no doubt Claudine will be held as a hostage to prevent us interfering with Hassan's plans,' Gunn said getting up to recharge Peter's glass.

'What happens now, John? When you get back to London, will you be kept on the case - if that's what you call it - or will others take over,' Peter asked as he took his drink from Gunn.

'I'm not sure, to be perfectly honest. Unless more information has come in, we're a bit stuck. Where has Hassan gone? If this hunt for Hassan is moving into a completely different part of the world, then I could well be pulled off it.'

'Will you be able to come sailing with us again when it's all over and tell us - suitably censored, no doubt - what happened?' Tricia asked.

'Yes, I'd like that, provided you don't think I'll cause any more damage to your lovely yacht!' Tricia jumped to her feet and disappeared below. Two minutes later there was a shout from the galley to say that supper was ready. The table in the wheelhouse had been laid so that they could all eat together while the autopilot held Osprey on her course and the radar scanned the sea to warn them of any hazard. Peter and Gunn took turns throughout the night to keep watch. The wind dropped back slightly which eventually added a couple of hours to their passage which meant that Osprey was not tied up at her berth on the Hamble until 9.20 the following morning. Gunn helped Peter give the yacht a good clean up and then after disconnecting his telephone, he said his goodbyes and pushed the trolley with his bag into the yacht club car park. He threw his bag in the boot of the TR6, pushed the telephone into its bracket between the two front seats, plugged it in and put his gun in the door pocket beside him. The car started at the first twist of the ignition and while it warmed up, Gunn rang the office and told Simon Peters that he would be in later that afternoon. He let in the clutch and drove slowly out of what was now an almost deserted south coast village.

*

The Olympic Airways flight OSA 541 from Moscow arrived on schedule at 11.30 in the morning of 30th July at Athens Airport and the majority of the passengers followed the signs to baggage collection and customs. A few took the right hand channel to the transit lounge for connecting flights. Major Petrovsky went over to the information desk and confirmed the connecting flight to London and then wandered through to the Duty Free shops to kill time until the flight was called. The TV monitors announced that the flight was boarding and Major Petrovsky went through with the other passengers - mostly British who had been scorched and roasted by the sun in exceptional discomfort for a fortnight and were now returning to show off tans which were barely darker than those achieved at Brighton or Bournemouth, so hot had the summer been in Southern England.

The British Midland Airways flight BD 758 took off at 12.35 and landed at Luton where it arrived at 14.10 hours local time UK, which was two hours behind Greece. Major Petrovsky collected the one small suitcase from the carousel, went through the green customs channel and caught the bus to Victoria. From Victoria, it was only ten minutes by taxi to the Cumberland Hotel in Cromwell Road, where Petrovsky paid off the taxi driver and went in to the hotel just after four o'clock in the afternoon.

Petrovsky was well aware of the new home of British Intelligence and the constant up-dates of information from the Embassy in Kensington Palace Gardens had confirmed that although it was easy enough to run surveillance on a person going to Kingsroad House, it was impossible to pick up that person again. It was obvious that there were many exits from the building, but try - as indeed the KGB had - as they might, not one of these covert exits had been discovered. Indeed, a number of attachés at the Soviet Embassy had been compromised by loitering around the area.

Petrovsky changed and took a taxi to Sloane Square and then walked along King's Road until a right turn led through side streets to Kingsroad House. It was nearly 5.30 and the streets were beginning to fill with people making their way to buses and tube stations. Petrovsky watched the exodus of Express Delivery Services employees from Kingsroad House and sauntered in amongst them as they reached the pavement. The majority turned to the left which would take them in the direction of Sloane Square and it's tube station.

In the small knot of people, which Petrovsky had joined, only one turned right. As Petrovsky had nothing better to do until the British Airways flight left for Baghdad the next day, it would pass the early part of the evening to see where this particular employee of Express Delivery Services was going. Was that the only reason? Well,

210

perhaps he was tall and rather good looking and you never knew
your luck. Maria Ionides - the name that Petrovsky was using -
thought with half a smile as she pushed her sunglasses onto the top
of her long, dark hair and set about her self-imposed surveillance
task.

CHAPTER 16

Gunn preferred the A3 to the M3, but in the end drove along the M27 until it connected with the M3 and took that to the junction with the M25. He then turned south, or anti-clockwise on the London orbital motorway and entered London from the south-west through Kingston and Putney on the A3. The latter became the A308 - Fulham Road - and he turned right off that into Beaufort Street and then left to his small mews house in Elm Park Lane. The house had belonged to his parents and was their base in England for the thirty years that Gunn's father had worked for Euro-Pacific Construction in Hong Kong. His father had retired some ten years previously and settled in Sussex where his Australian-born mother ran a moderately successful race horse stud. Gunn had two elder sisters, both of whom were married and so the mews house had been given to him.

He parked the TR6 outside his garage and carried his sailing bag up the four steps to the front door. Like so many converted mews houses which had been designed to accommodate grooms, horses, carriages and hay, Gunn's house was on a number of split levels which gave him three small bedrooms, a lounge-cum-dining room, a bathroom, a shower room, two toilets and a workmanlike, fitted kitchen. It was 2.40 by the time he got home, so he dumped his bag in his room where Mrs Charlesworth would deal with it the next day when she came in to do the cleaning, washing and ironing and took a long cool shower before getting dressed in slacks and open-necked shirt.

He picked up his wallet and thin cotton wind-cheater and then sat on the end of his bed and checked the Polish 9mm Radom. Wherever Volkonoff was, Gunn was taking no chances and he checked the action of the automatic carefully, cleaning it with thin gun oil before wiping it dry. He worked the action, chambered a round and then removed the magazine and put another round under its steel lips. There was no safety catch, but cocking the action, as he had just done and then releasing the ringed hammer slowly, had withdrawn the firing pin. It could be reset into the firing position by flicking back the hammer, which Gunn had practised as an automatic reflex action every time he drew the gun from its holster. He placed it in the ankle holster, picked up his anorak and went out of the house.

He locked the garage doors and then turned left into Beaufort Street and left again into the King's Road. He stopped for a cold beer and a sandwich and then made his way to Kingsroad House. It was now 4.20 and the fierce heat of the sun - it had reached the lower nineties at 1400 hours according to the radio - had abated slightly. No one was following Gunn, but he went into the lift at the multi-storey car park and up to the top floor and from there into the British Intelligence Directorate.

Once he was in the building, Gunn went to Simon Peter's office. On the drive up from Southampton, Gunn had used a small tape-recorder to record everything that had happened since he arrived at Hamble on the Friday night and as he went through Louise's office, he placed the small tape on her desk. 'They're all in the conference room, John. They've only been there a couple of minutes and I was told to send you straight in.'

'More problems, Louise?'

'Yes, I think so. Are you alright?'

'Yes, fine, why?'

'Well, I was running the tape recorder for Alan's debrief. Hassan sounds an awful man and yet I can't help feeling sorry for him.'

'I know exactly how you feel; that's how I felt until he tried to kill me. Tends to polarise your emotions more clearly. He's kidnapped that girl too, which will complicate matters considerably, not to mention the misery and discomfort she'll suffer, at best - at worst, it doesn't bear too much thought.'

'Yes, you're right; come on, you're wanted in the conference room.' They went to the room together and Louise pressed the button outside the door. 'Mr Gunn's here.' The red light turned to green and the door opened. Gunn went to an empty seat and sat down. The Director was chairing the meeting himself.

'Please sit down, Mr Gunn. We hadn't started the briefing, so if there are any questions at the end which concern what has happened in the Channel Islands, we now have Gunn here to answer them.' Sir Jeremy knew the name of everyone in the Intelligence Directorate and it was rumoured that that included all the cleaning and maintenance staff. The small red lights appeared on all the microphones and then the Director began.

'Less than an hour ago, the US military surveillance satellite Vigilent III, which was monitoring the area of the Indonesian Archipelago, recorded the whole sequence of the Russian Task Force's engagement of the ship, Al Samak. By way of confirmation,

Putin has spoken to both Bush and Blair to explain what happened. All ten ships of the Russian Task Force have been destroyed,' one or two glances were exchanged around the table. 'Once again, Hassan has been underestimated and the Russian Navy - and the Task Force Commander in particular - have paid an appalling price for their complacency and incompetence. It might interest you to know that none of the Russian ships - except three SSN attack submarines - were at action stations. It is perhaps just as well that the Task Force Commander is listed as 'missing, believed killed' as a result of the action. I can't imagine that he is Mother Russia's favourite son at this moment.'

'It would seem, gentlemen, that Al Samak has a weapon-fit that in sophistication is a match for anything in the NATO or Russian Fleet. Allowances for exaggeration must be taken into account,' and then as an aside the Director added, 'we all know how easy it is to elaborate and enhance the capability and size of the opponent who has just beaten you in the boxing ring. The Russians are crediting Al Samak with a submerged speed in excess of forty knots, at least two forms of propulsion - one of which they claim is silent - an ability to dive to 1000 feet and a weapon-fit which consists of homing mines, sub-launched cruise missiles and the very latest homing torpedoes. They believe that the ship is also capable of deploying a most effective decoy noise-maker - they would have to say that it's effective because it completely fooled all of their sonar operators. They have no real idea where the ship is except to say that they think that it has gone out into the Southern Indian Ocean.' Sir Jeremy nodded to his Deputy, Miles Thompson, who pressed a button and a very large scale map of the Middle East, South Asia, the Arabian Sea and the Indian Ocean appeared on the screen in front of them all. The seats had been so arranged that all of them faced the screen.

'This, gentlemen, is the position where the Russian Task Force was destroyed. The Americans have a very effective MAD device, sorry, that's a magnetic anomaly detector, fitted to Vigilent III, which has been successful in the past in identifying the movement of Russian subs out of Murmansk and through the GIUK Gap between Greenland, Iceland and the United Kingdom. So far, the Americans have had no success in identifying the course or destination of Al Samak, which could mean a number of things. The MAD detector is not 100% effective against a highly experienced sub captain who really knows how to use variations in sea temperature and salinity to mask the movement of his boat. It's possible that the detector is not functioning at its best and worst of all, it's possible that Al Samak is fitted with some magnetic cloaking device which both we and the

Americans - and the Russians - are working on, but have yet to perfect for a submarine fit.'

'However, there is something that we know that neither the Americans nor the Russians do - correction, the Americans know it now because we have told them. We know where Al Samak is headed. Success in the intelligence world is 99% sheer hard work - just the same as police detection - and 1% luck. I might add,' Sir Jeremy threw in as another aside, 'and the alertness of mind to identify that 1% when it occurs. Fortunately, we do have such people here,' and the Director smiled, 'and an Assistant Director who gave the credit where it was due. The hard work was done by Simon and David and the flash of inspiration came from Louise.' Gunn looked at Simon who gave an almost indiscernible nod. 'It would appear that Al Samak is heading for an island in the Lakshadweep Group - here,' as a bright spot on the screen identified the position.

'The island was named 'Al Samak' as long ago as the 7th Century, when an Islamic missionary, who had been rescued from the sea in a fishing net, converted the islands to that faith. In 1992, the Indian Government sold this uninhabited atoll. I am told by Simon that Louise has bet her year's salary that the buyer was Hassan Hussein and I think that I would be prepared to join her in that bet. That is where we believe that the ship is headed, but why?'

'It would seem that this scheme of is now into its third or fourth double-cross - whatever that makes it. President Putin used a GRU officer to sow the seed of a scheme amongst disaffected members of the military who wished to remove him. We know now that the aim of this exercise was to uncover all those diehard communists whom he knew were plotting to remove him at the first appropriate opportunity. One of the conspirators - Volkonoff, it would seem - double-crossed the GRU officer's plans and succeeded in getting his hands on ten genuine nuclear missiles. These were to be sold to Hassan and the conspirators were due to collect their money and then disappear in Libya after acquiring new identities. It would now appear from the information passed to us, and the Americans, that Volkonoff has double-crossed his fellow conspirators and is determined to supply Saddam Hussein with a nuclear capability. Again, this came to us partially through luck and the timely deployment of our agents in Baghdad.'

'Volkonoff met a senior member of the Mukhabarat and discussed the arrangements for the transfer of five of the SS20 missiles from a ship called Spirit of the Sea which should reach Bangkok tomorrow. From Bangkok they are to be flown direct to Iraq. If they reach their destination, Saddam will be able to prevent any intervention in the Gulf with the threat of a pre-emptive nuclear strike against Israel, Saudi Arabia or the US or British Forces in their holding areas. Equally as important, is the need to prevent the other five SS20s getting to the Lakshadweep Islands. We are awaiting a report from the Americans who have reprogrammed the orbit of Vigilent III to overfly the position of the island of Al Samak to see what has been constructed there. It would seem that Hassan's intention is to fire the missiles at Baghdad and so achieve his revenge for the wholesale slaughter of the people of his Kurdish village, Sarikamis, and the appalling burns which he received from poisonous gas during that slaughter. You will all wish to know that USS Los Angeles has been re-deployed again to the Lakshadweep Islands. The Russian Southern Fleet is awaiting reinforcements from the Black Sea Fleet and will then sail north - with a certain amount of caution this time, I should imagine.'

'Richard and Donald, this has now moved very definitely into your area, but also affects James. I want to ensure continuity and I have no wish to add even more to your plate, Donald. Simon Peters will co-ordinate the planning to prevent both Hassan's and Saddam's efforts to start a nuclear confrontation in the Gulf. I want Alan and John to stay on this one and see it through. Any questions?'

'Yes Sir.'

'Yes, James; your question?'

'Do we have any idea who's commanding the ship, Al Samak?' James had resigned from the Royal Navy to join the Intelligence Directorate.

'Yes, thank you James, I should have included that. We got onto the Bundesgeheimdeinst for information about the disappearance of Al Samak as reported in that article which John Gunn found. The only light they could shed on the matter was to tell us of another investigation that was being carried out at the time, which uncovered a neo-Nazi infiltration of the three armed services. Only weeks before the ship was stolen from the yard of Deutschmetal, two officers in the Bundesmarine were forced to resign their commissions. Both of these officers were in the Unterseebotdienst - a Commander Steinbaum and a Lt Commander Schwendler. Both of these men vanished. Commander Steinbaum produced the best result of any submarine commander on his 'Perishers' Course' - that term will be familiar to James, but perhaps not to all of you.'

'The Perisher's Course is the course, which all Royal Navy Submariners have to pass if they wish to achieve command of a submarine. The strain which the SAS acceptance course puts on the physical stamina of a man is the equivalent of the mental stress placed on aspiring sub commanders - why the name? because you either pass with flying colours or perish for ever. Steinbaum was considered to be brilliant and would have been assured of Flag rank if he hadn't been a Nazi. We know that Hassan has supplied the neo-Nazis with arms and explosives in the past. Our guess is that Steinbaum and Schwendler are captain and first officer of Al Samak.' There were no more questions and so the briefing was terminated.

'John,' Simon turned to him as they left the conference room, 'go home and get a good night's rest. We've got to sit down and work out what's to be done. Wear your bleeper and if we need you I'll buzz, but otherwise be here at 0830 tomorrow.'

'OK; what's the news on Claudine's father, Alan?'

'Oh, he's fine; he's as tough as old boots and he'll be out of hospital in a few days. Apart from his overriding worry about his daughter, he was keen to go and sort out the insurance company who've been difficult about paying up for the total loss of his boat. I left him with a very official government letter confirming that his boat had been destroyed. He had already phoned up to place an order for another boat with the boat builder who built the previous one.'

'Well, that's encouraging; now all we have to do is find Claudine. See you both tomorrow morning.' That was to prove to be a forlorn expectation.

It was 5.30 and Gunn joined all the EDS staff as they left the building. Whereas the majority of the people leaving the building either turned left towards the tube station or went straight ahead to cut through to King's Road, he turned right after descending the broad flight of half-a-dozen steps and crossing the narrow, paved forecourt of the building. He had switched on the small pager in his pocket and decided to walk back to his mews house in Chelsea.

Gunn's social life in London was a very hit and miss affair. He had spent scarcely more than a handful of nights at his house in the last nine months and most of his casual relationships had given up ringing the house only to hear yet again the recorded voice of his answering machine. Since his recruitment into the British Intelligence Directorate he still found it difficult to separate his work from his private life; this was hardly surprising as the former intruded so frequently into the latter that it was almost impossible to have such a luxury as a private life. Even a holiday, when it was taken, was certainly not sacrosanct and if the requirement arose, only cursory apologies were made for interrupting what was a privilege and not a right.

It was a Monday; Monday evenings in London tended to be dull, particularly in the summer. Few, if any people stayed in the city at weekends and those who returned on Monday morning in time to go to work spent Monday evenings recuperating from the activities of the weekend.

Gunn was toying with the choice of picking up a take-away and putting his feet up in front of the TV or taking himself out to one of the many bistros in the Fulham Road - the term 'bistro' rarely meant good food, wine and informality, but more often than not, in his view, indifferent food and wine at over-inflated prices - when to his surprise he realised that he was being followed.

His training had taught him to develop an instinctive habit of checking and he found that he now did this completely automatically, but had not expected a positive result that evening. He was walking west along South Parade and had intended to join the Fulham Road and then turn left into Beaufort Street. Instead, he turned left into Old Church Street and headed south towards the river; his tail turned left

It was now a shade after ten to six and at the end of Old Church Street was a pub named the 'Cavalier' which had benefitted greatly from the fine weather that summer because it had a minute forecourt which had been packed with white-painted, wrought iron tables, chairs and candy-striped umbrellas. These, in their turn, had been packed with clients since May and the pub had had a most financially rewarding summer. The pub had a fair cross-section of London humanity, which varied from the occupants of the very expensive property around Cheyne Walk, through the passé Sloane Ranger/Hooray Henry crowd to yobbos with earrings who patronised the place, craving attention to what they considered was their expression of nonconformity, but in reality only placed them in the uniform of the adolescently immature - or so the colour supplements had decided. Apart from the poseurs and those who went to laugh at the poseurs, there was a small majority of people who patronised the pub for its location - a view of the Thames - and its good food and drink.

As Gunn approached the pub, he saw that there were not only empty seats outside it, but a completely empty table. He assumed that the reason for this was the usual Monday evening syndrome that it was too early for the regular clientele and those who had been drinking ever since lunchtime had finally collapsed or left. He went into the pub, which was relatively empty like the area outside and was spotted by the landlord. It seemed ironic to Gunn that the only people who seemed to remember him where maitre d's, publicans and the lady in his local dry cleaning shop.

'Hello, John; haven't seen you for some time. What'll it be?' and then answering his own question, 'cold lager?'

'Thanks Harry, that'll do fine, and you?'

'Just a half of the same, thanks.' Gunn paid, taking the opportunity to assess his companion who'd followed him from Kingsroad House. She had followed him into the pub and was standing within arm's reach along the bar. As Gunn looked in her direction, she gave him a radiant smile which he could do little but return as he gathered his tankard of lager, took a sip and then walked out of the bar and laid claim to the empty table. A minute later, his 'tail' appeared at the door and looked round at the occupied tables; except Gunn's, all had two or three people at them.

She walked straight to his table and asked, 'do you mind if I sit here?' Gunn half rose from his seat and then sat down again as she held out a hand saying, 'no, please don't get up.'

'Not a bit, please have a seat.'

'Thank you, do you live in London?' The accent was there, but it was still excellent English and that explained the forthright manner - depending on the reason for following him. Two British people sharing a table in a foreign country could quite easily avoid speaking to each other for the duration of the shared encounter.

'Yes I do; you're visiting England?'

'Oh yes; I only arrived today and I have to leave tomorrow. I'm a free-lance journalist. My home is in Athens and tomorrow I fly to Baghdad.'

'Did you say this was your first visit to London?'

'Oh no; I visited London two or three times some years ago when I was at college in Bournemouth learning English.'

'It must've been a good college.'

'Sorry?'

'That was a compliment; your English is not only idiomatically correct, but also almost word perfect.'

'Thank you.'

'So, you're going to Iraq to report on what will probably be the next Gulf War?'

'That hasn't happened yet,' and she opened her shoulder bag and produced some brand of Greek cigarette - all the right props Gunn thought cynically.

'Do you have a light, please?'

'No, 'fraid not; stay there and I'll get you a box from the bar.'

'Please don...'

'No bother; don't let someone pinch my seat,' and Gunn walked into the bar. He caught the landlord's eye and mimed the action for lighting a match. The box was on the bar as he reached it and he paid and took out his mobile and dialled Simon's number, keeping one eye on the immediate area outside the door although he couldn't see his table. Simon answered.

'Telepathy, I've just rung through to our exchange to page you,' and with that the pager in Gunn's pocket bleeped. He switched it off. 'Where are you?'

'The Cavalier.'

'On your mobile?'

'That's the one; go on, you go first. Do you want me back in the office?'

'No; no need for that. One of the reps from the company office of our competitors in London' – (the Russian Embassy)- requested a meeting with one of our reps from the old office' – (that meant either MI5 or 6) - 'to let us know that they've sent a representative in the same line of business but on the military side' –(GRU not KGB) - 'who's due to do business in the Gulf. We've been given the name of the hotel and the flight details for tomorrow. This time it seems that we are not in competition, but there is a wish to co-operate to complete the current contract to ensure that errors like the most recent one do not reoccur. Their rep is staying at the Cumberland Hotel in the Cromwell Road and the name is Ionides. As you are almost certainly going to the same area to finalise this contract, the vice-chairman' – (the Deputy Director) - 'would like you to give the rep the once over. Now, why were you ringing?'

'Just checking in before making any plans for the night.'

'Thank you. See you tomorrow at 8.30; bye!'

'Bye!' and John ended the call and walked out to the table with no more thoughts of take-aways and TV.

*

George Gresham awoke from a deep sleep to the sound of a subdued knock on the door to his cabin. He switched on the bunkside light and looked at his watch. He'd been asleep for nearly six hours; it was always the same. As soon as the opportunity arose for him to sleep, he deprogrammed himself and went into a dreamless sleep.

'Come in!'

'Sorry to disturb you, Sir.'

'Come in, Hal. Go on. tell me we're no longer going for an RV with the Fleet at Guam.'

'That's right, Sir.'

'Right; sit over there. That looks like a long signal, but so that no time is wasted has Frank done the 'expedite' if one is required?'

'It is and he has, Sir, but he'd like you in the control room.'

'Right; give me a quick summary of that,' and George Gresham pointed at the long signal.'

'Al Samak has destroyed all ten ships of the Russian Task Force sent to intercept and sink it; that includes three, Sierra class nuclear attack submarines...'

'Jesus Christ on a bicycle! What's that sonofabitch armed with? Sorry, go on.'

'Our previous orders are cancelled and we are now required to identify an intercept point with Al Samak and inform Flag Officer 7th Fleet soonest. On no account, and this is repeated, Sir, is Los Angeles to engage Al Samak. Our task is to locate and confirm that Al Samak is headed for the Lakshadweep Islands...'

'The what?'

'Lakshadweep, Sir; used to be called the Laccadives. They lie just to the north of the Maldives.'

'Right, thanks; I'll take that,' and George Gresham took the signal and went up to the control room. His First Officer, Lt Commander Frank Mareno, was standing by the chart table with Lieutenant Pete Baker, the navigating officer. 'What the hell has this ship got in the way of weapons, Frank, if it can take out an entire Russian Task Force? No, on second thoughts, don't answer that; let's just see what's expected of us. Give me a couple of minutes to digest this and then I'll be with you.'

'Very good, Sir.' Five minutes later, Commander Gresham looked up.

'So bring me up to date on what you've done, Frank.'

'Sir; we received that new set of orders when we were here,' and he pointed a pencil to a position fix on the chart. 'That was 08°52' North, 134°12' East at exactly 2004 hours. Lieutenant Baker, here, has done the navigation calculation. I've checked it and confirm his calculations. We have been given Al Samak's last known position at 1800 hours today when the Russian Task Force was sunk. It seems that British Intelligence has identified the location where the ship is headed and our task is to achieve an intercept and confirm the ship's course towards the Lakshadweep Islands. We have been told to assume that the ship is at maximum submerged speed which our technical experts consider to be more than thirty, but less than forty knots - real helpful that sort of estimate!'

'But you've got a problem; your expression gives you away. OK, what's the problem?'

'We can't achieve an intercept unless we go to operational emergency maximum speed.'

'If we do, where's the intercept?'

'Here, Sir; 225 miles sou-sou-east of Sri Lanka at 03°04' North, 83°22' East.'

'What speed have you credited this ship with?'

'Forty knots, Sir.'

'Well done; how close is it?'

'If we use our max op speed, Sir, we can do it with 58 minutes to spare.'

'What're we doing now.'

'40.5, Sir.'

'Increase to 45 knots now.'

'45 knots, Sir, was instantly repeated by the petty officer driving the sub and smiled glances were exchanged around the control room. All the men in the control room were well aware that to go to max op speed under non-operational conditions required specific authority from the Flag Officer Seventh Fleet.

'Pete, give me an ETA at the intercept point and then I'll take a quick glance at your selected course. Hal, send a signal to Flag Officer Seventh Fleet giving the location of the intercept and my orders to go to max op speed.'

'0002 hours zulu on 2nd August, Sir,' came from the navigating officer.' The term 'zulu' indicated Greenwich Mean Time which was used for worldwide military operations rather than local time.

'There you are, Hal; there's your time, now Pete, show me the course,' and the two men bent over the chart while the bullet-shaped hull of the most successful attack submarine in the Western Navies bored through the sea at nearly 51 mph to the intercept point with Al Samak.

*

The distance to the airport at St Malo was only 62 miles and the four man crew of Hassan's twin-engined Lear jet had been given perfectly adequate warning to have the aircraft fuelled and airspace clearance for the flight to Colombo via Rome and Dubai. Apart from the blinding flash and a rapid increase to the airspeed as the blast and shock wave accelerated the helicopter towards the Brittany Coast, no other effects of the destruction of Sardrière Island had affected the helicopter and Hassan had never looked back once.

Claudine was suffering considerable cramp pains from being handcuffed to the frame of the seat, but had it not been for the handcuffs, she knew that she would have gone with Rashid out of the starboard door of the helicopter. As it was, she had been hanging from the handcuffs with nothing but the sea beneath her feet until the co-pilot had regained control. She had seen John Gunn on the jetty below as it flashed beneath them, but the last she'd seen of her father was as he lay on the floor of the wheelhouse on Osprey after he'd been shot. Air traffic control at St Malo gave the helicopter landing clearance and as soon as it was a couple of feet from the tarmac of the helipad, the co-pilot flew it across the apron to where the Lear jet was positioned outside its hangar.

Customs clearance was not required. As soon as the helicopter came to a halt, the steward of the Lear jet ducked under the blades and climbed into the back. He produced a hypodermic syringe, pulled up the sleeve of Claudine's blouse, swabbed the skin and plunged the needle into her arm. Her eyes closed before the needle was withdrawn. The keys for the handcuffs had left the helicopter with Rashid, but in seconds the whole rear seat had been unclipped and was carried out of the helicopter with Claudine on it. She was taken across to the Lear jet and bundled in just as an airport official drove up in a white DCV with a flashing orange light on top.

Hassan was already aboard his aircraft and the French were well aware of his fanatical dislike of being seen. The airport official waved to the steward who waved in return and then pressed the switch to close the door. The steps folded into the aircraft and with a 'thunk' the door closed. The aircraft started to taxi towards the runway and by the time it had reached the holding position, the steward had cut through the tubular frame of the helicopter seat, carried Claudine to one of the armchairs and strapped her in. He then checked that the young stewardess had provided Hassan with everything that he wanted and opened the door to the flight deck.

'All secure aft, and ready for take off,' he reported.

The pilot released the brakes and taxied onto the runway acknowledging the final clearance as he did so. He turned the handwheel which guided the nosewheel of the aircraft onto the centre line and then pushed both throttles fully forward. The twin-engined jet lifted into the sky and turned towards the east.

CHAPTER 17

Gunn walked out from the cool, dark bar into the bright light of the small terrace in front of the pub, holding the box of matches, which he'd bought for his table companion. There were now no less than four youths sitting at the table doing what they did so well when the target was female and well outnumbered. John heard the lewd remarks as he came out of the pub and saw that everyone else was pretending not to notice what was happening.

'Not again,' Gunn groaned inwardly; this would be the third time in as many days. She looked up, saw John and stood up which prompted the yobbos into action; the two on either side of her stood up and one attempted to put his arms round her to the accompaniment of more lewd encouragement from the other two. It was difficult to see what happened because it was done so quickly. One moment the two youths were molesting the woman, the next, one was lying unconscious on the paved terrace and the other was writhing in agony with his hands clasped to his groin. The other two half rose to their feet; Gunn's foot caught one in the backside and he emptied the remains of his beer over the other's head.

The youth whom Gunn had kicked, sprawled on the ground beside the two already there. The pub clientele were in fits of laughter; the youth with the beer rinse turned in a rage of anger towards John where he walked straight into a stiff arm jab, applied with the heel of Gunn's hand, which struck him about four inches above his sternum. The precise aim of the blow and the force behind it choked the youth who was momentarily unable to breathe and clutched his throat gasping for breath. Gunn placed the box of matches on the table, spun him round, grabbed him by the collar and the wide, immitation leather belt and 'bum-rushed' him off the terrace. The youth, who'd been kicked, had vanished and the other two Gunn dragged out onto the pavement.

Gunn's 'Greek free-lance journalist' was back at her seat as though nothing had happened and Gunn returned to his original seat. He smiled at the rousing cheer from the other occupants of the pub terrace and those who'd come out of the bar to watch the entertainment and he'd no sooner sat down than Harry appeared

224

with a fresh pint of lager and something red and fizzy in a wine glass for his table companion.

'On the house, John... and Miss; if you ever want a job as a bouncer, come and see me!' Harry lowered his voice slightly, 'take care, Sir, there are more where that lot came from and they've mugged some of my clientele on their way home. The police try and help out by being around, but they're short of men and can't keep an eye on just this pub.'

'Thanks for the warning and the drinks, Harry.'

'Thank you for my drink.'

'Pleasure, Miss.'

'Do all journalists in Greece learn that form of unarmed combat? Incidentally, my name's John.'

'Maria Ionides, and yes, a large number of women, especially in Athens, learn various forms of self-defence as assaults from men like that,' and she indicated with a movement of her head in the direction which the yobbos had gone, 'happen all the time.'

'Your matches.'

'Oh, thank you,' and Maria shook a cigarette out of the packet, which was still lying on the table. Gunn struck a match and cupped the flame in his hands to prevent the breeze blowing off the river from extinguishing it. She bent forward and placed her hand over his as she lit the cigarette.

'I don't know whether you are aware of it, but your employers - who don't live in Greece - have declared your entry into the UK en route for Baghdad.'

'Oh!'

'Now it just so happens that you and I are involved on the same case, mission - whatever you call it in the GRU - and it seems that we are likely to meet up in Baghdad in our efforts to deal with Volkonoff and the stolen missiles. I have just been instructed to contact you at the Cumberland Hotel, where you are indeed registered under the name of Ionides, but I would be interested - if perestroika stretches that far - to know why you followed me earlier this evening.'

'Chance; after booking in at my hotel, I decided to have a look at the new building occupied by the British Intelligence Directorate and I arrived there as a group of you were leaving the building. I thought you looked interesting and you went a different way to everyone else, so I decided to follow you. How long did it take you to realise that I was following you?'

'About a couple of hundred yards, I think.'

'Damn! I've never been much good at surveillance; in training, I was always spotted because I was not only taller than all the other women, but most of the men as well.'

'I bet you did well in the unarmed combat lessons.'

'Yes,' Maria laughed and Gunn saw a perfect set of teeth to match her striking good looks. He looked at his watch; it was just after 6.15.

'You have to go somewhere else?'

'No, I was just wondering if you would like something to eat and was going to offer to take you out to supper.'

'Thank you, I'd like that. Is that what your employers told you to do?' It was Gunn's turn to laugh.

'No, when they spoke to me on the phone in there, they had no idea that you were sitting out here. Now, another drink here, as it's a little too early to eat, or would you like to come back to my house where you can shower, bath or whatever and have a drink before we go out and find a restaurant?'

'I must admit that the thought of a bath after being handled by those smelly men is very tempting. How far away is your house?'

'No more than 500 yards; come on, we'll be there in a couple of minutes and within five you'll be up to your neck in a steaming bath.'

'Sounds tempting,' and both of them finished off their drinks and left the Cavalier's terrace. The walk took eight minutes and by the time the bath was ready it was nearer twenty minutes than the optimistic five, forecast by Gunn. He went down to the split-level dining room/sitting room where he found Maria looking through his rather sparse collection of books.

'Bath's ready; like a glass of champagne to take in with you?'

'What luxury! yes please; will you bring it up?'

'Yes, sure; use the bedroom opposite the bathroom to dump your things. You'll find a fairly large towelling dressing gown behind the door. I'll dig a bottle out of the fridge and bring it up.' Maria disappeared up the stairs while Gunn went to the kitchen and retrieved a bottle of champagne from the fridge. 'Oh well, not exactly Dom Perignon,' he muttered, twisting off the wire cage from the cork of a very acceptable brand of Australian champagne, 'but what's twelve or so thousand miles between friends, especially when one of them's got a figure like Maria Ionides.' The cork burst from the bottle with a satisfying pop and he filled a couple of slender, fluted glasses. Gunn went up the stairs and paused outside the bathroom door. 'Bath OK?'

'Yes lovely, thank you.'

'There's a little table outside the bathroom; I'll put your champagne on it. 'I'm going to take a shower.'

226

'Wait a moment, please.'

Gunn paused with champagne in hand and then the door opened to reveal Maria wrapped in the large towelling dressing gown, which he'd put in the bathroom for her.

'It's alright, I've finished so you can use the shower.'

'There's another bathroom, unfortunately. Go on take your time, there's no hurry.'

'Won't you join me?' and the dressing gown fell to the bathroom floor.

'Now that's an offer I can't refuse.'

*

Gunn looked at his watch; ten to eight. He was propped on the pillows in the double bed of his bedroom and Maria lay across him with her head on his stomach and her hand in his groin.

'Ready for some supper?'

'Just once more, please.'

*

The two of them left Gunn's house in the mews just before 8.30 and turned left towards the embankment and then right once they reached it so that they were walking beside the river. It had only taken a shade over ten minutes to reach the river and if Gunn hadn't been quite so relaxed after his love-making with Maria, he might have noticed that they were followed - indeed they had been ever since they left the Cavalier. The tail had waited outside the mews house while the two of them had made love, first in the bathroom and then after drying each other, in Gunn's bed.

'There's a restaurant beside the river?'

'Yes, there are one or two, but the one I'm aiming for, which I haven't been to for some time, is at the Chelsea Marina. It's only a few more minutes walk, but I can get a taxi if you would prefer.'

'Oh no, I prefer to walk; it's such a nice evening and I've got a good appetite after all that exercise,' and Maria laughed as she squeezed his arm. She seemed to match his stride with ease and it was no more than five minutes before they arrived at Giovani's Place. The good weather had given many others the idea of eating out and they were lucky to get the last table on the outside of the restaurant, overlooking the river and the boats in the marina.

Gunn ordered a light, white, chilled 'chianti' and they both choose an antepasta and main course. 'Are you allowed to tell me how you were selected for this particular scheme?

'I think so, but it would make it easier for me if you were to tell me how much you know.'

'Yes, I think that's reasonable,' Gunn agreed as their pasta dish was delivered to the table. He took a sip of the chianti to give himself time to get the sequence of events in order. 'By absolute chance, we discovered that ten missiles were on the Trans-Siberian railway and at the same time a different investigation found the connection between the arms dealer, Hassan Hussein, and the theft of a submersible ship from a German boatyard. Incidentally, when were you last in touch with your people? No tricks to that question!'

'Yesterday evening; I left Moscow at 8.30 - that would have been about 5.30 your time - this morning. The flight landed on time at Athens and I connected to Luton on a British Midlands flight, a bus to Victoria and a taxi to my hotel where I arrived some time after four this afternoon. I then had a bath, changed and took a taxi to Sloane Square. From there I walked to where I spotted you leaving that Express Deliveries building. Do you wish to interrogate me further?' was added with a mischievous smile, 'I think I might enjoy being tortured by you.'

'I've got a very special line in torture for gorgeous Russian agents.'

'Oh, yes please; I'm not sure I'll last through supper!'

'Give me a break, Maria. I'm finding it hard enough to concentrate with you sitting next to me. Now, what the hell was I talking about...you see, you temptress, you've scrambled my brains. Oh yes....timings; my poor brain was trying to struggle with time zones before I was distracted.' Their empty plates were removed and the waiter topped up their glasses. 'When you got to your hotel, was there a message for you to contact your Embassy? - you don't of course have to answer that, but I've a sneaking suspicion that you are unaware of a major turn of events in this missile saga.'

'Lumachine con cozze?'

'Thanks, that's for me,' Gunn answered, as the waiter arrived with their main course.

'And the spaghetti all'ouva for the lady.' The restaurant had a reputation for its excellent fresh mussels, so John had chosen that, served with egg pasta and Maria had been very frugal and chosen what was sometimes known as the 'poor man's spaghetti'; it had no meat sauce and was served with Pecorino Cheese. The interlude had given Maria plenty of time to work out her reply, if necessary, to Gunn's question.

'No, I have spoken to none of my people since arriving in England. Why?'

'Or while you were making your connecting flight in Athens?'

'No; what has happened?'

'You were briefed on the deployment of the Russian Navy to intercept and, if necessary, destroy Al Samak with its cargo of missiles.'

'Yes, of course.'

'But you haven't been told the result of that?

'No, well.. let me see, the earliest that could have happened would've been.....I see what you mean about the time zones now.'

'About 1330 hours Moscow time, which would have been about 1230 Athens time and 1030 UK time. I was told at about four this afternoon.'

'So can you tell me what has happened; is the ship destroyed?'

'No, I'm afraid not. The entire Russian Task Force of seven surface ships and three submarines has been destroyed by Al Samak.' Maria gasped and one or two heads turned from adjacent tables.

'That can't be right, I mean....'

'That information came from the Russian President to the US President and our Prime Mnister and is confirmed by satellite surveillance.'

'Where's the ship now?'

'That's anybody's guess, but heading for the Middle East is a fairly certain bet.'

'How did you know that Volkonoff was in Baghdad?'

'Someone saw him there and told us.'

'So what will be your mission?'

'Nothing that prolongs Volkonoff's continued existence, I hope.'

'Yes, I see; then both of us do have a similar task.' The news of the Russian Task Force had not spoiled Maria's appetite and her plate was now empty. This was confirmed when she accepted the offer of the menu to look at the sweets and chose fresh strawberries and cream. Gunn ordered coffee for both of them. It was now just before ten and the long summer evening had turned to night. The small wrought iron lamps on each table gave a pleasant intimacy to each table on the terrace.

'However,' Gunn continued, 'I was in the middle of telling you what we knew so that you could decide whether you were going to tell me why you were selected for this mission.' Maria made no comment as she ate her strawberries. 'Hassan Hussein has - or perhaps I should say had - a base on an island he bought, off the coast of Brittany. It was a phenomenal place with an underwater cavern for this ship of his and thousands of tons of stored arms and ammunition. That island has now been destroyed....'

'You did that?'

'Yes...and Hassan has disappeared in his helicopter. Now, that tells you what has happened since last Friday. What have you been up to?' The strawberries were finished and a generous spoonful of cream was being stirred into the coffee. It seemed to Gunn that not even the privileged members of the GRU were able to lay their hands on the luxuries, which the western world took for granted.

'I think you know quite a bit of the background to the scheme which our President decided to use to identify those who wanted to remove him - by force if necessary. I know that he has spoken two or three times to the US President and your PM,' Gunn's nod confirmed this, 'so I won't go over all that again. I was chosen because he wanted someone outside the KGB and an unknown personality. I am a major in the GRU and until September of last year, I was used for various assignments in connection with visiting foreign VIPs, diplomats and business men.' With her looks, figure and sexual athleticism, Gunn had little difficulty in imagining what those assignments would have been.

Whilst the Russian intelligence machine could be as subtle, · obtuse and cunning as any in the world, on other occasions it employed the same finesse as a brain surgeon using a chain saw - but it worked. Nearly every visiting male or female was put through the 'honey trap'; if it worked, it saved the KGB a great deal of effort. Time and again, despite repeated warnings, the KGB had succeeded in blackmailing foreigners with tape-recordings, videos and photographs.

'I was briefed by our President and I, with a team of fifteen officers in the GRU put the plan into operation. It all went perfectly until the chief conspirator recruited Volkonoff into the conspiracy; after that everything went wrong. Real SS20s were substituted for the fakes which we had prepared, Volkonoff killed those people in your embassy in Beijing, he killed more people in Hong Kong and now we believe that not all the missiles are on Al Samak.'

'I'm not in any way saying that you won't be able to handle it, but that's quite a task for anyone to take on, on their own.'

'Yes, well, I was warned that if anything went wrong, I would have to go and pick up the pieces. We have the same saying as you do; I opened the lid of Pandora's Box and it's my job to close it. Those were the President's exact words.'

'What time does your flight depart tomorrow?

'Terminal 3, 0930 hours.'

'So you'll have to be there no later than 0830. We'll walk or take a taxi to my house and collect my car. We can then go and get your things from the Cumberland Hotel. Stay the night at my place and I'll take you to the airport in the morning. How's that?'

'Yes. I'd like that.' Gunn paid the bill and the two of them walked out onto the wide pavement of the river embankment. It was twenty to eleven and full dark. Gunn paused to see if there were any taxis coming.

'Thank you for that very nice meal; can we walk a little way to shake it down a bit?'

'Yes, sure; we'll turn left in a couple of hundred yards and then go through Chelsea Park Gardens.' They crossed over the road and headed north towards the gardens.

As they walked towards Paulton's Square, they were overtaken by a motorbike which turned right into the King's Road and stopped some three hundred yards further on, opposite the King's Head pub. Without removing his helmet, the rider walked into the pub and was immediately spotted by the four yobbos whom Gunn and Maria had ejected from the Cavalier earlier that evening. The four youths left their drinks on the bar, walked out of the pub and after putting on helmets, mounted two motorbikes. The three bikes went west along King's Road until they reached the junction with Old Church Street and then turned left following the first motorbike which turned right after a hundred yards into Paulton Street and stopped. All three turned off their lights and waited. The five youths saw the couple cross over Paulton Street and head towards the King's Road.

Gunn and Maria paused as they reached the King's Road, crossed to the island and then continued to the other side where they turned left followed by a right into Chelsea Park Gardens. It was now a quarter to eleven and there were very few people around. Gunn heard the motorbike turn into the square behind them. Seconds later, he was knocked to the pavement by a crushing blow which had been aimed at his head, but which landed between his shoulder blades stunning him rather than splitting open his skull. As he fell to the pavement, two of the youths riding pillion jumped at Maria knocking her to the pavement where she cracked her head against the kerb and was then punched and kicked into unconsciousness by all four of them, while the fifth youth, who was holding the sawn-off shot gun, stood over the inert Gunn.

Two of the occupants of the houses on the east side of the gardens saw the assault and both went to their phones to ring the police. Maria's blouse was ripped off and the bra holding her large, firm breasts was cut away with a razor sharp knife. Fired with alcohol and lust, one of the youths could restrain himself no longer and at the sight of the ample breasts, started to undo his belt. The other three ripped open her slacks and pulled them and her knickers down together.

Gunn had been hit by the butt of the shotgun and could see the man standing beside him with the gun held in both hands. Had the butt connected with his head, he would have been either dead or unconscious with a split skull, as it was, he had fallen in a semi-foetal position on his left side. His right hand was only a few inches away from the gun in the holster on his right ankle. The man standing over him shouted hoarsely at the others to 'get on wiv'it'.

Maria was naked and two of the youths had pulled their trousers down. Gunn eased the big automatic from its holster, thumbing back the hammer as he did so. The man standing over Gunn was paying more attention to the rape than the person he was supposed to be watching. Gunn pointed the automatic over his left shoulder and fired. The 1450 feet per second muzzle velocity of the Radom and the 9mm steel-jacketed bullet slammed the man back against the chain-link fencing where he subsided slowly to the pavement, the sawn-off shot gun falling from his hands. Somewhere in the distance was the sound of a police car siren.

The four men about to rape Maria froze at the sound of the shot, turning towards where Gunn now lay, propped on his elbows on the pavement, the Radom held in both hands. The next two shots hit the youths who were watching the rape, hurling them both some two or three yards before they fell to the pavement. The two men who had dropped their trousers were immobile, hampered by the trousers round their ankles. One, involuntarily, put his hands over his genitals, like a soccer player in a 'wall' attempting to save a penalty shot. The fourth bullet hit him just there, going through both his hands, which was immediately followed by another,which hit him in the head; he was dead before he hit the pavement. The other youth opened his mouth to scream and the last bullet went through it and blew half his skull off. The sound of the siren increased in volume and shouts came from the houses closest to the scene. Gunn got to his feet; all five of the youths were dead. He returned the automatic to its holster and knelt beside Maria, removed his anorak and covered her with that and her slacks.

The sirens rose to a crescendo and lights swung into the square, tyres screeched and car doors slammed. Four policemen ran towards Gunn, who was now propped against the metal fencing. Bright torches were pointed at him.

'Please make sure you've called an ambulance, the young lady here should be taken to hospital as soon as possible,' Gunn said loudly shielding his eyes from the glare. 'These five men are dead and there's a loaded shot gun over there somewhere,' and he waved his arm in the general direction of the fence to his left. 'Could the senior officer here please look at that,' and Gunn held out his BID identity card, and then added, 'I'd be most grateful if someone could help me to my feet.'

The card was removed from his hand while he sat, still blinded by the torches. On the periphery of the blinding glare, he could see a crowd gathering. Another police car arrived with an ambulance and then the torches were pointed away from him and two policemen helped him to his feet. He saw the doors of the ambulance close and it drove off with the blue light flashing.

'Can you walk, Sir?'

'Yes, I'm OK, thanks.'

'We'd like to get you away from here as quickly as possible.'

'Suits me,' and Gunn was led over to the first police car and lowered himself painfully into the back; the whole area of his shoulders and neck felt as though he was carrying a red hot yoke, but better than a smashed skull, he thought, as he got into the car. The doors shut and the car drove the short distance to Chelsea Police Station. He was helped out of the car and taken into the station and upstairs to a comfortable office where a Police Superintendent was waiting. His card was handed back to him.

'I wish to God you'd keep this sort of business off the streets of this country.' John Gunn looked at the Superintendent.

'Would you, by any chance run to a cup of tea?' The man's mouth opened to say something, but at a nod, a constable left the room. 'Superintendent, what happened out there had nothing to do with my line of employment. That was nothing more or less than an example of the sort of vicious assault that happens every night in this and many other cities in this country. Tonight there were two or three major differences; the woman those yobs assaulted and attempted to rape is a member of the Russian Secret Service with whom we are currently co-operating. If I hadn't been armed, she would have been raped and possibly killed, as indeed would I, because we could both identify them. The fact that they are all dead saves the British taxpayer the burden of sending them to trial and accommodating them in prison.' The young constable handed Gunn a cup of tea; it was hot, sweet and didn't taste much like tea, but it was one of the most reviving drinks he'd ever had. 'Have you phoned the number on this card?'

'Yes we have...Sir,' the 'sir' was produced a little reluctantly.

'Good; may I now dictate a statement to someone, which will cover every detail of what happened tonight and then I would like to go to the hospital where you've taken Miss Ionides. I can come back tomorrow and sign the statement as I only live just round the corner.'

'What did you shoot them with, Sir?'

'This,' and Gunn produced the Radom from its holster and then returned it. There was silence and some shuffling of feet.

'Right, to whom do I give my statement?' The Superintendent jerked his head and a plain clothes detective - Gunn assumed - led him back downstairs to an interview room where he gave a full account of everything that had happened since he left Kingsroad House earlier that day.

*

Commander Steinbaum woke with a start to find Dieter Schwendler standing by his bunk. 'What time is it, Dieter?'

'Just after four, Sir. You asked me to call you.'

'Yes, of course; haven't slept so well for ages. Where are we?

'A couple of hundred miles to the south-east of the island of Bali.'

'Any sign of pursuit?'

'None at all.'

'We won't get lucky like that a second time. Right, I'll be in the control room in two minutes.' Schwendler left the cabin and Steinbaum showerd, shaved and dressed in a fresh set of whites before going up to the control room. He checked the inertial navigation plot on the chart and then walked round each station chatting to the duty watch and noting all the readings on the myriad of dials, gauges, VDUs and digital readouts. He then turned to Schwendler and thanked him, allowing him to leave the control room and get some sleep. He went to the officer of the watch and told him that he was going down to the reactor and engine room. After visiting the engine room and reassuring himself that everything was running properly he returned to the control room. His visit had taken him nearly half-an-hour and by the time he had completed it an idea was forming in his head.

Steinbaum had decided that even if the Russian Navy and anyone else searching for them didn't know of the existence of the island of Al Samak and thought that the ship was making for the Middle East, the course would be almost identical from the islands of Indonesia. When he reached the control room, Steinbaum walked over to the chart table and stared at the chart covering the Indian Ocean. He picked up the dividers and opened the points to measure 1000 miles - the distance Al Samak covered every 24 hours. He placed one tip on the 0400 hours plot and then swung the dividers across the Indian Ocean to the east coast of Africa, then north to the Horn of Africa and then east to the Lakshadweep Islands; 5½ days compared to 2½ on the present course planned. Steinbaum reached for the long steel ruler for drawing passage rhum lines. He turned to his navigating officer.

'Please mark the current plot,' the officer had been expecting this and was reading the latitude and longitude digital readout above the chart table. As the Captain stepped back from the chart table, the navigating officer bent forward and using a metal vernier scale, marked the plot at 0458 hours. Steinbaum placed his ruler on the chart and drew in a new course line which spanned the southern Indian Ocean to a point to the north of Madagascar, then north to the island of Socotra off the east tip of the Horn of Africa and then due east to the island of Al Samak. 'That's your new course, Lieutenant, please give the necessary instructions to the coxswain.'

'Very good, Sir.' The Lieutenant marched the parallel rules across to the compass rose and ordered, 'new course; 270°.'

'270 degrees it is, Sir.'

'Now let's see if you can find us,' and then aloud Steinbaum said, 'officer of the watch!'

'Sir!'

'You have the control room. I shall be in my cabin.'

'Aye, aye, Sir,' and Steinbaum smiled to himself at the incongruity of the traditional British Naval acknowledgement.'

*

A thousand miles to the north in the Celebes Sea, a very similar scene was taking place in the control room of USS Los Angeles. The Captain, Commander George Gresham, was also standing beside the chart table when his radio officer came into the control room. 'Any luck, Hal?'

'Yes, Sir; here's the reply. It seems that you had the same idea as British Intelligence. They got on to the Germans who came up with the names and backgrounds of the Captain and First Officer of Al Samak. It's all there in the signal, but it looks as though we're up against a couple of neo-Nazis and you'll see that Steinbaum - that's the Captain - was the most talented sub skipper in the Bundesmarine.'

'That figures,' George muttered to himself, reading every word of the signal as he tried to think himself into the mind of the man commanding this extraordinary submerging ship. Still deep in thought, he handed the signal back to Lt Commander Tudor with a 'thanks' and transferred his attention to the chart. He glanced over his shoulder at the sonar station; Leading Seaman Murphy was off watch. 'If Murphy's not asleep, will you ask him to come and see me in the control room,' the Captain asked the officer of the watch. Murphy had already acquired a reputation after winning the crate of Budweiser - to be received at the end of the current deployment - and so there were more smiles as the ratings in the control saw the potential for another opportunity to win the jackpot with the correct guess about the movements of the submerging ship.

'You sent for me, Sir?'

'Yes, son; I'm about to have another guess at this ship's course. You were the only one in Angeles who got it right last time so it's only fair to let you have a crack at this one, same stakes, same prize. You in on this one?'

'Yes, Sir.'

'Good; here's the situation. The ship is somewhere in this circle. It's heading for this island, here, in the Arabian Sea. In this area, here, is the depleted Russian Southern Fleet and Angeles is here. We know that the captain of this ship is said to be the most skilled German sub skipper since the Second World War - he's also a Nazi by inclination, if you think that's relevant to this problem. Right, son, you've got all the information that I have - no, sorry; one other point. It would seem that there is no immediate deadline for getting these missiles to this island. You are Unterseebot Kapitän Steinbaum,' the captain's imitation of a theatrical German accent brought smiles all round the control room, 'what course would you take? Just so there's no accusations of cheating, this is my idea, written on this bit of paper. Lieutenant Baker is excused from this problem as he can't afford to lose concentration for a moment while we're moving at this speed.' Take your time and then write your solution on the scribble pad.'

Twenty minutes later, Murphy indicated that he was ready and held out his piece of paper, which he'd torn from the scribble pad. 'Talk me through your solution, son; I'll look at this afterwards.'

'Right, Sir; I found this harder than the other because in the end it came to a fifty/fifty choice between two courses, each of which has its advantages and disadvantages. The skipper's problem is to avoid the Russian Southern Fleet; a fleet that has now been alerted to the capabilities of the ship and isn't likely to make the same mistakes as that task force commander. So he either goes for the open sea, making it a hell of a task to find him, or he's sneaky. From here to here is the main shipping route from South-East Asia to the Red Sea and Suez Canal,' and Murphy swept his hand across the Indian Ocean and the Arabian Sea from Malaysia to the Gulf of Aden.

236

'There's a constant stream of ships on this route and, on balance, I think I'd use them to mask my movement. I think that he will look for a big tanker or container ship, preferably twin screw like his ship, and then he'll sit right underneath it. It could also give the Ruskies a hell of a problem. If he sits under a big ship it's almost impossible to attack him without destroying the ship above him, while he's free to fire all his weapons. That's my choice; he'll go for the sneaky one and hide under another ship.' Commander Gresham produced his solution.

'I reckon he'll go for the open sea and head for the coast of Africa and then cut north-east so that he approaches the island from the opposite direction from that which is expected. So this is what we're going to do; we will continue to that intercept point as already planned, where we will wait for six hours and listen for him. If he's not there we will move south-west to this point to intercept him if he's taken a course across the Indian Ocean. Thank you Murphy, we'll see who wins that second crate.

*

Spirit of the Sea had had an uneventful and fast passage from Hong Kong and as dawn broke on 31st July, the anchor was dropped in the waiting area outside the mouth of the Chao Phaya River. Here the ship would have to wait until the pilot arrived to take it up the river to its alongside berth. The skipper contacted his agent shortly after eight in the morning and the agent, in his turn, made a long distance call to Baghdad. The time in Baghdad was just after 4.30 in the morning when the 'phone call was put through to Volkonoff's room at the Hilton. He grunted, replaced the phone and went back to sleep.

That was the second call he'd received that night; the first had been at 2.15 on his arrival back at the hotel after satiating himself in a brothel to which he'd been introduced by a member of Saddam's Security Police. He had taken the call in the lobby, which had been from his colleague at the Russian Embassy in London. The man had thought that Volkonoff was dead and on discovering that he was alive, had agreed readily to supply him with information in return for the large sum of money promised as a reward.

In another room in the Hotel, the second message was recorded and an alarm buzzer woke the occupant of the room. He reached over, wound back the tape and replayed it. He did this twice and then got up and put a call through to London on his mobile. The duty officer's 'phone rang in Kingsroad House where it was just after two in the morning. The duty officer had been told to contact two

237

people, Simon Peters and Donald Hastings. The former had been in bed for only an hour; there had been some hasty tidying up required after the incident in Chelsea. He acknowledged the 'phone call and went back to sleep.

Donald Hastings was still in Kingsroad House preparing the Director's brief for the PM on the US and UK troop deployment in Saudi Arabia and Kuwait which was required for 0830 hours. He acknowledged the message and made an amendment to the brief. There was little doubt that the President Bush and the Prime Minister Blair intended to invade. If they didn't get the next phase of the operation right, within 24 hours, Saddam Hussein would be in possession of a nuclear capability in direct contravention of Resolution 1441 and Bush and Blair would have the justification they wanted for armed intervention.

CHAPTER 18

Just as Gunn was finishing his statement, the door of the interview room opened and the police sergeant who'd helped him to his feet at the scene of the assault, stuck his head round the door. The detective-sergeant switched off the tape recorder. 'The young woman was taken to St Thomas', Sir; we can give you a lift there if it's of any help.'

'Thanks, Sergeant; that'd be most helpful. I'll be with you in a couple of minutes.' As soon as he had finished the recorded statement, Gunn used his mobile. He dialled the duty officer, but was put straight through to Simon Peters who was still in the building. 'Do you want me to come into the office now?'

'No, John, no need; it's all been taken care of and cleaned up. We've told her people and they are planning to move her later to-morrow into their place. I'll see you tomorrow morning.' Gunn replaced the mobile in his pocket and went out into the courtyard at the back of the police station. He climbed into the back of the Volvo which immediately moved off and turned right out of the gates, heading for the Thames embankment.

'The Superintendent means well, Sir, but he'd just been speaking to the Commissioner who'd given him a bit of a hard time on another matter. There isn't a man on this station who wouldn't thank you for what you've done tonight. That bunch has been mugging and menacing people on our patch all summer and every time we put them in court the prosecution is destroyed by a bunch of do-gooders who claim that society is responsible for the behaviour of those louts. I only wish that it was their daughter who'd been raped.'

'I don't suppose my employers will be overjoyed about me scattering dead bodies around the streets, but your point is the only valid one, Sergeant; how would you feel if it was your wife, daughter or girlfriend who was being raped. Thanks, that's very good of you,' this was added as the police car drove up to the casualty reception of St Thomas' Hospital. 'I'll call in tomorrow and sign that statement for you,' and Gunn waved and turned towards the brightly-lit entrance of the casualty department.

Gunn went to the reception desk and asked the woman sitting behind it if he might see Miss Ionides who had been admitted earlier.

239

'I'm sorry, Sir, there's a policeman on duty outside her room and you won't be allowed to go in.'

'I'm delighted to hear there's a policeman on duty; would there be someone available who could escort me up to that room so that I can identify myself to him.' The receptionist pressed a bell push and eventually a hospital porter appeared, who reluctantly accepted the task of acting as Gunn's escort. Outside the private room on the surgical ward was a young policeman. Gunn showed him his BID identity card.

'Right, Sir; the desk sergeant radioed to say that you were on your way. There's a doctor in there with her at the moment.'

'Thank you,' and Gunn quietly opened the door and went into the darkened room. The white-coated doctor was bending over the bed and even Gunn's rudimentary knowledge of first aid had never included the practice of holding a pillow over someone's face as a form of resuscitation. The man turned as Gunn entered the room, reaching inside the white coat. In the open doorway, the young constable stood with mouth agape. To Gunn's right was a steel trolley with metal bowls, drugs and other medical paraphernalia. He propelled the trolley across the room, grimacing with the sharp stab of pain this sent shooting across his back as he dropped into a crouch. The trolley struck the 'doctor' and momentarily distracted his attention.

He had produced a silenced automatic from inside the white coat and Gunn saw to his horror that the first shot was being aimed at Maria. The assassin evidently intended to complete his assignment before disposing of any obstacle impeding his escape. Out of the corner of his eye the fake doctor saw the big automatic appear in Gunn's hands and realised, too late, his error. The elongated barrel of his gun started to swing away from the patient in the bed towards the greater threat posed by the man crouching on the floor. Gunn fired twice; one bullet went into the man's stomach and the other into his right shoulder. The automatic fell from his hand and he slumped over the trolley, scattering its contents, and then fell to the floor. Gunn turned to the constable who had been watching this from the door.

'Shut the door and don't let anyone in!' The young man stood with his mouth still open, fiddling with his lapel radio mike. 'Do as you're fucking well told!' Gunn shouted at him, which produced the desired effect and the door closed behind the policeman. Gunn moved to the side of the bed and looked at Maria. It seemed that she was sedated and breathing evenly. He pushed the trolley out of the way and grasped the groaning assassin by the tie and pulled his head

240

off the ground. 'I only hope for your sake that you understand English, because if you don't, you're dead. Can you understand me?' There was a feeble nod of the head. 'I want to know who sent you to do this. I'm going to count to three and then the next shot will go here,' and Gunn jabbed him in the groin with the automatic. 'One...two...'

'I..I had...phone call. Man met me.....oh for chrissakes get a doctor, my gut's falling out.'

'I'm waiting; who met you? Have you done this for him before? Come on, the sooner I get the answers, the sooner you get medical attention.' Gunn could hear voices raised in argument

outside the door. 'I got to two,' and Gunn prodded the man's groin again with the barrel of the Radom.

'Think he's a Russian...followed him after he'd paid me.. half that is.. other half when it was done. He didn't go to their Embassy, but he went to a club where I saw him meet a man I know's from that Embassy. For the love of God get that doctor or I'm a goner, that's all I know.'

'No it's not; where and when were you to meet this character to get the other half of the payment?'

'Different place... bar by the gents at Waterloo.'

'When?'

'You bastard, get me...'

'When?'

'One thirty, tomorrow afternoon.....' Gunn got up and checked Maria again and then went to the door and opened it. There was quite a gathering which included the two policemen from the car which had given him a lift to the hospital and what looked like a very irate doctor and several hospital administrative staff. Gunn beckoned the police and the doctor into the room and pushed the door firmly closed in the face of the rest of the people. 'Your patient is unharmed, no thanks to the security of this hospital. This character,' and John Gunn pointed with his foot, 'was in the process of suffocating the patient - as witnessed by both me and the constable outside that door. He's been shot in the shoulder and the gut and imagines that he's justified in demanding medical attention,' this comment had been directed at the doctor. 'Incidentally, can you prove that you're a bona fide doctor?'

'Er.. no, but those people outside the door....'

'Alright doctor, can you see if you can do anything for this man,' Gunn turned to the police sergeant. 'His gun is over there, Sergeant. Can you stay here while I go and make another phone call.'

'Yes Sir, don't worry, we'll take care of the lady.'

241

'Thanks,' Gunn returned the Radom to its holster and took the mobile from his pocket and went out of the room to the central nursing station. He dialled and the duty officer at Kingsroad House answered. 'Is Foxtrot One still there?'

'Affirmative.'

'Please connect me.'

'Wait please... you're through.'

'Foxtrot two; I'm at the hospital. Our main competitors have had a go at her. I believe she should

be taken to our own clinic. I'll wait here until she's collected to make sure there are no more cockups and then call at the office before going home. Fifteen minutes... fine. Second floor, surgical ward. Thanks, bye,' and Gunn ended the call.

Gunn returned to the private room where the young constable was doing a herculean job of keeping out the hospital administrative staff. As he reached the door, it opened and a stretcher was wheeled out with a body on it, pushed by two hospital orderlies. Trusting no one now, Gunn pulled back the sheet, which exposed the ashen face of the hired assassin. Gunn flicked back the sheet and walked into the room.

The doctor turned; 'he's dead. You killed him. I hope you sleep well at nights with your conscience.'

'And you, doctor, need to get your priorities in life right; that rubbish which has just been wheeled out was a hired killer who has probably murdered more people than you've had hot dinners. He was attempting to kill that patient of yours who had just survived an attempted rape.' A bleak expression replaced the indignant one on the doctor's face and he turned without another word and walked from the room. 'We're removing her to a private clinic, Sergeant. Our ambulance should be here in about ten minutes. Thanks for all your support and help. I'll wait here until the ambulance comes, if you want to return to your patrol car.'

'Right Sir; hope you don't have any more excitement before the night's out.'

'So do I,' and the two policemen left the room. Maria Ionides had slept peacefully through all the hiatus, but the beating she'd been given that evening ruled out any possibility of her following Volkonoff to Baghdad. The door opened and the young policeman put his head round the door.

'Ambulance crew's come to collect the young lady, Sir.' Gunn got up and went to the door. He saw Simon Peters with them and opened the door wide.

'Come on, John; I'll give you a lift in my car back to your house which'll save you coming into the office. You can tell me on the way what the hell's going on.' The stretcher reappeared with Maria tucked up snugly on it and still fast asleep. They followed it to the lift and went down to the ground floor where Simon signed the papers for removing the patient and then they both followed the stretcher out to the ambulance. The doors closed and the ambulance moved away. Gunn got into the passenger seat of Simon's Renault Megane and they left the hospital and crossed back over the Thames.

'After you'd passed the message to the Russian Embassy about Maria Ionides, someone there hired the killer I found in her room. The man admitted that they had used him before. He's due to be paid the remaining amount of money at 1330 tomorrow in the bar at Waterloo Station next to the gents. Do you want me...'

'No, I must leave that to James Rayner and his boys. Is this Volkonoff?'

'There was enough time. If he has an informer at the Embassy, that person had time to ring him in Baghdad, be told what to do and then put it into action.'

'Yes, that must be right. I must now go back to the office and let the Russians know what has happened and that their agent is in no fit state to travel let alone take on Volkonoff. Here we are,' and Simon drove into the mews and stopped outside Gunn's front door. Off you go, I'll just wait to make sure that there are no more unwelcome surprises.' Gunn got out of the car; his shoulder injury was really stiffening up. He opened the door and went into the house. After a quick check all round he went back to the front door and gave Simon a thumbs up and then went back upstairs and turned on the shower before getting undressed.

The shower stall was full of steam when he returned after discarding his clothes. He stood in the shower under the jets of piping hot water for a reviving ten minutes, turning it from hot to cold and then towelled himself dry and went to his bedroom. Five minutes were spent cleaning the Radom after which he refilled the magazine and worked a round into the chamber. Gunn had a final walk round the whole house, noting all the 'tell-tales' he had left behind - the exact position of a door, a desk drawer, a book in the book shelves and the tins in the larder and then, no doubt much to the irritation of the doctor at the hospital, placed the Radom under his pillow and fell into a dreamless sleep.

*

243

The sonar operator in the control room of Al Samak reached out and turned one of the dials on the console in front of him. He listened for a few more minutes and then took off the headphones and went to the small library of books behind the chart table. He removed a volume of the Lloyds Registry of Shipping, returned to his station and opened the book at the index. Having found what he was looking for, he then turned to the relevant reference in the book. The officer of the watch walked over to the sonar operator who looked up from the book and then explained what he was doing. The two men spoke for about five minutes and then the officer of the watch picked up the telephone and dialled the captain's cabin. There was no answer; the officer glanced at his watch; 0805. He dialled the wardroom and a steward answered. Yes, the captain was there and just finishing his breakfast.

'Captain speaking.'

'Sir, officer of the watch; no urgency Sir, but we have an idea which we'd like to discuss with you.'

'Who's 'we'?'

'The sonar operator and myself, Sir.'

'Right, I'll be in the control room in a couple of minutes, thank you,' and Steinbaum replaced the phone, returned to the table and finished his coffee.

'Problems, Sir?' Schwendler inquired.

'I don't think so, but I'll let you know!' he put down the empty cup and was just about to leave the ward room when he paused; 'have you spoken with our five guests?'

'Not yet, Sir.'

'Take a visit to their ward room - they should all be at breakfast by now - and have a cup of coffee with them. I'll give you a ring if I need you in the control room.'

'Very good, Sir.' Steinbaum left the ward room, turned left and left again and then went up the companionway to the control room; submerged it was always referred to as the control room. When the ship was on the surface, it immediately became the bridge. Discipline on Al Samak reflected the training of its captain. The ship was run as a warship and as soon as the captain appeared in the control room he was saluted by the officer of the watch, which he returned.

'Right, let's hear this idea, please.'

'Sir,' replied the officer of the watch, 'sonar has informed me that he has a contact which he believes is the Japanese oil tanker, Shimojima.'

'And why do I need to know about that?' The watch officer didn't feel very sure of himself now that he was confronted by the

244

captain and was wishing that he hadn't thought of interfering with the nautical handling of the ship.

'The ship has a displacement of 100,000 tons and twin screws; it commutes regularly between Darwin and the Gulf. It's now heading for the Gulf in ballast. It's speed is 25 knots - we can do that on our APU - and we... I, wondered whether you would wish to consider the possibility of positioning Al Samak under the tanker which would completely mask our presence. It would also make it impossible for the Russian Fleet to engage us without damaging the Japanese tanker, whereas we would not suffer that impediment for the use of our offensive weapons.'

'And so you would have us hide like some sort of...cur, to sneak past the Russians?'

'Just an idea.....Sir.'

'And a brilliant one, Lieutenant! Why didn't I see that as the obvious solution to fool those dolts out there. Well done! I think we'd better go and have a close look at this ship, just to make sure. Sonar! Bearing to contact?'

'65°, Sir.'

'Right; coxswain!'

'Sir!'

'New course; 282°.' The small wheel spun clockwise and Al Samak banked to starboard as the hydroplanes heeled the ship over in exactly the same way as the ailerons on an aircraft's wing banked it.

'Blow main ballast! Come to 60 feet! Reduce revolutions for 15 knots! The orders were repeated at the various stations around the control room. 'Lieutenant, please ask Lt Commander Schwendler to come to the control room.'

'Yes Sir!' and the call was put through to the passengers' wardroom.

'Six zero feet, periscope depth, Sir.'

'Thank you; up periscope!' Steinbaum grasped the handles, flicked them open and then spun the monocular to commence his search from for'ard. Two miles ahead, right on the bow was the stern of the huge tanker and with little difficulty Steinbaum could read the name, Shimojima. He completed his search through 360°. 'Down periscope! Blow main ballast! 120 feet. Revolutions for thirty knots!'

Within fifteen minutes, Al Samak had closed the two, mile gap and once underneath the tanker, matched speeds and trim to bring the submerged vessel within twenty feet of the leviathan above it. Schwendler appeared in the control room. 'Change of plan, Dieter.

We defeated them with deception last time and I think we may be able to repeat that.'

'What the hell's that above us, sir?'

'That, Dieter, is the Shimojima, which is going to sneak us past the Russian Fleet!'

*

As soon as Simon Peters had dropped Gunn, he used his mobile to contact James Rayner. The latter had a small town house off Belgrave Square, which was worth a couple of ransoms. The Rayners had a large estate in Nottinghamshire; during the week, James Rayner lived in the family town house and returned at weekends to the estate. He was at his house, which saved Simon Peters from the irksome task of getting communications to page him and then wait for the return call. 'Sorry to bother you, James; can you come into the office.'

'Yes of course; I'll be there in ten minutes,' and the 'phone went dead.

James Rayner appeared in the office only two minutes over the promised ten. He was dressed in a dinner jacket and told Simon that he'd just had a rather successful evening on the Black Jack table at Whites. Simon Peters explained the Volkonoff connection at the Soviet Embassy, the move of Maria Ionides - alias Petrovsky - to the Directorate's clinic and the meeting at the bar on Waterloo Station.

'Right, got all that; you leave it with me as it looks as though you've had a very long day, Simon. You go home and I'll see you in the morning. What time are you coming in?'

'I'm briefing John Gunn at 8.30.'

'I'll have some sort of a response from the Russians for you by then.'

'Many thanks,' and Simon left the office after locking everything away and drove home to his house in the Claremont Estate at Esher where he climbed into bed at 1.30 in the morning. An hour later, he was woken to be informed of the call to Volkonoff from Bangkok.

*

Claudine de Carteret awoke to find herself in a very comfortable bed in what appeared to be the room of a five-star hotel. There was the gentle hum of air-conditioning and the view through the ceiling to floor windows was straight off the front cover of an exotic travel brochure. Beyond her balcony, the sky was a pale washed-out blue; dazzling white coral sand stretched from the edge of emerald green grass to the clearest aquamarine sea which Claudine had ever seen or

246

imagined. The sun was already high and its brilliance shimmered on the calm surface of the lagoon. Just beyond the opening to the sea at the far side of the lagoon, there were two dug-out fishing canoes with outriggers and coloured, patch-work crab-claw sails.

She got out of bed; her jeans, blouse and sweatshirt had vanished and she was wearing her bra and panties. There was a large fitted bathroom with a jacuzzi bath, a small lounge and when she tried them, none of the doors was locked. She opened the balcony windows, and the heat hit her like a physical blow. She closed them and retreated into the cool temperature of the room.

There was a knock at the door in the lounge. In the bedroom, at the end of the bed was a length of brightly woven cloth, which she wound round herself and then she returned to the lounge and opened the door. Outside the door were two very dark-skinned, female staff dressed in saris with a trolley which they pushed into the lounge. On the trolley was the sort of breakfast that a top, five-star hotel might have provided. Once the table had been laid, one of the women beckoned to Claudine who followed her into the bedroom. The woman opened a fitted wardrobe to reveal every imaginable form of fashionable female apparel for a tropical climate.

'Do you speak English?' Claudine asked, but the heads were politely shaken and with delicate hands clasped together in front of their faces in a namatsi display of deference, bowed themselves out of her room.

Having not eaten for what seemed like 24 hours, Claudine did good justice to the spread of iced fruit juice, fresh fruit, hot rolls and a piping hot plate of bacon and eggs. After her second cup of coffee, she went into the bedroom and examined the content of the fitted wardrobe. Her skin was well tanned from the unusually hot English summer and the amount of time she spent at sea with her father. There was a choice of no less than ten swimsuits and bikinis and so she selected a bikini, shorts, blouse and beach shoes and there was even a choice of three pairs of sunglasses.

She opened the door and walked out into the corridor. She found herself in the most perfectly designed mansion in the classical style with double staircases curving up to the first floor from a wide, cool hall paved in large green and white-veined marble tiles. Everything was painted in brilliant white except for alcoves and doors which mirrored the same shade of green as the marble on the floor. Most of the furniture was off-white rattan, with glass-topped tables and light, flower-patterned cushions and upholstery. Brass-scrolled fans spun from the ceiling blowing the cooled air around each room.

She walked out of the front door, immediately grateful for the sunglasses, as the glare from the sun reflecting off the white paint everywhere was blinding. Everywhere she looked were coconut palms, some of which were seventy or eighty feet in height. In between the coconut palms were all the other species of palms and ferns; royal palms, traveller palms with perfectly symmetrical fronds forming a fan, oil nut palms and fan palms. Brilliantly coloured tropical plants, hibiscus and flowers bloomed in profusion everywhere.

'Where the hell am I?' Claudine wondered as she explored her surroundings.

None of the buildings Claudine could see rose above the height of the coconut palms. Parked under the graceful, pillared portico was a small jeep with a candy-striped sun awning; the keys were in the ignition. She got into the car and started the engine; with the exception of the two girls who had served her breakfast, Claudine had seen no one else. She drove down the short drive and turned right. The neatly surfaced road wound through the palms; on her right was the lagoon. The first turn off to the right led her to a large, white rectangular building, which was as ugly as the mansion was beautiful. However, it was completely hidden by the surrounding palms and as Claudine drove round the building, he saw that it was a hangar.

She parked the jeep and walked to the side of the hangar facing the lagoon. The large steel doors were open and inside were two, twin-engined sea planes. From the hangar, a concrete ramp ran into the lagoon. Each seaplane sat on a tricycle undercarriage and at the back of the hangar were winches to haul the machines out of the water. At the far end of the hangar was a helicopter, fitted with floats and sitting on a dolly, which ran on rails down the concrete ramp. Men in overalls were working on the machines, but no one paid any attention to Claudine as she inspected the place.

She returned to the jeep and drove back to the 'main road' and turned right again. The road led next into an area of small round, white-walled huts with conical, rush roofs. Around these were saried women and small children and in the centre of what appeared to be this 'staff accommodation' was a larger, open-sided hut of identical design which was serving as a school room as Claudine stopped beside it, but could have easily served a multitude of purposes. The class of some twenty children turned to stare at Claudine until their attention was recalled by the woman who was teaching them.

The road led on through the palms to what seemed to be a cul-de-sac, but when Claudine reached the point in her jeep, she saw that the road turned through a right angle to the left. Directly in front of her was a channel, cut through the rock and coral. The channel was about fifty metres wide and led from the sea towards a collection of buildings two or three hundred yards away on the left. She got back in the jeep and drove along the road, which followed the side of the channel. Just before the channel reached the buildings, it was blocked by a very substantial set of lock gates set into reinforced concrete.

Claudine turned off the road and got out of the jeep. She walked over to the lock gates. To her right was the channel from the sea with strategically placed leading lights and to her left was the dry dock - presumably for the ship Al Samak . All round the dry dock were buildings, none of which rose above the height of the palms and when the ship sank down onto its wooden chocks, nothing would show above the top of the palm fronds. On either side of the dry dock were rails and at first Claudine thought these were for cranes, but on closer examination saw that there was a canopy, rather similar to those which slide over outdoor swimming pools, which covered the ship entirely once it had sunk down inside the dock. There were a number of men both inside the dock and in the maintenance area and even as she watched, the canopy started to move over the dock.

'Preparations for the arrival of the ship,' Claudine murmured as she turned and walked to the jeep.

The road ran round the dock area and then came to another group of buildings and concrete aprons; there was very little imagination required to guess the purpose of this area. In the centre of each of the concrete aprons was a round aperture about thirty feet across with a metal covering over it. One of the covers was pulled back and Claudine parked the jeep and walked over to it. She was watched, but no one attempted to stop her. Below the aperture was a silo, some seventy feet in depth with wide exhaust ducts for the thunderous burst of flame, raw power and thrust from the solid fuel missile rocket motors.

Further along, the road wound around row after row of bunkers in which, she presumed, the ammunition and arms were stored from which Hassan supplied his clients around the world. Beyond the bunker area, which must have covered at least 20 acres, she came to what she judged to be the 'executive accommodation area'. This looked not unlike the villa and apartment developments in Spain and Portugal which she'd seen advertised in colour supplements and included a small marina where there were motorboats, sailboards and small sailing boats.

She had now completed the circuit of the island and was at the other side of the lagoon. The sun was somewhere directly overhead, so Claudine decided to return to the luxurious mansion and then go for a swim in the lagoon. There had been no need for security because there was no where to go. She had no idea where she was - Seychelles, Maldives, the islands off Thailand whose names she couldn't remember or anywhere in the millions of islands of the Malaysian/Indonesian archipelago. It was July, or nearly August - but then how long had she been drugged? - it was hot and not over humid and so she judged that she was in the tropics in the northern hemisphere, but as she had no idea how long the flight to the island had taken, she had no idea whether she was in the Pacific or Indian Ocean.

There was still no one in the house and so she collected a large swimming towel from her room and walked down the path at the back of the mansion to the bleached coral sand which was almost white hot. Keeping on her beach shoes, Claudine walked into the water before removing them and then threw them back onto the sand. The water was like warm silk and she walked out amongst the brightly coloured parrot and angel fish which darted out of her way as she swam strongly out into the lagoon.

'No, there was no point in locking me up,' she thought, 'particularly if you were a devout Muslim, because you wouldn't expect a woman to be able to fly an aeroplane.'

*

By eight o'clock, Volkonoff had breakfasted and packed his small bag. He had been told that the airline booking desk would be opened at 8.15 and, 'no', there was no other travel agent open before the one in the Hilton. Impatiently, he walked up and down the reception area, which became more and more crowded as the minutes ticked by. The phone call in the early hours of the morning had warned him that the KGB was after him. A young woman walked across to the counter from a 'staff only' door. She unlocked the hatch, let herself in and switched on the ticketing computer.

'Yes Sir, can I help you?'

'I have a most urgent business appointment in Bangkok; what would be the first direct flight and failing that, a connecting flight to get me there as soon as possible.'

'Right Sir, what flight status do you want,' the woman asked as she started to tap in the information to the computer.

'Sorry?'

'Do you wish to fly first class, business or economy?'

'Preferably first or business, but I don't mind economy if that's the first and only seat on a direct flight.'

'Right, Sir, I won't keep you a moment. Cash or credit card?'

'Credit card; American Express.' More people moved up to the airline counter and one irritating man lent over it and interrupted the woman by asking from where the bus to the airport left.

'In fifteen minutes from the front entrance, Sir,' she replied without becoming in the slightest ruffled.

'There's a first class seat on Air France flight AF 568 to Sydney which leaves at 10.30. It has an hour and a half stopover in Bangkok.' She looked at her watch. 'Will that suit you?'

'Yes, I'll take that.'

'One way or return?

'One way.'

'That'll be $3,058. Thank you,' and she took the proffered American Express card, filled it in, pressed down the lever and returned it to him to sign. 'Thank you, Sir; your ticket will be waiting for you at the Air France check-in desk at the airport. The bus leaves in five minutes. Now, who was next, please?'

By the time the airport bus moved off, the information of airline, flight number and ETA Bangkok had been passed to Kingsroad House from where it was relayed in a flash precedence signal to the resident BID agent in Bangkok. Volkonoff's sharp edge had lost its keenness; he never noticed that the man who had irritated him by asking about the airport bus, was, in fact, not on it.

CHAPTER 19

Gunn's alarm woke him at 7.30; he started to get out of bed and was given a painful reminder of the blow from the butt of the shotgun. He went down the stairs and into the kitchen where he put coffee in the percolator and took two croissants out of the freezer and put them in the microwave. He then went back upstairs, showered, shaved and dressed in a tropical lightweight suit. He pulled up his right trouser leg, strapped on the holster and removed the Radom from under his pillow. The armourer at the Directorate had not been exaggerating; the gun was a man-stopper. He placed it in the holster, wrote a note to Mrs Charlesworth, his housekeeper, and went down to the kitchen. He switched on the radio and then poured himself a cup of coffee. The radio was broadcasting the 7.30 news summary which included, as the second to last item, the information that an unidentified young woman who'd been the victim of a vicious mugging the previous night had subsequently died of the injuries while in St Thomas' Hospital.

Gunn smiled; the Directorate had been at work ensuring that the contact at the Soviet Embassy believed that the assassination had been successful. Gunn put the breakfast things into the sink to rinse from where, as always, they would be removed by Mrs Charlesworth and washed again. He closed the front door, reversed the TR6 out of the garage and then closed and locked the doors. First stop was at Chelsea Police Station, where the desk sergeant produced the typed statement, which Gunn read and then signed. He drove the short distance to Kingsroad House and parked the car on the fourth floor. He took the lift to the top floor where he let himself into the Directorate.

It was 8.15; he didn't have an office and neither did any of his colleagues. Every department had an empty office, which was available to the field agent currently being employed should he need it, but it was well known that the Director's views were that field agents should be in the field, not in offices. This suited them admirably and in Gunn's case, if he ever wanted anything done in the way of clerical work, Louise always seemed to be able to make time to do it for him.

'Morning Louise, is Simon in?'

'He should be here any second. I gather that he was disturbed twice in the night.'

'The old Director was singing your praise yesterday in no uncertain fashion. Do you think that will mean a nice Christmas bonus?'

'Oh shut up you cynic! I hardly dare say this, but the whole thing was achieved completely by chance.'

'Often the case, so I'm told.'

'No really... here's your coffee.'

'Many thanks.'

'It was just like that when I stumbled on the island.'

'Sorry, I'm not with you; just like what?'

'I had just handed a mug of coffee to David Pettigrew and saw that a drip had fallen on the map we were looking at. I got a tissue from my handbag and bent over the map to wipe off the drip. It had fallen on this series of dots in the ocean to the west of India,which I'd never heard of before. I asked Simon if he'd ever heard of them, which he hadn't, and then he asked if they were within the arc, which David had drawn on the map. They were, so he told me to go and find out what I could about them.'

'Well, you struck gold that time.' The door opened and Simon came into the office.

'Morning everyone; sorry I'm late. There was a shunt on the Kingston bypass at the A24 underpass. I briefed Alan last night and had to re-brief him on the phone at six this morning to divert him from Baghdad to Bangkok.'

'You didn't get much sleep then.'

'No, not a lot, but once I get you out of this city, John, I shall be so bored I'll probably have to take up a second job. Come in to the office and I'll tell you what's happening and what's required of you. How's the back?'

'Fine, thanks.'

'Has old sawbones in the medical centre seen it?' The Directorate had its own small medical centre which could cope with life stabilising first aid, minor surgery and was particularly expert at removing bullets. It kept all the field agents current with every type of immunisation and was an annex of the Directorate's own clinic which was collocated with the training centre at Maidenhead.

'No, I didn't think it was worth it.'

'You probably won't take my advice, but here it is anyway, pop in and see him. Apart from the fact that he's got some fantastic embrocation for twisted and strained muscles - I've frequently used it when I've strained my back in the garden - it's important that a record is made of all the bumps you get as it affects compensation, pensions and medical discharges. Boring, I know, but I've now said it and I won't repeat it!' Both men sat down in comfortable armchairs in Simon's office and Louise brought in Simon's briefing folder. 'Is all the Bangkok stuff in here, Louise?'

'Yes, Simon; I'll just bring your coffee and then leave you in peace.'

'When does John's flight go?

'The flight's on Thai Airways International TG 642 departing from Terminal Three at Heathrow at 1330 hours. It arrives at Bangkok at 1000 hours local time tomorrow; the flight time is thirteen hours and twenty minutes. John will have no hold baggage and he can delay boarding until 1300 hours. I have warned Transport that we may well require the Gazelle and that will be standing by from 1200 hours. There is a Queen's Messenger on the flight and if John gives me his gun now, I'll see that it goes into the Classified Diplomatic Bag. The Queen's Messenger will be sitting in seat 3A and B - the extra seat is reserved for the bags. The freight leaves on the BA flight which should' - and Louise checked her watch - 'be taking off about now. John's contact is a Mr Ratchasima who will meet him at the airport. John is also booked for a visit to Cyphers and Codes, Communications and the Armourer.'

'Sorry, Louise, I missed that; could you say it all again, please?' She hit Gunn on the head with her shorthand notebook and left the office.

'She's been carrying a torch for you ever since you threw coffee over her at your first meeting. Now, time is short. How well do you know Thailand and Bangkok in particular?' Before Gunn could reply, Louise returned with Simon's coffee, which she placed on the low table between the two men and then left the office closing the door behind her.

'My father and mother went there regularly on business trips and always stayed at the Oriental. As children, my sisters and I were taken there for two or three holidays; a fairly standard package - a couple of nights in Bangkok, two or three days at Pattaya, then off to Chiang Mai to see the elephants and finally four or five days on the island of Phuket. Once I left Hong Kong to go to university, which was immediately followed by the army, I never had any cause to return to Thailand, so I'm a bit out of date.'

'Right, that gives me a starting point; my briefing goes on until about tenish, which will be followed by the other departments. You are an unknown quantity to Volkonoff and the criminal fraternity of Bangkok and therefore your cover will be as an executive of your

254

father's company - which you very nearly were. We have spoken to the chairman, Peter Wyngarde, and your brief from the company will be waiting for you in your room at the Oriental. You are merely inspecting Euro-Pacific Construction's site where they are building yet another hotel to join the hundreds already there. Your contact, Mr Ratchasima, has also been enrolled onto the payroll of Euro-Pacific, so it will arouse no suspicions for him to meet you at the airport and be your constant guide, whenever you should need that sort of help. There's a lot of stuff in this folder you will be taking with you to read on the flight. Bangkok is probably one of the most difficult cities in the world to get to know, as are all the customs of the people.'

'I'm going to concentrate on Bangkok's infamous reputation; vice. The reason that you need to know some background on the seamy side of life in Thailand is because our records not only show that Volkonoff's contact in Bangkok, a Mr Thannamarong, is now the godfather of that city's criminal community, but he contacted Thannamarong by phone from the airport before he left Baghdad. It is only very recently that the government of Thailand has realised that the country is facing a crisis, which it is already, probably, too late to reverse. This is the view of some, not all, sociologists, doctors and behavioural scientists.'

'The main source of foreign currency to Thailand is the tourist trade and the main earner of that trade is what is spent by the tourist on every form of vice, prostitution and drugs. For hundreds of years, the Thais have abused their women by using them as sex objects; I ought to add, at this point, that that is a western point of view. The Thai female doesn't see it that way and considers that she has the upper hand and merely uses her body to get her way. It is an accepted way of life in Thailand for men, both married and single, to make regular visits to prostitutes. This practice is condoned by both wives and girlfriends, but in the last twenty years, prostitution has become really big money. It all started in a privately owned street called Patpong, which runs between Silom and Suriwong Roads.'

'Twenty years ago, this used to be an area of sedate nightclubs, but now every single building is a massage parlour, brothel or go-go bar and there is a Patpong 2 and 3. In Patpong 3, it's all gay bars. Incidentally, any women you see on the streets loitering with intent are probably not women at all, but transvestites - or kra-toeys as they are called there or kai-tais in Singapore and Banshees in Jakarta. Did you get to see Boogey Street before it was cleaned up by Lee Kwan Yu?'

'No; sorry, not old enough.'

'Right; but I must warn you then how beautiful some of these transvestites can make themselves.'

'No need – I heard of a guy on a Hong Kong rugby tour who lost $100 - Singapore, I hasten to add - on a bet about one of those. She - or it - was the spitting image of Brigitte Bardot and he fell in love - or perhaps it was lust - at first sight. The older hands in the Hong Kong fifteen then called 'her' over to the table in the street and whispered something, whereupon the mini-skirt was hitched up revealing a diminutive set of male genetalia, to the great mirth of all. The poor creature had presumably taken such a quantity of female hormone drugs that those visible signs of the gender at birth had shrivelled away to something of the size that even a self-respecting male squirrel would be ashamed.'

'I was caught in almost the same way, John. You will, of course, know that Bangkok became the leading 'R and R' centre for the American troops on leave from Vietnam. New areas of vice blossomed overnight along the New Petchburi Road around the area of the Soi Asoke intersection. This area became known as 'The Strip' and contains some of the fanciest brothels in Bangkok. One which I was shown had both walls and ceiling covered in mirrors and a switchboard by the bed which controlled lights, air-conditioning, music, video projector and a mechanism which made the bed undulate. The fanciest of these is the House of the Rising Sun - which I'm told is about the only thing which doesn't rise in that place - and this is where Thannamarong hangs out.'

'For those with really warped tastes in sex, there's another strip of bars and brothels at Klong Toey in Bangkok's port area on the Chao Phaya River. The story goes that if you suffer from 'brewer's droop' with a prostitute in this area, you could end up with a broken bottle pushed in your face to encourage you to perform better. Unlike the massage parlours of the Wanchai in Hong Kong, the Thai girls will give you a massage with their whole body - for some unknown reason this is known as the 'B-Course' - these are genuine massages, but inevitably lead onto other things for which the client pays more and more at each stage.

There are special package tours organised from Europe and the USA - Germany is the worst culprit - for a fortnight of non-stop sex, pornography, perversion and drug abuse. However vivid your imagination is on the subject of sexual deviation or perversion, multiply it by at least a factor of ten and you can guarantee that that form of sex will be for sale in Bangkok, or Pattaya, which has become so blatant in its sex exploitation of tourists, that couples can be seen fornicating within yards of the main road along the sea front. Pattaya now delights in the nickname of 'Sodom by the Sea'.'

'The tragedy of all this is, firstly, a human one; young children are born and bred into vice and prostitution. They understand no other way of life and they are corrupted beyond any form of physical or mental cure. Incidentally, perhaps I ought to add at this stage, John, it is not only the male who is responsible for this demand for package sex tours in Thailand, although until five or six years ago that was the case. The fastest growing interest in sex tours is currently coming from the females of the so-called civilised world. The second tragedy is that this trade has corrupted every level of society in Thailand from the peasant to, some rumours have it, the Thai Royal Family. It is such easy and plentiful money that no one is able to resist sticking a hand into the honey pot and it is known that the 'godfathers' of crime and vice rackets have friends in very high places.'

'With all these sex package tours there are plenty of free gifts which come as no extra charge - syphillis, gonorrhea and Aids, to name but three. To that you can add every other form of contagious disease including, believe it or not, leprosy, which is not contagious but is endemic to Thailand; that is the third tragedy. The Thai medical authorities have no figures for the incidence of Aids or the spread of the HIV virus. A short while ago, it was estimated that there were some 300,000 carriers of the HIV virus and a World Health Organisation projection from this put the figure at over 2 million carriers by 2005.'

'Then the real shock came; three months ago, a medical examination of young men being called up for military service showed that 15% were infected by the HIV virus. This showed a 300% increase over the same examination done a year previously. Interpolate that level of infection and the rate of increase and the resultant figure measures the potential victims of Aids not in fractions of millions, but in tens of millions. Again, John, this is an unofficial view because there are no reliable statistics or figures; you can imagine what this would do to the Thai tourist trade. Unless a cure for Aids is found very soon, Thailand - like parts of Africa, India, the Philippines, Indonesia and the Caribbean will be ravaged by the disease by the year 2020. The king of sex and porn in Thailand is Mr Thannamarong; he is Volkonoff's buddy and the two of them make a right horrific pair.'

'Your mission is to destroy the nuclear warheads of the SS20 missiles which have now been separated from the propulsion and guidance system and re-crated for air freight to Baghdad in a fake

Saudia 747 which is scheduled to leave Bangkok airport at 1030 hours local time on 3rd August. To assist you in that, the vital part of your mission, the freight, which Louise referred to, consists of four, HVMs - that's....'

'A high velocity missile.'

'Of course, I was forgetting that you were a Gunner ...how familiar are you with them?'

'Totally ignorant as the whole project was in the research and development stage when I left the army.'

'OK, just a quick bit about the HVM, because you've got a half hour slot with the armourer who has persuaded the Royal School of Artillery to lend us an HVM simulator and what he called a 'drill round' - a term which he said you would understand?' Gunn nodded. 'Good; I believe that both its predecessors - the Blowpipe and the Javelin - required considerable dexterity and therefore expensive practise in the case of the former and almost equal dexterity and nerves to maintain the cross wires on the target in the case of the latter.'

'That's a pretty fair judgement.'

'The HVM - I'm told, is a genuine 'fire and forget' missile, which even makes the highly successful American, Stinger, obsolete. It can cope with ECM, chaff and flares; it can see - like a smart bomb - it can hear and it can feel; and - as its name implies, it reaches Mach 3.5 in flight.'

'It must be bloody expensive'

'It is, but in comparison with the training aids, practice rounds and simulators of its predecessors and its 100% hit rate, is no more expensive and represents better value for money. I hasten to add that I'm quoting from the defence sales blurb, but the armourer says that its performance damn nearly makes the low flying aircraft obsolete and as for a helicopter - it's rather easier than shooting clay ducks in a fun fair's shooting gallery.'

'I'm sure the armourer will tell me, but what's this 'see, hear and feel bit'?'

'Ah, even I understood that; the first pressure you take on the trigger activates a miniature TV camera which looks at the aircraft and instantly compares it with stored information on a chip. That stored information contains the profile of that aircraft - and hundreds of others - seen from every angle, so it doesn't matter how it manoeuvres, once you've pointed the eye of the missile at that aircraft and told it 'that's your target', it will never let go until its rocket motor stops. In the same way, I gather, every aircraft has a sound signature and an air-disturbance signature - its wake as the

258

blurb put it. The missile senses all of this and follows it to destruction. The only thing that could divert it is if an identical aircraft flew between it and the target, but even then its sound and wake might be different and if it is an identical aircraft, presumably it's also an enemy one, so it matters not if the missile hits it.'

'Surely its very high speed might be a disadvantage, Simon. If the target aircraft spots the missile, and makes the correct hard, six or seven 'G' turn, the missile will overshoot?'

'The cunning little bugger can even cope with that on two accounts. Firstly, the development of an entirely new solid fuel has made the efflux of the motor barely visible and certainly not on a battlefield with all the other distracting activity and explosions, so, unlike the Stinger, there is no characteristic flare on launch for the pilot or his navigator to spot. Correctly sited, there is no indication of launch and the engagement is all over before the aircrew know what's happened. Secondly, if the target starts to turn, the brain in the missile deploys air brakes, which slow it down so that it can damn nearly turn inside the arc of the target's turn.'

'What price being a fast jet pilot. OK, you've sold it to me.'

'We would like you to destroy the warheads on the ground if you can; if not, then use the missile and do it over the sea. Almost all the aircraft leaving Bangkok climb out over the sea, so hopefully that won't be a problem. Your second priority is to kill Volkonoff. You will be on your own as Petrovsky - you know her as Maria Ionides - is hors de combat. Volkonoff will be able to call on a vast network of thugs, gunmen, criminals, informants - you name it - which stretches into every geographical and sociological corner of Thailand. Ratchasima you can trust implicitly; he and his wife only had one child; a daughter. She was a superb dancer and exquisitely beautiful until she came to the attention of Thannamarong and resisted his advances; perhaps he may tell you how his daughter died and you will then understand his motivation.'

'Alan Paxton will be operating out of our safe house above Rama Jewellry and will keep a very close eye on you and give you all the information and equipment you need to find and destroy both the cargo and Volkonoff. Don't underestimate the danger of this mission. Don't begin to think of any form of 'fair play'. There is no such thing in the dirty game we're employed to play. Shoot Volkonoff in the back or anywhere else and do it with my best wishes and for poor old Tim Driscoll. Any questions?'

'None.'

'Luck doesn't come into this, so I won't wish it to you. Just make sure you get back here in one piece. Leave your gun with Louise. I'll see you on the helipad at 1200 hours.' Gunn left the office, placed the Radom and two extra magazines on Louise's desk and went out into the corridor.

*

James Rayner was admiring the excellent displays of precious and semi-precious gemstones in the Geological Department of the Natural History Museum. 'I regret to say that my weakness is Jade, Mr Rayner. What about you?'

'Diamonds, Mr Kamarov.' The Museum had only just opened and was almost deserted. 'A certain amount of co-operation is needed between us if we are to prevent a disaster in the Gulf. You will know that Petrovsky was attacked last night and taken to St Thomas' Hospital.'

'We do.'

'You should also be aware that you have an informant in your embassy who passed on that information about Petrovsky's arrival, her mission and the assault and attempted rape. Last night, an attempt was made to assassinate Petrovsky in the hospital. The assassin was a hired killer who can identify the man in your embassy who hired him. They are due to meet at 13.30 today, so that your man can pay the killer the second half of the contract fee. I want you there with me so that you can see the transaction.'

'Where's Petrovsky?'

'She's in a private clinic, from where she will be able to leave very shortly. She is not seriously injured and only received mild concussion and some bruising. She will, of course - in the opinion of our doctors - be unable to fulfil her mission. Volkonoff is no longer in Baghdad. We know where he is; not even the Americans know that. We have sent someone to carry out the same task, which Petrovsky was given. We are asking you to leave it like that for the moment to give our agent a clear field to deal with the problem. If he fails, then, of course, we will supply you with all the information, which we possess and hand the task over to you.' A small group of children had arrived and squeals of delight were coming from the very realistic displays of volcanoes and the earthquake simulator.

'We will give Mr Gunn 48 hours and then we will send in an operative. You will be told this operative's name. I will come with you to this meeting at 13.30. Once the man is identified, you may leave the matter in our hands. I'm told that your man Gunn did well to save Petrovsky's life last night. We are grateful for that. Now where do I meet you to deal with this other matter?'

'Embankment tube station, 1300 hours.'

260

'Very well, I'll be there.'

'Have you seen the dinosaur exhibition? I can recommend it.'

'Oh, thank you, but we have plenty of them in Russia and they are all trying to obstruct the course of perestroika,' and with a cheery wave, the cultural attaché of the Russian Embassy walked towards the exit, pausing only momentarily at the display of jadestone.

*

James Rayner arrived at the Embankment station, used his Oyster card on the swipe pad at the gate and walked down the steps to the level of the District and Circle lines and then crossed to the escalators to go down to the Northern line. He never once checked to see if Kamarov was there as he knew that it was completely unnecessary. As he reached the platform, James felt the wind on his cheek as the approaching train compressed the air in the tunnel like a piston in a pump. It burst out of the darkness into the light of the station, there was a piercing scream, the screech of metal grinding on metal as the wheels locked and the train slid along the track to a premature stop, only one and a half coaches out of the tunnel.

A crowd gathered immediately and after turning off the current, two uniformed station staff climbed down to the rails off the platform. One of them shook his head and climbed back onto the platform and started to push the crowd back. A familiar voice came from just to the rear of his right shoulder.

'We knew who it was, Mr Rayner.' James turned and Kamarov was standing beside him. 'You provided us with the last bit of evidence, which we needed. He was the duty officer on the night the information came from Moscow of the imminent arrival of Petrovsky and the nature of her mission. He's dead; you've just witnessed his execution. Goodbye Mr Rayner,' and Kamarov was soon swallowed in the throng of lunchtime commuters and tourists.

*

The USS Los Angeles had rounded the northern tip of Brunei an hour previously and the town of Kota Kinabalu was now abeam to the east. ETA Singapore was just before 0400 hours the next morning and the submarine's ETA off the north of Sumatra was 0900 hours followed by an ETA at the intercept - if there was anything to intercept - at midnight. The nuclear attack submarine was being propelled through the water at a speed faster than that of a World War 2 torpedo. Everyone in the control room and throughout the boat was keyed up to a high state of alertness and concentration and no one more so than the navigating officer who held the life of everyone on board in his hands. If the submarine hit anything at the speed it was going it would probably go straight to the seabed.

'Control room, this is the turbine room, Lt Commander Butler; is the Captain available?'

Commander Gresham moved over to the microphone and picked it up.

'Captain speaking.'

'We have a problem with the for'ard, main shaft bearing, Sir.'

'I'll be with you in two minutes.'

'Thank you, Sir,' and the address system clicked off. The Captain left the control room, went past the reactor compartment and into the diesel generating room. He closed the watertight door behind him and then went down some steel-runged steps and through another door into the turbine room where he was met by Lt Commander Dan Butler, the submarine's chief engineering officer.

'What is it, Dan? Sounds like bad news.'

'Yes, 'fraid it is, Sir.'

'Right, let's hear the worst. Is there anything you want me to order immediately to prevent possible damage?'

'Yes Sir; can we reduce revolutions to 40 knots?' George Gresham moved over to the PA microphone and gave the instruction to the control room. Before entering the turbine room, The Captain had taken a pair of ear defenders off a hook outside the door. The electronic ear defenders allowed normal conversation to be heard, but excluded sound which reached damaging decibel level. The whine of the heavily muffled turbine reduced with the revolutions.

'What's the problem?'

'It's right there, Sir, where you're standing. The main bearing temperature of the turbine is approaching danger level. Can't recall, Sir, that I've ever seen emergency op max speed used for so long before, but if that temperature doesn't stabilise we'll have a seized bearing. We can take that bearing out of service, but that means using the electric motors.'

'What's the temperature doing now?'

'It seems to be steady.'

'Right, I'll hold her at that.' George Gresham picked up the microphone and spoke to the control room. 'If we stay at this speed, what's the new ETA at the intercept?' The reply was instantaneous, the question having been anticipated by the navigating officer.

'0410 hours; we will miss Al Samak by three hours, Sir.'

'Thank you for that Mr Baker,' and the Captain replaced the microphone.

'That means we've screwed up, does it, Sir?'

'Not necessarily; we've assumed that this ship will maintain maximum speed and that might not be the case. Right, you nurse that bearing for me, Dan, and don't you hesitate to tell me if that temperature starts to go up again.'

'Yes Sir; sure am sorry....'

'Don't be,' the Captain interrupted the apology, 'it's just the 'ole lady's' way of telling us to take it easy. There's a long way to go yet. Thank you, Dan.' The Captain left the turbine room, closed the door, removed the ear defenders and then swore..loudly. When he got back to the control room, he found that his navigating officer had been pouring over charts and almanacs and had worked out a course which made use of every known current and set which might help their overall speed and reckoned that he might be able to reduce the three hour deficit by an hour to an hour and a half.

The Captain thanked him and stared long and hard at the chart covering the Eastern Indian Ocean. No one in the control room was over anxious to offer advice, sensing the bitter disappointment of their Captain. Faced with the remnants of the Russian Southern Fleet deployed to the west of Sumatra, what would he have done, had he been commanding this extraordinary ship which had just sunk ten of the latest Russian warships in almost as few minutes?

His eyes drifted across the north coast of Australia. Darwin.... he'd been there 18 months ago before he was given command of Los Angeles. He'd been on the staff of the US Defence Attaché in Canberra and had flown up to Darwin to assist with the protocol of a visit by four ships of the Seventh Fleet which were due to carry out an exercise with the ANZUS ships. Needless to say, no nuclear powered ships were allowed anywhere near the harbour. It was a very deep water anchorage and not far from the oil tanker terminal. From Darwin to the Gulf was damn nearly a straight line - give or take a few chunks out of Indonesia, Sri Lanka and India. George Gresham rolled a pencil between his fingers, a sign with which his crew were familiar as it heralded a decision.

'Send a signal to Fleet! I want to know what tankers have left Darwin in the last 48 hours. I want to know course and destination and, if possible, speed and tonnage. Precedence is FLASH. I shall be in my cabin; please let me know as soon as the answer is received,' and the Captain left the control room.

*

The wheels of Air France 747 Flight AF 568 touched down on the runway at Bangkok's Don Muang International Airport in a torrential tropical downpour at 20.32 hours local time. It was full dark and had been for well over an hour. For those passengers continuing to Sydney, it was an hour and a half's stopover while the aircraft was refuelled. There were only eighteen passengers leaving the aircraft at Bangkok and the baggage was already arriving on the carousel as the passengers reached the baggage claim area from immigration. Volkonoff had no luggage to collect and went straight through the customs green channel and out into the arrival area. He continued towards the split-level arrival and departure area and as he reached the glass doors which opened automatically, he was greeted by a short, smartly-dressed Thai in a light-weight business suit.

'Mr Thannamarong's greetings, Sir. I am your driver,' he added, taking the proffered hand baggage from Volkonoff. 'You will be staying at Mr Thannamarong's house, but only if that is convenient, and we will go there as soon as you are ready.' Volkonoff paused, looking down at the short Asian and waited until the greeting process was finished.

'Have you got the packages which I asked Mr Thannamarong to arrange?'

'Yes, they're in the car.'

'Good; please drive me to the docks where I wish to visit the ship Spirit of the Sea.

'Very good, Sir; please follow me,' and he was guided only a handful of yards to where the very latest 500 Series Mercedes was parked in an area specifically forbidden for any parking. There were two policemen doing their best to ignore the presence of the car. Volkonoff refused the seat in the back and got in beside the driver. Old habits died hard and the KGB training had taught him not to sit in the back, but if given the choice, beside the driver where the man's hands could be seen the whole time. The Mercedes pulled away from the kerb and joined the teeming traffic and rain on the multi-lane, toll Phahol Yothin Road. It was a 45 minute drive into Bangkok, 13 miles to the south, and it would be at least an hour's drive through the Bangkok traffic to the docks on the north bank of the Chao Phaya River.

The deluge lasted all the way to the docks and turned the vivid neon lights of the vice capital of the world into an impressionistic blur of colour and humanity. The canals, with their community of boat people, were deserted while the whole city waited for the rainstorm to cease, which it did just as the Mercedes reached the docks. As they drove into the docks, great swathes of mist swirled around the car, illuminated by the high, overhead lights. Spirit of the Sea looked just like an ocean mirage, as only the top half of the vessel was visible above the layer of mist lying on the water's surface. The car came to a stop at the foot of the companionway. Volkonoff got out of the car before the chauffeur could get round to open the door for him. He took the plastic bag, which contained the packages, from the chauffeur, picked his way round some puddles and then climbed up the planking of the companionway to the deck of the vessel. There was no one around, but that was of no concern to Volkonoff who knew his way to the captain's cabin. The door opened at the turn of the handle and he went into the dimly lit cabin. There was an over-powering, sickly-sweet-burnt smell of opium. The diminutive Chinese captain, who looked about sixty, but was probably nearer forty, rose from a sweat-stained couch and walked unsteadily towards his visitor.

Volkonoff's face reflected his revulsion which even penetrated the drug-sodden fog of the captain's brain and he altered course, unsteadily, and went to a bell push which he pressed and then returned to his couch. Volkonoff backed out into the comparatively fresh air outside the cabin where he bumped into an equally small man whom he recognised as the first officer. No words were spoken; the first officer beckoned and then turned and walked for'ard. The hatch cover of the hold immediately for'ard of the bridge had been partially removed and a tarpaulin had been rigged over the gap to keep the rain out. The first officer led the way down the steel-runged steps into a hold lit by low-wattage bulbs whose dim light barely penetrated any distance into the damp and evil-smelling darkness.

When they reached the foot of the steps, the first officer operated a switch, which turned on some rather more powerful lights, illuminating the cargo. The only cargo in the hold had been the five SS20 missiles and the area had been used as a workshop to remove the warheads from the remainder of the missile. On the starboard side of the hold were five sturdy wooden crates, none of which had been sealed in accordance with Volkonoff's instructions. Volkonoff walked over to these and inspected the contents; inside each was a warhead. Taking his time, Volkonoff took a multi-purpose tool from his coat pocket and undid the metal panels of the warhead on the nearest crate. The warhead arming mechanism, multiple re-entry vehicle targeting controller and all other systems checked out correctly.

He removed one of the packages from the plastic bag and a roll of adhesive tape. He taped the explosive charge and its radio-activated detonator to one of the brace struts inside the warhead. Volkonoff delved into the bag again and removed the transmitter, which was rather smaller than those used for controlling model cars, boats and aeroplanes. He switched the receiver from 'armed' to 'test' and pressed the button on the transmitter after extending the little stub aerial on the receiver and transmitter. A green light lit, indicating that the detonator had received the transmission. He switched the detonator from 'test' to 'armed' and then closed up the panels and moved to the next crate.

Two seamen, whom Volkonoff hadn't noticed, appeared out of the darkness and started to nail down the lid of the first crate. This process continued for the next forty minutes while Volkonoff took meticulous care to check all the warheads and then fit an explosive charge to each. Everything else to do with the missiles had been lowered over the side of the ship and was now at the bottom of the South China Sea. While the last of the crates was being sealed, the hatch cover was removed. Volkonoff climbed back up the steel ladder and watched as the five crates were removed from the hold and lowered onto a flat-bed truck by the ship's derricks. Once the crates had been secured on the truck, Volkonoff went down the companionway to the dock, spoke to the driver of the Mercedes and then returned to the ship and headed for the captain's cabin.

He went into the cabin followed by the first officer where he removed a small leather pouch from his pocket and handed it to the sailor. The captain was incapable of rising from the couch and was more than happy to leave the completion of the deal to his first officer. The pouch was opened and the contents carefully poured out onto a small piece of cloth, which had been produced from the first officer's pocket. The uncut stones looked very ordinary in the dim light and little better when the first officer switched on a slightly brighter desk light. All the stones were examined with the same care that had been applied to the warheads. The Chinaman was satisfied. The stones were returned to the pouch and Volkonoff went down to the dockside.

He ignored the Mercedes and walked along the dockside beside the ship. He found what he was looking for after some forty or so yards; the fresh water supply to the ship. He turned the large circular valve down to stops and then undid the hose connection, standing out of the way as the back-flow of water flooded out onto the dock. Volkonoff took a pair of rubber gloves from his pocket and a small wooden box, no bigger than that which would hold five dice. The rubber gloves were pulled over the large hands and he then slid open the top of the box like a child's pencil case. From inside the box, he removed a glass phial, which he placed with great care inside the 3" nozzle of the fresh water supply. The hose end was pushed into the nozzle and the glass phial broke as Volkonoff quickly screwed tight the locking connector. He turned on the water supply, pulled off the rubber gloves and after throwing them into the water he walked back to the Mercedes.

'Take me to Mr Thannamarong; the lorry will follow you.'

'Very good, Sir,' and the two vehicles headed north up the expressway to the Petchburi intersection where they left the expressway on the slip road and headed east along the New Petchburi Road, paralleling the Saensaep Canal towards the teeming streets and gaudy lights of the Strip.

CHAPTER 20

Both 'Communications' and 'Cyphers and Codes' occupied the top floor of Kingsroad House. Communications was staffed by a mixture of ex-military communicators from all three Services and some very bright young graduates who had been involved in post-graduate research right at the cutting edge of electronic wizardry, when recruited into the Directorate. With the promise of reasonable freedom in their area of research and a generous budget to finance it, this group of young men had come up with some astonishing inventions using miniaturised silicon chip technology.

Gunn was shown the various bits and pieces which had been requested by Alan Paxton and which had accompanied the HVMs on the BA flight to Bangkok. The method of operation of each was explained in layman's language. Alan had selected a variety of bugging and listening devices, secure speech facilities, hand-held radios, car tracking devices and an HF radio for direct communication back to Kingsroad House.

Once that briefing was finished, it was straight down the corridor to meet up with David Pettigrew and his department, where he was given recognition codes and one-time pads. At 11.15, he went down to the basement of the building to the Armourer's department, where much of what Simon had said was repeated, but he was able to examine the weapon and hold and operate it on the simulator.

It was ten to twelve when he finished and he then went back up to the 15th floor, which was the helipad on the roof of the building. There was a small, glass-fronted lounge where Simon was waiting for him with his hand baggage. 'Did you bring your car into work?' Gunn produced the keys from his pocket and handed them to Simon. 'Right, I'll see that it's locked up in your garage.' Out on the roof in the bright mid-day sun, the whine of the Gazelle's turbine could be heard through the double-glazed glass.

'Bye, see you soon,' and Gunn turned and headed for the door.

'Bye,' and the 'good luck' was swamped by the sound of the gas turbine as the door opened. Gunn climbed into the seat beside the pilot and the rotors started to turn as he clipped the shoulder straps into the waist turnbuckle. He reached over his head and pulled the headset and boom mike onto his head and pressed the intercom.

'All set, thanks.'

'Right, Sir,' and the pilot switched frequencies and spoke to air traffic control at West Drayton. The Gazelle lifted off the roof and quickly gained altitude as it headed west towards Heathrow where it landed four and half minutes later. The EDS van was waiting by the helipad and he was taken round to Terminal Three where he checked in at the Thai Airlines Business Class desk. He was the last passenger and the flight had already had its final call, so he went straight from passport control to Gate 26 where there were some anxious stewardesses waiting to hasten him onto the 747. The aircraft door was closed behind him as he went aboard. His seat was 60H at the front of Business Class on the starboard side of the upper deck; 6I was unoccupied so he had both seats to himself. A dainty Thai stewardess stopped by his seat and presented him with an orchid and a hot towel. She was followed by another as the aircraft started to roll back from the Gate.

'Champagne, Sir?'

'Yes please.' He took the long, fluted glass of chilled champagne and the proffered menu. The engine note increased and the 747 turned under its own power and joined the queue of aircraft waiting to take off. Twenty-five minutes and two glasses of champagne later, their turn came and the 747 didn't pause on the threshold, but as soon as it was on the runway and rolling the flight engineer pushed all four throttle levers to maximum power and the big aircraft quickly gathered speed and lifted off, banking and turning to port away from Heathrow Airport.

*

Claudine swam strongly in an effortless freestyle stroke for nearly ten minutes, which took her two-thirds of the way across the translucent water of the lagoon. She paused and regained her breath, swimming on her back in the same direction towards the break in the horseshoe-shaped coral around the edge of the lagoon. The gap was about forty metres across and she knew that she was approaching it as she could feel the movement of the waves coming through the gap from the sea outside. The two fishing canoes were pulled up on the sand and the crews were repairing the nets. Her feet touched the sand and she walked slowly out of the sea towards the fishermen.

The men paused for a moment in their task and then continued as she approached across the sand. Claudine's pace quickened as the sand began to burn her feet, which brought smiles to the faces of the men mending their nets. One of them reached into the nearest canoe and produced a small piece of woven coconut frond matting which he placed on the sand in a fair imitation of Walter Raleigh's gallant gesture; Claudine stepped gratefully onto it and thanked them remembering the namatsi with both hands placed together in front of her face. Lots of smiles and gleaming white teeth, but nothing else.

'Can any of you understand me?' she asked slowly in English and then, on the off-chance, repeated it in French. More smiles and vigorous shaking of heads, so it would have to be sign language. She was trying to place the ethnic origin of the men; very dark skins, straight black hair, rounded as opposed to aquiline features and, most surprising of all, some of them with blue and green tints to the iris of their eyes. She pointed at the boats and made sign language to ask from where they had come. They still hadn't spoken and she was trying to get them to do so to see if that could indicate their origin. She could see that they understood her question and they started to discuss the answer. The language they spoke she had never heard before, but the intonation had a ring of familiarity to it.

The fishermen pointed and glancing up at the sun which had passed its zenith, she judged that they were pointing due south. Pictures drawn in the sand of a sun and moon produced a voyage time of, say 12 to 14 hours - a sun, and a little bit of a moon. Claudine did some mental arithmetic; say about five knots as the outrigger canoes were not streamlined in design, but otherwise had all the quick sailing characteristics and performance as the multi-hulled cats and trimarans in which she had sailed. That meant that where they lived was somewhere between 50 and 70 miles to the south.

This was proving a great source of amusement to the fishermen and all had gathered round Claudine. Did they live on an island? This was quite easy to mime. What was it's name? Again, not difficult as she told them her name and led on from there; this led to all the men wanting to tell her their names. They came from the island of Tilacam - they might have said the proverbial Timbuktu for all the good that did except that it sounded as though it came from the east side of the Indian Ocean and not the west. She wrote her name in the sand with one of the wooden bobbins, which the fishermen were using to mend their nets and then said 'Tilacam'. So they wrote it and made her even more confused as the writing went from right to left and was of Arabic script. There was a much older man who had been watching all this without saying a word who now moved forward to the front of the circle around Claudine and politely held his hand out for the wooden bobbin.

They all turned as an outboard motor started up on the other side of the lagoon. Claudine begged the older man to continue, indicating a clear patch of sand. He bent down and appeared to ponder. She

270

snatched a glance over her shoulder and saw a motorboat approaching fast across the lagoon. The old fisherman appeared to be doodling in the sand with the tip of the bobbin. The high-revving whine of the outboard grew in volume and then died as the motorboat was run up onto the sand. Two men jumped out and the fishermen fell back. The men came to the gap left by the fishermen and called Claudine.

'Miss Carteret! Will you please come back with us as it is time for lunch.' It all sounded so incongruous, like being scolded for playing with the wrong group of children. She started towards the men from the motorboat and then turned and thanked the fishermen. The old man was still squatting on his haunches and in the sand in front of him was a perfect outline of the major landmasses of Southern Asia. The wooden bobbin lay on the sand with its tip pointing to a collection of dots in the sand to the western tip of India. On an impulse, Claudine stepped forward and took the old man's hands who looked up at her with the clearest of blue eyes and a conspiratorial smile as he swept the piece of coconut frond mat, on which she had been standing, across the picture in the sand, obliterating it.

Claudine climbed into the boat and the two men pushed it back into the water. The boat returned across the lagoon to the spot where Claudine had entered the water. She was helped from the boat, thanked her two escorts and after putting on her beach shoes, walked back to the mansion. Lunch was indeed ready and the same two women were waiting to serve her on the wide veranda. No other place was laid. Beside her place was a coconut with the top sliced away and two straws projected from the hole in the top. The rim of the coconut was decorated with sliced fruit and frosted sugar and inside was a tantalisingly refreshing concoction of iced coconut milk, white rum and tropical fruit juices. There was a wooden bowl of fresh, cold rock lobster tails, a small glass bowl of mayonnaise, freshly baked French bread, an avocado salad and a huge dish of fresh fruit. Pushed firmly into a silver bucket, packed with ice, was a bottle of the driest, chilled white wine.

There was still no sign of her host; as Claudine ate the delicious food, she went through the process of taking stock of the situation. Why had she been brought to this island? The answer was presumably for the same reason that she'd been kidnapped and taken to Sardrière Island. She could be used as a hostage to frustrate any attempt by John Gunn's organisation to deal with Hassan Hussein. In that case, rather like the books she'd read and films she's seen of the exploits of prisoners of war, it was her duty to try and escape.

271

Sitting on the island living in the lap of luxury was going to be of no help to anyone except Hassan.

Right, so what had she discovered so far? Firstly, she was being watched; secondly, she knew where she was and her 'host' was unaware of that. Thirdly; if she attempted to escape, it would have to be by air as any other means of transport was too slow and she would be caught before she'd gone more than a few miles - it was either that or she had to destroy all three aircraft. Whatever she decided to do, it must be done quickly before any routine was established for holding her captive on this island. Would she be able to fly that twin-engined amphibious plane?

She had achieved her private pilot's licence after 44 hours on a single-engined Cessna 152 Aerobat at the flying school adjacent to the airport on Guernsey. That had been two years ago and she had kept herself current, but always on the same or very similar aircraft. Where would she fly the aircraft? Always presuming she was capable of starting it, getting it down the ramp onto the water and then taking off from the water. Taking off from water had to be completely different to the grass runway on which she had practised her circuits and bumps. What had she got to achieve? She must get away from Hassan so that she didn't hinder any plans afoot to prevent him getting his hands on the nuclear missiles and she had to get a message to John Gunn's organisation to tell them that she was no longer held hostage by Hassan. How on earth was she going to do that? She had no money, no identification, she didn't have any 'phone number.

John had told her that he worked at Kingsroad House. She had a number of friends who shared flats in London; if she gave them a message and asked them to deliver a note to the office block, would that work? Doubtful, then again, if she reached the Indian mainland, it might be possible to get in touch with the British Embassy - or High Commission, as India was a member of the Commonwealth. If she could convince them, perhaps they would send a message to London. Would that work? It would have to; there was no other way.

Claudine had only sipped at the delicious coconut drink and had left the wine alone as she wanted a clear head to put the plan, which she was developing into action. She finished her lunch and went up to her room. Unpleasant thought or not, she had to assume that there might be both cameras and microphones bugging her room and so nothing must be done to alert Hassan's security system. When she got to her room, it had been cleaned and tidied. She opened the fitted wardrobe and looked casually through it, examining various dresses and items of clothing as though out of idle curiosity. After half-an-hour, she knew exactly what was there and what she wanted to take with her.

That task completed, she went downstairs and out to the jeep which was still parked in front of the mansion. She drove the other way round the circuit to the small marina where she'd seen the boats. Here she met the two men who had brought her back from the other side of the lagoon; one of the men, rather clumsily, pushed a small radio out of sight under a canvas boat cover. Claudine smiled at them and asked if she might take one of the sailboards out on the lagoon. She was asked if she knew how to sail it and detected a certain disappointment when she confirmed that she could and wouldn't need any instruction. She asked them if there was anywhere that she was not allowed to go which was answered with mildly embarrassed shrugs and the indication that she could go where she wished.

Both men watched as she stepped down nimbly from the wooden pontoon onto the fibreglass board and asked them to cast her off. This they did; she pulled up the rig, took hold of the wishbone and pulled it in slightly as she guided the board away from the pontoon and out into the lagoon. As soon as she was clear of the other boats and dinghies, she pulled the sail in close-hauled and the light board with its multi-coloured sail skimmed across the clear water. Out of the corner of her eye, she saw the two men get into the outboard motorboat and heard the engine start. There was a constant on-shore breeze of about 7 or 8 knots as the heat of the small landmass sucked in the comparatively cooler air over the sea. The breeze was perfect for what Claudine wanted to do; she wanted to get another look at the hangar and then sail a course along what might be her take-off run to see if there were any obstacles or rocks to be avoided. She held the board on the starboard tack across to the opposite side of the lagoon to the hangar and then spun it round, stepping adroitly round the mast, and did a broad reach across the lagoon again before turning onto a dead run with the triangular sail held in front of her and all her weight on the back of the board. The run took her towards the hangar; the wide doors were open and there wasn't a soul to be seen inside the building. At the back of the hangar was the small yellow battery trailer with the thick power cable she would need for starting the engines.

Some transfers and logos on the aircraft and equipment around it announced that it was a Mckinnon Super Widgeon Amphibian, but it was totally alien to Claudine who was used to single-engined Cessnas, Pipers and Beechcraft. It had a deep 'V', stepped marine hull and what appeared to be a retractable tricycle undercarriage. It was a high-winged monoplane with sponson floats towards the tip of each wing and large, picture windows on each side, which reached back as far as the trailing edge of the wings. As far as Claudine was concerned, as she studied the left-hand of the two machines, it might have been Concorde parked in the hangar. She transferred her weight, pulled in on the rig and brought the sailboard onto a port tack out into the lagoon again. It looked like a formidable machine and perhaps it was stupid to even consider an attempt to escape in it. These thoughts went through her head as she sailed close-hauled along what would be her take off run out towards the gap in the coral.

The fishing canoes had gone and she couldn't even see a sign of their sails as she cut across the small waves coming in from the open sea. She changed course back towards the hangar as she heard the motorboat and then saw it as she turned onto a run. The motorboat returned to the pontoon as she headed back towards the hangar. The aircraft on the left, as she looked at the hangar, appeared to be ready for flight. The one next to it had the metal engine fairings unclipped. The helicopter also looked as though it was ready for flight.

Both of those aircraft would have to be put out of commission if she was to have any hope of getting away. If she could impose a minimum of an hour's delay on any form of pursuit by air, she had a chance of getting to one of the other islands if she didn't crash and kill herself in the attempt. She took the sailboard right up to the lip of the concrete ramp and then turned away and made for the marina again. Claudine brought the sailboard into the pontoon, dropped the rig into the sea and stepped off onto the wooden planking. She bent down and picked up the painter and made the board fast to a cleat.

Claudine went over to the two security guards, thanked them and told them that she was rather tired and was going back to her room for a rest. They complimented her for the way in which she had handled the sailboard and offered to take her out water-skiing if she so wished. She told them that she would like that and waved goodbye as she climbed into the jeep and then drove back to the mansion. She had no idea if there was a camera in her room, but decided that she would have to take that risk. She turned on the shower and made other appropriate sounds as though she might be going to take a rest and then very quietly got dressed in some light cotton slacks, trainers and a greeny-coloured T-shirt. There was a baseball-type hat with a large peak and a mesh covering to go over the head. Claudine put her hair up on top of her head and crammed the baseball cap on top of it. She turned off the shower and went into the small lounge.

She opened the windows, went out onto the balcony and closed them quietly behind her. Below the balcony was the roof of the veranda. She climbed over the side of the balcony and lowered herself down to the full stretch of her arms; the veranda roof was about a metre below her feet. She let go and landed soundlessly on the bitumen and gravel-covered roof. Keeping close to the wall, she went to the left-hand end of the veranda roof and repeated the procedure to get down to the ground. She paused to see if any alarm had been raised. If it had, she couldn't hear it, so she made her away across the grass and then through the shrubs, hibiscus and palms towards the hangar. Again she stopped to see if she was being pursued, but it seemed that the whole island was resting during the mid-afternoon heat of the day. There were no vehicles parked on the small parking area at the back of the hangar. She went up to the side door and tried the handle; it wasn't locked and she opened it and went into the building. On her immediate right were some office buildings with glass fronts to them so that those inside could see what was happening in the hangar; still no sign of anyone.

Claudine walked over to the amphibian and slowly went all round it, making herself recall all the things which she used to look for in her pre-take off checks. The ailerons, flaps and rudder were all locked with red-flagged pins and there was another inserted into the pitot of the airspeed indicator.

She found the spring-loaded flap behind which lay the connection for the battery-booster power cable. She ran her hand along all the fairings and wing edges, checking for a proud rivet, improperly secured panel or any other fault, which might spell disaster in the air. After completing her circuit and checking the tyres of the three wheels and the hydraulic brake leads, she paused and listened; not a sound. A set of boarding steps was positioned by the door in the fuselage. She climbed these, opened the door and entered the aircraft.

There were seats for five passengers and then a bulkhead between the passenger compartment and the flight deck. She presumed that she had arrived on the island in one of the three aircraft. She remembered boarding the twin-engined jet at St Malo and guessed that that particular aircraft must be kept on the mainland of India or wherever there was a suitable runway. She moved forward to the flight deck and looked all around out of the windows before she sat in the left seat. 'Thank God,' she murmured as firstly she saw that all the instruments were labelled in English and secondly, when she spotted the pre-take off and landing check-list, it was also printed in English on flick-over, plastic-covered pages.

She picked up the check-list; from the cover she discovered that the Widgeon had first flown in 1940, in the Second World War, when it had been used as an anti-submarine patrol aircraft. The abbreviated account explained that of the original 176 built, some 70 had been converted and upgraded with two, 270hp Lycoming engines giving the amphibian a speed of 180 mph. She ran her eyes across the instruments; lots more than those in a Cessna, but provided she didn't let them overawe her, they all had very similar functions to those with which she had become familiar. She glanced again out of the window, reminding herself not to become so engrossed in the task that she forgot to check to see if anyone came into the hangar. She read quickly down the engine-start procedure, running her fingers over the appropriate switches, levers, dials and buttons. The first time she did it, it took some time as she had to confirm that she had correctly identified the right control or indicator. The second and third time, her hands started to go automatically to the right places.

There was a clock on the panel in front of her, which indicated that it was just after four. Now for the crucial test; 'is there any fuel in the machine?' she muttered, as she checked all round to see if she could see anyone. 'Hell!' she thought, 'here we go,' and pressed the main power switch, ensuring that neither her hands nor feet were anywhere near any of the controls. She was fairly certain that all of these would be hydraulically assisted and she had no wish to damage any of the control surfaces by trying to move them against the locking pins.

The panel in front of her came to life to the accompaniment of the whine of the fuel pumps and the hydraulic motors. Four fuel tanks; two main and two reserves and all needles were climbing across the gauges to indicate a full load of fuel.

The artificial horizon, bank indicator, compass, altimeter, airspeed, course/fine pitch indicator, carburettor heat, generator and magneto warning lights, suction pressure, oil temperature and pressure and a small host of others she had yet to identify came to life. As far as she could tell, the aircraft was ready for flight. She identified the lever to retract the undercarriage which she would have to operate as soon as the amphibian floated clear of the concrete ramp and then once more for luck, went through the start-up procedure. There was no point in wasting any more time and so Claudine switched off the power, climbed out of the aircraft and as she walked towards the door through which she'd come, she made note of a red-painted panel on the wall where various fire-fighting implements were hanging, including a large axe. She went out onto the road and strolled back along it, as though she had been for a walk towards the islanders' accommodation.

As the white-painted mansion came into view, so did a group of men standing beside two jeeps. It was evident that she had been missed as all heads turned in her direction, as if on cue; she waved and walked towards the security guards.

'Where have you been, Miss Cartaret?' Claudine recognised the man who had given her the injection on the aircraft at St Malo.

'I've just been for a walk along the beach on the other side of the building where the planes are kept. Have I done something wrong?'

'No; how did you leave the house?'

'I'm sorry; I don't understand you. I set off from the veranda and walked through the palms.'

'You told Yacoub,' and her interrogator nodded towards one of the men who had been on duty at the marina, 'that you were going to take a rest.'

'And I did; on the lounger on the veranda, but it was rather hot and windless, so I walked to the beach. I can't see why you're bothered. I've no way of getting off the island and even if I did I haven't the faintest idea where I am except that I must be somewhere in the Western Pacific from the look of the islanders.'

'How did you get from your room to the veranda?'

'I jumped out of the window.'

'That's not funny; you're in serious trouble, Miss Cartaret.' Her inquisitor was becoming rattled.

'No, I don't think so. I think you're in trouble. I've done nothing out of the ordinary; you and the other guards have failed to monitor whatever equipment has been watching me. I...' but she got no further as the disembodied voice of Hassan came from the deep shadows of the hall.

'Miss Cartaret is right, Idrissu. You weren't paying attention, otherwise you wouldn't need to ask all these inane questions. All the security staff will report to my office now. Dinner is at 7.30, Miss Cartaret,' and the figure in the shadows turned and made for a door on the right of the spacious hall.

*

'FLASH signal, Sir!' George Gresham woke with a start from a troubled and confused dream, which he'd often had ever since he was a child. He was chasing someone or something, the identity of the quarry was never revealed in this recurrent dream, but everything he used - his feet, a car, a motorbike and even a horse in one instance - seemed to be firmly jammed at dead slow. He took the signal and thanked the petty officer. He placed the signal on his desk and doused his face in cold water to wash off the perspiration induced by the dream and the airless atmosphere of the cabin; he switched the air-conditioner to a higher setting and read the signal.

Fleet had produced the response in record time; two tankers had left Darwin in the last 48 hours, one headed for Brunei and the other to Kuwait; both in ballast. George Gresham ignored the information on the ship headed for Brunei and concentrated on the second one; name, Shimojima, registered in Liberia; 100,000 tons dead weight - its fuel carrying capacity; present position - it was in latitude and longitude and he glanced up at the world map on the wall of his cabin - south-east of Yogyakarta on the island of Java; speed 25 knots.

'Damn you, Murphy! Five gets you ten you've best-guessed me again.' George Gresham pulled back the curtain and left his cabin. The atmosphere in the control room was charged with anticipation as all the duty watch knew that the FLASH signal had been received. 'Mr Baker, if Al Samak's position was this' - and he showed him the signal - 'at the date/time/group of the signal, please let me know at what time it would be at our intercept point if it's making 25 knots.' Lt Pete Baker was holding a calculator in his hand as the question was asked and his fingers darted across the keys.

'0742 hours on August 2nd, Sir.'

'Thank you, Pete.' George turned to the officer of the watch.

'Please acknowledge this signal. No change to course or speed. It's just possible that Al Samak is using a 100,000 ton tanker, Shimojima, to mask her move past the Russian Southern Fleet. Please ensure all watches are briefed. That's all.'

'Aye, aye Sir.' The Captain paused as he was about to leave the control room and turned towards the duty watch who all became intensely interested in the equipment in front of them.

'It's known as Murphy's Law,' and he left the control room.

*

The fourth and last of the Russian Southern Fleet's Sierra Class Nuclear attack submarines had left the passage through the Selat Sunda, between Sumatra and Java, and on the orders of the Soviet Admiral was undertaking a zig-zag patrol pattern two hundred miles to the south of Java at a depth of 500 feet. The patrol pattern crossed the Java Trench which had a depth of over 7000 feet. The new watch had been on duty for a little over 15 minutes and the senior sonar operator was fine-tuning the passive sonar receivers.

What he needed to check out his equipment was a nice reliable sound emission source on which to calibrate; and he now had it. The sonar signature of the churning twin screws of the large tanker was as familiar to him as the signature tune of a TV soap would be to his opposite number in a Los Angeles Class hunter/killer submarine. He was just reaching for the tape to slot into the computerised comparator, when he paused; something was wrong. It was just as though one instrument was playing out of tune. He adjusted the volume and sensitivity of the headphones and listened.

*

Five miles away, the towed array sonar of Al Samak had already identified the Sierra Class submarine and Axel Steinbaum was bending over the sonar station with the headphones held tight to his ears. He removed them and returned them to the operator whom he patted on the shoulder. He stretched and turned to his first officer, Dieter Schwendler. He nodded in answer to the raised eyebrows; 'that's her - the last one.'

'Do you think that they will detect our presence below this monster?'

'You know my motto, Axel, 'never base a decision on an hypothesis, only on fact'. We must assume that the sonar operator on the Sierra Class is good at his job. He will detect the anomaly between the known sonar signature of a twin screw, 100,000 ton tanker and the signal which he is receiving. It will only be a matter of minutes before the captain of the Russian Submarine is informed and he makes the decision to get us out from under the tanker and destroy us. Sonar!'

'Sir.'

'Have you input the sonar signature of the submarine into the computer?'

'Affirmative, Sir.'

'Enter it into the captor mine arming computer.'

'Aye, aye Sir.'

'Depth?'

'500 feet.'

'Stand by to release port and starboard mines.'

'Standing by,' came from the weapons officer.

'Range?'

'4000 metres and closing.'

'Speed?'

'32 knots.'

'On my count.....five..four..three..two..one..release!'

279

'Port and starboard mines released.'
'Time to detonation?'
'186 seconds, Sir.'

*

On the Sierra Class submarine, the captain had just been summoned to the control room by the officer of the watch. The captain entered the control room and asked the officer of the watch for a briefing. He was told of the suspicions of the sonar operator, went to the sonar station and listened to the headphones. 'What's the range to the tanker?' the captain snapped.

'1000 metres and closing, Sir.'

'Dear God!' - biblical oaths weren't frowned on since the start of perestroika - 'are you mad? Helmsman!' he shouted, 'right full rudder, seal all watertight doors, close up to action stations! I.....' but that was as far as he got because the last of the 186 seconds had just ticked away and the two captor mines had detonated, one on the port side and the other on the starboard side of the Russian Sierra Class submarine. Neither of the mines was more than five metres from the hull of the submarine and both exploded about 15 metres for'ard of the leading edge of the submarine's squat sail.

The simultaneous explosion of two lots of nearly 300 pounds of Semtex explosive severed the entire bulbous nose of the submarine for'ard of the sail and the forward speed of the boat snapped it open like the top of a flip-top, Zippo lighter. No submarine had been built to withstand that extent of damage and it was immediately engulfed by the sea and carried to the bottom of the Java Trench, 7000 feet below, where the remainder of the hull crumpled like an aluminium beer can, crushed within the giant fist of a pressure of more than 100 tons per square inch.

*

A thousand metres astern of the Shimojima, the sea erupted in a boiling mass of foam and a startled lookout on the port bridge wing reported the phenomenon to the officer of the watch, who noted the ship's position and then went onto the wing to study the area through his binoculars. Presumably a World War Two mine which had been activated by the passage of the tanker. A lucky escape! He drafted a signal to the ship's owners and then buzzed the captain in his cabin.

*

In Al Samak, the sonar operator had removed the headphones - to avoid damage to his eardrums - and had switched the sonar

280

receiver onto the loudspeaker. All of the men in the control room heard the explosion and the unmistakable noises of the submarine breaking up. In spite of his fascist/Nazi leanings, his catholic childhood in a Bavarian village made Captain Alex Steinbaum cross himself as he left the control room.

CHAPTER 21

The bright morning sun was shining through the windows of her bedroom when Maria Ionides awoke. A nurse had just drawn the curtains and now came to the bed and slipped a thermometer under her tongue and held her wrist to take the pulse. As soon as the thermometer was removed, Maria sat up and looked out of the windows. A sweep of well-kept lawn, interspersed with azaleas, rhododendrons, beeches and cedars sloped down to a river. On the other side of the river were fenced meadows, where cows grazed. 'What is this place?' she asked the nurse who had just completed writing up her temperature and pulse on the clipboard at the foot of her bed.

'Riverview Park private clinic, Miss Ionides. You've been under sedation for just over 24 hours after arriving here the night before last. It's the 1st August today; your breakfast will be here any moment. Would you like a newspaper?'

'Yes please; where's Riverview Park, nurse?'

'About 8 miles from Maidenhead; I'll just get your breakfast. Your clothes are all in the wardrobe and the doctor will be up to see you in just under an hour. You may leave whenever you wish and we will provide you with a car and driver to take you to London - if that's where you wish to go. We would like you to wait until the doctor has seen you just to check that the mild concussion which you suffered from the blow on the back of your head will cause you no problems. It is, of course, entirely up to you if you wish to wait for the doctor to see you or not.....' the door opened and a trolley was wheeled in with a breakfast which would have done credit to a five star hotel. 'Ah! here's your breakfast; I'll just get you a newspaper and then we'll leave you in peace.' The nurse returned seconds later with the paper and then left, closing the door behind her.

Maria waited for a few moments and then climbed out of bed - even the nightdress she was wearing was new and fashionable - and walked to the door. It wasn't locked and there was a carpeted corridor stretching the length of the building with stairs and a lift in the centre. Maria closed the door and went over to the table by the windows and poured herself a fruit juice from the laden trolley.

She did more than justice to the breakfast trolley, realising that she hadn't eaten since supper in Chelsea with John Gunn, and then took a bath in the en suite bathroom. Her clothes had been washed and everything was still in her handbag. She dressed and used some of the make-up which had been provided in the bathroom. The phone beside the bed rang and she picked it up cautiously.

'Is that Miss Ionides?

'Yes,' cautiously.

'Miss Ionides, I work in the British Intelligence Directorate and am currently controlling John Gunn on his task in Bangkok. I've been told that there is no medical reason why you shouldn't leave Riverview Park immediately and I expect you will wish to continue with your task. What happened to you after your dinner with John might be somewhat hazy, to say the least, and I wonder if you would like to meet me for lunch when I can set your mind at rest.'

'Thank you, Mr.........'

'Smith'll do.'

'Thank you 'Mr Smith'll do', and Maria smiled as she heard the laugh, 'I'd like that. Where do I meet you?'

'Cocktail bar of the Hilton at 12 o'clock.'

'Very well; I'll see you there, bye,' and she replaced the phone as the door opened to admit a white-coated doctor.

'How are you feeling, Miss Ionides?'

'Fine, thank you. Am I fit to leave?'

'I'll answer that after a couple of quick checks; that alright with you?'

'Yes, go ahead.'

'Can you just sit on the bed please.' Maria did and the doctor produced a small torch, which he shone into her eyes and then got her to follow with her eyes the tip of a pen, which he removed from his pocket. 'Any dizziness, queasiness or difficulty in concentrating?'

'I haven't tried the last one, doctor, but 'no' to the other two.'

'Right, you'll do, Miss Ionides. Here are some pills, which will help if you have any headaches. There's a car waiting outside the front door. Goodbye,' and he held out his hand which Maria shook and picking up her handbag, she followed him out of the room. The driver dropped her at the Cumberland Hotel in the Cromwell Road where she changed and then caught a taxi to the Hilton. The cocktail bar was on the mezzanine floor and she entered it a couple of minutes after midday.

'Hullo Maria; Simon Smith'll do!' She turned and took the proffered hand. Simon Peters gave the drink order to a hovering waiter and led her to a small table by the large windows overlooking

283

Park Lane. Their drinks arrived. Simon picked up his, raised it slightly with a softly spoken, 'Na'strovia!' and sipped the gin and tonic.

'Tell me all about Monday night, Simon.' So he did, in detail, and before they parted after lunch, he told her how to make contact with Gunn in Bangkok.

*

The lighting and texture of materials used in the interior design of Bangkok's Don Muang International Airport made everything glow in golden and copper hues like its palaces and temples. The Thai Airlines 747 had landed 12 minutes late at 10.12 and Gunn followed the other passengers into the extending tunnel parked tight up against the aircraft door. Just before he reached the moving walkway, a breathless stewardess caught up with him and handed over a Heathrow, duty-free plastic bag. 'A gentleman sitting in Royal Orchid Class noticed that you'd left this behind, Sir.'

'Thank you very much, I'm sorry to have been the cause of that energetic dash of yours.' He was rewarded with a big smile.

'That was no trouble, Sir,' and then the dreaded, 'have a nice day.' Without any hold baggage, he went straight from immigration, through customs, to the meeting point where he spotted a man in slacks and open-necked shirt holding a small placard with Euro-Pacific Construction printed on it. He went over to him; 'Mr Ratchasima?'

'Mr Gunn from our London office; how do you do. I don't know how much you know of our ways in Thailand. We never refer to people by their surnames; always the first name or the first name and second name. My first name is Aree - like all first names, it has a meaning; mine means 'compassionate' - and so all my western colleagues call me Harry. I hope you will call me Harry.'

'Mine's John, Harry, and thank you for that lesson in Thai customs; although I've been to your country a number of times, that hadn't been explained to me before.' The two men were walking towards the public taxi stand next to the meeting point when Harry pointed at his duty-free bag.

'You were wise to bring that as imported spirits are expensive.

'Yes, I'm told that Dubai Airport's the best value for duty-free.' The correct recognition signal had been given and acknowledged. There were half-a-dozen people in front of them at the taxi stand, but these were quickly carried away by the waiting queue of taxis and Harry gave directions to their driver and they both settled back in their seats for the drive to the Oriental Hotel.

For many years, the Oriental Hotel had been voted the best in the world by various tourist companies and travel magazines and certainly Gunn remembered that his parents supported that view. It occupied one of the best sites in Bangkok, overlooking the Chao Phaya River and the mandatory tourist visit to the Floating Market on the Bangkok Yai Canal departed from its boat landing stage. Everything about the hotel was the epitome of luxury, comfort and efficiency from its swimming pools to its scenic penthouse restaurant and four-poster beds.

Harry went up to John's room on the 16th floor with him, where he announced, with an apology, that he intended to take Gunn to the Euro-Pacific Construction site which was within walking distance and they would then have lunch at the hotel after that. Gunn dropped his hand baggage on the suitcase stand, changed out of his lightweight suit into slacks, trainers and cotton shirt. He went into the bathroom, removed his Radom from the wooden box of King Edward VII cigars in the duty-free plastic bag, checked the magazine and the round in the chamber, strapped the holster to his ankle and placed the gun inside it. He returned to the bedroom, transferred his wallet from his jacket pocket into the rear pocket of his slacks and then said, 'right, I'm ready, Harry; let's go.'

They walked out of the hotel and turned left onto Chareon Krung New Road and within a distance of 400 metres passed two hotels, the post office and the Portugese Embassy. Less than 200 metres beyond that, at the junction of the Chao Phaya River and the Phadung Canal, was the site acquired by International Leisure Plc for yet another five star hotel. The huge billboard rising above the fenced-off site, showed a computer-graphics impression of the new hotel and the company logo of Euro-Pacific Construction. At the entrance to the site, Harry showed his pass and both of them were issued with fluorescent yellow safety helmets and ear protectors.

They had walked a few paces onto the site when the security guard at the entrance caught up with them and asked them to go back to the site office at the entrance. Puzzled, Harry led the way back where they were met by Euro-Pacific's senior engineer in Bangkok. He recognised Gunn. 'Hello John! I didn't think that it could be anyone else. So you've finally decided to settle down to a respectable profession instead of rushing around the world shooting people. When did you leave the army?'

'Hello Justin; yes, I've stopped shooting people and I left the army about a year ago. You know Harry Ratchasima?

'The name, yes; the face, no; nice to meet you Harry,' and they shook hands after which Justin turned to Gunn again.

You're at the Oriental I presume?'

'Yes, I've just checked in.'

'Fine, well, Diana and I'll come round and do our best to keep you away from the fleshpots of this amazing city. Oh! nearly forgot; the security guard was a bit worried because his man on the gate says that he's already checked in a Mr Ratchasima. I expect he put a tick against the wrong name. Must get back to work. Nice to see you John... Harry,' and with that he climbed back up the steps to the site office.

'Come on John, I'll take you round the site,' and Harry led the way towards the towering framework of steel, glass and concrete. They stepped into the construction lift, which ran up an enclosed gantry on the outside of the building. On the top of the building was a crane, which grew in height with the building. When the framework was complete, the crane was dismantled and the trunking in which its steel support had been built became one of the six lift shafts of the hotel. They went up to the 20th floor; above that was the crane and a further 25 floors yet to be built.

'You were telling me about first names and surnames, Harry; what's your wife's first name?'

'Sumalee.'

'And does that have a meaning?'

'Yes, the prefix 'Su' means good and 'malee' means flower, so 'Good Flower.'

'Do you pass these names on to your children?'

'Oh yes, we just change prefixes and suffixes to suit ourselves.'

'Do you have children?'

'Yes; a son and a daughter.' The lift had about another 30 feet to go.

'What have you called them?'

'My son is Damrong - that means 'proud' and my daughter is Thongmalee - 'golden flower'.'

'And your wife and children are all well?'

'Yes, thank you.' The lift came to a halt with a jolt and the steel-mesh gate swung open. Harry indicated that John should go first and then he followed him onto the rough concrete of the 20th floor. It was extremely hot and the humidity had to be hovering around the high nineties, Gunn thought, as he put on his sunglasses to protect his eyes from the blinding glare of the sun reflected off the concrete. The shadow of the boom of the crane swung across the concrete towards him, slowed and then stopped. Gunn glanced at his watch and saw that it confirmed that it was only a few minutes after mid-day and the sun was right overhead. The hoist and pulley block were travelling along the boom, imitated by the shadow on the concrete. Gunn turned to Harry who had stopped some 20 feet away to examine a very ordinary steel girder sticking out of the concrete and had his back to John.

There were three other construction workers on the top floor with them. Two were looking at Gunn and the third was looking up at the boom of the crane speaking into a small radio. Gunn glanced up and then hurled himself sideways as 4 tons of steel hopper filled with concrete crashed onto the spot where he had been standing, bounced and then went over the side of the building still attached to its pulley and wires and hurtled towards the ground 200 feet below.

The door of the lift slammed shut. No sign of Harry; presumably he had taken the lift. What had happened to the real Harry Ratchasima? Gunn wondered as a bullet whined off the thick steel girder behind which he was now crouched. Another bullet dug into the concrete by his foot and ricocheted into the cage surounding the lift gantry. The crane operator was firing a rifle from the side window of the tiny cab on the vertical shaft of the crane some fifty metres away.

As 'Plan A' had failed to squash him under four tons of pre-mixed concrete, it seemed that 'Plan B' was to shoot him or hurl him over the side of the building - or both. The three men rushed towards his steel girder. Gunn drew the Radom from its holster and fired three times. The man nearest to Gunn stumbled and then pitched forward over the unprotected side of the building; the second man had not achieved sufficient momentum with his move towards Gunn and he was thrown on his back, a deep red stain spreading over his chest and the third fell to his knees clasping his stomach.

Silence from the crane cab and then the operator appeared and started climbing at a frantic pace down the steel ladder. Gunn raised the Radom, still held in both hands, and fired.

The crane operator stopped climbing and then, like a film switched to slow motion, let go of the ladder, arched over backwards and fell to the concrete. Gunn went to the lift where there was a stack of labourers' tools - shovels, crowbars, barrows and all the other paraphernalia of construction sites. He grabbed a shovel, swung back the blade and brought it down on the thick cable carrying power to the electric motor on top of the lift gantry. Showers of sparks flew from the severed cable and the motor stopped. He went over to the man whom he'd shot in the stomach.

'Where's the real Harry Ratchasima?' No answer. 'There's every chance that you might live if you answer my question. If you don't, then you'll still live, but the next two bullets will turn you into a sexless vegetable. Do you understand what I'm saying?' A nod; 'where is Harry Ratchasima?'

'With Thannamarong at.....at... Rising Sun.'

Gunn went over to the larger of the two men and removed the coarse leather construction gloves from his hands. Even so, it was a struggle to get his hands into them. He walked to the edge of the building, grasped the steel wire and started to lower himself hand over hand. It was laborious and exhausting, but he slowly made his way down. The other wire beside the one he was climbing down started to vibrate. Gunn paused in his descent and looked down. Sixty or seventy feet below him, the pseudo Ratchasima, who had failed, and knew he'd failed to answer correctly the questions about his family, was also using the wire to reach the ground. There was a group of people around the spot where the hopper had crashed to the ground and another group around the body of the man who had taken a dive off the top of the building.

Gunn speeded up his descent, the heat from the friction was reduced slightly by the grease on the wire and the skin on his hands was saved by the strong gloves. He reached the ground only seconds behind 'Ratchasima' and before the bewildered workers could grasp what was happening, ran after him as he headed for the site entrance. Gunn discarded the gloves, hard-hat and ear-protectors as he ran.

When he reached the road, 'Ratchasima' was at least 100 metres away, heading back towards the Oriental Hotel. In the quarter of a mile or so to the Hotel, Gunn reduced the gap by half. 'Ratchasima' ran round the side of the Oriental between the two swimming pools and across the road to the landing stage where boats of every size were taking on or dropping off passengers from river and canal tours. He went straight to a motorboat and jumped in beside the driver who had seen his approach and started the engine. It pulled away immediately heading south down the Chao Phaya River.

Tied up to the landing stage were four, slim canoe-shaped boats, each with huge converted car engines pivoted on the stern with long, gleaming prop shafts; one had chrome exhaust pipes like a waterborne dragster. Its owner was a young man with long hair, stylishly tied in a pony-tail, who would have looked perfectly in place on the film set of an Errol Flynn pirate extravaganza. Gunn went up to him. 'Is this the fastest boat in Bangkok.' The youth smiled and nodded. 'Catch that motorboat over there,' and he pointed, 'and I'll give you enough money to buy another boat.' A grin split the youth's face from ear to ear and the suped-up engine roared into life. Gunn climbed down into the boat and sat up by the bows as directed by his driver. No sooner was he on the seat than the boat took off like a rocket almost catapulting Gunn off his seat.

The motorboat was almost half way to the Krumg Thep Bridge and at least 600 metres ahead of them as the slim-hulled boat started in pursuit. Gunn held onto the thwart, convinced that imminent destruction faced him as they leapt clear of the water every time the boat crossed another's bow wave. His driver was completely unconcerned as he stood in the stern with a perfect sense of balance on his waterborne dragster. They gained quickly on the motorboat and Gunn could just make out 'Ratchasima's' face as he turned to look at the pursuing boat.

The river was full of every type of boat and it was almost impossible to keep track of the motorboat as it swung over to the right-hand bank of the river. As it went under the bridge, Gunn estimated that they were about 300 metres behind the motorboat. The deep shadow of the bridge flashed by, followed by blinding sunlight; the roar of the engine subsided and his driver tilted the prop clear of the water.

They'd lost the motorboat; there wasn't a sign of it anywhere. His driver plunged the prop back into the water and swung the boat out into the centre of the river to get a better view. The boat could be anywhere; tucked close in to the hull of a bigger boat or screened by the large number of boats emerging from the Bangkok Yai Canal and the Floating Market. The boat spun round and they headed for the entrance to the canal, weaving in and out of the boats. Here, it was impossible to go fast as the canal was choked with boats, similar in design to the one in which Gunn was sitting, but laden with fruit, vegetables and every other form of merchandise for sale.

His driver spotted the motorboat and pointed. It was about 400 metres away, but it might as well have been 400 miles as in between was an uninterrupted sea of boats. His driver tilted the engine down bringing the prop clear of the water and walked nimbly forward to Gunn and asked him if he thought he might know where the boat was going. 'Do you know a club called the Rising Sun?' A grin and a nod indicated that he did.

'We go by boat, look,' and he started to draw a plan on the bilge boards of the boat with a wet finger. 'Here is Chao Phya and here, Floating Market. Rising Sun is on Klong Saensaep' - Gunn knew that klong was the Thai word for canal - 'and he must come out from Floating Market on Klong Bangkok Yai - here,' and he indicated on his map which the sun was doing its best to dry up. 'We go wait here, under bridge and he will come - you see.' Gunn shrugged and smiled.

'You're the boss, you find them.' His driver grinned in reply and returned to his engine. The prop swung down into the water, the boat spun round in its own length and went back to the main river. They went back past the Oriental and then followed the broad river in a long left-hand bend until they reached the Memorial Bridge where Gunn's driver pulled into the deep shade on the right hand bank. He pointed to the golden spires of a temple on the left-hand bank about 400 metres away and told Gunn that the motorboat would appear just the other side of the temple and would have to come towards them. Gunn looked at his watch; it was now 1.20 and he was grateful for the shade provided by the wide Prachathipok Road over the bridge above them. The humidity was really oppressive and the clouds were building up into heavy, high-piling cumulo-nimbus, threatening thunder and a torrential downpour. His driver looked up at the sky as a distant rumble of thunder could be heard above the subdued roar of traffic over their heads. Gunn looked at his watch again; 1.35.

'Any minute he come, you see,' and he was right because at that exact moment the motorboat appeared and the first great fat drops of rain splattered onto the surface of the river. The boat turned towards them and approached along the right-hand side of the river.

'What's your name,' Gunn asked.

'Ringo,' and the driver held up his hands to display the collection of gold and gem-stone encrusted rings.

'Ringo, these men are dangerous. They may have guns and will use them. If you stand up you will be a big target to hit. The man you saw get into that motorboat has already tried to kill me so he will try again.'

'You have a gun?' It was a polite question and Gunn produced the Radom.

'That's fine,' was the grinned response. The rain was heavier and a light mist was rising from the surface of the river.

The engine was ticking over slowly. The motor boat was nearly at the bridge and Gunn realised what Ringo was going to do. While the motorboat went under the bridge, they would move down the north side of the bridge and then burst out from under it behind their quarry. The rain was now a downpour and visibility steadily reduced. The engine roared and they surged forward skimming along the north edge of the bridge until they reached the last span and then Ringo swung the boat hard to port and opened the throttle wide. The motor boat was 50 metres in front of them and now angling towards the left bank of the river to turn north up the Phadung Canal at the junction overlooked by Euro-Pacific's construction site. Two heads turned in unison only seconds before Ringo roared past the motorboat and turned across its bow. The engine note of the motorboat increased in volume as it swung away.

'Ratchasima' was holding an automatic, but it was impossible to tell if he'd fired as the noise of the deluge of rain on the water's surface seemed to drown all other sound. He had fired and had hit Ringo as Gunn could now see the blood running down his arm, washed by the rain. The bullet appeared to have scored across his left shoulder. Ringo shook his head indicating that it didn't matter, but that was not what his eyes indicated. He swung back towards the motorboat, weaving from side to side. Gunn braced himself in the bottom of the boat, back jammed against the thwart and held the blade foresight on the driver of the motorboat. He fired twice. The plastic windscreen shattered and the driver was thrown back against the seat and then toppled over the side of the boat. There was a shriek of delight from behind Gunn, followed by some sort of war cry and that was followed by the most incredible feat of boat handling that Gunn had ever seen.

The motorboat had swerved out of control as its driver went overboard and 'Ratchasima' had to lean over and grab the wheel to prevent the boat ramming at full speed into one of the bridge supports; in his right hand was the automatic. Ringo drove his canoe straight at the motorboat, completely ignoring the threat of the gun pointed in his direction. Gunn saw rather than heard the gun fire as the cacophony of the deluge on the water and the car horns of the jammed traffic above them blotted out all other sounds. There was a momentary wisp of burnt cordite as two shots were fired, but neither of the bullets hit Ringo. Gunn was convinced that their boat was going to ride right over the motorboat and was preparing himself for the inevitable ducking. At the last moment, Ringo spun the boat in almost exactly the way that a downhill skier would execute a full-Christiana halt and raised the ten foot long prop-shaft clear of the water with its 14", three-bladed propeller a spinning blur at the end. The motorboat shot past and the prop shaft lowered. 'Ratchasima's' head disappeared in a pink spray as the propeller and torrential rain acted like a liquidiser of skin, bone, muscle tissue, brain and blood.

The motorboat roared south down the Chao Phaya River driven by the headless trunk behind the wheel. 'Come on Ringo, we'd better get back to the Oriental and I'll get the doctor to look at that shoulder of yours.'

*

Claudine glanced at the ornate gilt clock on the mantelpiece in the hall; a shade after 4.30. Something like 2½ hours of light left. The

291

aircraft in the hangar had a maximum speed of 180 mph, according to the information on the front of the flight check-list. That capability would get her as far as the other islands before the darkness made a sea landing impossible. Hassan's head of security and all the guards had been summoned to a meeting after which, no doubt, a much closer watch would be kept on her movements. These and other thoughts went through Claudine's head as she went up to her room. By the time she reached it, her mind was made up. It had to be done now.

Decision made, she went into the bedroom and collected together a few items of clothing, which she had identified earlier that afternoon. She placed these in a rafia bag she found in the bottom of the wardrobe and left the house by the same route as the previous occasion. The hangar was still deserted and the doors were open; 4.45. Claudine took a deep breath to steady her nerves and then walked over to the amphibian, opened the door and put her bag of clothes inside.

She went over to the fire point by the side door into the hangar and removed the large axe. The first blow of the axe against the 'V' hull of the second amphibian, went straight through the thin metal which was most satisfying, but warned Claudine of the fragility of both the aircraft hulls. A few more blows and she had opened up the whole of the front of the aluminium fuselage. Two blows of the axe destroyed the starboard aileron and then as she walked round the tail of the aircraft to get at the helicopter, two more blows severed the galvanized wire, which operated the rudder.

Claudine climbed into the cab of the helicopter and systematically smashed all the instruments and then went to the tail and destroyed the rotor. Back in the cab, she severed any electrical cable she could and then returned to the back of the hangar where she dropped the axe and picked up the towing hook of the battery starter. She pulled this round to the port side of the aircraft, opened the spring-loaded cover, pushed in the multi-point connector and pressed down on the clamping handle. The connector was about 18" below the pilot's side window and she prayed that she'd be able to reach it from inside the flight deck; two minutes to five.

Claudine pulled the steps clear of the door and then did all her pre-flight checks, removing red-flagged locking pins from flaps and ailerons, chocks from the wheels, clearing the pitot tube of the airspeed indicator, ensuring that the engine air intakes were clear and checking all the fairings once again. She climbed into the aircraft closing the door behind her. Time was of the essence now as someone might appear at any moment. She sat in the left hand seat and checked that she could reach the battery cable connector - just! 'Now, go for it,' she said out loud. Her hands were sticky with sweat, which she wiped on her cotton trousers.

Parking brake on, master switch on, fuel switch on, fuses in, prime engines and lock, mixture to rich, throttle free and set to a quarter open, magnetos on, carburettor heat set to cold, props to coarse pitch, 75% flaps - all the dials were now registering - altimeter to zero, radio on, but what frequency? 'to hell with that!' Claudine muttered. Operate starter - the prop swung, a puff of blue smoke, 'start damn you!' she cursed and the check list fell from her lap as there was another puff of smoke and then the Lycoming engine fired and settled into a steady rhythm. She retrieved the check list, deafened by the shattering roar of the port engine inside the hangar. Starboard throttle, starboard starter button - instant response and now sound reverberating all round her. Rpm to 1000, hydraulic pressure in the green and oil pressure rising to within tolerances. Generator warning light out, suction reading above 3" of mercury, magnetos checked for 'dead cut' - no drop in engine rpm - she wiped the sweat from her forehead and checked the security of the safety harness.

Claudine shut her mind to any interruption by security guards and concentrated on the task of getting the McKinnon amphibian out of the hangar. With brakes still on, she opened the throttles to 75% power and the whole aircraft rocked and strained to be released. She eased off the power, leant out of the side window and pulled up the clamp of the battery booster cable, which fell clear onto the hangar floor. Brakes off and a quick burst of power to overcome inertia and the amphibian rolled forward towards the lip of the concrete ramp down to the sea. The nose wheel went over the lip and the aircraft trundled down to the water as Claudine used her left hand to steer the nose wheel in a straight line into the water.

The amphibian floated clear of the ramp and Claudine operated the lever to retract the undercarriage; three green lights; windscreen wipers on. No more hesitation, no practce runs, this was it. Half her mind told her that all the dials were registering correctly while the other half saw the group of men running towards the hangar from the mansion. A gout of water warned her that the shooting had started; time to go. Both throttles to maximum power, right hand clasping the rounded knobs on top of the levers, left hand on the control column - no 'feel' in the rudder yet. Speed increasing rapidly - 30...40... 50mph - a thump somewhere behind her, but no time to worry what damage the bullet had done, the far side of the lagoon raced towards her; life in the control column and the rudder pedals;

Claudine eased back gently on the column, one bounce, another and then the amphibian was airborne.

The sickle of white sand swept by below the wing tips as Claudine eased further back on the column and adjusted the trim wheel to keep the aircraft climbing. She kept the compass on 180 degrees as the amphibian climbed into the evening sky; 5.08. Was that really the time? she asked herself as she retracted the flaps and ran her eyes over the instruments as she went through the post take-off checks. She brought the amphibian onto level flight at 1000 feet and trimmed out the aircraft. She changed from coarse to fine pitch and checked that the mixture was at 'lean'. All dials were in the green sectors. She checked all round her, but the sky was clear. Time to see if she could raise anyone on the radio. She turned the dial on the radio fit between the two flight deck seats; static, then garbled speech and then a clear acknowledgement from Victor Tango 52 to Cochin air traffic control. 'Where the hell's Cochin?' Claudine asked the empty seat on her right. The high wing configuration of the McKinnon enabled her to read her own recogniton letters and numbers - VT 235. She pressed the transmit button. 'Hello Cochin air traffic, this is Victor Tango 235.'

'VT 235, please identify yourself. What type of aircraft and your destination. We have no record of your flight plan.'

'VT 235, twin-engined amphibian. I have escaped from an island to the west of India where I was being held as a hostage by a man called Hassan Hussein who owns his own island. I have no idea where I am and require assistance. Could someone contact the nearest British Consulate or High Commission?'

'Roger VT 235, please confirm heading, speed and altitude.'

'VT 235, 180° at 1000 feet and speed is 135 mph.'

'Roger, VT 235; turn right onto 200° for radar identification.' Claudine eased forward on her right foot and banked the amphibian onto the new course. 'VT 235 this is Cochin, we've got you. Remain at 1000 feet, all other aircraft will be kept clear. Come left onto 115°. Can your amphibian land on a hard runway?'

'VT 235, I should think so.'

'Roger, you have 228 miles to go and we will talk you down. Airport security has contacted British Consulate in Bombay. What is your name?'

'Roger, thank you Cochin; my name is Claudine Cartaret. Will you tell the British Consulate that I'm no longer a hostage with Hassan Hussein and would they get that information to British Intelligence in London.'

'We'll pass that message, Miss Cartaret. Good luck; Cochin air traffic.'

'Thank you Cochin; VT 235.' Claudine checked the clock on the instrument panel; 5.35. Another hour or so should see her close to her destination. Would the British Consulate get through to London? Doubtful, but worth a try, Claudine thought as she once again looked all round her and then checked all the instruments for what seemed the hundredth time. Below the amphibian, the sea turned to a coppery-pink hue as the sun sank towards it behind the twin-engined plane.

*

'Stop engines! Secure all departments to silent routine.

'Aye, aye, Sir; engines stopped,' and the USS Los Angeles settled into complete silence as it drifted 1000 feet below the surface of the Indian Ocean at Latitude 03°04' North, Longitude 83° 22' East. Only forty minutes earlier, during the routine period of deploying the floating aerial to receive and transmit, the submarine had been told by 7th Fleet of the sinking of the fourth of the Russian Southern Fleet's hunter/killer submarines. Leading Seaman Murphy was at the sonar station.

'I have the Shimojima now, Sir,' he reported.

'Range?'

'15,000 metres, speed 22 knots.'

'Thank you. Secure to action stations.'

'Aye, aye, Sir,' from the first officer.

'Weapons officer!'

'Sir.'

'Prepare all four tubes for Mark 48 ASW torpedoes.'

'All four for forty-eights, aye; aye, Sir.'

'Range?'

'11,000 metres - I've got Al Samak, sir; coming up on the VDU comparator now.' The Captain of the Los Angeles went and stood behind his sonar operator as he displayed the sonar signature of the Shimojima from the sub's computer stored records and then below it, the signature being received by the passive sonar. Murphy leaned forward and pointed with his finger to the anomaly indicating the presence of another vessel beneath the large tanker.

'200 feet; bring her up real smooth and quiet,' the Captain directed the seamen operators of the planes and trim. The first officer checked the film in the general purpose periscope. 'Range?'

'8000 metres.'

'Depth?'

'550 feet.'

'Stand by with the flood lights.'

'Aye, aye, Sir; standing by.'

'Up periscope!'

'Range 5000 metres.'

'Depth 200 feet and steady.'

'Bearing to target 163 degrees.'

'Roger to that,' and the Captain spun the periscope onto the bearing.

'1000 metres.....800.....600... 400...200.'

'Floodlights!' and George Gresham pressed the motor drive of the camera.

'Target overhead.....receding...200...400,' the lens of the periscope followed the course of the two ships.'

'Floodlights off!' The first officer came forward and removed the film from the periscope and handed it to the petty officer who was waiting to take it for processing. Ten minutes later he returned carrying three, ten by eight inch monochrome prints which showed a bow, flank and stern view of Al Samak. George Gresham took the flank shot and placed it in front of Leading Seaman Murphy. 'Well done, son; that's your second crate of Budweiser,' and he patted him on the shoulder.

CHAPTER 22

Simon Peters and Maria Ionides parted company outside the Hilton; he took a taxi and she chose to walk to Knightsbridge Tube Station. She got out at Gloucester Road, turned left onto Cromwell Road and walked to the Cumberland Hotel at the junction with Collingham Road. Having collected her key from the small reception desk, she went up to her room on the first floor and opened the door of her room. Colonel Anatoly Kamarov of the Sixth Directorate of the KGB and incidentally, Cultural Attaché at the Soviet Embassy in London, was sitting in the only armchair. He smiled, but didn't get up. 'Hello Mr Kamarov,' Maria greeted him without pausing, as she threw her handbag onto the bed. 'New instructions for me?'

'Just a slight alteration to our plans, my dear. Do sit down and I will tell you all.' Maria looked round the room and then indicated with her eyes that it might not be wise to talk in the hotel bedroom. 'Oh, that's alright,' Kamarov laughed, This room's been checked and is clean.'

'But British Intelligence know where I'm staying.'

'Of course, we told them.'

'You don't think that they might have placed a bug in my bag or clothes while I was unconscious at their clinic near Maidenhead?'

'I very much doubt it, as the British have this extraordinary sense of chivalry, which has been their downfall on more than one occasion. Fortunately we don't suffer from any such weaknesses. However, to be on the safe side, just let me have your bag and we'll run this gadget over it and then you.' Kamarov produced a small black gadget of the size of a pocket calculator and which looked very similar to an electrician's voltmeter. He plugged in a lead, which had a small probe on the end of it. The handbag was emptied onto the bed, each item was checked and then the bag itself; the needle never moved. Kamarov came over to Maria and ran the probe all over her; she gave no indication of her anger as his hand stayed unnecessarily long in between her thighs. 'No, just as I thought, you're OK. We've had to change our plans. I will be replacing you and will leave on the flight to Bangkok leaving at 4.15. It's unfair to send you on a mission when you've suffered an assault such as the one you had the other night. We have confirmed with Moscow that you're to stay here and

297

take three days leave and then return to Moscow via Athens. Your tickets are all booked; here they are,' and he threw across the ticket folder to where Maria was sitting on the bed.

'Very well, comrade Kamarov; as the weather is so pleasant, a few days holiday would be much appreciated.'

'That's settled then; I must get back to the embassy, collect my bag and then go to the airport.' Kamarov got out of his chair and went to the door.

'I'll walk a short way with you, comrade, as there are one or two things which I'd like to pass on about my short stay in the hands of British Intelligence and whatever that machine of yours says, I'd prefer to talk on the street.'

'Your sense of security is commendable, comrade,' and the two of them left the room and went down the stairs to reception and then out into the street. It was a very hot afternoon and the temperature was well up in the eighties. The pavements were packed with tourists as Maria and Kamarov made their way back along Cromwell Road to Gloucester Road Tube station.

'What is it that's bothering you, Major Petrovsky,' Kamarov asked as the two of them made their way around a throng of young tourists who were taking up the whole of the pavement. Kamarov and Maria stepped out into the road to get round them. Three buses in a row came towards them and Maria reached out to pull Kamarov back onto the pavement, but he stumbled and fell forward right under the wheel of the first bus. Brakes screeched, passengers in the bus screamed as they cannoned into each other and then the second bus slammed into the first one and the third only just succeeded in stopping with its front bumper touching the rear one of the second bus.

Scores of people milled around the buses and in no time a policeman appeared and covered Kamarov's pulverised head with a newspaper donated by one of the many ghouls watching from the pavement. No one had noticed Maria who was now walking back towards the Cumberland Hotel. No one would ever know that Kamarov was dead before the wheel of the bus squashed his head and shoulders and obliterated the wound in the back of his neck made by the needle sharp point of her steel nail file. Maria turned and glanced back and it was only then that she answered Kamarov's question.

'You were bothering me, Colonel Kamarov, and that's evened the score for your attempt to get rid of me and the innocent man in the embassy whom you murdered to cover your own treachery with Volkonoff,' and she continued on her way back to the hotel. She

298

stopped by a group of three telephone kiosks; the phone card one was unoccupied and she went in, pushed her card into the slot and tapped out the number on the buttons. The phone rang in a building in Grosvenor Square. When the call was finished, Maria returned to the hotel, asked reception to make out her bill and call a taxi. She went up to her room, packed her suitcase and by the time she returned to reception, the taxi and her bill were waiting. She settled the former and got into the latter. 'Heathrow, Terminal 4 please, as quick as possible,' and the taxi pulled out into the afternoon traffic on Cromwell Road.

*

Gunn and Ringo were soaked to the skin and left small pools of water as they walked through the reception area of the Oriental. At the desk, Gunn asked a young girl to contact the hotel doctor. She confirmed that he was a guest at the hotel and was occupying the room reserved for executives of Euro-Pacific Construction. The two of them were directed to a treatment room on the mezzanine floor where a middle-aged doctor examined Ringo's wound. 'What caused this?'

'Most unfortunate accident, doctor,' Gunn replied, 'this young man was my driver and was helping a colleague whose propellor had fouled some netting. I really don't know how it happened; somehow his friend pressed the starter before this man was clear of the propeller. He's very lucky not to have lost both hands and half his face.'

'Looks more like a bullet wound,' the doctor muttered as he cleaned it, applied a freezing agent as a local anaesthetic and then put six stitches in the wound. 'You'd better come back in a week to have those out. Are you paying for this,' he asked turning to Gunn.

'I will, if the management of the Oriental insists, but I thought that this service was provided free.'

'It is, for guests, but I expect we can include Ringo here who takes many of our guests on boat trips.' The doctor smiled, 'just as well it wasn't a couple of inches to the left,' and then let his nurse escort them out of the room.

Gunn gave Ringo a $100 note which was equivalent to ten times the standard charge for a Floating Market boat trip which was usually about 200 baht.

'Where can I contact you?'

'In day time, you leave message at kiosk on pontoon if I am not there.'

'And in the evening?'

'I drive a taxi; it's a radio one - here, I've got a card,' and Ringo dug in his pocket and produced the card. 'Now I must get back to work; goodbye Mr Gunn.'

'Take care of that arm; I'll be in touch.' Gunn went over to the lifts and went up to his room, where he discarded his sodden clothing and took a shower while he considered what he'd learned since his arrival in Bangkok.

Thannamarong had got Ratchasima and from him had found out about Gunn's arrival in Bangkok, the recognition code and the Euro-Pacific Construction cover. There must have been another spook at the airport, John supposed, watching the meeting point. If that hadn't gone without a hitch, presumably a message would have been sent to Thannamarong and curtains for Ratchasima. The capture of Ratchasima must have been a very recent event as it appeared that there had been little time to find out a great deal of Ratchasima's background - hence the lack of knowledge about his family and the error of letting the security man on the site gate check off his name when the reception on the 20th floor was being set up.

He turned off the shower and dried himself off with a towel that was large enough for a baby elephant. He draped the towel around himself and went into the bedroom and picked up the phone; it was time to make contact with Alan Paxton. Gunn paused, with the phone half raised. On the dressing table was the English language Asian Times; two-thirds down the front page, an article had caught his eye because the name of the ship, Spirit of the Sea, was in bold print. He replaced the phone and picked up the paper. The bold print read, 'MYSTERY DEATHS ON SPIRIT OF THE SEA. It appeared that two customs officials had arrived on the ship late on the night of 31st July to clear the ship's cargo before it sailed with the high tide at 0630 hours on 1 August. Every member of the crew was dead and the ship had been sealed off while a team from the city's health authority investigated the mystery.

'Volkonoff!' Gunn said aloud and dropped the paper back on the table. He picked up the phone again, paused and then undid the mouthpiece. Sure enough, there was the bug, which he left alone. He got dressed in the only change of clothing he possessed and went down to reception where he picked up a phone in one of the many booths.

'Rama Jewellry, can I help you?'

'Yes, I hope so; can you tell me if you have any pigeon's blood rubies of at least 3 carats. I'm flying to America tonight and I don't want to waste time visiting jewellers unless I know that they have the quality of stone I want to buy.'

'I'm sure we can help you, sir. Will you wait one moment please?' and the phone started to play music as she placed him on hold.

'Salaams.'

'Salaams you old fraud,' John Gunn's reply was the final check with Alan Paxton that the contact was genuine. Only the two of them knew that greeting. 'Can we meet?'

'Bobby's Arms in Patpong 2, off the Silom Road, in 15 minutes.'

'See you there,' and Gunn broke the connection. He dug out the small Bangkok guide book from his pocket and checked the directions which he'd been given by Alan; barely a mile from the Oriental. He went back to his room, switched on the radio and removed the magazine from the Radom. He inserted the spare magazine and put the other one into his electric razor case. Gunn turned off the radio and left the room. He reached Bobby's Arms exactly 15 minutes after his call to Alan Paxton and saw him propped against the bar of the English style pub holding a tankard of beer. Whilst the interior decor of the pub was exactly what might be found anywhere in an English pub, that's where the similarity ended, as far as Gunn was concerned, as he had yet to find a pub in England that provided such a host of pretty young waitresses.

'Have you got a tail?'

'No; what's happened to Ratchasima?'

'I was hoping that you were going to tell me that,' Alan replied as he caught the barmaid's eye and pointed to his beer. 'I saw Ratchasima at 7.15 this morning. He told me he was going down to the Euro-Pacific site to have one more look at it to make sure that his cover looked genuine. Who met you at the airport?' Gunn told him what had happened and finished by asking if there had been any changes to the plans to fly the warheads to Baghdad. 'Yes, it's been brought forward to tomorrow. The information from London is that various bits and pieces of aluminium tubing have been discovered by a UN Inspection Team in Iraq. These tubes could have been used in the enrichment process of uranium and this has been grabbed by both the President Bush and our PM who are also maintaining that there is proof of Saddam trying to buy large amounts of 'yellow cake' from Nigeria – that's the raw….. oh, OK, as Gunn indicated that he knew what 'yellow cake' was. It now seems that the USA is determined, whatever the other members of the Security Council say of invading Iraq. Blair and that spin-doctor of his have even produced a document that proves he can launch a WMD strike within 45 minutes. From where? and with what? the other members of the Security Council are asking….particularly Jacques Chirac and

Gerhardt Schroeder. This rhetoric from the USA and UK may well be Volkonoff's reason for bringing the flight forward by 24 hours. Have you had anything to eat?'

'No.'

'The meat pies here are excellent. I've got the car in the car park behind this place and I'll take you to the site we've recced for the HVM missiles. Every flight takes off towards the sea, but now and then they use a different runway. I therefore plan to have you in one place with two missiles and myself at another with the other two,' he paused as Gunn's tankard of beer and meat pie arrived. 'You and I will be in touch by radio and the third radio would have been with Ratchasima at the airport who would have given both of us a count down on the movements of the fake Saudia 747. That plan will have to be changed. We must get Ratchasima away from Thannamarong. Sadly, first things first; the priority is the destruction of those warheads. Pie alright?

'Yes, very tasty; what was it? Pye dog!'

'Shut up, John! This place has a reputation for the excellence of its steak pies.'

'Sorry, it was excellent.' Gunn finished his beer. 'Come on Alan, time's not on our side,' and the two men left the pub and went down the ramp to the car park. They got into Alan's hired Toyota Celica and he drove north through the city past the University and the Royal Bangkok Sports Club, round the gardens of Siam Square and then onto Phaholyothin Road which led out of the city to Don Muang Airport. Alan checked his mirror constantly and remarked, once they had passed the Victory Monument, that they were not being followed.

'As you probably know, John, the whole of Bangkok and the area around it is criss-crossed by canals and waterways and is therefore as flat as a pancake. It took some time to find a suitable place to position you.'

On either side of the road were deep ditches and squared-off paddy fields, interspersed with clumps of coconut palms and groups of houses. Alan slowed down and turned right off the main road towards a group of houses with wooden walls and thatched rush roofs. The road was metalled for a short distance and then turned into a rough track as they approached the houses. The track branched and Alan took the right-hand fork; now Gunn could see the ruins of a pagoda, a central spire with collapsed remains of others around it. The ground rose slightly and when they both got out of the car, Gunn was surprised that a small increase in elevation gave them a such commanding view of the surrounding land. Alan

Paxton led the way into the ruins, heading for the main conical spire in the centre. Great chunks of the small-brick masonry had collapsed which made it possible to climb up the outside of the spire. Alan stopped and pointed to the north where an aircraft was climbing steeply towards them.

'That was well timed. Just watch this aircraft - it's a jumbo, which is even more convenient - and you'll see the sort of target it will present to you. To-day, the weather is by no means ideal and tomorrow it could be worse, low cloud and so on.'

'So what do I do if I can't see the aircraft?'

'We did think of that and the boffins at British Aerospace came up with a brilliantly simple and obvious solution. The recognition chip in the brain of the missile is programmed for all the characteristics of the Boeing 747-400, which is the aircraft which the Iraqis will be using. Even if you can't see it, you will hear it and the talk down on the radio will ensure that you get the right aircraft.'

'Provided that we have someone on that radio. Just imagine the disaster if we got the wrong aircraft and brought down a jumbo full of passengers.'

'I agree that it doesn't bear thinking about, but we have thought of that. Ratchasima had obtained an airport security pass and was going to follow every move of that fake Saudia 747 so that there was no possibilty of you getting the wrong one; if we can't find him, his wife had already volunteered to handle the airport end, but that will be a last resort. If there is any doubt, then you will be told not to fire and Plan B comes into action.'

'Oh yes, and what's Plan B?'

'Plan B is bad news; the Russian Aircraft carrier - Baku by name - from the Southern Fleet, which has performed so successfully to date, and which is now deployed on the southern extremity of the Gulf of Thailand, will fly off two Forgers to intercept and destroy the Saudia Boeing 747. Incidentally, you won't have heard that the Southern Fleet lost the fourth and last of its hunter/killer nuclear subs.'

'No, I hadn't heard that. What price an incorrect identification by the Russian pilots? You're right, that is bad news. What happens if we can't get hold of Ratchasima or if we do, he's in such bad shape that he can't carry out the task and we don't use his wife?'

'If that's the case, then I will do the airport job as best I can. If the aircraft takes off in the wrong direction, then I will have to cope with that as well.'

'That's not going to give you much chance of getting away from the scene of the missile launch. No, I don't like that at all. I think that

Ringo would do that airport job extremely well if that's what it comes to.'

'How do you know that you can trust him?'

'I don't, but I'm going to use him this evening to get Ratchasima.'

'Sure that's wise; he sounds a bit of a cowboy.'

'Which I reckon fully qualifies him for the job. No Alan, you stay out of this as you might well have to pick up all the pieces if I screw it up. I'll get in touch and let you know the score on Ratchasima. If you haven't heard from me by six, tomorrow morning, then assume that we've failed and you're on your own. Make sense?'

'Yes, I suppose it does. Come on, it's nearly 5.30 and you've got to get hold of Ringo. I'll drop you at the hotel.'

Thanks, Alan, just drop me around the Rama Hyatt and I'll walk to the Oriental. Now, before we leave here, where does that track go?'

'Nowhere; it stops just beyond the ruins and then there are only footpaths between the rice fields until you get to the canal.'

'Where does that canal go?'

'Eventually, it goes as far as the city. Why?'

'I'm not happy about driving into this fire position, using a radio, firing a couple of missiles and then coming out by the same route I went in on. Does that canal go under any road bridges?'

'Yes, about three miles further south, you can join the expressway from a road which crosses the canal.'

'Would it be possible for me to have a driver who could drop me off at the firing position and then take the car to that bridge and wait for me?'

'Yes, that's no problem. I'm sure that Harry Ratchasima's wife, Sumalee, would do that if we're not going to use her at the airport; she's helped out with tasks like that on many occasions. What about a boat?'

'That I must leave to you. Can you fix me up with one of these outboard jobs you see everywhere?'

'That's no problem; come on, we'd better go and look at this bridge over the canal.'

'Got any more 9 mm bullets?'

'Yes sure, in the car.' It was just getting dark as Alan dropped Gunn in front of the Hyatt. He drove off as Gunn went into the hotel, through the foyer and out of the side entrance into Silom Road.

Gunn went round to the river pontoon in front of the Oriental where he was told that Ringo had already gone and would now be in his taxi. Gunn used his mobile and dialled up the number on Ringo's card and waited as the phone rang at the other end. It was answered. 'Victory Taxi Service, where you want to go?'

'May I speak to Ringo, please?'

'Ringo driving taxi. Who want him?'

'My name is John Gunn. Please ask him to come to the Oriental Hotel as soon as possible.'

'You stay at Oriental?'

'Yes.'

'What room number.'

'1642.'

'Ringo there in five minutes. Goodbye,' and the connection was broken. In fact it was seven minutes later that Ringo walked into the foyer where he was spotted by Gunn.

'Hello Ringo, I need your help again.'

'Same as this afternoon?'

'Probably.'

'Guns?'

'More than likely.'

'You FBI?' This was said in a conspiratorial stage whisper that was rather more distinct than the hotel PA system, but in just the same way that no one pays any attention to PA announcements in a hotel, not a soul appeared to hear Ringo's remark.

'No, I'm not FBI; come on, let's go and see what's happening at the House of the Rising Sun.'

'Came ready for tonight, Mr Gunn.'

'Sorry, what d'you mean? and its John.'

'Ah! I like name Johnny. Look,' and Ringo showed him a very slim, flat-handled switch-blade knife which he produced from the belt slot on the waistband of his jeans.

'That's neat; come on,' and the two of them left the hotel and John got into the back of Ringo's red Datsun taxi. Ringo drove east to the Mitaphap Expressway and then took the slip road after they had crossed the Seansaep Canal and turned right onto the New Petchburi Road. They took another right turn and then Ringo drove in through a set of gates up to a most imposing building which carried no flashing neon signs like the majority of the clubs, topless bars and massage parlours in that area. Whatever the Rising Sun was, it certainly catered for those with expensive tastes, Gunn judged by looking at some of the cars parked outside the building, but he was only half right in this assessment.

'Are you allowed to park this taxi here?'

'Yes, no problem.' He parked the taxi and then both of them went into the club. Ringo explained that the club did really well because it catered for all pockets and tastes. Here, a taxi driver like he could rub shoulders with some of the wealthiest men in Bangkok and both parties felt perfectly at ease. The Rising Sun was a number of clubs all under the same roof and Ringo led Gunn from one bar to another, to gaming rooms, massage bathrooms, pornographic movie rooms, and live porn floor shows. Gunn saw no sign of Volkonoff. Ringo explained that they had now looked at all the places, which he had been to, the other part of the building was expensive.

There were hostesses everywhere, but at the entrance to the 'expensive part' as Ringo had described it, the hostess who met them might have walked off a film set. Inside, the whole atmosphere changed to one of subdued lighting and plush seating. Even Ringo's bravado seemed to have deserted him as they were escorted to a table set back from a small dance floor where an exotic and erotic floor show involving no less than four completely naked women was in progress.

Two hostesses appeared at their table and sat down. A waitress served the table with iced champagne and glasses. The sparkle returned to Ringo's eyes who was no longer overawed by the atmosphere of the place. With a flourish of drums, the floor show ended, the women disentangled themselves from each other and the lights around the room were raised a couple of watts. Volkonoff was sitting by the small dance floor with another man; there were no less than six hostesses at the table.

Gunn nudged Ringo who was taking a keen interest in the pretty hostess who already had her hand inside his tousers. Gunn pointed at the table, but it was his hostess who supplied the information. 'That's Mr Thannamarong.' Gunn turned to Ringo and told him to stay at the table, enjoy his champagne and his hostess, but to be ready to leave instantly.

'I am going to find my friend and then we will take him to his home,' Gunn finished. He turned to his hostess and raised his glass of champagne. The gesture was either misconstrued or accepted as some sort of invitation because the girl immediately rose from her seat, took his hand and led him from the room. Gunn had already seen a handful of couples leave the room by the door through which she led him. They both went up in the lift to the second floor. The interlude in the lift was used by his hostess to show him that she was wearing nothing under her dress.

They went to a door at the end of the corridor, which opened into a bedroom and large bathroom with jacuzzi and massage bath. As they went into the bedroom his hostess let the dress fall to the ground, turned and placed her arms round him. Gunn placed his fingers on the side of her neck and then pressed hard against the pressure point. The naked girl went limp in his arms. He carried her to the bed where he placed a gag in her mouth. He opened the fitted wardrobe, which was filled with every form of sex aid and fetish object. He picked out a length of cord and two leather straps, which he used to tie her hands and feet. The cord he used to tie her to the bed to minimise the possibility of any alarm being raised.

The lift was just coming up as he reached the doors, so he started down the stairs. The lift doors opened and another couple emerged and headed off down the corridor. There was nothing on the first floor except rows of doors just like the floor above. On the ground floor, there was subdued noise coming from the door through which he and his hostess had come. He turned to the left and tried the door at the end of a short corridor; inside was the small foyer of what appeared to be a high stakes casino. No one saw him so he closed the door and walked back along the short corridor to the corresponding door at the other end. He paused and listened; there were voices, but he couldn't identify what might be behind the door. He tried the door and it opened. There was a small foyer just like the casino. He had walked into the club's security centre.

The door was ajar ahead of him and led into a room, which seemed to be stacked with television monitors. On his left was an office, which could well be that of the duty security officer, or whatever he was known as, because Gunn couldn't read the Thai script on the door. He went to the door and opened it. The reason for the lax security was revealed. The security officer was engrossed in watching what appeared to be a hard porn movie on a TV. Gunn realised that it was the live porn floor show which he had seen earlier and that there were probably cameras in every room, including the one he'd been in with his hostess. Beside the man, the switch to operate the solenoid lock on the door through which Gunn had just come was switched to 'off' which, fortunately, was probably the same position as the man's brain.

The guard turned as he went into the room and reached for a pump-action gun. His feet were pulled from under him and he fell off the chair. Gunn stamped on the wrist of the hand holding the weapon and then bent down and pressed the same pressure point on the side of the neck. Once he had removed the pump-action gun, he went back into the foyer and looked into the other room. There were two men on duty. Gunn went in and hit one over the head with the stock of the pump-action and levelled the barrel at the other who had jumped out of his chair and was reaching for an identical weapon. 'Turn round!' The man did and was rewarded for his co-operation with a blow on the head. Gunn dragged both of them into the other room and bound them using wire, which he ripped from all the electronic security gadgets. The head security man was regaining consciousness. Gunn pulled him up and sat him in the chair.

'Can you hear me?' A nod; do you speak English; again a nod. 'Listen carefully. You have a man here called Ratchasima. I want him and you will tell me where he is. Get it right and you will live; get it wrong and you will die first, whatever happens to me. Understood!' Another nod; 'get up!' He did. 'Where is he?' Speech this time.

'On the second floor.'

'Which room?'

'The one right at this end on the right.'

'If that's wrong I'll come straight back here and shoot you. Turn round!' and he went the same way as the other two. Gunn hurriedly tied him up, not making a very thorough job of it and then went back into the other room. At the other side of this room was a door which led out to the front of the building. He walked back along the corridor and opened the door into the nightclub; the lights were dimmed again as more bodies writhed around on the dance floor. Gunn went to the table and to his surprise found Ringo still there. 'Come with me and bring your girlfriend.' No second invitation was required and the three of them left the room. The girl thought this was perfectly normal and that a foursome was being set up. As they left the darkened nightclub, Gunn saw with dismay that Volkonoff was no longer sitting at the table next to the floorshow.

The three of them went up in the lift to the second floor and then Gunn led the way along the corridor to the last door on the right. As they reached it, he turned round, put his hand up towards Ringo's hostess in what appeared to be an affectionate gesture and then pressed firmly on the same pressure point. Ringo's faced registered his astonishment as she collapsed to the floor. Gunn propped her against the wall and then tried the door. It was locked. He stepped back to the other side of the corridor, took a pace forward to gain momentum, raised his foot and drove it into the door where the blade of the lock held it shut. The lock burst out of the woodwork and the door swung open. The room was identical to the one in which Gunn had been at the other end of the corridor. On the bed lay a man who was unconscious or dead. Gunn went over to the bed and felt for the pulse on the side of the neck; it was there and quite strong. He had no idea if the man was Ratchasima.

'Come on, Ringo, give me a hand,' but there was no response and as Gunn looked up to where Ringo stood, perfectly still, he saw a silhouette in the doorway which, from its size, could only be Volkonoff.

Gunn dropped into a crouch to present as small a target as possible and started to reach for the Radom, when his world exploded in intense pain and then unconsciousness. Milli-seconds before he collapsed, his last coherent thought was the bathroom; the bloody bathroom! Why hadn't he checked?

*

'VT 235, this is Cochin air traffic. You should have the coast in sight now. Your heading is correct and you will see a lake to the south of the city. Your altitude is correct. We will be talking you down onto the glide path within the next ten minutes. We have a pilot in the control tower who has experience of your aircraft; Cochin air traffic.'

'Thank you Cochin; VT 235.' Cochin had kept in touch with Claudine every five minutes of her flight. The light was now fading fast. Claudine started preparing well in advance for the landing. She read through all the checks and actions again and familiarised herself with all the relevant dials and switches on the instrument panel.

'VT 235, Cochin air traffic; this is the last message before we start the talk-down. We have a message for you from the British High Commission in Delhi. Your information is understood. You will be catching the Air India Flight AI 042 to Delhi. We will delay that flight for your arrival. We assume that you have no hold luggage to transfer; Cochin air traffic.'

'Thank you Cochin, that's a great relief; no luggage; VT 235.' All the indications were correct; she breathed a sigh of relief.

'VT 235 this is Cochin, Captain Abbasbeg, Miss Cartaret; I will be doing your talk-down. From now on you don't have to acknowledge instructions. Turn left onto 90°...mixture control from lean to rich and descend to 800 feet. Excellent.... flaps to 75% and bring the trim forward to help you. Turn left onto a heading of 75° and descend to 500 feet.......good, that's fine....check that your carburettor heat is on. Well done, you're right in the middle of the glide path. Be ready for some buffeting against the control surfaces; lower the undercarriage.' Claudine did as ordered; only two greens. She reversed the switches and tried again; no change. The nose and port wheels were down but no starboard wheel.

'Cochin, VT 235; I am going to overshoot, I say again, I am going to overshoot; malfunction of starboard undercarriage. I'll come back to you.'

'Cochin, roger, climb to 1000 feet and turn onto a heading of 180°.'

'VT 235.' Claudine switched the mixture from rich to lean and pulled the throttles to maximum; adjusted the trim and climbed back to 1000 feet heading due south.

'Cochin, there's nothing in the circuit, VT 235, and you are clear in all directions. Let us know when you've done your checks.'

'VT 235.' The voice from Cochin was calm and in no way indicated the anxiety of those in the control tower as the last of the light started to disappear. Claudine undid her harness and then pressed the switch to lower the undercarriage; two greens again. The port and starboard wheels of the tricycle undercarriage were right beside the flight deck. She climbed out of her seat into the starboard one and pressed her nose to the plexiglass window; the starboard wheel was up. The amphibian started to bank to starboard. She climbed back into her seat, levelled the aircraft, raised the undercarriage and pressed the transmit button. 'Cochin, VT 235, the starboard wheel is jammed. Is it possible to wind it down?'

'Cochin, yes it is, but on that aircraft it takes time and you need someone to assist you as there is no autopilot. The light has almost gone, so you must come down on the lake, which is now on the right in your three o'clock position. The altitude of the lake is 56 feet: set that now on the altimeter.'

'VT 235,' and Claudine set the altitude.

'We will bring you into the lake from ten miles out on a course of 60°. Surface wind is 8 mph from 60°. Turn right now onto 270°.'

'VT 235,' and Claudine refastened her harness and then banked the twin-engined amphibian to starboard and watched the compass swing round. She levelled out on the new course.

'Turn right onto 360° and don't bother to acknowledge unless you wish to. That's fine; now right again onto 60°. Good, you're doing fine. OK, here we go for the landing sequence. Mixture to rich.... carburettor heat on...flaps 75%....speed 100 mph.... descend to 800 feet. That's fine... acknowledge if you can see the surface of the lake.'

'VT 235, I can see the surface and there's a helicopter below me in my ten o'clock position.'

'Sorry, VT 235, that's one of ours which is waiting to lift you back here after you've landed.'

'VT 235,' and Claudine saw the helicopter turn sharply away as it was given a very abrupt order from the control tower on another frequency.

'Descend to 500 feet, speed 80 mph........that's fine, fine... two miles to go, 200 feet.....no problems, you're spot on....100 feet and 70 mph......half a mile to go, it's all yours.' The last of the sun's rays gave a deep red tinge to the surface of the lake. The amphibian came in towards the edge of the lake and for one dreadful moment Claudine thought she was going to undershoot and hit the bank. Bushes and scrub flashed past under the wings, then water......down, down... cut the throttles and spray flying past the window.

'Bugger!' Claudine swore as she realised that she'd forgotten the wipers and switched them on. Spoilers up, speed coming down and the amphibian settling on the water's surface; she was down. She increased the revs and brought the aircraft to the side of the lake. 'Cochin, this is VT 235, many thanks for your help. Aircraft and pilot both safely down,' and Claudine killed the engines in turn and then switched off the magnetos and the main power switch.

CHAPTER 23

Commander George Gresham awoke feeling refreshed; it was 6.20 in the morning. Just a few more minutes peace before he showered and shaved. USS Los Angeles was 20,000 metres astern of the Shimojima and Al Samak. The submarine could adjust both the pitch and profile of its five-bladed propeller to alter its cavitation signature and had done so to make sure that their's wasn't the same fate as the Russian Southern Fleet's submarines. There was a knock outside his cabin. 'Come!' The curtain was pulled back and the duty signaller came in.

'FLASH signal for acknowledgment, Sir.'

'Thank you,' and George propped himself on one elbow as he read the signal. 'The shit'll hit the fan now! Thanks Jackson, acknowledge it. No reply,' and he signed to indicate that he'd read the signal. He swung his feet off the bed, sat up and then reached to the bulkhead behind his bed and unclipped the microphone on the boat's PA system. He paused, collecting his thoughts and then flicked the switch. 'Now hear this; this is your Captain. I have just received a signal from Fleet. It seems that the USA will be at war with Iraq in the very near future unless Saddam complies fully with Resolution 1441. The President is trying to get the rest of the Security Council to sign up to a new resolution authorising military action against Iraq. No other information is available at this time. That's all,' and he switched off the mike. His first officer appeared at the door. 'Hello Frank, I thought our wise guys at Langley had ruled out that scenario.'

'Yea, me too; what price wisdom!'

'Look, can you do a check with all heads of departments; I'd like to know as soon as possible if any of the guys on this sub have family, relatives or friends in Iraq, Kuwait or Saudi.'

'Right, Sir; just to keep you informed, that's me for a start. My sister's married to the commercial attaché at our Embassy in Kuwait.'

'Thank you for letting me know that. Let's pray this doesn't turn into another Irangate fiasco. I'll be in the control room in half-an-hour.' Frank Mareno left his cabin and George looked at his watch; 2 August - 0200 hours - Saddam about to receive a load of nuclear missiles. It didn't bear thinking about.

The metal-ribbed floor of the van was extremely uncomfortable and he was face-down on it. Every time the van hit a bump, he banged his head. Slowly, Gunn came back to painful and uncomfortable consciousness. His hands and feet were tied and he was gagged. It was dark, and he appeared to be in the back of an open van, which had a tarpaulin strapped over the back. He wasn't alone. There was certainly one other body in the back with him. Gunn moved around and found that there were two other bodies. Ratchasima and Ringo? The one next to him was Ringo. Dead or alive? Gunn wriggled over and pinched Ringo. There was a slight response, so he pinched again, harder. That produced a more positive response and Ringo began to move. Gunn's eyes were now getting their night vision. The van was being driven along a lighted road and some of that light filtered through small cuts and tears in the tarpaulin over the back. He could just make out Ringo's features; the eyes were open and he was gagged like Gunn.

Gunn turned over putting his back to Ringo, hoping that he hadn't been too badly injured and would understand what he was trying to do. He wriggled forward a little along the floor of the van and hoped that Ringo wouldn't misinterpret what he was about to do.

Had they taken Ringo's knife? Gunn moved about until his hands found Ringo's belt. He found the belt slot and worked his fingers into it. The knife was still there. The binding on his wrists was painfully tight and his fingers were already swollen. Carefully he pushed the end of the knife handle and it started to move. It came clear of the belt slot and fell to the floor of the van. Gunn turned over more on his back and groped about. 'Got it!' he muttered into his gag. He turned back to Ringo who was now fully conscious and with their faces only inches apart, Gunn used his head and eyes to try and get Ringo to turn over so that his bound wrists were towards Gunn.

The message was understood and Ringo turned over, followed by Gunn who then felt along the knife handle until he found the catch. He made sure that he wasn't going to stab himself when the powerful spring was released and pressed the catch. The switch-blade clicked out. He moved back towards Ringo, feeling with the fingers of one hand for the binding on his wrists. It seemed to be some sort of plastic-coated cord - like a washing line. With great care, Gunn brought the blade into contact with the cord and started to saw at it. It seemed to take an age and he had no idea where they were going or if they might stop any second. The cord parted. He moved away a little as Ringo started to flex his wrists. The movement increased and the next moment the knife was taken from his hands and his bindings were cut. Gunn reached up and pulled away the sticking plaster holding the gag in his mouth. The van slowed and then turned off the road onto another. Ringo cut away the bindings on his feet and then those on Gunn's. They both turned to the third body. Whoever it was had also regained consciousness. The bindings were cut away and the gag removed.

'Ratchasima?'

'Yes, are you Gunn?'

'Do you like rubies?'

'What? Oh yes, but only if they're as red as pigeon's blood.'

'I'm John Gunn and this is Ringo who came with me to the Rising Sun to get you. Right, that's the introductions dealt with, now to get out of here,' and right on cue, the van slowed and then turned left onto a track which bounced them around in the back. Gunn reached down, but the Radom had been taken. He turned to Ringo. 'Quickly, cut an opening in this.' Ringo's knife went through the tarpaulin with no difficulty and slit it from one end to the other and he then did a cross-cut. They all looked out. They were driving down a track. There were ponds on either side of the track and some low buildings ahead of them. It was Ratchasima who whispered.

'This is Pak Nam. This place is a crocodile farm where they breed the animals for commercial purposes - you know, shoes, belts and handbags. There are thousands of the creatures here and I think we are scheduled to be their next meal. Very convenient, not a trace of us left.'

'Ringo,' Gunn whispered, 'you take that side and he pointed to the right where the passenger would be. 'I'll take the other the moment this thing stops.' Ringo nodded. The van went through a central part of the farm and then pulled up beside pens, which were open to the salt water in the mouth of the River Chao Phaya. All three of them could see the reflection of light from the eyes of the sixteen foot long monsters, lying on the mud among the roots of the mangroves. Gunn and Ringo jumped over the side of the van and waited. The two cab doors opened. On Gunn's side a trousered leg appeared, a hand on the door and then a head. It was unlikely that the man ever felt a thing; Gunn reached forward, grasped his chin and the back of his head and with a sharp twist, broke his neck. There was a strangled gurgling sound from the other side of the cab. Gunn went round the front of the van to find the passenger lying on the track with his throat slit from ear to ear.

'Mustn't disappoint the old crocs must we. Come on, Ringo, give me a hand,' and the two of them carried the bodies over to the low wire fence and after swinging them backwards and forwards, hurled them down to the crocodiles. Both were dragged away and vanished beneath the surface of the rising tide. Gunn looked at his watch; 3.50. 'How long will it take us to get back to Bangkok?'

'The farm's just off the old Sukhumvit Highway to the south-east of the city. We'll be back in half an hour. Come back to my place,' Ratchasima offered, 'and we can contact Alan from there. Here, John, is this yours?' and he handed him his Radom.'

'Yes, thanks, where was it?'

'On the floor on the driver's side. He must have dropped it there when you adjusted the angle of his head.'

'How are you feeling,' Gunn asked Ratchasima.

'Still a bit fuzzy-headed; they used drugs on me and I've no idea what I've told them.'

'Not much and nothing that's of any use now. I'll tell you what happened on the way back to the city. You drive Ringo.' The three of them got into the cab of the van. Ringo turned it round, drove back to the metalled road and then joined Route 3, the old Sukhumvit Highway.

Ratchasima told Gunn that he had a flat in a large apartment block just off the old race course road, by the university where he lived with his wife. Before going to the flat, they went back to the Rising Sun. There were still cars parked outside the club despite the government ruling that all clubs had to close at midnight. Ratchasima explained that it would have to be a very brave or stupid policeman who raided the Rising Sun as many of the senior police officers were taking bungs from Thannamarong. Ringo's taxi was still parked between a Mercedes and a Seven Series BMW. They parked in the road and Ringo and Gunn went in, got into the taxi and drove it out.

Outside the driveway, Ringo paused; Ratchasima got in and they then drove to his flat. Ratchasima had explained that he really was known as Harry and Gunn explained how Ringo and he had met. In the flat, there was a tearful reunion between Harry and his wife Sumalee and then tea was produced for all of them while Gunn rang Alan Paxton; it was just after five. Ratchasima explained that he was perfectly fit and capable of doing the airport task that morning, but was grateful when Gunn suggested he took Ringo as a minder to watch out for Volkonoff and Thannamarong, both of whom could recognise him. They would all have their own cars, Alan told him, which were currently parked outside Alan's flat above Rama Jewellery.

Alan asked them to meet him at his flat at eight. From there, Alan and Gunn would go direct to their firing positions with the HVMs and Ringo and Harry would go to the airport. Two small radios would be used by Ringo and Harry to keep in touch with each other whilst the larger radio would be left in Harry's car in the car park reserved for airport staff where Ringo would be positioned with binoculars. After these plans had been discussed, Harry offered them the use of his bathroom to shower and shave and by the time this was finished and Sumalee's breakfast had been eaten, it was 7.30 and time to leave. Ringo drove the taxi to Alan's flat through the early morning traffic.

The entrance to the flat was through a door beside Rama Jewellery and then up two flights of stairs. Alan's flat door was open and he was on the phone as they arrived. He put the phone down and turned to them. OK, the HVMs are in the cars. Your's John is the Toyota Celica we drove in yesterday; Sumalee, here are the keys. Harry, you and Ringo have got the Mercedes van with the 'Airport Services' sign painted on the side. Here are the keys which include one for this flat. The scheduled take off time is still 1030 hours. Harry, yours is the most important task; there must be no confusion about the aircraft before either John or I fire. If there is, we abort; understood?'

'Yes, that's quite clear.'

'You've got the geiger counter?'

'Yes.'

'Sumalee, are you happy about the meeting place with John.
You only saw it in the dark last night.'

'That's alright, I know that area well as I was born very close by.'

'Good; John, your boat is in position and has a full tank of petrol. That's all. We meet back here when it's over - one way or another.'

The morning rush hour in Bangkok on Thursday 2nd August was building up as the three vehicles left Alan Paxton's flat. It was a fine judgement as to what time to be in position. Whilst it was sensible to get into position in good time, the longer each of them was there, the more the chance of discovery. They were heading against the flow of traffic and by 8.45, Sumalee had turned off to Gunn's firing position and at 9.05 he and Alan received a radio check from Harry. At 9.30, Gunn recognised Ringo on the radio who gave them a report that the Saudia 747 cargo had landed on schedule and was now being refuelled. The flight was on the listings for commercial departures as Flight SV 904. The aircraft registration was RP-64AL and this was stencilled on both wings. The information was acknowledged by both firing positions.

Sumalee stopped the Toyota by the ruined temple and Gunn opened the boot and removed the two launchers with their pre-loaded missiles. One by one, he carried them up the side of the temple spire to the launch position he'd selected and laid the two missiles down on the crumbling masonry with his radio. He then climbed down to the ground and jogged along the track, between the paddy fields, to the canal. The boat was tied to a flimsy wooden pontoon which jutted out into the canal. There was a similar pontoon on the other side of the canal and the two, presumably, were used for some ferry system. Gunn got into the boat, pumped the black rubber bulb on the fuel line, pulled out the choke and pressed the starter. The converted 1300 cc Ford engine fired immediately and when he pushed the choke in, settled to a steady tick-over. He switched off the ignition and ran back to the temple. Sumalee was waiting with the engine running and he held up his thumb; she waved in acknowledgement and drove back to the expressway.

That morning, the sky was a brilliant blue with high cloud. Gunn looked at his watch; 9.50. He checked both of the launchers and prepared them. Each tube was extended like a telescope, the sight folded out of the side of the launcher. He cocked both weapons; this was rather like the action on an old frontier Winchester rifle, however, in the case of the HVM, the lever motion powered up the silicon chip circuit and capacitors. Both launcher test lights glowed green when Gunn pressed them to indicate a 'go' for launch. It was now 10.02. The radio came to life.

'Cargo positively identified and loading and fuelling complete. The repaint of the Iraqi 747 is an amateurish job and the Iraqi Airways colours can still be seen in places under the green, blue and black of the Saudia livery. I am now back with the vehicle and can see the aircraft which is in the process of being turned round by a tractor prior to engine start.'

After the initial acknowledgement that they were all in position, there would be no more from the two firing positions. It was getting very hot indeed, stuck up on the side of the temple spire and the sweat started to trickle down Gunn's face as he raised his binoculars and looked towards the point at which the aircraft would first appear. He wiped his face and hands on his shirt; 10.26. 'Aircraft now taxiing out to runway 190. South position, it's coming in your direction.'

'Roger,' it had been agreed that that information would be acknowledged.

'There are three aircraft waiting to depart; a Thai Airways 747, a Cathay Pacific 747 and the third one is the Saudia 747. The Thai 747

317

is now rolling for take off....it's clear of the runway and should be visible...now.' It was; Gunn saw the aircraft climb into the sky towards his position. He had no difficulty in reading the registration letters and figures. The sound of police sirens came from the direction of the main highway; Gunn swung the binoculars round and focused them on the road. 'The Cathay Pacific 747 is moving out onto the runway.'

There was an airport security vehicle coming south down the dual-carriageway; it had a direction finding aerial on the roof and was escorted by three police cars. This and three other radio-direction-finding vehicles were constantly manned at the airport and at least two of them must have achieved a rough bearing on their first transmission. This was the reason for no acknowledgements from the firing positions except for the identification of the runway, which was to be used by the Saudia 747. The next turning point on the expressway was some four miles further south on the road ,which Sumalee would be using.

'The Cathay Pacific 747 is rolling....clear of the runway.' It came into view and climbed steadily towards the Gulf of Thailand and then turned to the east. The sirens faded into the distance and the oppressive humidity seemed to envelope and press down on Gunn. He wiped his face and hands again; his shirt was soaked in sweat. He could hear the sirens again. They became louder and louder as they came up the nearside of the expressway.

'Saudia 747 is moving onto the runway... it's turning straight into its take-off run.....nose wheel clear.... its off the runway.' The sirens had stopped. The aircraft came into view climbing towards Gunn. Registration RP-64AL and he could even see the crossed scimitars and palm tree on the green-painted tail; Gunn swung his binoculars across the sky. No other aircraft in sight. He picked up the first launcher and pointed the sight at the fake Saudia 747. He activated the sensors of the HVM, following the aircraft round and keeping it constantly in the centre of the sight. An alarm like that on a digital watch sounded; the computer brain was telling him that it had recognised the target and was ready to fire. Gunn pressed the trigger. There was a muffled thump, a woosh and the missile had gone. He dropped the launcher and picked up the second one. Instant recognition and the second missile was on its way. He threw both launchers to the ground and scrambled after them. Sirens screaming again; he picked up the two launchers and ran with them and his radio through the ruins of the temple, along the narrow path between the paddy fields to the line of coconut palms on the bank of the canal.

An explosion and fireball in the sky to the south of him; he threw the launchers and radio into the boat. The police sirens were even louder. Gunn walked along the pontoon, climbed into the boat and lowered the prop-shaft as he steadied himself in the stern. He pumped up the pressure again, set the choke to half and pressed the starter. The engine fired and died and thick blue smoke came from the exhaust. Mixture too rich; sirens now screaming as the police cars came down the track off the expressway. Choke in, press starter; the engine fired...men in blue uniforms running towards the canal...another burst of blue smoke and then the engine settled into a steady rhythm.

Gunn cast off the painter, lowered the spinning propeller into the water and the boat moved rapidly away from the pontoon. He slowly increased the revs and the boat responded instantly, leaving the pontoon and ruined temple out of sight in a matter of seconds. He could no longer hear any sirens. Eight minutes later, he saw the canal bridge, over which there was a steady stream of traffic heading towards the expressway. He pulled the boat into the bank just short of the bridge, de-telescoped the launchers, slung them over his back on their slings and then climbed up the bank to the road carrying his radio. The Toyota was parked at the top of the bank with the bonnet open. The moment Sumalee saw Gunn, she got out of the car, shut the bonnet and opened the boot. Gunn threw the launchers into the boot and got into the passenger's side. Sumalee started the Toyota and pulled out into the traffic, heading towards the expressway.

Thirty-five minutes later, they reached the Pethcburi Road intersection and just after crossing it, Gunn spotted what he'd been looking for; a large dustcart. He asked Sumalee to pull in behind it; he opened the boot, took out the launchers and threw them into the open maw of the monster, which was grinding and pulverising the rubbish. The launchers disappeared from sight as the dustmen reappeared, pushing large metal bins towards the cart.

Sumalee pulled out into the traffic again and five minutes later turned down a side road and then into an area of lock-up garages by two apartment blocks. She drove up to one of the many garages, stopped and handed Gunn a key. He jumped out, opened the garage and Sumalee drove the Toyota in. The door was locked and both of them went out onto the road and Gunn hailed a taxi. They got the taxi driver to drop them at the top of the Silom Road and from there, they walked to the flat over Rama Jewellery. Sumalee opened the door with her key and they went up the stairs to the flat. She used the same key in the door at the top of the stairs and they both went in; they were the last to arrive. The door closed behind them.

'Well, I think that completes the party!' Gunn dropped to the floor and turned, reaching for the Radom, but he was staring into the wrong end of a bulbous silencer on the end of an automatic; at the other end was Volkonoff's right hand.

*

British Airways Flight BA 042 to Bangkok landed 70 minutes early; the Airbus 340 had gone unserviceable and had been replaced by a Boeing 747. The longer range of the 747 and the chaos in the Gulf, which had already cost British Airways one aircraft, accounted for the non-stop flight and the early arrival. Maria was in the meeting area just before 12.00; the whole airport was swarming with armed police and soldiers. Her first task was to go to the left luggage facility where she produced the key which she'd been given in Moscow and opened container 343, removed the small box and left the key in the lock. After this, she went to the information desk and asked what was happening and was told that there had been a terrorist attack on an aircraft, which had crashed into the sea. Feigning horror and concern because a relative had been scheduled to catch a flight from Don Muang Airport that morning, she was told that it was a Saudia commercial flight with no passengers. She could hardly contain her pleasure on hearing that Volkonoff's plan had failed. She thanked the man at the information desk and went over to the telephones and dialled Rama Jewellery. 'Rama Jewellery, can I help you?'
'Yes please; I'm looking for good quality rubies, at least 3 carats and as red as pidgeon's blood.
I'm flying back to America shortly and I'm short of time, so I'm ringing round to save a wasted journey.'
'It's just as well you phoned, Madam. I regret to say that we've sold out and there seems little chance of getting stones of that quality for at least a week. Is there any other stone you'd be interested in?'
'Yes, would you have any star sapphires?'
'Yes, indeed and excellent quality.'
'Thank you, I'll drop by later on.' Maria replaced the phone and ran with her trolley to the taxi rank and went straight to the front of the queue. 'Please forgive me, but I had a relative on the plane that crashed. I must get to the hospital.' The acting and the tears ensured her a seat in the first taxi and as it pulled away she directed the driver to Silom Road and offered to double his fare if he could do it in less than forty minutes. The taxi left a few hundred baht's worth of rubber on the tarmac by the taxi stand and within 3 minutes was on the expressway heading south to the city.

The girl who answered the phone at Rama Jewellery had responded to Maria's recognition sequence with the coded message, which had warned her that the opposition was on the premises, someone was listening to the conversation and help was needed immediately. Out of sight of the driver's eyes in the rear-view mirror, she opened the box which she'd collected from left luggage and removed the 9 mm Walther. She checked that a round was in the chamber, removed another one from the box of 9 mm bullets and squeezed it into the magazine. She tucked the automatic into the waistband of her jeans behind her back and put the bullets into her bag.

'How much longer, driver?'

'About ten minutes, I think.'

'Faster please!' The poor taxi driver thought that he'd been doing pretty well. Well, if it was faster she wanted, it was faster she could have, he thought, and rammed his foot down on the accelerator. Eight-and-a-half minutes later she stopped him a hundred yards short of the jewellery shop and gave him 500 baht - instead of the 70 baht, which the meter registered. Maria looked at her watch as she walked quickly towards the shop; 12.50. A 'closed' sign was in the glass and steel-shuttered door. She walked past and used the key, which Simon Peters had given her to open the door. She took the Walther from her waistband and flicked off the safety as she walked quietly up the stairs. She heard the 'cough' of a silenced gun and then a woman screamed. She put her ear to the door of the flat; Volkonoff was speaking.

*

'What you have just done has deprived me of my old age pension. I see little reason why I should be well-disposed to any of you. If you think that you can rush me and that at least one of you might get to me, just try it; nothing would please me more. Mr Thannamarong has offered me a job here in Bangkok which he assures me will recoup my losses within a year. I thought you would all like to know that before I execute you; your execution will upset the KGB, MI6 or CIA, who or whatever organisation you all work for,' and Volkonoff raised the gun and fired.

Harry Ratchasima had seen that it was aimed at Gunn and pushed him hard at the last minute. The bullet hit Harry in the right arm and Sumalee screamed. The gun came up again, the skin on the knuckle whitened and Volkonoff fired. The bullet went into the floor beside Gunn and a look of surprise appeared on Volkonoff's face. Gunn dived across the room for the Radom; he had no idea what had happened to Volkonoff, but wasn't prepared to sit like a plaster duck at a fun fair shooting gallery any longer. He picked it up and swung towards Volkonoff who was having difficulty in raising the silenced barrel of his automatic. Gunn fired three times and Volkonoff's face dissolved into a bloody mess, his knees crumpled and he pitched forward onto the floor. The door opened and Gunn swung the Radom to cover it.

'Hello everyone, hope I arrived in time!' and Maria walked into the flat and put her finger up to her lips as she shut the door. They all heard someone coming up the stairs.

'Volkonoff!' was called from outside the door. Maria snatched it open, fired twice and Thannamarong fell through the doorway. Gunn walked over to the body of Volkonoff and bent down. Maria's shot had gone through the door, through Volkonoff's left arm and into his heart. He stood up and went over to her and kissed her.

'Thanks, I think we all owe you our lives. Whatever kept you, or were you planning a dramatic entry!' Maria returned the kiss.

'One good turn deserves another. Simon 'Smith'll do' told me how you saved my life twice in London.'

'Who?'

'I asked him on the phone, 'Simon who', when he rang me at the clinic in Maidenhead and he said,'Smith'll do'.

'Ah! that explains it. Well I'm not sure about saving your life twice, but I might have saved you from the proverbial 'fate worse than death' and on the second occasion, perhaps I did.'

'Are we allowed to join in this conversation?' Alan asked as pulled out his mobile. 'I think London might be interested to know of the success of this mission. Well done everyone; we haven't had the pleasure,' and Alan introduced himself to Maria. Harry introduced himself and his wife and then Ringo came over and was very obviously smitten by the tall and very attractive woman who had saved all of them. Harry's wound was a flesh one which Sumalee bound up and then he went down to the shop where he found that all the staff had been tied up and locked in the manager's office.

'Express Delivery Service, can I help you?'

'South-east Asia Services Manager or his deputy, please; it's the regional manager in Bangkok.' It would be 5.30 in the morning in London.

'Manager, South-East Asia.'

'I thought you'd be pleased to know, especially in the light of recent news in the Gulf, that the contract we were after has been successfully signed and completed in both respects. We have suffered no losses in the clauses of the contract and the matter is very satisfactorily concluded. We are much in debt to the consultant whom you sent out from London. We now await further instructions to conclude this business transaction.'

'Thank you for all of that and my congratulations to all concerned on such a successful conclusion. Can I take it that the opposition to our contract has been eliminated?'

'It has, as has the business associate here in Bangkok.'

'Excellent; some news for you. Our consultant, who left the Channel Islands by helicopter, is back with us after a most dramatically successful disengagement from our competitors in that field. Further instructions will follow shortly. Thank you all again and well done; goodbye.' Alan Paxton replaced the phone and turned to John.

'Claudine de Cartaret has succeeded in escaping from Hassan Hussein. The boss is very pleased and congratulates all of you. We will receive further instructions shortly.'

'Now that all that's over, can someone tell me whether that fake 747 went into the sea,' Gunn asked. For answer, Alan went over to the TV and switched it and the VCR on.

'They've been showing this on TV ever since it happened. Some tourist happened to have a camcorder handy and has made a small fortune by selling the tape to the Thai Broadcasting Services. We've recorded it, in fact we'd only just done that when our uninvited guest arrived. There, that should be it,' Alan had wound back the VCR tape and now pressed the 'play' button. There was black and white horizontal rain and then the screen cleared and a wobbly picture appeared which was very evidently shot by an amateur.

It showed the 747 with its registration crystal clear on the underside of the wings. The strike of the missile was so quick that Alan Paxton rewound the tape and then put it on slow motion. Slowed down, the approach of the first missile could be seen as it struck the starboard wing root and went straight into the fuel tank. The wing broke away just as the second missile hit the port outboard engine nacelle and exploded. The whole aircraft mushroomed into a white, hot ball of flame and plunged into the sea seven miles off the coast.

'Well, I don't know about everyone else, but I think this calls for a small celebration,' Gunn announced. 'A late lunch on the Oriental's Riverside Terrace is called for, preceded by some very cold champagne,' and they all left the flat and walked to the Oriental Hotel.

CHAPTER 24

The bleep of Alan Paxton's mobile interrupted the meal of smoked salmon, fresh asparagus, caviar and chilled champagne. He left the table on the Oriental's Riverside Terrace, but was back in less than three minutes. 'Our instructions will be coming through on the secure fax in half-an-hour; time for one more glass of champagne and then I think we'd better get back. The 'shop staff' has cleared up the rubbish in the flat.' Fifteen minutes later, they all walked back to the flat and Alan set up the fax to decode the scrambled input from the machine in London. The warning light came on and then the machine started.

'SITUATION - Al Samak is now within 250 miles of its destination and its progress is being monitored by the SSN - USS Los Angeles. ETA of SS20 missiles at Al Samak Island is approx 2200 hrs local (two hours behind local time Bangkok). Hassan will assume that his location is now known to us and therefore we must assume the worst case that he will attempt to unload the missiles from the submersible ship, transfer them to the silos and launch as soon as possible. The estimate of launch time is midnight today, 2 Aug 90. USS Los Angeles is equipped with Tomahawk SSM missiles which can destroy the SS20 launch silos with great accuracy as 'Vigilent', the US military satellite, has transmitted high-definition photographs of the island. We have learnt from Miss Cartaret that there are at least 100 indigenous Lakshadweep islanders, with their families, employed on the island. Every possible effort is to be made to rescue these islanders before the destruction of the silos. USS Los Angeles will launch it's first salvo of Tomahawk missiles at 2359 hrs today.

MISSION - Your mission is to rescue the Lakshadweep islanders from Al Samak Island before 2359 hrs today.

EXCECUTION - Gunn and Ionides will leave Bangkok at 1730 hrs on a British Airways 747; the pax have been sent to hotels on the pretext that the aircraft has become unserviceable. Your ETA at Cochin Airport is 1800 hrs (Cochin local time). At Cochin Airport you will be met by Miss Cartaret who will brief you on the island of Al Samak, the security guards, and the location of the islanders and their families. You will transfer to an Indian Air Force C-130 which will fly you to Tilacam Island, where you will drop by parachute.

This will be a 'Hi/Lo' descent; it is known that Hassan has radar, so you will jump at 27,000 feet - the routine altitude for over-flights by commercial aircraft - and delay to 2000 feet. Tilacam is 54 miles south of Al Samak Island and you will be transported in local fishing boats, which have been fitted with outboard motors. Your ETA at Tilacam is 1900 hrs and at Al Samak is 2100 hrs; that gives you two hours and 59 minutes to secure the islanders into the fishing boats and leave before the Tomahawk strike. If you discover that the launch of the SS20s is to be earlier than 2359 hours, then you are to send the appropriate codeword in these orders with a time of launch for the Tomahawk missiles. On no account,(rpt) no account, are the SS20s to be launched. The priority is the destruction of the SS20s and you will, if necessary, have to accept casualties to both yourselves and the islanders.

ADMINISTRATION, COMMMAND and SIGNALS - Miss Cartaret will deal with items under these three headings when you RV at Cochin. Miss Ionides should make contact with the KGB Station 26, in Bangkok, which will confirm Moscow's orders for her to take part in this operation. Good luck. Exclam.'

Alan finished reading the fax and then looked at his watch. 'Nearly 1630 hours; you've got an hour to catch that flight. Come on, Maria, you'd better make that call.' Maria made her phone call; the conversation in Russian only lasted for a few minutes and then she replaced the phone and turned to them.

'I was asked if I knew where the MI6 safehouse was and I told them that I was speaking from it and then put down the phone!'

'We've got to move anyway, Maria, as rather too many people know about it now,' Alan commented. 'Right, collect anything you want to take. I'll drive you both from here to the airport via John's hotel so that he can collect his things. Time to say farewells everyone. Ringo, keep in touch with Harry and we'll see if we can put you on a retainer - that's if you'd like to work with us.'

'Yes, I'd like that Mr Paxton.' As soon the farewells were over, Gunn and Maria left the flat with Alan Paxton. They stopped at the hotel while Gunn went up to his room and collected his hand baggage and Alan settled the hotel bill. On the way to the airport, Alan told them both to leave their guns with him and he would arrange for them to be sent back to London. 'I'm quite sure that Claudine will be issuing you with all that when you get to India.'

As soon as they arrived at the airport, Alan went to the BA desk where he was told that the two passengers should go straight through to the departure lounge and to Gate 24 where the aircraft had already started its engines. They shook hands and Alan kissed

Maria and thanked her again. As soon as they were in the 747, the door was shut and the tractor rolled the aircraft back from the boarding tunnel. It was a 2½hour flight to Cochin and British Airways had provided three cabin crew to look after them. The 747 taxied out to the threshold of runway 190 and turned immediately into its take off. The cabin lights were switched off as the aircraft climbed clear of the airport and Gunn and Maria asked for them to be left off so that they could both sleep as the remainder of the night promised to be a long one.

After the champagne at their celebratory lunch, it only seemed like two minutes to Gunn before he was being woken by a stewardess who told him that they would be landing in less than ten minutes. He doused his face and hair in cold water in the miniscule toilet and shaved to help freshen up. The 747 was making a wide turn to starboard out over the Arabian Sea as it sank towards the Indian Continent. The Jumbo touched down and was greeted by a small car with flashing orange light, which led it away from the airport terminal to the far side of the airport, which was used by the Indian Air Force. Out of the window, Gunn saw the Hercules C-130 with its engines running and a tanker waiting to refuel the 747 for its return flight to Bangkok. The aircraft came to a halt, the door was opened and a set of steps was manoeuvred into place. Gunn and Maria said goodbye to a rather mystified crew and left the plane, which the airport ground-handling staff was already refuelling. At the bottom of the steps was Claudine de Cartaret in a khaki flying suit.

She embraced Gunn and shook hands with Maria as she led them both across to the C-130. Conversation was impossible, so the three of them boarded the C-130 by the crew door and strapped themselves into the canvas jump seats. As soon as the door closed, the noise of the four turboprop engines increased and the aircraft rolled forward and turned onto the taxiway. The Indian Air Force loadmaster climbed down from the flight deck and came back into the fuselage to do his final pre-takeoff checks. In front of them, in the centre of the fuselage, were their parachutes. They were provided with three headsets and once these were plugged in to the aircraft intercom system, they were able to speak to each other.

Claudine explained that the equipment they would need - weapons, explosives and radios etc - had been taken to Tilacam on the aircraft which did the tourist flights from Cochin. Very briefly, she told Gunn and Maria about her escape from Al Samak and what had happened since her arrival in India.

The flight to Tilacam was only 35 minutes and as soon as the C-130 was airborne and climbing, they removed the lap straps and started to put on the clothing and equipment for the drop. Insulated suits, breathing apparatus, helmets, goggles and gloves, chest-mounted altimeter and stopwatch; they checked each other while Claudine explained that she had done a sport freefall course, but nothing like the descent which she was about to undertake. Maria told them that she had likewise done freefall jumps before, but nothing from above 8000 feet.

The loadmaster appeared, wearing similar clothing to them and breathing apparatus as would all the flight deck crew. He held up his hand with fingers spread; five minutes to go. They were led to the port fuselage door and the loadmaster fastened the safety strap round his waist. The jump order was Maria, Claudine and then Gunn last. The bleak, empty interior of the fuselage was filled with the glow of the red light by the port door. The loadmaster warned them of the impending depressurisation; their goggles misted over and then cleared as the outside temperature of minus 50 degrees Celsius matched the inside of the fuselage. Red off, green on! and Maria had gone; Claudine followed with Gunn close behind her.

There wasn't a cloud in the sky and Gunn could see both of the women clearly in the brilliant light of the moon. Within six seconds of exiting the aircraft, they were at maximum descent velocity and after 15 seconds, Gunn was able to identify a bright, illuminated cross on a dark lump in the moon-lit sea. Ten thousand feet - they would now be able to breathe with relative ease; 6000 feet...5000...4000 and then first one and then another rectangular freefall chute opened below him. He reached across and pulled his own chute release toggle and was rewarded with a comforting jerk as the chute deployed. He reached up to the control lines and steered his chute towards the glowing cross.

As he came closer and closer to the ground, Gunn saw that the cross was formed by hundreds of people holding burning torches. On the beach were some twenty, outrigger fishing canoes; all three of them landed on the soft white sand between the boats and the human cross. Gunn spilled the chute and then removed the harness and protective clothing as the temperature was now 30 degrees Celsius. By the time this task was complete, all three of them were soaked in sweat and surrounded by the islanders of Tilacam. Claudine called the other two over and then introduced them to the headman of the island, then the Imam - who was the interpreter - and then the head fisherman whom, Claudine explained, she had met on Al Samak.

Now able to think and speak coherently, away from the deafening roar of the aircraft engines, Claudine briefed Maria and Gunn on the remainder of their orders and then led them down to the boats, where all the equipment they might need had already been loaded. Each boat had a crew of four men, a 150hp outboard motor and four fuel tanks. Each boat could take eight passengers - or ten at a pinch - and there were twenty boats. Claudine explained that twenty was a fairly usual number for a fishing fleet visiting the fishing grounds around Al Samak and, hopefully, wouldn't arouse the suspicions of Hassan's security system.

Claudine had declined to take a weapon as she had said that it was as much a liability to her own side as the opposition if she was armed. There was a Kalashnikov for Maria and an Enfield SA 80 assault rifle for Gunn; explosive charges and timers - in case the Tomahawks failed, they were told, and radios; one, with a spare, to communicate to the USS Los Angeles and small, hand-held radios for them to communicate with each other. The plan was simple; the fishing boats would go to the usual place by the opening in the coral atoll into the lagoon. The three of them would swim ashore with their equipment in waterproof, buoyant bags; the Imam would also go with them to act as interpreter throughout the operation. Gunn would go to the missile silos and determine the state of readiness for launch; the two women would go to the village with the Imam, round up the islanders and lead them back to the boats where Gunn would rejoin them. At the airfield on the island of Agatti, the Indian Air Force had deployed three Jaguar, all-weather fighters, and there were two Sea King helicopters from the Indian Navy; the former to provide air cover in case Hassan had succeeded in repairing either his amphibian or the helicopter and the latter to assist with the evacuation, if required.

It was 19.18; the plan was already eighteen minutes behind schedule and there were 54 miles of open sea to cover. The three of them, with the Imam, climbed into the head fisherman's boat, engines started up all round them, the beach was thronged with torch-waving islanders and then, led by their boat, the fishing fleet moved out through the breaking surf into the deeper water beyond. Once through the surf, the throttles were opened up and the light craft, drawing almost nothing, skimmed over the surface of the calm water towards Al Samak.

*

Commander Steinbaum left the control room after asking Schwendler to invite the Russians to come and join them in the officers' wardroom for a drink. He went to his cabin first to have a hot shower after being in the control room for almost twelve hours. There were less than fifty miles to go and he had then succeeded in his task; a task for which he'd been promised a million pounds

Sterling. He would return to his village in Bavaria and having bought the farm, which he'd always wanted, he would make a generous donation to the Neo-Nazi Party. The thoughts made him whistle a rousing German marching song as he towelled himself vigorously. An entire Russian task force and four submarines; he doubted if there was a naval commander alive who could boast of an achievement of that magnitude. He looked in the mirror; white polar neck sweater, immaculate dark blue uniform with the Unterseebot motif on his left lapel. He left his cabin and walked the short distance to the wardroom; the five Russians were already there being entertained by Schwendler.

'Good evening, gentlemen; you must forgive me for not socialising before now, but we have had an eventful voyage which has kept me tied to my bridge. However, that is now nearly all over and we should be at our destination in about two hours. A remarkable boat, don't you agree?' Like many a submariner, he used the term 'boat' purposely because it always annoyed the surface navy. It was Simeon who answered him.

'Remarkable, Captain; is it possible to tell us where that destination is which we will reach shortly?'

'In general terms, yes, Mr.....er?

'Bukharin.'

'Just so: Mr Bukharin; we are in the Arabian Sea, approaching an island which is owned by Hassan Hussein - with whom I believe you negotiated the sale of ten, SS20 missiles.'

'As we understood it, Captain,' Rokossovsky interrupted, 'the missiles were to be sold to Gadaffi and we would be picked up off the coast of South Yemen and then flown to Tripoli.'

'You are....?'

'Marshal Rokossovsky.'

'Ah yes, ex-Marshal Rokossovsky, well, it will be no surprise to you as a man who has defrauded others to discover that in this sort of game, where we play for very high stakes, nothing is ever quite as simple as it, at first, seems. No, Gadaffi will not get these missiles; a far more deserving case has been found. They are being given, absolutely free, to Saddam Hussein, who has slaughtered thousands of his own population. Don't worry, gentlemen, I'm sure you will receive your money for the part which you have played. I have never known my boss not pay his debts in full.'

'What are we supposed to do on this island in the middle of the Arabian Sea?'

'Mr Samsonov? would I be right.'

'General...er..yes, I'm Samsonov.'

'Yes, I thought so; what you do is up to Hassan Hussein and I have not been told of those plans. I do know that you will all leave the ship when we dock and I advise you to have all your things packed because there will be someone waiting to escort you off the ship as soon as we arrive. I hope that you have all enjoyed your voyage with us, but unlike the pilot of a commercial airline, I can't say that I hope we'll see you again. Please forgive me, gentlemen, but I must return to the bridge, which is my place of duty for the procedure of bringing the ship into dock. Goodbye!' and Steinbaum left the wardroom.

*

'Assuming that it maintains its present course and speed, Al Samak would seem to be making for this island,' and Lt Pete Baker touched the chart with the points of his dividers. 'If that's the case, it will have to surface in about 25 minutes as the sea bed shoals rapidly from 12 miles out.'

'Thank you, Pete,' his Captain acknowledged and turned to his first officer. 'Frank, have we had that signal yet from Fleet?'

'It's coming in right now, Sir,' and at that moment the signal was brought into the control room and handed to the Captain who read it and then turned to his weapons officer. 'I'll be bringing the boat to action stations shortly; I want all torpedo tubes loaded with Harpoon and the first salvo of four Tomahawk in the for'ard vertical launch tubes.'

'Aye, aye, Sir.'

'Frank.'

'Sir.'

'Sound action stations and secure the boat for silent routine; I'll speak to the crew.'

'Aye, aye, Sir.' Commander Gresham picked up the mike on the PA system.

'Now hear this; this is the Captain. This would seem to be the final phase in our task to shadow the movements of the submersible ship carrying nuclear missiles for use in a Middle East conflict. That ship has almost reached its destination where it's expected to unload the missiles for immediate firing. It's our task to prevent the launch of those missiles. We are going to carry out this task in conjunction with both British and Russian agents who are at this minute, like us, approaching the island. Their task is to evacuate the islanders before we launch our Tomahawk missiles. Our secondary task is to destroy the submersible ship and finally to render any assistance necessary to the sea evacuation of the islanders. The time is now 2230 hours;

missile launch will be at 2359 hours at the latest and possibly earlier if we receive instructions from the personnel on the island. As soon as the submersible ship docks, we will close to within 50 miles of the island. Thank you for your attention, that's all.'

*

Simon Peters had warned his wife Audrey that he would be staying in the office for yet another night. It was just after five in the evening. Alan Paxton had phoned him from Bangkok to confirm the departure of Gunn and Ionides to Cochin and to say that he'd been informed by the Captain of the British Airways 747, on his return, that the C-130 had taken off from Cochin within five minutes of their arrival. There had been a steady exchange of calls between Langley, Virginia, and Kingsroad House, both to tie up the details of the task allocated to the USS Los Angeles and to update the British Intelligence Directorate on the progress of the operation. That information was reaching the CIA Headquarters at Langley from the floating aerial of USS Los Angeles via satellite to the 7th Fleet and via satellite again to the USA. The phone rang; it was the Director's PA who asked him to come to his office. Louise's eyebrows went up as he told her where he was going.

'Bad or good news?' she asked.

'I've no idea; he's been a bit livery throughout this whole operation. I'll soon know,' and he left the office and took the lift up to the Director's office. He was greeted by Melanie, the Director's PA, as he went into her office, who asked him to wait a moment. She went into the Director's office and emerged almost immediately to call him in. Simon went into the office to find Sir Jeremy Hammond and John Dempster, the Director of the CIA, sitting in comfortable chairs around a glass-topped coffee table.

'Hello, Simon; I'm sorry to drag you away when your operation is reaching such a crucial stage. I don't think you've met John Dempster.' Both men had stood up as Simon went into the room.

'We met at a cocktail party in Washington three years ago, Sir, when you were chairing a Congressional Inquiry, just before your appointment as Director of the CIA was announced.'

'You've a good memory Mr Peters and catch me at a disadvantage; I'd forgotten that meeting.' Simon shook hands with the CIA Director and all three men sat down.

Simon Peters returned to his office twenty minutes later and sat down at the desk. Louise put her head round the door.

'Everything alright?' she asked anxiously.

'Yes, everything's alright. I often wonder in what mad moment I chose to become involved in this intelligence business. The pay's not that marvellous, the hours are dreadful, holidays get interrupted and I'm almost guaranteed a gutful of ulcers by the time I'm 45. John Dempster, the Director of the CIA is up there with the boss. He's just....' but the phone rang and it was Communications asking him to come up immediately to see the signal arriving from USS Los Angeles.

*

For what seemed the twentieth time, Gunn looked at his watch; 2145 hours. They were still some five miles away from the island of Al Samak and were now 45 minutes behind schedule.

The engines of two of the fishing boats had packed up after less than thirty minutes, but the remainder had proved to be reliable. His anxiety about the time was interrupted by an extraordinary noise, which terrified the Tilacam fishermen in his and other boats. It sounded like someone beating a huge cauldron under water. Gunn was as mystified as the frightened islanders. It was Claudine who came aft along the narrow boat and told them what it was.

'That has to be Al Samak...' and even as she spoke, the calm surface of the sea some hundred metres away boiled and then burst asunder as the streamlined bridge of the submersible boat broke through the surface. 'The noise is made by the high-pressure air blasting the water out of the ballast and trim tanks. I last heard that when I was crewing in a race off Cherbourg and the French had just launched their latest nuclear submarine - Diamant, I think, which had the number S604 painted in red on the conning tower....sail or whatever its called. It was doing its acceptance trials we were told and surfaced right in the middle of the yachts in the race, very nearly capsizing two of them.'

In exactly the same manner, two of the outrigger canoes came very close to being capsized by the surfacing Al Samak. As the ship rose out of the sea, Claudine spotted the leading lights of the channel cut through the coral to the dock and pointed them out to Gunn and Maria. As the ship rose further and further out of the water, the bridge slowly changed shape as the variable structure of the ship started to change it back into a surface cargo vessel. Their canoe swung away to port, followed by all the others and they soon lost sight of the ship as it was hidden behind the coconut palms on the spit of sand which jutted out into the sea between the lagoon and the deep water channel into the dock.

The head fisherman who was guiding their canoe towards the opening in the coral around the lagoon, eased off the throttle of the outboard motor and let the canoe drift. He spoke to the Imam who, in turn, spoke to Gunn.

'He says he does not think it would be wise to go any closer to the shore as it might arouse suspicions. He says to swim from here. I am ready to go.'

'Thanks,' Gunn acknowledged. 'Both ready?' and nods confirmed that Claudine and Maria were ready. The four of them slipped over the side of the canoe into the warm water and swam towards the sand, towing their waterproof bags behind them. It was only a 200 yard swim ashore and once on the sand, they unpacked weapons and radios, synchronized watches and then they all moved off into the palms towards the islanders' village and the missile silos beyond it.

*

Using a ceremonial scimitar, Hassan Hussein had personally beheaded the head security officer who had failed to monitor Claudine de Cartaret's movements on the afternoon of 1st August and failed to secure the hangar, so allowing her successful escape from the island. His aircraft engineeers had worked round the clock to make both the amphibian and the helicopter airworthy; the fuselage of the aircraft proved to be relativeley simple and was repaired within four hours, but the smashed instruments, electronics and tail rotor of the helicopter had proved to be beyond the capacity of the aircraft workshop on Al Samak. None of Hassan's men dared approach him, such was his fury at being out-witted by a young woman and none of them wanted to suffer the same fate of the head security officer.

Whilst the engineers worked on the repairs to the aircraft, the remainder of the workforce prepared for the arrival of the ship with the SS20 missiles. Hassan himself was in the dockyard superintendent's office and everyone was keyed up to fever pitch as the ship surfaced off the coast of the island. He had demanded a report every five minutes from his air defence officer who was responsible for the island's radar and early warning system, the Soviet SA-4, 6 and 7 missile launchers and the 30mm Gatling air defence machine guns. His entire island was on full alert in the expectation of an attack by either a combined or single nation assault from Russia, the USA or the UK. All the islanders had been confined to their houses in the village and were being guarded by a section of the security force.

Every over-flight had been reported by the air defence officer and the flight timings compared with Thursdays of previous weeks. No anomaly had appeared. The arrival of the fishing fleet had been reported by the observation post at the entrance of the channel, but as yet there was nothing to indicate outside interference with his plans. His missile officer had assured him that he could have the first two SS20s ready for launch within 1½ hours of the ship docking and the remaining eight would follow in pairs at twenty minute intervals. Every major conurbation in Iraq, south of Kurdistan, had been targeted and the prevailing north-westerly wind would carry the radiation south-east away from his homeland.

His ship, Al Samak, was now at the entrance to the channel; the dock had been flooded and the lock gates were open. He watched with admiration at the skill of the captain of the ship as he guided it, unaided by tugs, into the channel. Messenger lines snaked down from the deck of the ship; these were spun round large winch drums which pulled out the steel warps which, in turn, were wound rapidly onto the drums and then acted as brakes to halt the forward motion of the ship.

Frustratingly slowly, the bows came through the lock gate into the dock; the forward motion of the ship was now entirely from the winches hauling it into the dock. On deck, the hatch covers were already off and the self-stowing derricks had been raised in preparation for the removal of the missiles.

The dock superintendent told Hassan that the stern of the ship was in the dock and the lock gates were being closed. The leading lights were extinguished as was the floodlighting of the dock channel. The ship stopped, the gates closed and the dock superintendent clutched-in the gas-turbine-driven pumps which would empty the dock in six hours. Even as he did this, the first of the long wooden crates containing an SS20 missile swung over the side of the ship and was lowered onto a trailer. The quick-release buckles were undone and the trailer was towed away to the silos to be uncrated and then lifted clear and lowered by crane into the silo. Once in the silo, the fins would be fitted, the inertial guidance system would be programmed and the target data for the MIRV warhead would be fed from the launch control computer into the warhead-arming computer. Unable to contain his impatience any longer, Hassan left the dockyard control office, much to the relief of the superintendent, and went out onto the dock to watch the unloading of the missiles.

Another derrick was lowering the companionway into position on the port side of the ship and Hassan could see the group of five Russians standing on the deck with their suitcases. Another trailer with a crated missile moved off and the derrick swung back to delve into the hold for the next one.

The companionway was locked into position; a small minibus pulled up at the foot of it and the Russians started to descend. Hassan could hear some shouting in the distance, which irritated him. The Russians reached the foot of the companionway and looked towards the frightening, masked character in a flowing bernous. Hassan walked towards the five men who did their best to get into the bus; he was used to this physical show of revulsion and it no longer bothered him. The shouting increased in volume and a small jeep drove towards Hassan from the missile launch site. Hassan's missile officer jumped from the jeep as soon as it came to a halt and ran to Hassan and, in terror that he was about to suffer the same fate as the security officer, told Hassan that the first two crates contained no missiles, only scrap metal. The Russians had heard the announcement and looked at each other, mirroring the apprehension of the missile officer; with one voice, they all said the same word, 'Volkonoff!'

Now dead, Volkonoff had achieved the only good deed he had ever done in his life - in error. In his greed to be paid twice, both by Hassan and Saddam Hussein, he had just bought Gunn, Maria and Claudine an extra few minutes of time to save the islanders of Tilacam and a nuclear holocaust in Iraq.

CHAPTER 25

The hangar, from which Claudine had taxied the amphibian less than 24 hours previously, was brightly illuminated with fluorescent lights. Half-a-dozen men were working on the helicopter which looked as though it was unlikely to fly again and certainly not in the next 24 hours. They decided to select the place near the hangar where they had stopped as the RV where they would meet after the two tasks had been completed. It was easily identifiable and the technicians working in the hangar would have no night vision and would be unable to see what was going on outside. The two women and the Imam disappeared among the palms on Gunn's right while he made his way round the hangar towards the missile silos on the left side of the dockyard.

The full moon was like a fluorescent globe itself and even under the canopy of palm fronds, Gunn could see his way without any difficulty. As he came out of the trees onto the tarmac road, which ran all round the island, he was able to identify an air defence missile launcher on a circular concrete plinth. There was a steady hum coming form the remotely fired launcher indicating that it was 'live'.

Gunn crossed the road and went into the palms again towards the area to the left of the dockyard where Claudine had told him that he would find the two silos. There was little difficulty in identifying the area as there was no attempt at concealment and there was also a great deal of noise coming from that direction. The area was floodlit by banks of lights on metal pylons. Gunn paused in the deep shadow cast by this lighting. There were two crates lying on the concrete with their tops removed, but he couldn't see inside either of them. All the men were wearing green overalls and orange safety helmets. As he watched, a small diesel tractor appeared from the direction of the dockyard, towing a trailer with another crate on it. As soon as it reached the silo apron, it was attacked by a small army of the green-overalled men who broke open the lid and then collapsed the sides of the crate revealing the dull grey paint and red markings of an SS20 missile.

The jib of the mobile crane was extended and small panels on either side of the missile were removed, revealing strong-points attached to the missile frame to which the sling on the end of the crane cable was attached. The clamps holding the missile onto the wooden trestles were undone and then the crane raised the missile, nose first, off the base of the crate. Guide ropes had been secured to the base of the missile and as soon as it was vertical, the jib of the crane extended until the SS20 hung over the mouth of the silo. It then slowly disappeared into the silo as another crate arrived. The same procedure was followed and in less than eight minutes, the second missile had been lowered into its silo.

Gunn checked his watch; 23.05. It was only twenty minutes since they had separated at the RV and it was most unlikely that all the islanders had been rounded up. The first two crates were dragged over to the area of the concrete apron just in front of where Gunn was hiding amongst the palms. He could now see inside the crates; pieces of scrap metal. Gunn assumed these were the fake crates substituted for the real ones in Hong Kong by Volkonoff. The second one was towed over and the driver jumped off the back of the tractor and bent down to disconnect the trailer. Gunn hit him very hard indeed with the butt of the SA 80 and then dragged him into the palms. He pulled off the overalls, squeezed into them, removed two, one pound Semtex charges with attached timers from his waterproof backpack which he set for a forty minute delay and picked up the safety helmet which had fallen on the ground.

There was shout from one of the men at the mouth of the silo who was pointing towards the dock area. Gunn waved, jumped into the seat of the tractor and drove towards the dock. For only a few yards, he was out of sight of both the missile launching area and the dock. He stopped the tractor, jumped out of the seat and wrenched the flexible fuel line out of its jubilee clip. At the dockyard, beside the ship, were two more crates waiting to be collected. He made his way back to the silos where the workmen were waiting for the arrival of the next two crates. Two men were carrying a missile fin each and as Gunn watched they disappeared through the entrance to what had to be stairs or a lift down to the bottom of the silo.

Gunn walked over and picked up a fin and followed. It was the entrance to a stairwell, which went down by flights to the foot of the silo. The other two men were a couple of flights ahead of him. When he reached the bottom of the stairs, there was a two-foot thick door, which was open, between the two silos. He went through into the far silo where there was a technician waiting for the fin and it was taken out of his hands. The panels at the base of the missile had been removed and the technicians were peeling off the thick, black sticky duck tape, which covered and protected the edges of the fins. No one paid any attention to him.

Right at the base of the missile, by the rocket motor venturi, were ceramic extensions, which jutted into the rocket efflux and were connected to the movable flaps on the end of the fins. From his military experience of missiles and their propulsion and guidance systems, Gunn presumed that these ceramic 'flaps' substituted for the airflow over the missile control surfaces until adequate airspeed was achieved for the latter to become effective. The Semtex charge fitted neatly inside a slot under the ceramic flap made it completely invisible to a cursory inspection.

Gunn went through the thick, steel door into the other silo. The fins were fitted and the panels were being replaced. The technician reached for the screwdriver, which had been placed on the concrete ducting under the base of the missile. It wasn't there because Gunn had picked it up and it was now held behind his back. The man looked around and then went over to a tool-box, giving Gunn just enough time to slip the Semtex charge into the same place on the ceramic flap.

He left the silo and made his way back up the stairs to the surface. Someone had retrieved the tractor and now two more missiles sat on their trestles to one side of the launch area. It was 23.32; Gunn went to the palms on the fringe of the concrete apron, discarded the tight overalls, picked up his bag and the SA 80 and made his way towards the RV.

*

As Maria and Claudine approached the islanders' village, they easily identified the security guards because they were the only people moving around; they counted six who were patrolling around the perimeter of the buildings. All the guards were wearing some form of dark overall, which differed little from the damp flying suits worn by the two women. The guards were armed with Kalashnikov sub-machine guns; the only difference between them and Maria was the peaked combat hat the guards were wearing. Maria told Claudine and the Imam to wait amongst the palms on the edge of the little village and she walked forward toward the first of the guards who was some 25 metres away. He spun round as he heard her footsteps raising the Kalashnikov as he did so, but almost immediately lowered it as he mistook Maria for one of his colleagues.

He spoke to her in Arabic, which she didn't understand and so she made a non-commital noise which might have been construed as anything from a greeting to acknowledgement. He made a gesture towards the small, thatched-roof huts, turning away from Maria for an instant and that ended his guard duties as the metal skeleton butt of Maria's sub-machine gun was rammed into the nape of his neck. She stooped and picked up the combat hat and weapon. She put on the hat, returned to Claudine and the Imam and handed over the Kalashnikov.

'Fire it into the air, Claudine, as a signal if you need help.

You and the Imam start getting the people out of bed and onto the beach. I'll try and get rid of the other guards,' and she turned and went back towards the centre of the village. The addition of the hat completed the confusion and Maria had little difficulty either finding the other guards or of disposing of them. She then went back to the others where she found men going from hut to hut waking the occupants. As the islanders appeared from their huts, bewildered, they were led towards the beach. Maria looked at her watch; it was after 23.30. 'We must speed this up,' and she and Claudine went from hut to hut urging the people to hurry. Maria turned to Claudine; 'look, you go and lead all those we have at the moment to the RV to meet up with John and then we can, at least, start the evacuation of the islanders. I'll keep chasing them along from here.'

Claudine moved away through the huts while Maria went into yet another hut to rouse the occupants. As she reappeared, she was met by the Imam who told her that all the islanders were now on the move to the RV. Four men were rushing from hut to hut doing a final check and Maria waited until they reported to the Imam that the village was clear and then they all left the village and made their way through the palms towards the RV. It was now 23.47. Gunn was waiting at the RV with the aerial extended on the large radio. He explained that he'd been back to the silos and that the launch site had been cleared and the countdown had started. Claudine had gone on ahead to the beach to signal the fishing canoes and as Gunn saw the islanders head in that direction, he picked up the handset of the radio and sent the codeword to USS Los Angeles.

Fifty miles away from the island, the codeword was picked up by the submarine's floating antenna and the sea above the vertical launch tubes of the Tomahawk missiles erupted as the first two missiles were blasted to the surface by compressed air. The solid-fuel rocket motor accelerated the cruise missile to 650 mph and then the ram-jet propulsion took over as the missile swooped down to within twenty feet of the surface of the sea and its pre-programmed brain guided it to the missile silos. No sooner had the first salvo left the submarine than the second followed while the launch tubes were reloaded. The air defence radar on Al Samak Island identified the missile launch and the air defence officer ran to warn Hassan Hussein of the in-coming missiles, but Hassan had left the launch command post.

The message was passed to the missile launch officer who made the decision to accelerate the remaining seconds of the countdown and reached for the two plastic covers of the firing switches. He lifted the covers and placed a hand on each switch as both silos reverberated with shattering explosions just seconds before the two cruise missiles plunged into the silos and exploded. The second salvo followed the first and then the two following salvos struck the ship as it settled in the dry dock, and blew it apart.

The last of the islanders had just been carried to a canoe as the first missile struck and a fountain of white-hot flame poured into the sky from the mouth of the silos as the SS20 rocket fuel ignited. Gunn turned as he heard the unmistakeable sound of aero-engines in amongst the cacaphony of sound. As the last canoe was pushed away from the beach into the surf, with Gunn, Maria and Claudine and a group of children aboard who had become separated from their parents, the second amphibian left a white streak of phosphoresence across the lagoon and then climbed into the night sky.

*

Simon Peters had told Gunn that Louise had held him to his promise to take her out to dinner and asked Gunn to join them. The restaurant chosen by Louise was Giovani's Place in the Chelsea Marina. Claudine had returned to Guernsey to inspect her father's new boat after extracting a promise from Gunn that he would fly over and stay with them. He had dinner with the de Havillands and Celia and her husband, Robin, where she was told what had happened since her chance sighting in the bogie-changing shed in Erlian.

The Indian Navy had found five Russians on the island of Al Samak who, on the advice of the British Intelligence Directorate, had been put to work helping the people of the Lakshadweep Islands. Nothing had been seen or heard, or remains found, of Hassan Hussein, but the amphibian had gone and as more and more troops were sent to the Gulf and the world press focused on the impending conflict, he was forgotten and no one noticed the return of Hassan to the village of Sarikamis in the hills of Kurdistan.

*

Gunn walked into the restaurant and spotted Simon and Louise at a table on the outside balcony. He walked between the other tables and joined them. 'Three's company tonight, Simon?' Gunn enquired with a smile.

340

'No, the fourth's right behind you,' and Gunn turned, half-rising from his chair; it was Maria, looking stunning and turning all the male heads in the restaurant. 'Ah! Maria,' Simon welcomed her and then rather more quietly after they were all seated. 'John, you know this very attractive addition to our table as Maria Ionides, President Putin knows her as Major Kristina Petrovsky of the GRU, Boris Samsonov as Kristina Kuchinsky and the Americans as Diedre Bates of the CIA. She told me that she learnt Russian and joined the CIA so that she could get rid of that dreadful name!'

OTHER BOOKS FEATURING JOHN GUNN
BY BRIAN NICHOLSON

GWEILO

The theft of a birthright has been the motive for murder since Jacob usurped it from his elder brother, Esau. The birthright to the immense riches of Hong Kong will be stolen at midnight on 30th June 1997 from the descendants of the first settlers on that inhospitable, fever-ridden island of decaying granite, as a result of the signing of the Anglo-Sino Joint Declaration in 1984. Not only the New Territories will be handed back to China - acquired by Great Britain in the 1898 treaty - but also Hong Kong Island which was ceded to Great Britain in perpetuity after the first Opium war in 1842, thus forming the birthright of the descendants of those intrepid traders and settlers who had arrived in Hong Kong - 'a place of sweet water' - under the straining canvas of the triangular sky and moonraker topsails of their lean-hulled trading clippers.

In 1986, two years after the signing of the Joint Declaration, the reactor at the Chernobyl nuclear power station exploded. The subsequent meltdown and escape of radioactive material turned the surrounding area for hundreds of square miles into a deserted wasteland of mutant plants and animals and humans riddled with cancer. The world reeled in horror and condemned the corrupt and decaying Soviet Union for its crass incompetence. But one man in Hong Kong, whose ancestor had disembarked from the first of the clippers to anchor in Victoria Harbour and whose father had died for Hong Kong, tortured to death by the Japanese occupation force in 1943, saw the Chernobyl disaster in a different light. It offered the solution to his all-consuming fury at being dispossessed of his inheritance and betrayed by his own country. If he and his descendants couldn't have Hong Kong, then no one would have it - least of all the Chinese.

ASHANTI GOLD

An investigation into the disappearance of an ineffective operative, from the now-defunct Secret Intelligence Service at the British High Commission in Accra, reveals a conspiracy to overthrow the governments of West African countries by subversion, terrorism and tribal civil war.

The cruelty and corruption of the 18th century Portugese, Dutch and British slave-traders who raped West Africa of its human and mineral resources, is easily surpassed by that of 21st Century, power-hungry, West African exiles, ruthless arms dealers, diplomats and politicians on both sides of the Atlantic who are involved in the conspiracy.

Governments can be brought down by subversion, terrorism and civil war. Terrorists need weapons which must be bought with money....lots of it. Gold is money......and in Ghana is the priceless horde of Ashanti Gold ingots in the vaults of the Bank of Ghana and the richest gold mine in the world is at Sawaba in the Ashanti Region where nuggets as big as walnuts can be illegally panned from the Ofin River and then sold to dealers abroad......just as was done during the 18th Century slave trade.

FIRE DRAGON

The slaughter of half a million Communists by Indonesia's President in the 1950s is a weeping sore for Arief Sulitsono (Alias Dr Ramano Rusman) the illegitimate son of Aidit- the Communist leader - who is determined to return Indonesia to a Communist Dictatorship. He realises that he can do nothing against the power of the USA unless he and other developing countries of NAM possess nuclear weapons. He therefore enters into a conspiracy with the North Koreans to help them avoid US interference with their nuclear weapons programme.

Fortuitously, he stumbles on the enormous treasure amassed by Admiral Yamamoto and hidden in the islands off Irian Jaya and uses this unlimited funding to build a rocket launch site on Waigeo Island on the Equator. From this rocket launch site he plans to place the North Korean nuclear warheads in geo-stationary orbit out of reach of IAEA inspection and US satellite surveillance and available to any country resisting US interference.

Rusman's plan unravels because there are other clues to Yamamoto's treasure and his launch site is being built on the most likely epi-centre of a cataclysmic earthquake. This is John Gunn's fourth assignment for the British Intelligence Directorate where he is confronted by man-eating dragons in 'the ring of fire'.

THE AUTHOR

Brian Nicholson's life has been almost as exciting and eventful as that of John Gunn. Apart from flying, sailing, scuba-diving, skiing, renovating classic cars and being a talented artist and writer, he has led an unusually exciting and successful life as a soldier. This has varied from active service to negotiator extraordinary in Beijing to rescue the 1984 Anglo/Sino Joint Declaration on the future of Hong Kong. As the personal Military Adviser to Ghana's Flt Lt Jerry Rawlings, he assisted in the planning of the military intervention in Liberia in 1991. As the Defence Attaché in Jakarta, his highly successful expedition to unlock the mystery of what happened to the ill-fated, WW2 Australian commando raid – 'Operation Rimau' - on Japanese shipping in Singapore received wide press coverage at the time.

His first book, 'GWEILO' focuses on a conspiracy to prevent the return of Hong Kong to China. His second book, 'AL SAMAK' is about Saddam Hussein's efforts to prevent the invasion of Iraq in 2003. The third book, 'ASHANTI GOLD' uses his exciting exploits in West Africa as a colourful backdrop to a novel about the chaos and corruption in the African Continent. The author's latest novel 'FIRE DRAGON' uses material from his time as a Defence Attaché in Jakarta. This provided an ideal backdrop for a plot around Indonesia's communist history and North Korea's single-minded determination to develop a nuclear weapon and the means of delivering it.

He is currently writing John Gunn's fifth assignment for the British Intelligence Directorate.

ISBN 142511267-6